Bet...
Theirs w...
the winds...
the ...

Fiery Tempers
Fanned by Years
of Hope . . .

Rage erupted within her. All the years of waiting for him, the endless lonely nights of imagining the happiness they were to share, the anticipation of his joy upon discovering she was carrying his child. All of this to add to nothing? She cursed. Enraged beyond feeling, she spewed forth words like mud from a spring flood. It was the anger and frustration of a lifetime of denial, of waiting, of dashed hopes and irreparable dreams.

Throughout the tirade Raleigh was silent, his face impassive. . . .

When she was through and stood, shaking with emotion before him, he said simply, "May I go now?"

Her voice was cold, expressionless. Empty. "You may go to hell."

THEIR PASSION WOULD DIE A THOUSAND DEATHS—UNTIL AT LAST IT COULD LIVE FOREVER!

Tame the Rising Tide

VIRGINIA MORGAN

PUBLISHED BY POCKET BOOKS NEW YORK

Another *Original* publication of POCKET BOOKS

POCKET BOOKS, a Simon & Schuster division of
GULF & WESTERN CORPORATION
1230 Avenue of the Americas, New York, N.Y. 10020

ISBN: 0-671-81043-X

First Pocket Books printing August, 1979

10 9 8 7 6 5 4 3 2 1

Interior design by Cathy Carucci

Printed in the U.S.A.

For Peter Mallory
at Crookings

Book One

Chapter 1

The pains were lasting longer now, and the respite between them growing shorter. Beth bit the grizzled edge of the blanket she had wedged between herself and the hard wooden side of the wagon. She moaned as one of the wheels struck a rock, bumping the wagon, sending a sharp pain through her belly.

The child inside her kicked and she cried out.

"I don't want to hear nothin' out of you," her father said, and slapped the reins once again across the horse's back. The cart jolted as the animal responded. Beth moaned again.

"Nothin', you hear?" Abraham Talbot growled. "We're almost there. You can see the lights up on the hill."

Beth gripped her belly. It was keg-hard. She squeezed her eyes shut and said nothing, waited for the relief that would give her just enough time to catch her breath before the next tightening. When it came she glanced at her father. His face was gray and bleak, as barren as the leafless trees that cast their

3

skeletal shadows in the late-October dusk. His skin, still tan from the long Catskill summer, gave no clue to his thirty-five winters upriver; no clue to the meanness that was in his being, except perhaps for the absence of any laugh lines around his eyes. Beth had seen his meanness, had watched it sap the life from her poor mother until she withered and died before her youngest son was barely off her breast. It was a meanness that went beyond severity, even cruelty, into something that fouled the soul. It was an ugliness of the spirit that no amount of churchgoing or Bible reading could conceal, and Abraham Talbot had passed it on to his oldest son, Ansel.

Beth hated them both with all the imprisoned passion of her fourteen years.

She hated them almost as much as the devil child that now savaged her body for release. Soon, soon she would be free of it. The memory of that night, the shame, the lies, the pain . . . A sharp contraction brought her back to the present. She was grateful.

"Pa! It hurts somethin' awful. The wagon bumping makes it worse."

"Well now, maybe you'd 'uv liked Mrs. DeWitt to send a coach for you? Hmmm? I guess that's the kind of gratitude I should have expected from the likes of you. It isn't every man's whore-daughter who gets to have her bastard in a manor house, now is it?"

Beth started to cry, only partly from the pain. "The Lord knows I'm no whore," she said softly. "The Lord knows."

"I got my suspicions about what the Lord knows and what he doesn't," Abraham said. "But if my beatings only brought you to lying, then you and the Lord keep your covenant and I'll take my purse from Mrs. DeWitt for your sinning."

Beth prayed silently, trying to block out her father's voice and the pain. They were almost at Clearview, the DeWitt manor. Beth had seen the grand brick-and-stone mansion on the bluff above Rhinecliff only twice before, and then only from the road gates.

She remembered the Negroes most clearly. They wore fine outfits and looked more like revelers than slaves when they came out to the wagons for the produce. She had seen Regina DeWitt only once, when she'd strolled down to the gates to survey the wagons and nod to the tenants. It seemed odd to Beth that all she remembered of the woman was that she had red hair and carried a lavender parasol; odd because this was the woman who would soon become the mother of Beth's child.

Beth's nails dug into the wagonside as Abraham halted the rig at the entrance to Clearview. Two black men with torches said something that Beth couldn't hear and then the massive gates were swung open. The wagon jogged forward. The two slaves ran alongside, guiding the horse up the carriage path. Despite the pain, Beth's eyes widened as they approached the house. It was the many windows that awed her. There were only four in the Talbot cabin, and small ones at that. The winters across the river were hard. Abraham Talbot had trouble enough keeping the cabin warm without losing heat through more windows. A house filled with light had always been Beth's dream. Several times in the summer she had slept outdoors just so she could wake up in the morning bathed in sunlight. The pleasure had been so great, she thought she would never forget it. Now she could not call any of it to mind.

The Negroes guided the horse around to the rear entrance where a tall man in a frock coat was waiting on the steps. Behind him stood Regina DeWitt.

"Thank you, Jacob. Luke." She waved her hand, dismissing the slaves. When they were gone, she said, "You may bring her inside, Abraham."

Beth was surprised to hear her father's Christian name spoken so familiarly by Regina DeWitt. She knew they had met three weeks earlier to make the arrangements, but it still sounded odd.

"All right, 'Lisbeth," her father said gently. He took

her arm. "We're here now, honey. Everything's going to be all right. Don't you be frightened none."

Beth tried to jerk her arm back, but Abraham gripped it tighter without ruffling his manner. Neither Regina DeWitt nor the tall gentleman at her side noticed.

Beth began to slide across the seat, then stopped suddenly and hugged her belly. "I can't," she gasped.

The tall man came down the steps quickly. He pushed Abraham to the side and put both his hands on Beth's swollen stomach. "How long has she been having pains?"

"Well, I don't really know."

"We'd better get her inside fast. Here. Help me carry her."

Beth felt the tall man's arm gently circle her. "It's all right, child. I'm a doctor. I'll wait until the contraction passes." He kept his hand on her stomach. When it began to soften he said, "Now."

"I can do it myself," Beth said tightly as her father reached to support her. She walked up the stairs, through the doorway, and found herself face to face with Regina DeWitt. She had never been that close to a real lady before. It was almost frightening.

"How do you do, ma'am——?" she began. Then her voice broke and she clutched herself. A tremor pressed her body and suddenly a puddle of liquid began to spread across the polished floor. Beth stared at it, incredulous, shamed beyond all knowing. She wanted to apologize, run, hide. A new contraction slammed her into immobility.

"Oh, God, Stanton," Regina said with disgust, "she's going to have it right here in the hall if you don't get her in there soon."

The doctor took Beth's arm. "We're going right into that room." He pointed to a door a few yards away. "Can you make it?"

"I——" She stared at the floor, unable to think.

"Damn it, girl," Abraham said sharply. "The doctor's askin' you a question."

Stanton glared coldly at Abraham Talbot, said nothing. Then he took Beth's arm. "That was your waters, child. The baby is coming soon." He guided her slowly down the hall. "Mrs. DeWitt, I think neither you nor Mr. Talbot will be needed. I'd appreciate the assistance of your maid, though. You did say that she could be trusted?"

"Implicitly. I'll call her at once." Regina picked up a small bell from the hall table and shook it three times. While she did, she watched with only the faintest discernible touch of envy as the doctor helped Beth onto the large four-poster bed.

Beth was aware of Regina's gaze and even through the haze of mounting pain was struck to wonder about it. Was she thinking of the child her own body hadn't nurtured to life? The child who'd died three weeks before and would now be replaced by a spawn of sin? That was the arrangement, wasn't it? She'd heard her father and Mrs. DeWitt's maid, Leonora, talking about it last week when they thought she was asleep, after they'd thought the rhythmic squeaks of Pa's hardwood bed could be drowned out by a crackling fire.

Dr. Stanton went to close the door. "I'll let you know, Mrs. DeWitt. Don't tire yourself standing and waiting. Have a glass of sherry. It will do you good."

Regina looked past him to Beth. Her face was slightly drawn, but other than that, and the shadows beneath her eyes, there was little evidence that she had ever suffered any physical discomfort or illness, least of all the loss of two children. Beth had been taught that money couldn't buy health or happiness, but looking at Regina DeWitt belied that. She felt her belly begin to tighten, and squeezed her eyes shut. A lot of things she'd been taught had already proved lies. Money *was* important. With money her mother wouldn't have died; with money they both could have been free. Someday, Beth vowed, she was going to have it, and she was going to get it any way she could.

"I hope it won't be too difficult," Regina said as she turned to leave. There was as much feeling in her voice as if she were asking Beth to close a window.

Beth opened her eyes and stared directly into Regina's. "It won't be," she said. And from that moment she knew that no matter how great the pain, she would not utter a sound.

The doctor asked Regina to send her maid with the towels and hot water, then closed the door. He tore a piece of cloth and looped it around the bedpost near Beth, secured it with a knot. "You can pull on this," he said. "It helps when you have to bear down." Then he turned to the table in the corner and began removing ominous shiny instruments from his black bag.

There was a light knock on the door. Regina DeWitt's maid entered. Beth looked away. She didn't like Leonora, hadn't trusted her from the first time she'd come to their house. Beth had heard Abraham · tell her brother, Ansel, that Leonora was the only woman he'd ever met who understood there were other things to do with her mouth than gossip.

Beth pulled back unthinkingly when Leonora reached out to touch her.

"I'm not going to hurt you," Leonora said coolly. "But you're not going to have a baby with all those clothes on. I'll help you. Better clean you up a bit too."

Dr. Stanton put another instrument on the table. Beth shivered.

Peter Avery's sister had her baby cut out of her and nearly died along with the infant. Peter was Beth's dearest friend. He was two years her senior and his mother hated Beth's father, but from his eighth birthday on they'd shared secrets that few brothers and sisters, or even lovers for that matter, would ever share. He had told Beth his sister, Elmira, had festered for a year after the operation. She'd come back home to live, too, because her husband wouldn't take care of her. Peter read to Elmira when she was ailing, every night. He was good at that. He read to Beth too, poems he'd copied from a book in the fancy Dunham house where he went every day after school to chop wood. The poems of Andrew Marvell were Beth's favorites. When Abraham had taken her out of school two years ago to tend her baby brother, John, Peter taught her how to read and copy the letters. His father was a fairly prosperous merchant, and Peter was the only boy in Shokan even to *think* of entering King's College. Beth missed him now more than she could have imagined possible. In all the world she'd known, he was the only person beside her mother who had ever said he loved her.

He'd told her a little about what having a baby would be like because he had overheard his mother talking to Elmira when she was expecting. Mrs. Avery had said that when the pain got really bad you could stop worrying, because the baby was surely just about born.

"When it gets that bad," Peter had said one day sitting by the river, "try to think of something else."

"Like what?" Beth asked. "Having General Washington to tea?"

Peter grabbed her, held her fast, and tickled her cheek with a soft reed.

"Stop," Beth giggled. "I'll have it right here and then you'll see all the good your thinking of something else will do."

"Well, that's what you get for smart-mouthing," Peter said, releasing her. "I'm being serious."

"And that, Peter Avery, is probably your biggest problem." She tossed a pebble into the stream. "You need to be more like me. Carefree."

"Ha! Carefree, you? You may fool some people with your grins, but I know you too well."

"Oh, Peter." Beth gripped his hand tightly. "I'm scared. Truly I am."

Peter put his thin arms around her and stroked her hair. Tall and blond, with clear gray eyes and the seriousness of those twice his age, he never failed to comfort Beth. Though it had only been a year since he'd begun shaving his whiskers, which even untended would not yet fully cover his chin, he was already far too mature to any longer be considered a boy.

"There's nothing to be scared of. I told you I'd marry you in a year, when I had the money put aside. We'll raise that baby fine, far away from here."

"And you know that's nonsense. One life down the well doesn't mean two. I'm not taking you with me. Good things are going to happen to you, Peter Avery, and my heart cares too much for you to stand in their way. Besides," she looked away, "there's not going to be a baby to worry about."

"What do you mean?"

She told him what she'd overheard between her father and Leonora.

"Mrs. DeWitt is going to pretend that your baby is hers?" Peter asked, amazed.

Beth nodded. "Her husband is due back from Paris next month, and the way I understand it, he wouldn't be pleased to learn that his wife had brought another dead baby into the world. From what Leonora said, Mrs. DeWitt took to screaming like a madwoman when they told her the child was stillborn. It appears James DeWitt has hinted that either she produce a DeWitt heir or else he would seek a better ground in which to sow. And Regina DeWitt would not be happy to give up life at Clearview."

"So your baby—"

"Is going to be hers, and a fine purse to my father to keep the secret." Beth laughed bitterly. "And the cursed little bastard will grow up lookin' down his nose at the likes of us."

Peter said nothing.

"See," Beth chided, "you are too serious. This will all be over in a few weeks and then we can pretend it never happened. I can go back to fattening you up with my corn biscuits and turkey."

"But it has to happen first." He smashed his fist into the ground beside him. "Damnit. I don't want

you to suffer one minute for that woman. You're worth
a dozen of her."

"Not with this baggage, I'm not." Beth patted her
stomach.

Peter grabbed her shoulders roughly. "Don't talk
that way. I—" He leaned forward, for a moment unsure, and then gently kissed her.

Beth turned away. "You shouldn't have done that,
Peter. I'm tainted and I know it."

"God loves you. You've done nothing wrong. You
have to believe that. You have to stop punishing yourself. If anyone should be punished it's that—"

"Peter, I don't want to talk about it." She stood.

She didn't want to think about it either, but like
garden weeds pushing up between the onions, that
night would return again and again to haunt her.
She could still smell the whiskey, feel the rope that
bound her wrists above her head. And the hands, the
hands tearing her nightdress, humiliatingly fondling
her breasts, touching, squeezing, probing her all over;
the hairy sweat-drenched body rubbing against hers in
vile assault as her own futile screams echoed hollowly
in the empty cabin. She looked down at her wrists
where bluish scars from the ropes were still visible,
and she shuddered.

Peter was on his feet instantly. He grabbed her
hand. "Promise me you won't suffer for *her*."

"Oh, Peter," Beth laughed. "I'll have enough just
suffering for me."

"When I cut my arm last winter and old Doc Steiner
was sewing it, I kept the pain away with reciting in
my head. I mean, I just kept saying poetry lines over
and over and before I knew it, I was bandaged. It
might help you when your time comes."

"I can understand sayin' the Lord's Prayer, but
reciting poetry . . ." Beth shook her head. "I don't
know. I can't imagine me birthin' to 'The Definition
of Love.' "

"I can," Peter had said, "I really can . . ."

Remembering, Beth gripped the cloth Dr. Stanton

had looped on the bedpost. *This is for you, Peter,* she said silently.

> *Therefore the love which doth us bind,*
> *But Fate so enviously debars,*
> *Is the conjunction of the mind,*
> *And opposition of the stars.*
> *Therefore the love which doth us bind . . .*

On her third silent recitation, the baby slid into the doctor's unexpecting hands. It was a girl.

The child was small and the doctor had to slap it twice before it cried. Regina Dewitt was not pleased.

When she saw the child she said: "For seventeen pounds sterling, she could have at least produced a healthier specimen." She ignored Beth entirely.

Beth sipped the cup of tea Leonora brought and remained silent. The doctor had said he'd put a sedative in it, but not until the room began to swirl out of focus did she realize it was something to make her sleep. Hazily, she was aware of Leonora holding a neatly swaddled bundle and asking: "Have you a name for her?"

"She'll be christened Adrianne," Regina said. "James expressed a fondness for the name before he sailed."

"Shall I take her to the nursery, or—"

"No, the nursery is fine. Minnie is there. She has enough milk to fatten all the infants in Kingston."

"Won't she wonder where the child came from?" Leonora asked.

"Minnie doesn't wonder." Regina assured her. "She's a very happy slave and intends to stay that way."

Beth attempted to focus, but couldn't. Even the voices began to grow muted. She heard the door close as Leonora left.

"I trust your payment is sufficient to keep tonight's activities behind sealed lips, Doctor Stanton," Regina said.

"I delivered you of a girl child on the twentieth day of October in this year of our Lord seventeen eighty-three," the doctor said politely.

"Fine." Regina smiled. "I do hope you'll be able to attend the christening."

"Of course."

"How soon can the girl be readied to leave? I want her and her loutish father out of here as soon as possible."

Beth fought to open her eyes, but felt herself slipping into swampy darkness.

"Why, I—I thought she was going to stay a few days. I've given her a sedative."

"All the better. She won't be disturbed by the wagon ride and if they leave by dawn they'll probably be in time for the morning Rhinecliff ferry."

"But—"

"I haven't paid you for 'buts,' doctor. I want her out. I'll send in her father. You can give him any instructions on her care." With that Regina left the room, closing the door sharply behind her.

"Doctor . . ." Beth said softly, her voice sounding cottoned and slurred. "My stomach . . . it's still swollen. And . . . and I still hurt."

"You'll be fine," he assured her. "It takes time for the abdomen to recede."

"But the pains. They're—"

"I'll give your father some sedative to take along. It'll help you with the afterpains. And be sure to get good soups and rest."

Beth felt her stomach tighten. "But, doctor—" she began.

Abraham Talbot entered the room. His coat was tossed over his shoulder and he reeked of whiskey. "Mrs. DeWitt said I can take her home now," he said.

"Yes, but you should be careful getting her into the wagon and it would be best if she's bedded down. I've given her a sedative."

"Anything you say, doc," Abraham Talbot smacked his pocket and there was a jingle of silver. "A good night's work is always worth a little trouble." He went to the bed. "Hey, girl, we'd best be movin'. Your bundle's gone."

The last thing Beth remembered was her father's lean muscled arms slipping beneath her; and the stink of whiskey breath driving her into blackness.

Chapter 2

Regina DeWitt watched the Talbot wagon drive through the Clearview gates in the sparse light of dawn. She wanted that to be the last she'd ever see of the girl or her repulsive father, and knew she would have to do something to assure it. Abraham Talbot was not the sort of man who'd remain satisfied with a simple bargain when one of this sort offered such lucrative possibilities. A man like that didn't have to stoop very far to become a blackmailer. No, she couldn't leave it to chance. Her marriage and Clearview were at stake. She had managed to keep James in contented ignorance and their union intact for three years, and she had no desire to change things. If she could conceal two affairs, and an outrageously foolish but exciting encounter with the devilishly handsome young son of James's closest financial associate, William Eckert, she certainly could make sure there would be no question about the legitimacy of their daughter.

"Leonora," she said, "tell Doctor Stanton I would like to see him before he leaves."

Leonora nodded, stifled a yawn. When she returned with the doctor, Regina asked that they be left alone.

Leonora nodded and left. She was tired, it had been a long night, and had she not heard her mistress direct the doctor to bolt the door, she would have gone straight to her room. Instead, she positioned herself outside and pressed her ear against the polished oak. One could always count on the most interesting revelations from behind bolted doors at Clearview.

"I can't take the chance," Regina was saying.

"But you paid him handsomely," the doctor said. "I don't see any reason why he'd bite the hand that fed him."

"He's the sort that gets hungry too often."

"You mean blackmail?"

"That's exactly what I mean. The man's crude, but not stupid. I want him out of the valley before James returns."

"What are you suggesting?"

"I happen to know that a few of my tenants were Tory sympathizers, and Abraham Talbot was one of them. If word of this were to leak out, from a reliable source, I don't believe Mr. Talbot or his family would be likely to remain in their present lodgings."

"Isn't that a little severe? The newspapers are calling them robbers, murderers, and incendiaries. I've heard of two families in Dutchess County who merely gave lodging to wounded British soldiers and were beaten unmercifully by their neighbors."

"Talk like that will have *you* suspect, doctor."

"Surely my loyalty is not in question."

"I do not doubt your patriotism. I'm merely asking for your assistance. No one will question your word, especially when people are so eager to find the traitors who guided the British to hiding places for a lot of silver and jewels that are sorely missed."

"But how can you be sure that he—?"

"I have my informants," Regina said curtly. She settled back against her pillows. "I'll sleep easier knowing that you'll handle the matter. I want that family run out to Halifax, where the rest of the traitors are, within a fortnight. Now if you'll excuse me, I need my rest. I just had a baby daughter, you know. And Governor Clinton will be coming for dinner in little more than a week."

Leonora heard the latch unbolt. She raced down the hall, managing to round the corner and reach the servants' stairs before the doctor's weary footfalls echoed in the hall. Standing there, breathing heavily, she tried to think of how she would warn Abraham before Mrs. DeWitt set her rumor aloft. Lord knew the man wasn't a *real* Tory. Sure he'd done a bit of playin' the sides, but for the silver the British paid him, who wouldn't?

She fingered the locket he'd bought her, thought of how his hands had fastened it and what had happened afterward. It would be a long ride, but she'd get up to Shokan tomorrow, somehow.

The rocking of the ferry woke Beth. The river was choppy and that would mean they weren't likely to dock easily. Sometimes the wind drove the ferry so far downstream it took a whole hour to get back to Kingston.

She opened her eyes slowly and tried to lift herself up on her elbow, but the tightening in her belly stopped her. She hoped the pain would let up soon. It would take at least another hour to get home from Kingston in the buggy. She put her head back down and tried to think of a poem.

It's all over, she told herself. *All over.* She felt herself falling back to sleep. And then, like a nightmare that had no end, she once again felt life inside her.

Beth snapped awake and cried out.

Abraham, who was standing alongside the wagon as the ferry docked, leaned over and slapped her. "Quit that," he whispered harshly.

"But, Pa—"

"I don't want to talk about nothin' here, you understand? I'm known on this crossing and I don't aim to feed everyone's empty hours on the river with tales. So you just keep still."

Beth fought back tears until sleep took her once again. When she awoke next, it was nearly sundown and she was in her own bed.

And a baby was moving inside her.

Abraham had pulled the curtain across the section of the room she shared with her brothers. On the other side she heard little John whining for his dinner and Ansel cursing as he prepared it, but paid no attention. She placed her hands across her still swollen belly, and shivered.

It was still there. Kicking. Oh, God, was this to be her punishment for wanting the child dead? When she'd missed her first moon-blood, she'd rolled down Krom's Hill in the hope of dislodging the devil seed, but all that had happened was that she scraped her knees and elbows. Was she to be possessed forever?

She felt a scream rising inside her, but stifled it. She hadn't dared to see the Reverend Whitford since the night it happened, but she had prayed for salvation. She'd read the Bible whenever she could and had taken at least six psalms to memory. Was this then not her punishment, but perhaps her reward?

Beth began to sweat. She felt light-headed. The room, her candle, and washbasin, appeared to move. She massaged her stomach. How could she have been so ignorant? God wanted her to have *this* child, the way he wanted Mary to have hers. Of course, that had to be it! From sin would come salvation. This was God's child, not the devil's. From far away she heard little John calling her father.

"Pa, Beth's gone and wet her bed all over."

Beth heard her father's boots, but kept her eyes shut. She didn't want to see him. Not now, not when she was preparing for God's work.

"Ansel!" His voice was gruff when he called to his older son. "Get a cloth and soak it in the rain barrel and bring it here. I think Beth's feverin'."

"Feverin' now? What next?" Ansel said disgustedly.

Beth heard the squeak of the latch as her brother went outside to the rain barrel.

"And you might as well fill up her pitcher while you're there," Abraham Talbot called after him. He handed John the pitcher and told him to bring it outside to his older brother.

John came running back inside. "Pa! Pa! Miss Leonora is coming up the path. And she's on a horse!"

"Leonora? Here now?"

"What am I supposed to do with this rag?" Ansel said, holding the dripping cloth away from him as if it were a dead rat. "Mop *her* brow while you entertain your lady friend?" He stared arrogantly at Abraham. He was tall for his seventeen years, and already wore a full beard and mustache that made him look even older. His hair was pitch-colored and hung lank about his shoulders as if wet. His eyes were a chillingly incongruous ice blue.

"Give me that. I don't need any wise mouth from the likes of you." Abraham took the cloth and placed it carelessly on Beth's forehead. "Here." He reached in his pocket and took out a handful of coins. "Buy yourself a pint or two and stay with your buddy boys for a while, eh?"

Ansel winked. "Anything you say, Pa!" He smacked John on the bottom. "You best be hoppin' into bed before Pa sends you out drinkin', too."

There was a knock on the door. Abraham quickly put his hands into Beth's pitcher and splashed some water on his face, smoothing the surplus back over his hair.

Beth moaned softly.

Abraham gave Ansel a shove. "Go on, now. And to bed with you, John."

"But—"

"Now!"

There was no further argument. Abraham went to the door. Beth heard Ansel greet Leonora and apologize for leaving; heard the door slam. She gritted her teeth. She knew what was coming next, what always came next when Abraham sent John to bed and Ansel out drinking. The walls of the cabin were too thin for secrets. Abraham had built the structure before Beth was born. It was to be a temporary shelter for his wife and son while he worked on their real home, a two-story farmhouse with room enough for a half-dozen young ones, a porch for sitting, and a larder large enough to store a winter's goods. But before it even got started, Abraham had drunk away the money to build it. The half-dozen young ones didn't come, there never was time for sitting, or enough stores to fill even a week's larder, and the dark make-shift cabin became the Talbots' permanent residence.

"What in God's name are you doin' here tonight?" Abraham asked. There was the rustle of fabric as he took her in his arms. "Not that I'm complainin', mind you, but I didn't expect you until next week."

"I came because there's something I got to tell you."

"Well, you sit right down here on my bed and un-burden your mind while I undo some of these laces so you can breathe properly after your ride."

"Abraham, there's no time for that tonight."

Beth heard her father's voice grow husky. "There's time, but it's got to be now. Ansel won't be drinkin' forever and I expect Beth will be comin' round shortly. Come on. I contained myself at the manor, but I sorely missed nippin' those buds on your titties. There. Now that's much better. You go on talkin' and I'll just give 'em a bit of a lickin'."

"Abraham, stop," Leonora pleaded. "I've come to warn you that you're in danger."

"Huh?"

There was the rustle of petticoats. Leonora stood, began to pace across the bare planked floor, her shoes making hollow little clicks. Beth's stomach contracted violently. She bit down hard on her pillow to muffle a groan.

"It's Mrs. DeWitt," Leonora said. "She's going to have you driven from the valley, or jailed, by having

Doctor Stanton pass the word about your dealings with the Tories."

There was a sharp slap and Leonora yelped.

"You're lyin'," Abraham said. "You're playing me for some sort of a game or money."

"I'm not, honest," Leonora swore. "I wouldn't have ridden all the way out here just to tell a tale."

A cork popped and Beth could hear her father guzzle a long draught of whiskey. "That's the truth, you say?"

"I swear it. She wants to make sure that nobody ever finds out the child isn't hers."

"How did she find out about my little deals with the British in the first place, eh? There's only one way far's I can see."

"Ow. Abraham, you're hurting me. I never told her nothing. You know she has informers."

"Damn fancy bitch. Thinks she can just go and buy everything. I'd like to——"

"You haven't got a chance in hell of doing anything that'll ever cross a DeWitt. Believe me, I know it."

"Hmmm. And knowin' her, she's not likely to waste much time in setting this scheme in motion. That means I've got to get me and mine ready to leave. There are a few in this valley that still got strong feelings about Tory scouts—and they've got plenty of powder left for their rifles, too."

"Oh, Abraham," Leonora wailed. "What's going to happen to us? You said we were going to get married in the spring."

"Well, now, that looks as if it's going to have to be another season, doesn't it? I don't know what time spring comes round in Halifax."

"I don't care," Leonora said bravely. "Whatever season is all right with me. I'll pack my things and meet you in Kingston tomorrow."

"Whoa! Now there's no need for that. I haven't enough money to book passage for my family *and* you. I'll have to write for you once I get settled."

"But I'm ready to go with you. I—I love you, Abraham."

"Well, if you do," Abraham said softly, "you can say good-bye in a way that I'm not likely to forget."

"But, Abraham—"

"Why don't I just lay back here, rememberin' you, while you do it, huh? Come on, now. You know the way I like it . . ."

Beth was too numbed by what she'd heard and too sickened by her father's whiskey-fed pants of pleasure to be fully aware of the slowly increasing intensity of her contractions. But suddenly they gripped her mercilessly.

Her father's moan of release was almost simultaneous with her scream, and her second breaking of waters.

Chapter 3

Leonora entered the room first. She took one look at Beth and gasped. "Oh, my God, Abraham. She's having another baby."

"What nonsense are you talking?" Abraham raked his fingers through his hair. His whiskey-flushed face began to gray. "That's impossible." He walked slowly, apprehensively to the bed. "What's happening to you, girl?"

A beatific smile crossed Beth's face. Her long russet hair, still streaked from the summer sun, flamed across the pillow like a halo. "I'm having the Lord's baby," she said quietly. Her eyes had difficulty focusing; even the pain seemed to come from a dream.

Leonora put her palm against Beth's head. "She's fevering. You'd better get a doctor."

"There ain't a doctor 'cept in Kingston, and he wouldn't get here until morning. But maybe I can get Widow Brinks. She's good at nursin' and getting rid

of deliriums. I mean, that's what this new birthin' talk
is, isn't it?"

"Uh-uh." Leonora took a step backward, shaking
her head. "I never seen anything like it, but she's having a baby all right."

"It's—it's not natural," Abraham said nervously. "I
don't like it. It's devil's work."

"No, Pa," Beth said calmly. "The other was the
devil's; this one is the Lord's."

"Stop talking foolishness!" he shouted. He crossed
the room and pulled back the dividing curtain. He
shook John awake.

"What's the matter, Pa?"

"Get on your britches and see if you can get
Widow Brinks over here."

"Widow Brinks? But Pa, you said last week that
she was a witch. You said—"

"Never mind what I said last week. Just mind what
I say now. You go and tell her that Beth is feverin'
bad."

As John was dressing, Abraham and Leonora left
the room and Beth eased herself up on one elbow.
John's eyes widened as if he were seeing a ghost.

"I—" he began.

Beth put her finger by her lips and beckoned her
brother to come close. When he did, she put her lips
to his ear and whispered: "Go to the Averys'. Knock
on Peter's window, you know, the small one in the
back, and tell him I need him."

"But—"

"Just do it. And don't tell Pa." She kissed him.

"Are you going to die?" he asked.

She smiled and ruffled his hair. "Someday," she
said, "when I'm very rich and can afford to have im-
ported taffeta for my layin' out."

"Not before?"

"Not a moment before."

"John!" Abraham shouted. "What's keepin' you?"

"Comin', Pa." John kissed his sister. "You better
not be lyin'," he said, "else I'll never forgive you."

Beth waited until he was gone, then took the wet cloth Ansel had brought her and tied it in a knot around the bedpost the way Dr. Stanton had done.

Silently she began reciting.

She heard Leonora weeping as Abraham repeated his decision not to take her with him and began hurrying her out.

"Widow Brinks will be here soon. You'd best take off before it's more than Tory collusion I'm accused of and Mrs. DeWitt has my neck."

"You promise you'll send for me?" Leonora asked, sniffling.

" 'Pon my honor. Now off with you."

Beth stopped her reciting and listened as the sound of Leonora's horse faded into the fall evening. She breathed a small sigh of relief. She needed none of them. This was her child and she'd birth it by herself. She'd—

She gripped the cloth and bore down. Once, then once again, and the child was born.

A great peace filled her emptied body. Her heart soared with joy as she took the wriggling infant in her hands. Holding it upside down, firmly grasped by its heels as she'd seen the doctor do, she slapped its buttocks. The small, perfectly formed baby girl let out a lusty squawl.

Abraham came running. "What in the—?" He stood in the doorway, gaping.

Beth brought the baby to her stomach, cradling it with her arms. She was perspiring heavily and her voice was barely audible, but she smiled as she spoke. "Can you heat some water in the kettle so I can wash her, Pa?"

John came racing in. "Widow Brinks is coming just as fast as she—" He stopped when he saw the baby. "Where'd that come from?"

"From me," Beth said proudly.

"I thought you were feverin'," John said. "What kind of sickness gives you babies?"

"That'll be enough questionin' from you," Abraham

snapped. "You can get back in your bed. We're going to be journeyin' tomorrow and I'll need you to run errands."

"Pa," Beth said. "Can't I have the water? Please?"

Abraham looked uneasy. "All right. I'll get it." He stared at the child in his daughter's arms, then turned quickly away. "Now where in hell is that widow woman," he grumbled. He stomped out into the kitchen.

"Pssst." Beth signaled her brother. "Did you tell Peter?"

John nodded dumbly, fascinated by the red mewling infant in his sister's arms. "It's a girl baby, huh?"

"Yes. Now tell me, did you speak to Peter?"

"Uh-uh. He wasn't there. I saw Elmira, though, and she said she'd have him stop by in the morning."

The weariness Beth had been holding off seemed to crash around her. She sighed, eased herself back against the pillow. Morning. For all she knew her father would have them packed and gone before the cock crowed. She hadn't even thought of never seeing Peter again. The baby in her arms squirmed.

"Don't worry, little one," she whispered softly. "I'll take care of you no matter where we are." She ran her fingers gently over the baby's head, amazed by the sleekness of golden down that covered it like wet corn silk. She'd never felt a newborn baby before, and the wonder of it pushed all else from her mind.

As her father entered with the water, there was a knock on the door. He left the pan by the side of the bed and hurried to let in Widow Brinks.

"I came as quickly as I could," she said. Her voice was low and anxious. "How bad is the girl's feverin'?"

Abraham coughed. "Well, um, she's not feverin' so much anymore. It's—um— Well, she's in there."

Beth felt the widow's presence the moment she entered the room, and instantly it allowed her to relax. The woman was easily twice Beth's weight and nearly five times her age, with frizzy gray hair that framed her face like a thick winter fog. She smelled of fresh soap. It was a comforting scent.

"Why didn't you tell me she was having a baby?" the widow demanded.

"I—I didn't know," Abraham said. "You see—"

"I see that she has a baby, that's what I see. And I do not see any afterbirth." She moved silently to the bed. "Did you have another pain after the baby?"

"No . . . but I'm having one now," Beth said.

"Out!" the widow shouted at Abraham. "And get me *hot* water, not this tepid frog's spit." She put both her hands on Beth's belly. "Now this might be a bit painful," she said quietly, "but once it's over I know that you're going to be all right. You put your child to the breast now and hold her there. I'm going to push down on your stomach. And when I do, you bear down again."

Beth took the infant and placed its tiny mouth to her nipple. As she did, a strong tightening seized her body and Widow Brinks's hands pushed against her. She bore down and heard the widow sigh with relief.

"Well, now, all we have to do is clean you up a bit and you and your daughter can have a nice long nap." She took the baby from Beth. "You relax. You did a good job. I will cut the cord. There's nothing I like better than bringing babes into this world."

Beth watched the widow clean and swaddle the baby, then take a drawer from the bureau and put it alongside the bed. Lining it with a blanket, she placed the infant inside. "It's not a fancy cradle, but it's good enough for any newborn." Then she sponged Beth off and helped her into a clean nightdress. Abraham had long since left the house and gone, Beth suspected, to join Ansel at the tavern.

Widow Brinks fixed Beth a cup of tea. She pulled a chair up next to the bed and settled her large frame into it. She explained to Beth how to nurse the baby, diaper it, and gave her a formula for medicine to give in case of colic or fevers.

Beth thanked her. The Widow Brinks was one of

the few people who hadn't treated her as if she had the pox when her belly had begun to swell last July.

"May I hold my baby now?" Beth asked, putting her tea aside. She was tired, but the child was the most beautiful she had ever seen. To hold and feed a real infant the way some girls her age still did sock dolls was delight beyond any she could remember.

The widow lifted the infant from the drawer and placed her in Beth's arms. "She's sleeping now, but she feels your closeness. The more secure she feels, the less cryin' she'll give you. What name will she answer to?"

"Her name?" Beth was startled for a moment, then filled with a rush of excitement. Imagine naming another human being! Why a name lasted a body their whole life! She looked down at the tiny creature in her arms and ran her finger gently over her golden hair.

"Suzannah," she said proudly.

"That's a real fine name," the widow said, rising from the chair with difficulty. "I guess I'll leave you and Suzannah to get acquainted."

Beth thanked her. Then, noticing a small, rose-colored crescent, like a fairy-tale moon, on the back of Suzannah's neck, she asked the widow what it meant.

"Why that's just a little love mark. A piece of the Lord's jewelry to show that she's a special child."

"Oh, she is," Beth said in a rush. "I know she's special, she's—"

"Yours," the widow offered. She brushed Beth's hair back from her face. As she did a curious look came into her eyes. It was partly sad, but mostly unreadable. Beth wondered if it was because the widow never had any children of her own—or because she saw something in Beth's future. Everyone said that Widow Brinks had that kind of power, though she never talked about it.

Suddenly Beth desperately wanted to know what lay ahead; her future and Suzannah's. Never before had she dared to be curious—not even after the Gypsy woman at the fair had told her friend Anna that she would marry a handsome soldier and have wealth aplenty. The future had always frightened Beth and she feared it, the way a child feared the entering of a cave. She could handle any adversity once it came, but the unknown was more threatening. Then, too, knowing the future might destroy her daydreams about it. If misfortune awaited, why should she suffer before time? And if, on the other hand, her future held happiness, why spoil the surprise?

But the circumstances of her life had changed radically in the past few hours. She could no longer depend on their old rooster to wake her every morning, nor Peter Avery to teach her letters and poetry on Sundays. Within days, maybe sooner, her father could be caught the way Irene Smyth's father was and beaten, the whole family persecuted, unless they managed to escape downriver. And that would mean leaving the valley, and Peter. Dear Peter.

She clutched the baby tighter with one hand and reached out for the widow with the other.

"Widow Brinks," she said, a whisper so taut there was no disguising her desperation. "You have to tell me. I know you don't like folks asking you about the future, but—"

The widow's face darkened. "You were in church last week. You heard the reverend say that only servants of the devil try to see what the Lord has planned."

"I—I don't believe that. 'Specially not about you."

The widow gave a short bitter laugh. "I wish there were more in this valley thought the same."

Beth gripped the woman's hand tighter. "I won't tell anyone," she whispered. "I swear."

The widow gazed down at Beth. "You know," she said gently, "with that child in your arms, you look even younger than your fourteen years."

Beth kept her grip on the woman's hand. "Please?"

Without saying anything, the widow sat down and

turned over the anxious hand that clutched hers, spreading it palm up so that she could see it clearly in the flickering candlelight.

Beth held her breath as Widow Brinks's fingers explored her palm. She squeezed her daughter closer and the child gave a soft grunt. It was the present and she could deal with it. It comforted her.

The widow's voice changed, became deep and unfamiliar as she spoke. "I see travel, change . . . soon, very soon. You will not see the new moon through the windows of this house."

Beth swallowed hard, fought back the release of tears that threatened for no reason other than that she knew that what the widow said was true.

"I will tell you more," the widow said, "for you of all in this valley are entitled to know." The woman's eyes rolled upward and her lids half descended, as if in a trance. "Because you alone will risk your life to save mine and in so doing will alter your own forever."

"I—"

The widow waved her silent.

"You will grieve for two children taken from your breast, but fate will twist fortune so you will not be denied them forever." Her breath became heavier as she spoke, her voice deeper. "You will live a life of paradoxes. A beloved will become a friend, a captor will become your beloved, and a man of sin will lead you to salvation . . ."

Beth's heart began to beat heavily, thumping inside of her like some beast hurling itself against the bars of a cage. Fascination had replaced all fear. She wanted to cover her ears and hear no more, but dared not move.

The widow's face was tallow-colored and small beads of perspiration dotted her forehead. "I see you in the foulest of squalor, tearing bread from the mouths of rats. But also I see you in the finest of splendor, dining on porcelain from across the world. There will be oceans and ships, violence beyond my experience and love beyond my imagination. A secret of shame will haunt you and flesh of your flesh will comfort you. You will give life and take it . . . learn hard the ways of survival and never forget the price of failure." She paused and turned her face toward Beth. "But through all your days, and all your men, only one shall hold your passion . . . and in so doing shall control your destiny." The widow's head fell forward to her heaving chest.

Beth gasped, gripped the bodice of her nightdress. "Widow Brinks!"

Slowly the woman raised her head. "It's all right. I'm fine," she huffed. "That sometimes happens . . . afterwards."

Beth wrapped both arms around Suzannah and held her almost as a shield. "What you said—" she began, "it frightened me."

"I did not wish to frighten you," the widow said softly. "You *were* frightened and that is why you asked me to look ahead. I saw things I did not want to see, but others that I envy you. You must remember that even on the brightest day, there are shadows in the sun."

"Oh, Widow Brinks!" Beth put Suzannah beside her and leaned forward, burying her head in the widow's enormous bosom. For the first time since that awful night she let herself cry. Her tears fell unashamedly, loosened by the widow's slow comforting stroking of her hair.

"Cry, girl. No one sees a new life start or an old one end without tears."

Beth wept for a long while. Then, exhausted, she fell back against the pillow. The widow tucked Suzannah into her drawer-bed. As she was leaving, she withdrew some coins from her dress pocket and handed them to Beth.

"But why—"

"It's a present." She bent over and kissed Beth's forehead.

"I don't deserve any presents."

"Don't say that. You're a fine girl, and I know it. You see, I know your secret."

Beth's eyes widened in fear. "But—"

"It's all right. I know many secrets. Too many. You rest now." She smiled. "You're the closest I'll ever come to having a daughter, and I want you to know that. God love you." She picked her shawl up quickly and tossed it around her shoulders. Without a backward glance she left the room and let herself out.

Beth closed her eyes. The widow's prophecy nettled her consciousness, but fatigue obliterated everything. She slipped into a deep sleep.

The soft pressure of a calloused hand on her cheek awoke her. She opened her eyes slowly, then bolted upright. "Peter! How did you—?"

Peter Avery smiled, put the candle he was holding on the bureau and knelt down. "John let me in."

Beth looked anxiously to the door. "If my father comes back he'll . . ." She gripped Peter's hands.

"He's down at the Overlook Tavern with your brother. I saw them there when I rode up. It's not likely they'll be returning just yet."

"Oh, Peter." Beth pressed her cheek against the familiar roughness of his homespun shirt. "I'm so glad you're here. I thought I'd never see you again."

Suddenly everything was all right. Peter always made everything all right. She had counted on him for as long as she could remember, and he had never disappointed her. At sixteen, with his fine blond hair tied back in a gentleman's queue, his britches unpatched, and his leather boots, he looked more of a man than most in the valley, and knew more than just about all.

Because of it, Abraham hated him, and Ansel resented him, but their feelings had never stopped Beth from seeing him. Peter was the only one who knew what had happened that awful January night. And it had taken much pleading and more of her strength to stop him from committing murder to avenge her, though there had been times in the last nine months when she wondered if she had done the right thing.

"I came as soon as I could," he said. "How are you?"

Even by candlelight, Beth could see the consternation in his soft gray eyes. His hand stroked her face tentatively. His love was so evident. Would she ever, she wondered, be able to return it in kind? She told him quickly what had happened at the DeWitts' and about Leonora's visit.

"That means you'll be going too," he said, his voice rising with disbelief.

"I have no choice. I'm bounded by hell on all sides. You remember what happened to Irene's family after her father was driven out last month?"

Peter stood, began to pace. "No! I'll think of something. I'll hide you somehow."

"Don't be foolish. Your mother would never have me. Besides, there's not only me to consider." She said the last slowly, with a mixture of pride and embarrassment.

Peter appeared confused. "You mean John?"

Beth lowered her head, then brought her eyes up to Peter's slowly. She smiled. "Uh-uh. I mean Suzannah." She reached over and took the baby from the drawer, cradled her in her arms.

Peter's jaw dropped. He stared at the infant in disbelief. "But I thought the DeWitts were—"

"Shhh. You're not supposed to know that," Beth admonished.

"But— How?" Peter scratched his head, tugged uneasily at his vest. For the first time in a long time he looked his age.

"I had two babies," Beth said, and as she did a strange chill coursed through her. Like an echo that refused to die she heard the voice of Widow Brinks. *You will grieve for two children taken from your breast* . . . No. Not Suzannah. She wouldn't let her go. She hugged the child to her.

Peter brought the candle closer to look at the baby

and it began to cry. He backed off instantly and Beth laughed.

"They don't bite, you know. Haven't you ever seen one before?"

Peter shook his head. "Not that small."

Beth grinned. Then she heard the sound of hoof-beats and her grin vanished. "Pa and Ansel! They're coming. You've got to get out of here."

"I can slip out John's window. I left the horse out back, just in case." He knelt beside the bed. "I'll think of some way to keep you here. Both of you."

Beth reached out and touched his head sadly. "I don't know about this time, Peter. But I promise I'll come back."

"It's not right. It's not right you going away with *them*," he growled savagely.

"Peter, they'll be here any minute. You must leave."

"I'm going, but I'll be back first thing tomorrow morning."

"No." Beth gripped his hand tightly. "That'll only make things harder. You know how Pa and Ansel are."

"I—"

Beth put her fingers across his lips. "Don't be the stubborn cow you always accused me of being. Besides, I need your help. I don't know why I have the feeling, but I think Pa's going to try to take the baby from me before we get to the boat."

"What are you—?" Peter stopped. The sound of Abraham's laughter drifted in from outside. "They're here," Peter whispered. "I'd better go now."

Beth held his sleeve. "Follow us tomorrow. Don't let Ansel see you, but follow the wagon to Kingston. Please?"

"But—"

"I don't know what Pa has in mind, but I don't want to lose my baby. I won't rest or close my eyes unless I know you're going to be there. Please?" Beth brought her face close to his.

"I'll be there," he said. Then he raised her to him

and pressed his mouth gently against hers. She returned his kiss fiercely. When they parted, neither spoke.

Peter turned quickly and hurried to John's window. A few moments later he was gone. Beth heard his horse ride away as the front door squeaked open. She slid down between the sheets and put her fingers to her still-moist lips. She knew what the kiss had implied . . . just as she knew that for the first time in their friendship she was deliberately *using* his love!

Chapter 4

The baby was crying and the room was cold when Beth awoke. Abraham was shouting at Ansel to get out of bed.

"All right, all right," Ansel groaned. He sat up slowly, rubbing his temples. He was still dressed from the night before.

"We've got to get movin' if we want to make the boat out of Kingston tonight."

"Where are we goin', Pa?" John asked. He was standing by his bed in his underwear, shivering. He looked frightened.

"Journeying," Abraham snapped. "You get dressed and help your sister pack."

Beth said nothing. She placed the baby beneath the covers and put her in dry swaddling. She wished it was all a bad dream, but the crisp October morning destroyed all hope of fantasy. She too began to shiver.

Ansel belched loudly. "She ain't packing the bastard, is she? We'll have enough handling four layin' hens."

Beth felt the hatred pour through her like molten wax. "You shut your mouth, Ansel!"

Ansel stood, stretched, then smiled nastily and scratched his groin. "That's a lot of sass from the likes of you, ain't it?"

Abraham swung his arm and sent Ansel sprawling back on the bed. "That'll be enough of that. There's no time for feudin'. We got to get movin'. And whatever don't fit in the wagon gets left." He stomped from the room, the heels of his boots driving squeaks from the old floor.

Ansel got up and spit in his basin. He put on his boots. Recently he'd taken to blackening them and his leather vest, enjoying the sinister impression he felt it carried.

He made sure Abraham was out of the house before he walked to his sister's bed.

Beth straightened, held Suzannah protectively. "You keep away from me, Ansel."

"I just wanted to look at your little bastard," he said with a half smile.

"Get away!" Beth shrieked. "You hear me, get away!"

John began to cry and ran from the room.

"Why you trouble-makin' little tramp," Ansel said. He raised his hand and was about to slap her when Abraham entered.

"Ansel!" Abraham thundered.

Ansel whirled, bowed. "At your service, Pa." He grinned as he almost lost his balance.

"Let's get going. No more of this spattin' or I'll take the rod to you."

"I think you're forgetting that I'm a man now, Pa."

"Man or no man, you'll be standin' all the way to Halifax if you keep it up," Abraham said. He still had a good two inches in height on his son, and more muscles than years. He was a man that few in the valley wanted to find themselves up against in a brawl, but one that most self-respecting folks avoided.

"Okay." Ansel raised his palms. "I just wanted to see the little bugger."

"Get him out of here!" Beth shouted.

"Now you be quiet too," Abraham yelled. "And don't get hitched up to that little one, because it's not comin' with us."

Beth's eyes narrowed. "She's coming with us, all right, else I'm not going."

Abraham looked down at the hooked rug at the foot of Beth's bed, studied it for a moment, then looked up. "All right," he said, "she can come. But no more fighting."

"Okay." Beth nodded, looked warily at her brother.

Ansel spit in his basin and left the room.

Beth got up with difficulty and dressed. John helped her pack the big oak traveling chest that had belonged to their mother. Beth had hoped to keep the chest for her wedding things, but over the years it had become a catchall for everything she'd wanted to hold on to. It was the only thing in the house that offered her any privacy, and she kept the key to it in a small buttoned pocket in her shift.

There would be no room for anything but essentials. The fleeces she'd so carefully opened and sorted for carding and spinning would have to be packed, for who knew how long it would be before they would once again have sheep of their own. The wheel, she noticed, had already been taken out to the wagon. Pa wasn't about to leave anything behind that provided him with goods and comfort.

Beth stuffed the family's wooden trenchers and spoons inside the trunk, along with the candle mold and as many candles as John could find. Pa would have to make room for the pots and the big copper kettle. She took down the strings of peppers, dried apples, and rings of dried pumpkin from over the fireplace and put as many as would fit into one of the large bowls and covered it with another. What remained she gave to John to toss outside for the animals. She wrapped dried blackberry leaves, goldenrod, and sage in a cloth that was easily accessible so that they would have tea when they stopped. She missed the real tea that Pa used to bring home, but most folks hadn't had that since before the war. She stopped for a moment and realized a tear had slid down her cheeks.

Leaving the valley was more than just leaving the house and Peter. It was leaving all her dreams of the future and all her memories of the past. She ran her hand over the warm bricks of the oven and remembered gathering wet oak leaves to put inside so her mother could bake bread. Her Mama. Her beautiful Mama. In reverie she could still see her in frilled cap and flowered chintz, returning from church and letting down her voluminous rust-colored tresses only to swirl them up again in her plain working cap so that they wouldn't interfere with her cooking.

Beth glanced over at the bed in the corner of the kitchen where her mother had lain dying for so many months, where now her father brought women or snored off his pints. In some ways it was better that her mother wasn't alive, for Abraham would be no different.

She lifted the handwoven coverlet from the bed. Mama had been so proud of its complicated rose design. Now it was stained, unraveling at the edges. It wasn't worth carting, but it couldn't be left behind. Not after all the hours Beth had seen her mother put into it. Beth folded it carefully and brought it into her room and tucked it in the chest.

"Mama," she whispered softly. She patted the quilt, then quickly wiped her eyes. She had never seen her mother cry. Now she herself was a mother. There would be no more time for tears. She picked up Suzannah, wrapped her in a blanket, and walked slowly out to where Abraham and Ansel were stringing a hempen cover over makeshift wooden bows, making a poor but workable Conestoga wagon. The only real Conestoga Beth had seen was the one brought from Pennsylvania for the county fair. Peter's cousins, the Van Ryieks, made one like it when they moved to Albany. That one had four horses, each with a full set of bells, except, of course, the saddle horse. All the Talbot wagon had were two saddle horses. Beth wondered how the poor beasts were going to manage to make it to Kingston.

"Get your brother," Abraham shouted. "We're leaving as soon as I get the trunk and kettles."

Beth called to John. He came running, but she sent him back inside for his cap and scarf. October weather, like their father, was not to be trusted. She looked around to see if she could spy Peter, but saw nothing except the deep green darkness of the lavish pines.

When the trunk and kitchen equipment were loaded, Beth climbed aboard. John followed and huddled down beside her in the back of the wagon. She made a makeshift bed of blankets and pillows, wedged between the trunk and spinning wheel, and settled herself and Suzannah down upon it.

Ansel sat in front with his father. Abraham slapped the reins, and the horses started down the road to Kingston. Beth lifted a corner of the wagon cover and looked back, her eyes searching the woods for some sign of Peter. Seeing nothing more than unruffled pines, her heart sank, but only fleetingly. Peter had promised, and the sun would sooner fall from the heavens than for Peter to break his word.

Before they reached Hurley, the baby began to cry. Beth unfastened the bodice of her dress and brought the baby close. The child rooted anxiously, whimpering until its mouth found her nipple. Thoughts of Peter disappeared as she marveled at the pleasant sensations that filled her as she nursed. When the child fell asleep, uneasiness returned.

She put Suzannah beside her and lifted the hempen flaps absently so not to arouse any suspicion. As the wagon rounded a curve, she saw a doe spring out of the woods, noticed a flash of yellow through the green. Straining her eyes, she could make out Peter's roan,

Keeper. He was a large horse and it was no mean feat to keep him hidden. She smiled inwardly and patted Suzannah. Now she could relax.

They stopped to rest after an hour. Abraham built a small fire, gave each of them a chunk of hearth bread, and made a pot of blackberry tea. John brought Beth's portion to her in the wagon. Her thirst was incredible. She drank the tea in a single gulp. It tasted bitter, but she thought nothing of it until she downed her second cup and began feeling dizzy.

The sedative the doctor had told Pa to give her! She knew it instantly—but too late. She struggled to focus her eyes, as everything grew hazy. With effort she wrapped her arms around Suzannah and held her tightly. She wanted to scream out: "You'll never take her from me!" but her tongue was fuzzy; her lids like lead.

Don't worry, Suzannah, she said silently, Peter is watching out for us. She wondered what the dark shape forming before her was? It looked like a bear, all hairy-faced and mean. She tried to lift up her hand to push it away, but her arm wouldn't move. Then it reached down toward Suzannah, and Beth saw that the hairy-faced bear was her brother Ansel.

Somewhere inside her she screamed, and Ansel tore the baby from her arms.

Chapter 5

The wagon was moving and John was sobbing softly beside her when she woke. An acrid taste lingered in her mouth. For a moment she didn't know where she was. Then all of a sudden it came back to her. She bolted upright.

"Suzannah!" she cried.

John began to sob louder.

Beth gripped his shoulders. "Where is she?" she whispered hoarsely, almost unable to speak.

John sniffed, looked nervously forward where Abraham Talbot drove alone. "Ansel took her."

"Took her? Where?"

John shook his head, wiped his nose on the sleeve of his jacket. "I don't know. I heard Pa say something about some tanners."

"The Van Munditzes?"

"I didn't hear the name. It was after the fight and I—I got sick."

"Fight?" Beth felt cold. She squeezed her brother's arm so hard he yelped. "What happened?"

John's fear-filled eyes darted to the front of the wagon. "Pa will tell Ansel, and Ansel said he'd beat me good if I told you. He said he'd beat you too if you made trouble."

Beth pulled him down so that they both were lying on their sides behind the trunk. "He can't hear you out there above the wagon noise. Now you tell me what happened."

"It was terrible." John buried his face in his small hands. "There was blood all over the road."

"Peter!" Beth gasped.

John nodded and began to cry again.

"Stop that." Beth shook him. "Tell me what happened."

"Well, it was when Ansel was just getting on his horse and Pa was going to hand him Suzannah that Peter rode up. He asked Ansel where you were and what he was doing with the baby. Ansel told him it was none of his business and to move on. Peter said he wasn't going anyplace until he could talk to you. And that's when Ansel caned him. He hit him right in the side of the head. He was layin' on the ground and bleedin' when Ansel got off his horse and . . . and . . ."

"And what?" Beth demanded.

"And smashed Peter's leg with a rock."

Beth let out a cry.

Abraham turned around. "What's that?" he shouted, unable to see over the spinning wheel.

"Say I cried out in my sleep," Beth whispered.

John coughed and did as Beth told him.

"You tell me when your sister wakes up, hear?" Abraham yelled.

"Yes, Pa!" John looked at Beth, his eyes still wide with fright. "Pa would whip me if he knew I lied." His bottom lip began to tremble and Beth pulled him to her.

"Hush," she warned. "If you keep bawling he'll

know something's wrong. Now tell me quickly, what happened next?"

John shrugged, his thin shoulders rising to his ears. "I—I'm not sure. Pa gave Ansel the baby and said he should take her to the tanners and meet us at the docks in Kingston, and then he got the horses goin' real fast."

"What did Peter do then?"

"Do?" John looked confused. "Peter didn't do anything. He didn't even move. I think Ansel made him dead."

Beth covered her mouth to stifle a scream. Her mind raced. Not Peter! John was just frightened. He was a child. He always exaggerated. She had seen Peter wallop the pants off the Mallory brothers when they'd cornered her in Dame Riekel's barn and tried to get her to kiss them. He'd blackened Turp Mallory's eyes so bad he couldn't read lessons for a week, and Ben's nose was still a bit crooked from the encounter. And the Mallorys were older than Ansel.

"I don't believe it. Pa wouldn't let Ansel kill anyone."

"Ansel caned him and then threw the rock before Pa had a chance to stop him," John said. "Pa was mad about it, but once he looked at Peter he said we had to get out of there fast."

It wasn't true. Not Peter. But if he was hurt she had to help him. And she had to find Suzannah.

The wagon kept slipping in and out of focus. The sedative still held her, try as she did to fight it. Oh dear God, she had to find her baby.

Pa would try to stop her, she knew that. Her only hope lay in getting away before he found out. It would mean leaving John, but she had no choice. John was seven now and sturdy enough to be without a woman's tending. Besides, knowing Pa, there would be a woman in the house soon enough. But how was she to find Suzannah? And where would she get money enough to survive? Damn the fuzziness that clouded her head.

The wagon wheels hit cobblestone and Beth knew

that they had reached Kingston. There wasn't much time.

"John," she whispered. "Where did Ansel and Peter have the fight?"

"Where we stopped. By the bridge in Hurley. What difference does it make?"

"I've got to get there and find Peter, find out where Suzannah's gone to." She kissed his forehead. "I have to leave you."

"But Pa, he'll be hoppin' mad. You can't leave. Besides, Peter's most likely . . . dead." His voice quavered. She could see that he was trying to be manly about his argument, but just hadn't the years for it.

"I don't believe that," Beth said quietly.

The wagon rattled its way noisily down to the docks. Inside Beth hugged her brother and told him that as soon as possible they would be together again.

"But how will you know where to find me?" John asked. "Pa doesn't even know where we're going."

"He'll be in touch with Uncle Ephram. I'll find you. It might be a long time, though, but I'll send you kisses in my prayers every night. And you send some back to me. Okay?"

John nodded.

Beth raised herself and lifted the heavy flaps to peek out. "We're almost there," she said. "I'm going to need your help."

"But—"

"Shhh. I'm going to pretend to be asleep. More than likely Pa's going to get himself a few pints waiting for Ansel. When he's gone, that's when I'm going to leave."

"But he'll blame me for not telling him." John's lip began to quiver again.

"You say that I told you I was going to look for him, that's all." She tousled his hair. "He won't suspect anything. In fact, you can tell him that you were tired and took a nap."

John looked doubtful, but agreed.

"Now one more thing," Beth said.

"What's that?"

"I need some money. Pa's got a purse of sterling and a good many Spanish dollars in the lining of his jacket." She pointed to the coat that rested atop the spinning wheel. "I want you to tell Pa that you're cold and ask him if you can cover yourself with his jacket because I've got the blanket."

John was about to protest, but Beth stroked his head. "Just do it," she said. "The Lord will forgive you."

"I know that. But Pa won't."

"You'll pretend to go to sleep. You won't be responsible. Just act surprised when you wake up and I'm gone."

John did as she asked, pulling his father's heavy gray coat over him, hiding his head beneath it.

Beth slipped her hand quickly into the pocket and took out the purse. She counted out seven dollars and put them in her handkerchief, along with the coins from Widow Brinks. It amounted to almost eight dollars. That was more money than she'd ever had in her life, but would it be enough for Suzannah and her to survive? It would have to be. She lay down beside John and waited.

Abraham stopped the wagon in front of the Esopus Tavern. He took his jacket, threw it over his shoulders. Beth could see through partly raised lids that he was debating waking John. She was relieved when he decided against it.

She watched him walk into the tavern, knowing she might never see him again. She felt nothing. He was a bad man and would never be other.

She nudged John. "Wake up."

"I'm not sleeping."

"I'm leaving," she said, unable to ignore the new tears that welled in his already puffy eyes.

"It's going to be forever, isn't it?" His voice quaked.

"Forever is too long to wait to see an imp like you

again." The words came easily, but she swallowed hard. "Just remember to say your prayers."

She kissed him, hugged him to her, then almost brusquely pushed him back. "Now lie down and close those eyes. And remember, you didn't hear or see a thing."

John lay down, tried not to whimper. Beth opened the trunk they had packed so carefully and pulled out her mother's quilt. She would mend it properly and save it for Suzannah. She rolled and tied it with a piece of hemp. Then, giving John one last wordless kiss, she climbed out through the rear of the wagon.

When her feet hit the cobblestone, she felt faint. She was still weak from the birthing, weaker than she'd thought. How on earth was she going to get to Peter's? It was already nearing four o'clock and it would be evening before she was anywhere near the Hurley bridge.

A man and a woman passing by looked at her strangely. If she aroused too much suspicion, Abraham would track her easily. She tried to appear relaxed. Keeping her eyes on the tavern door, she hurried across the street and entered a small alley. Her heart was already pounding. Pulling her shawl over her head, she began the long walk.

On foot it would take her two days to reach Hurley in her present condition, but Peter was the only one who could help her find Suzannah. No walk was too long for that. But with Pa and Ansel looking for her she wouldn't be able to set out until after the boat left. The only thing she could do now was to keep out of sight until well after sundown.

She walked slowly down the river road, keeping clear of taverns where, from back alleys, the smell of ale and urine was sickeningly pungent. Weak and light-headed, she made her way up to the main street. Klamper's bake shop was the first store she came to. Faint and hungry, she went inside.

The trays that sat on the counter were almost empty, except for a few expensive pastries. Beth realized she'd had nothing but tea and hardtack all day. She took a few coppers from her handkerchief and bought herself a boysenberry tart, then sat down on the customer's bench to eat it. But instead of quieting her hunger, the tart increased it. She opened the handkerchief and bought another two tarts.

Mr. Klamper eyed her suspiciously. Girls Beth's age didn't have money to spend on three tarts for themselves. Beth felt his gaze, knew what he was thinking and started for the door.

"Just a moment, young lady," Mr. Klamper said sternly. "I want a word with you."

"I'm late," Beth said hastily. She dropped her tart and raced into the street. She ran without looking back and turned into the first alley she came to, her forehead beaded with sweat.

A cough from the shadows caused her to freeze.

"Well, now," a voice chuckled, "what have we here?"

Beth turned and looked down. A drunkard in tattered vest and stained leather breeches lay slumped against the wall. He beckoned with a gnarled finger. Beth stiffened. His stench was palpable.

"Don't be afraid, missy," he croaked. "I take good care of nice girls. Just come over here."

Beth looked out into the street to see if Mr. Klamper was following her. As she did, the handle of a cane snaked her ankle.

"It's been a long time since anyone stopped by." The drunk smiled and the stubs of yellow teeth glinted in the fading light.

Beth felt the cane tug at her ankle. She tried to free her leg, but lost her balance and fell to the ground.

"Now see what you've gone and done." The man began to push himself along the wall toward her.

Beth scrambled to her feet, stifled a scream. The drunk's cane swung forward again, but this time it missed and smacked the wall. Beth bolted blindly forward into the street.

"Watch where you're going, girl!" A man in a light-colored broadcloth coat held her arms. "You could have . . ."

Beth panicked. She didn't hear what else the man said. All she knew was that he was holding her and she had to get away, get to Peter, get to her baby, her God's child. She twisted free and began to run. Several people stopped and turned. She heard one call out to the man to ask if he'd been robbed. Her eyes had trouble focusing, the daylight seemed to be fading rapidly. Oh, dear Lord, she prayed, please don't let me faint.

Rounding the corner she stopped and leaned back against the wall of a building to catch her breath. She let her eyes close for a moment. When she opened them, Ansel was sitting astride his horse in front of her.

"And where do you think you're going?" He got down and came toward her. "Pa's been looking all over for you, and a hefty bit of his money. What were you up to?"

"Where's Suzannah?" Beth said, her eyes glaring.

"She's fine and taken care of," Ansel said. "And that's that." He reached for her but she stepped to the side. "Now come on, we've got a ship to meet and some questions to be answered."

"I'm not going with you."

"We'll see about that."

Beth brought her knee up hard and fast, sending Ansel doubled over to the ground. It took all her strength and for a moment she felt as if she too were going to fall. But then, from a passing carriage, a baby cried. And like some strange magical signal, Beth's breasts dripped milk. *A sign! A true sign!* her strength returned.

"You goddamn little whore," Ansel groaned. "I'll make you pay for this."

Beth moved quickly. Before Ansel could stand she was on his horse, her body flung forward, her mind desperately trying to blot out the pain that blazed inside her with a single name: Suzannah.

It was dark, the horse was wheezing and Beth felt as if she were about to lose consciousness when she finally reached Peter Avery's house. Her thighs were slick with sweat and blood. Viselike cramps gripped her abdomen. She dismounted with difficulty and made her way up the path to the door.

She had no idea of the time, but the large stone house was still lighted and Peter's horse had not yet been put into the barn. She curled her hand into a fist and knocked twice, lightly, upon the door. As she heard the clack of wooden clogs crossing the floor, she unthinkingly tried to smooth her wind-matted hair, straighten her dress.

The door swung open and Mrs. Avery, looking gaunt and pale, her white hair straggling out from beneath her cap, stood in the entrance. She narrowed her eyes, peered into the darkness. "Who is it?"

Beth stepped forward into the light. "I've come to see if Peter's all right," she said hesitantly.

"You!" Mrs. Avery's face darkened, contorted into a grimace of loathing. "Get out of here. Go away!" Her voice was rising slowly, brinking hysteria. "Go away!"

"Mrs. Avery, I must see Peter. Is he all right?"

"Haven't you and your brother done enough?" Violet Avery fairly screamed.

"What's happening?" Wilbur Avery came to his wife's side. Seeing Beth, he put his arm around Violet and drew her close, as if protecting her from some great evil. "Go away," he said calmly.

Beth reached out her hands in a pleading gesture. "Please. I didn't know he was going to get hurt when I asked him to follow us."

"But for the Lord's mercy, Peter would be dead now," Wilbur Avery said solemnly. "As it is, if he ever gets to walk again at all, he'll be crippled for the rest of his days on this earth."

Violet Avery began to sob.

Beth could not believe what she'd heard. Peter crippled? Peter who could climb South Mountain without winding? Who could dance six reels at the church without so much as a gentleman's rest? Not the Peter who could carry her across the Bushkill on his shoulders?

"I have to see him," she said more anxiously than before. "You must let me."

Violet Avery pulled free of her husband's protective embrace. "Never!" she said savagely. "You're not fit to breathe the same air as my son. He wants no part of you and your vile Tory-loving family, so go away and stay away."

"He didn't say that. He'd never say that," Beth cried. "I don't believe you."

Violet Avery stepped forward and without another word slammed the door shut.

Beth stared at it blankly, uncomprehendingly. Her knees were shaking and she'd begun to tremble all over. She fell back against an oak tree, forcing herself to breathe deeply. When she felt steady enough, she made her way to the Avery's well and drank two icy ladlefuls of water. They refreshed her and revived her determination. She had to get to Peter.

She knew the Averys were lying about Peter's not wanting to see her. He wouldn't blame her for Ansel's attack. She would wait until his mother and father were asleep and then tap on his window, as she'd done so many times in the past. She had to see him. He was her only hope of finding Suzannah.

In the moonlight, Ansel's horse was much too visible. All the Averys had to do was look outside to know that she hadn't left. With some difficulty, she led the animal into the woods behind the house and tied it to a tree. Then she walked back, ignoring the cramps that shot through her again and again, crouched in the shadows and waited.

By the time the house was dark she was perspiring again and shaking so violently she could barely steady her hand to open Peter's shutter. When finally she did, and looked inside, her heart sank.

Peter lay still upon his bed, a candle lamp burning on the table beside him. His eyes were closed and there was a wide white bandage around his head. She couldn't see his leg. She unlatched the window the way he had shown her four months ago when his mother had found out about the pregnancy and refused to let her come visiting. She called his name softly.

He moaned and his eyes fluttered open.

"Peter. It's me," Beth whispered anxiously.

For a moment his eyes focused. Beth smiled tentatively, reached out her hand. Peter raised his, but instead of trying to touch hers, he motioned her away.

"Peter!" She kept her shaking hand extended, unable to believe that he was not going to grasp it.

Peter wet his lips and tried to speak but couldn't.

"What is it?"

He raised his head slightly and with much difficulty said, "Go . . . go away. My mother will try to—" His words broke off in a grunt of pain as the bedsheet pulled across his leg.

Beth heard footsteps racing down from upstairs.

"Go quickly," Peter breathed. "And hide. The town knows about your father and—ow!" He turned his face and buried it in the pillow.

"But where will I go? How will I find my baby?"

Before Peter could answer, the door to his room opened and his mother rushed in. Dressed in a white nightdress and cap, clutching a flickering candle, she looked like a specter. When she saw Beth at the window she shrieked.

Beth drew back, stumbled and fell. Struggling to her feet she could hear Wilbur Avery's angry voice demanding to know what was going on. She bolted for the woods.

Mounting Ansel's horse, she rode blindly up into

the hills. Only when the faint light of dawn began to dilute the blue-black sky did she realize she was on Peekamoose Ridge, burning with fever and clutching her mother's rose-embroidered quilt in front of Widow Brinks's cabin.

Chapter 6

For six days and nights Beth knew only a twilight world of delirium, and the constant ministrations of Widow Brinks. The widow's soothing voice would ease the terror of Beth's fever nightmares and her herbal elixirs drew the fire from Beth's body. From morning through night, seemingly without respite, the widow battled the darkness that threatened to engulf her charge, and on the morning of the seventh day she triumphed.

Beth emerged from the siege just barely strong enough to spoon gruel to her lips. Her cheeks were hollow and her eyes rimmed with bluish shadows. Through her pallid skin, her ribs were in stark evidence. She could not sit up without assistance.

The widow smiled as Beth, propped up with several pillows, slowly ate a bowl of warm cornmeal sweetened with maple syrup.

"I've been here a week?" Beth asked incredulously.

"Physically, yes. Though I fear that spiritually you were places even the most courageous among us would not dare to go."

In the bright morning light the nightmare world she had emerged from seemed far away. Only the images of a bear stealing her baby and Peter in a welter of blood remained.

She put down the bowl and tried to sit up on her own, but fell back against the pillows.

"You have at least another week of bed healing, and then a full moon cycle before you're strong enough to move about as before."

"But I must find my daughter. My brother took her."

"I know." The widow nodded. "But a child alone cannot raise another child, especially in these hills."

"I'm not a child," Beth said indignantly.

"Your protest belies that," the widow said gently.

"But—"

"Oh, I know in many ways you're far older than your years, but it takes more than carnal knowledge and childbirth to make a woman. Meanwhile, leave what the fates have arranged for your daughter."

"You know where she is?" Beth asked anxiously.

"No, but I know she is alive and well."

"I have to find her. I want her back."

"You will have her—in time. That is the way it's to be. Nothing can change it."

"But when?"

"That I do not know."

"Can't you tell me more?"

The widow looked distressed, turned away. "No. And you must not ask me again."

"I don't understand."

"The future is not yours to understand."

"But it is yours. You can see—"

"What I see is not always to be spoken of," the widow said sternly.

"But I want my baby."

"Listen to me, and listen well. For her to rejoin you now, even if that were possible, would be to sentence you both to early graves. What has been ordained, painful as it is, must stand. Your child has a home now, which is more than you do. I will keep you here until you regain your health, but, much as I want to, I dare not have you remain longer."

Beth was confused, hurt. She hadn't had a chance to think of where she was going to live, but it had been so long since she had anyone to take care of her that the thought of being cast out and alone again caused unbidden tears to well. "I don't understand."

"You have been robbed of enough of your childhood. I am a pariah in these hills, and to live with me would make you one too. Besides, to remain here in Shokan would also be dangerous. Your father is being sought for much Tory pillage. The hatred of those who hunt him will spew out on you. You must have a home that will offer you safety, allow you schooling, and keep you out of sight of the DeWitts."

Beth's mouth dropped open. "What do you know of the DeWitts?"

"All that you said when you were in fever, which I imagine is everything."

"Is there nothing I can keep secret from you?"

"All that I know is secret," the widow said with a smile. "But it is no secret that Regina DeWitt can be a dangerous woman if streams do not flow her way. She believes you have fled to Halifax and it is best that she keep this belief. I will find a home for you when you are well. In the meantime, you will get strong and think of nothing else."

"But my baby," Beth protested.

"It will be time enough to think of her when you are able to take care of yourself."

In the days that followed, to her surprise, Beth found that she had little time to think of anything *but* getting well (though she rarely forgot a nighttime prayer for Suzannah). Widow Brinks plied her with tonics and guided her through curiously simple but effective exercises that renewed her strength remarkably. By Thanksgiving she was splitting logs and felt healthier and happier than she had in years. Widow Brinks refused to allow her to leave the ridge, even to sneak a nighttime visit to Peter, and had made her vow on her mother's grave to conceal herself should someone come visiting (an occurrence that happened but once when Dame Van Proctor came by for a remedy for her boils). Despite the restrictions, Beth felt a joyous contentment.

Evenings were spent around the hearth. The widow told Beth of growing up lonely and friendless in the mountains, her Indian mother and nature her only teachers, until she met Everett Brinks. He was a trapper who saw her ride into Kingston one day and followed her home.

"We were married two months later," the widow said, her face flushing slightly as she added, "and we honeymooned the next six in a cabin by the Bushkill."

It saddened Beth to think that so happy a couple could only have eight years before death parted them, and that life had given them no children. Her heart went out to the widow and she made a special effort (which in truth was no effort at all) to exhibit her affection as often as possible.

By the beginning of December, life with Widow Brinks had become most pleasurable. On blustery days, after the chores, she let Beth pretend to be a great French lady and would balm her hands and face with cucumber cream or soften her hair with a rinsing of egg. Neither mentioned Beth's leaving, though both accepted it as inevitable.

The inevitable happened before Christmas. The widow returned one day and announced she'd arranged for Beth to live with an elderly farmer and his wife and daughter outside of Kingston.

"Life there will not be easy," the widow warned, "but you will be schooled, and safe from those in these hills who still carry hate."

Beth wanted to protest, but knew the parting was no easier for the widow and so remained silent.

The widow handed her a sack. It was filled with beautiful fine fabric. "There is enough here for at least two dresses. I was saving it for Christmas but . . ." She let her voice trail off.

Beth could barely say thank you.

"I will take you to the Stillwells' tomorrow, providing the snow holds off."

"If it doesn't?" Beth asked, hopefully.

"The sled broke two years ago, so I suppose it would mean you'd be here until spring." The widow didn't smile, but her eyes did.

Beth lay awake most of the night, praying for snow. When she finally fell asleep, she dreamed of it. In the morning she flew from her bed to the shutters, flung them open.

The sky was gray, but the ground was hard and dry. The widow was already awake and had hitched up the wagon.

As they were ready to leave, the widow said: "Let us say good-bye here. It will be better."

Beth hugged the widow tightly and tried not to cry. But she was still only fourteen years old. Her cold cheeks soon dampened with tears. To her surprise not all of them were her own.

It was a long, quiet ride down.

The farm of Jacob Stillwell was small but well tended, with a large barn and corncrib set fairly close to the main house. To the rear of the barn stood a small slave shack and a copse of apple trees, now bare and gnarled.

The house itself was Dutch-fashioned, a single story with another built into the high, inward curving roof. The heavy board shutters on the windows were closed, though it was not much past midday, and Beth wondered if the house's cold exterior mirrored its owner's ways. The widow had said that the family was strongly religious, but was daylight an offense to the Almighty? Beth shivered beneath the heavy woolen cape the widow had given her.

Jacob Stillwell, a lean man of substantial years, with black and silver hair hanging loosely about his shoul-

ders, stood without smiling in the doorway as Beth
and the widow approached. His eyes were small,
dwarfed by bushy silver brows, but seemed to miss
nothing. They were scrutinizing eyes, made for in-
spections and judgments. Beth wondered how she
measured.

Jacob's wife, Hannah, stood behind him. She was a
good twenty years her husband's junior. Beth guessed
that she was no more than thirty-five, though her
blond braids were already streaked heavily with gray.
She smiled tentatively as the widow made brief introductions.

"Come inside," Jacob said. "Hannah, get the
widow and"—he seemed to falter over Beth's name—
"and *Beth* some tea."

"Of course," Hannah said quickly.

"Just a small cup," Widow Brinks said. "I must be
getting back."

"But not before you've seen Margaret. You haven't
seen her since she was an infant," Hannah protested.
She took two cups down from a shelf and placed them
on the table, then poured water from the fireplace
kettle into a beautiful copper teapot and set that beside them. "You just warm up here while I go out to
the barn to get her," Hannah said. She grabbed a
shawl from a wall peg. "Jacob, why don't you give
the widow and Beth some of my corn bread."

Jacob nodded. He turned his eyes to Beth. They
were still searching. "It's only two hours cool," he
said, waving his hand toward the bread tin. "Would
you like some?"

"Yes, please," Beth said.

"Child!" Jacob said sternly. "Your elders answer
first."

Widow Brinks gave Beth a quick look that said,
Don't-worry-he's-not-as-severe-as-he-seems, but Beth
had her doubts.

"We'll both have some," the widow said. She patted
Beth's knee beneath the table.

Jacob brought the bread and some jam. Beth waited

until the widow had taken a piece before reaching for hers. She noticed that Jacob, who sat down by the fireplace, was watching to see that she did.

Hannah returned, followed by a blond large-boned girl about sixteen. Beth regarded her warily as she removed her shawl, pulled at her skirt and apron, and straightened the muslin cap that was pulled over her up-pinned braids. There was something vaguely disquieting about the girl.

Hannah prodded her daughter slightly until she was facing the table. "This is our daughter, Margaret," Hannah said proudly.

"How very nice to meet you," the widow said.

"Margaret," Hannah said, "this is Widow Brinks." Margaret curtseyed.

"And Beth." Hannah lowered her voice, the way one did when discussing the departed. "Beth is an orphan and she's come to live with us."

Beth looked questioningly at Widow Brinks, but the widow deliberately avoided her eyes. Obviously the deception was necessary, but the widow could have at least warned her. Beth raised her head and smiled at Margaret.

Margaret returned the smile, with all the warmth of a copperhead. The Stillwells' daughter was obviously not pleased with the idea of an addition to the household.

"Won't that be nice?" Hannah asked her daughter.

Margaret kept her gaze leveled at Beth. "Yes, Mama," she said politely.

Beth wished she could move her chair closer to the fire.

"They'll be such fine company for one another," Hannah went on. "And it will be good to have another young one in the house." She patted her daughter's arm. "Margaret, when Beth finishes her tea, why don't you show her your room and where she can unpack her things."

"Yes, Mama," Margaret said tonelessly. Beth had the feeling that Margaret answered all her parents' questions affirmatively; that her agreeableness was an attribute brought about by her father's free hand with the leather switch, which hung ominously on a peg near the door.

"I'd better be going." The widow stood. Beth felt a lurch inside her stomach. She didn't want to stay with these people. There was a large wooden cross lying beside a leather-bound Bible on a stand in the corner, but there was no love in this house.

The widow kissed Beth on the forehead. "Behave yourself and make me proud of you. I'll visit again in the spring."

The spring! Beth wanted to scream. That was months away. She was about to say something, but the widow's eyes stopped her. She lowered her head. "Good-bye," she said softly, for they had already had their parting. It would be a long cold winter.

When the widow had gone, Beth followed Margaret upstairs to a large sloped-ceilinged room. There was an iron bed, covered in red-and-white chintz, against one wall, and a large chest of drawers against another. Near the door stood a tall oak cabinet, lined in cedar, for frocks and fine linens. And though there was only a single window, the room was well lighted.

"Your room is very lovely," Beth said.

Margaret pulled off her muslin cap and sat down on the bed, began loosening her braids. "Was."

Beth looked confused. "I'm afraid I don't understand."

"I said it was. It *was* my room. It's *ours* now." She said the word sarcastically.

"Oh. Well, I don't have to sleep here. I can sleep in the kitchen. It doesn't matter to me. Really."

"It's not up to you," Margaret said snippishly. "Nor to me, unfortunately. Mama wants us to be like *sisters*." She fairly hissed the word. "She wants to pretend that Matilda is still here."

"Matilda?"

"My *real* sister. She died when I was seven." Margaret laughed. "Though to tell you the truth, she never died for *them*. They still talk about her as though she were alive."

"I'm sorry," Beth said, shrugged helplessly. "I know it's hard to lose someone you love. My mother died six years ago."

Margaret began brushing her hair. "When did your father go?"

"My father? He's—" Beth caught herself. "Uh, I —I never knew him."

"Any brothers or sisters?"

"Uh . . . um, no. No, none."

Margaret eyed her suspiciously. "You certainly don't like talking about your family, do you? You're fidgeting. Papa says that people who fidget have the devil nipping at them somewhere." For the first time, Margaret smiled. "Do you?"

"Do I what?"

"Have the devil nipping at you."

Beth began to feel trapped, and didn't like it. She tilted her chin defiantly. "No, I don't."

Margaret studied Beth a moment. "How old are you?"

"Fourteen."

She dropped her hands disappointedly into her lap. "I should have known. Fourteen! Some sister. I wouldn't be surprised if you're not a woman yet."

If she only knew! Beth seethed inwardly. She was more woman than Margaret would be for a good many years.

"Well?" Margaret asked mockingly. "Are you or aren't you? Or don't you know what I mean?"

"I know what you mean," Beth said. "And yes, I am."

"Well, at least I'm not going to be saddled with a complete child." She sighed and resumed brushing her hair.

"I'm not a child," Beth answered tightly.

"You're fourteen. I'm going to be seventeen on the twenty-seventh of February," Margaret said haughtily. "That's a big difference."

Beth bit back the words she wanted to hurl at her. Why, the conceit! If only she could tell her what she knew, the snooty twig.

"It's *only* two years," Beth said, not really trying to keep her voice pleasant.

Margaret sighed again. "How can I expect you to understand? Oh, well, let's get on with getting you placed. You can put your clothes in the bottom drawer of the bureau, and if you have any frocks they can go in the cabinet."

"I haven't anything except what I'm wearing, an extra sacque, and a few underthings," Beth said.

Margaret made a face. "That's all? What do you go to church in?"

"I—I've been ill for a while. I've been saying prayers at the widow's."

Margaret laughed. "I'd like to see you try that here. You'd have to be ready for the minister's last words to miss church in this house. Papa thinks the devil just waits around on Sunday looking for victims."

"I've fabric for two skirts and an apron," Beth said, opening the sack the widow had given her to exhibit the material.

Margaret's eyes widened. "Why, that's velvet! And enough of it for a whole costume, too." She grabbed the material. "Where did an orphan like you get this?" Her eyes narrowed. "I'll bet you stole it, didn't you?"

"I did not! The widow bought it for me," Beth said defensively.

Margaret eyed her suspiciously. "Oh, did she now?" she said mockingly, holding the fabric against herself.

Beth pulled it back. "That's mine!"

"What's going on up there?" Jacob's voice cut through the room like a scythe.

"Now see what you've done," Margaret whispered harshly. "Nothing, Papa!" she shouted. "I'm just showing Beth the room." She closed the door and quietly fastened the latch. "Listen to me," she warned, "this is *my* room and as long as you're here you're *my* guest and subject to *my* rules. Sister or not."

"I don't have to——"

Margaret grabbed Beth's arm and squeezed it. She was stronger than Beth would have imagined and her fingers dug deeply into Beth's flesh. "Don't tell me what you don't have to do or you'll be sorry. Very sorry. Do you understand?"

Beth winced. "Let go of me."

Margaret released her. "That was just to show you who's boss."

Beth rubbed her arm, said nothing. How on earth was she going to live with this girl? Before she had a chance to speculate, Jacob called them to help Hannah with the dinner.

Beth took her fabric and folded it neatly. She cocked her head to the side and looked at Margaret. "It's mine," Beth said, "and I have *no* intention of sharing it."

Margaret smiled. "We'll see about that," she said sweetly.

Beth felt in her pocket for her handkerchief purse. She would have to make certain Margaret never saw *that*. Judging from first impressions, it seemed likely that the only way to do it was to keep the purse with her at all times.

At dinner—rabbit stew and creamed corn—Beth almost forgot the argument she'd had with Margaret, when Jacob Stillwell announced that he expected the girls to be to one another like Naomi and Ruth.

Margaret coughed. Beth nearly choked on her food. Neither glanced at the other.

"I expect," Jacob said somberly, "that Margaret, being the older, will set a noteworthy example for behavior that you, Beth, will follow."

"Of course she will, Papa," Margaret shot her a triumphant glance.

Jacob Stillwell looked at Beth. "We're a hardworking, churchgoing family, and I hope you'll not disappoint us as a member."

"No, sir," Beth said. She kept her head lowered, reluctant to face Jacob. There was something about his eyes that frightened her. Something uncomfortably familiar. It wasn't until bedtime, when she and Margaret were required to curtsey before him and say good night, that Beth realized what the familiarity was.

Jacob Stillwell had the same ice-blue eyes as her brother Ansel.

Chapter 7

The following months at the Stillwell Farm were hectic. But going to school again was exciting and there were enough new activities to keep Beth's loneliness and depression at bay. Even despite the cold, which grew bitter enough to freeze the water in her pitcher every morning, she managed to find a kind of pleasure in the farm chores, particularly those that put her close to the animals and far away from Margaret. Neither Christmas nor the New Year had sweetened *that* one's disposition, though for a while it seemed a possibility—after Clay Matthews had started coming around to help Jacob Stillwell mend stalls in the barn.

Clay Matthews was twenty-one and Margaret followed him like a shadow. He was slightly pudgy and sallow-faced, with a long nose that blared red in the cold, but he had a friendly manner and was good with an ax and always dressed well for church. The week he began work on the barn, Margaret fell in love.

Every night after that, bundled up in their bed,

Margaret would tell Beth another anecdote about her budding romance. In the most conspiratorial whisper —after making Beth cross her heart and hope to die should she disclose a word—she would describe in detail the glory of Clay Matthews's kisses.

"You wouldn't believe it," she said one February evening, blowing out the candle and burrowing under the comforter next to Beth, "but it was the most wonderful sensation I've ever felt. I do believe it was . . . *passion*."

"Passion?" Beth was impressed. She had only read about passion, in Peter's books. Never had she met anyone who'd really experienced it. Clay Matthews was the last person in the world she'd suspect of producing it.

"Oh, damnation," Margaret said disgustedly. "I should have known better than to try to explain adult things to a child." She rolled over, pulled the heavy quilt more tightly about her.

Beth waited patiently. Margaret wasn't that easily stopped when she started on the one thing her father would thrash her mightily for discussing. So far as Jacob Stillwell was concerned, anything that put a male and female in conjunction was dirty, "devil's foulness." Moreover, any part of the human body— barring face and hands—that was unclothed was lewd. Once Beth tripped and fell on the kitchen rug and her skirt pulled up far above her knees. Jacob, turning teaberry red, not only failed to help her to her feet, but swatted her with his switch and told her to compose herself or prepare for a thrashing. Margaret had received more than her fair share of those and Beth had no desire to partake of the experience.

But regardless of Jacob's feelings, and the risk of thrashings, or perhaps because of them, Margaret was the most romantically obsessed girl Beth had ever met.

Sometimes, when she thought Beth was asleep, she would light the candle and stand before the small cracked mirror above the bureau. There she would slowly unbutton her nightdress and admire her breasts, often running her fingers slowly around each nipple. Several times she had let the nightdress fall to her waist. Then, pressing against the bureau, she would cup her breast with her hand, squeeze it and toss her head back as if in ecstasy, on occasion gripping both breasts and kneading them until soft moans escaped her lips.

Recently, Beth noticed, Margaret was going to the mirror less and wriggling a lot more in bed, especially after she'd talk about Clay. It made Beth uneasy. When she asked Margaret why she was wriggling so, Margaret snapped that it was none of her business.

After Margaret had been silent for several minutes, Beth thought that perhaps this time she was miffed enough to remain quiet. But just as Beth was about to close her eyes, Margaret stirred.

"Are you awake?"

"Uh-huh."

"Well, do you want to know what happened or don't you?" Margaret asked.

It was impossible not to be curious. Though she had been violated and given birth to two children, Beth knew very little of love and lovemaking. Sometimes she would fantasize about Peter, but he was so real and proper it was difficult. More often she would imagine a dark-haired smiling stranger coming to whisk her off to a magnificent house where he would ply her with chocolate and passionate kisses. But though she knew the taste of chocolate, she had yet to recognize a passionate kiss.

"Of course I want to know," she said.

Margaret moved closer, took a deep breath. "Well, it was the most exciting thing we've done yet. Clay took me in the back of the barn—you know, where I told you I saw old Vly put his hand in Black Annie's dress?"

"Uh-huh." One of Margaret's other preoccupations was spying on the Stillwells' slaves.

"Well, he kissed me . . . the French way!"

"What's that?" Beth asked.

"It's the way the French people do it, and you know what they say about the French."

"No, what?"

"Oh, Lord. Don't you know anything? The French are lovers, that's what. They make love all the time. Different ways. Ways that make women their slaves."

"I wouldn't be anyone's slave," Beth said righteously. "No matter what he did."

"It's not being a slave like Vly or Annie, you nit."

"I don't care. If that's what happens when you get kissed the French way, I hope it never happens to me."

"You don't even know what it is. It's just a . . . well, a special kind of kiss."

"How special?"

"It makes you feel tingly all over. You see, you're supposed to open your lips and the man opens his. And then when you're kissing like that, he puts his tongue in your mouth and wiggles it all around. Then you do the same to him."

"It sounds disgusting."

"It's not. Come here, I'll show you.'"

"No." Beth moved back.

"Oh, come on, don't be a baby. I'll just show you what it feels like." Margaret reached out and pulled Beth toward her. "Just part your lips and—"

Beth broke free and covered her mouth with her hands. "No. I don't want to."

"All right, Miss Innocence. Stay a baby. I'm not going to tell you anything anymore!" She rolled over to her side of the bed.

Beth sighed, closed her eyes. She suspected that if Clay Matthews continued working on the Stillwell farm, Margaret's nighttime silence would be short-lived.

And so it was. Two nights later, as they were undressing for bed, Margaret called Beth's name. Beth was surprised and slightly embarrassed to see Margaret standing on the cold floor stark naked. Usually they slipped into their nightclothes before removing their underthings, as much for warmth as for modesty, and to see Margaret like that in bright candlelight was somewhat of a shock.

"How do I look?" Margaret asked. Shivering slightly, she turned sideways and tossed her hair back.

She looked better than most people would have thought, were they to judge from the clothes Jacob Stillwell made her wear. Her large firm breasts were milky white and dappled with the tiniest of freckles, and her belly was no more than a gentle rise above the golden mound of her womanhood.

"Fine," Beth said, confused. "Why are you asking?"

"I—I want to know how—" She stopped. "Never mind." She picked up her nightdress and slipped it over her head. Buttoning it quickly, she hurried toward the warmth of the bed.

"Want to know what?" What was the girl about? Beth wondered.

"Well, I want to know how I'd look to . . . Clay."

"Margaret! You wouldn't let him *see* you!" Beth gasped. "Why, I don't even think married folks do that."

"Some do," Margaret said offhandedly. "Ingrid Westheimer told me that she once saw her father and mother lying together naked."

"But they're not regular church people," Beth protested. "Your father said so just the other day. Remember?"

"There's nobody who goes to church enough to please Papa," Margaret said disgustedly.

Beth could hardly argue the point. Jacob Stillwell's obsession with religion was equaled only by his daughter's with sex.

"I guess you're right," Beth said. She kneeled on the bed and was about to get under the covers when Margaret stopped her.

"Hey. What do you look like?" she whispered.

Beth drew back. "Just like you, I guess," she said uneasily.

"Well, let me see, why don't you? I never saw another girl bare. Come on. It's not like a sin or anything. I just want to look."

Beth gripped the bodice of her nightdress. "No."

Margaret sat up quickly and grabbed Beth's hands. "I showed you what I look like, it's only fair."

"I didn't ask to see."

"But you looked, didn't you? And I know you weren't sleeping all those nights when I got out of bed to go over to the glass."

Beth flushed scarlet, but said nothing.

"I'll bet you liked to see me touching myself, didn't you?" Margaret said slowly. "Would you like to know what it feels like?"

Beth flung her hands outward and free. "You leave me alone, hear, or I'm going to tell your father about you and Clay."

Margaret moved back. "Oh, all right. Who wants to see *you?* You probably have nothing to look at anyway." She lay back and pulled the comforter over her head.

Beth sat up, waiting until she was sure Margaret was asleep before letting her own head touch the pillow. The rest of the night was filled with unpleasant dreams. For the first time in many weeks she forgot to pray for Suzannah.

In the days that followed, Margaret said little about her romance with Clay, but passed few opportunities to harass Beth, harassments that increased when it became obvious that Clay Matthews had more than a passing interest in Beth.

By March, Clay was coming to the Stillwell farm to court Beth, and Margaret's hostility had become unbearable. Whatever Beth was engaged in, be it carding or spinning linen or making candles, even milking the cows, Margaret would sabotage it. She would either snip the flax on the wheel when Beth was working it or dilute the lye so that Beth's soap would fail. Though Beth hadn't the slightest interest in Clay, nor offered him any encouragement, he persisted, to Margaret's mounting rage. It was a rage aggravated to no small degree by the fact that she was not happy to give up her widening explorations in passion, being still too proud to offer herself without at least the *pretense* of love. It all climaxed the day of the thaw.

Clay stood beside Beth as she finished milking the cow, waiting to carry the pail for her as she went down the road to sell quarts. (Jacob Stillwell was susceptible to the milksick and never drank any himself.) He'd just reached for the bucket when a thunderous rumble rent the air.

The cow started, nearly causing Beth to spill the day's quarts. "What in heaven was that?" she cried.

Before Clay could answer, there was another rumble, and hollering and shouting seemed to come from everywhere.

"It's the river ice! It's breaking up! Come on." Clay grabbed her hand.

"But—the milk. I can't leave now. Where are you taking me?"

Clay whooped. "Everyone leaves everything when the ice breaks. If you've never seen it, it's something to behold." He clasped her hand tighter and pulled her after him.

Outside the barn, Beth saw Margaret and her mother, followed by Vly and Black Annie and several Negroes from the neighboring farm, hurrying down the hill toward the river.

"Come on," Clay urged. "There ain't nobody working from here to Poughkeepsie now. Just listen to that rumble."

It was impossible not to. It was awesome, filling the air with tremors. When they reached the bluff that overlooked the river, the sight was as incredible as the sound. Huge blocks of ice crashed against one another, hurtling in the air, as the swollen river's unleashed waters flowed freely once again.

"There's bound to be partying in Kingston. Last year it was better than a county fair. Will you come with me?" Clay asked.

Beth saw that Margaret had turned around and was glaring at her. "Well . . ."

"Oh, please say yes."

"I'll ask Mother Stillwell, but I'll only go if we take Margaret with us."

Clay looked crestfallen.

Beth was adamant. "And you have to ask her," she added.

"I don't see why," he said grumpily, "but if that's what you want."

It wasn't what Beth wanted at all, but it was better than being stuck alone with Clay, better than fending off still more of Margaret's hostility.

Margaret was only half pleased with the invitation, but accepted nonetheless. Hannah Stillwell suggested they get on their way before her husband returned from fence mending, as he was not in favor of such frivolities. She made Clay promise to have the girls back no later than an hour after dark.

Kingston was already aglow with barnfires and merrymaking when they arrived. Margaret had made sure to sit next to Clay for the ride and had made the most of every bump in the road by pressing shamelessly against him. Beth suspected that their romance had stopped short of ultimate consummation not because of Margaret's morality but because of Clay's reluctance to be roped into wedlock.

Beth had never even kissed Clay. It was clear as they rode, though, that like a flower watered after a long drought, he was not immune to the pleasant pressure of a female body. When they reached the docks, he had removed his woolen scarf and looked as warm as a schoolboy after a sack race. Margaret was positively glowing.

An old woman by a small fire was selling sausages on a stick and Clay bought one for each of them. Beth was entranced with the rapidly burgeoning crowd, the music makers and vendors who appeared out of nowhere, the beggars and gentry, everyone excited by the maelstrom of crashing ice, the birth of spring.

There was much shouting and jostling, especially by the youngsters. Before Beth realized it, she had become separated from Clay and Margaret, which didn't upset her in the least. Standing alone on one of the piers, she gazed admiringly at a grand brigantine-rigged twin-masted sloop. Though she'd seen Hudson River sloops before, their mainsails full in summer breezes, she'd never seen one close up, nor one so grand.

The Golden Gull, as its gold-painted name proclaimed, was easily seventy feet in length, and festively colored in red, green, and blue stripes. Two seamen stood on the deck polishing the brass fittings that only recently had been swept clean of snow. One of them saw Beth and leaned over, shouted a friendly greeting.

Beth smiled, but turned demurely away. You didn't strike up friendships with strangers, no matter how pleasant they looked. She started walking back to where she'd last seen Clay and Margaret when a raffishly dressed young man in a buckskin coat, tight leather breeches, and riding boots stepped in front of her. He was lean and muscular, with chiseled features and piercing dark eyes.

"I beg your pardon," he said, tipping his hat and exhibiting a head of thick black hair, long on the shoulders and cut in a straight bang across the forehead. "I believe this belongs to you." He held out her handkerchief purse.

Beth gasped. Unthinkingly she grabbed it from him, clutching it tightly.

"Whoa. I didn't take it. I saw an easy-fingers pull it from you and I managed to retrieve it."

"Thank you," Beth stammered. "I'm just startled that someone was able to lift it from me without my knowledge." She blushed, thinking of the pickpocket's hand sliding into her skirt fold. She gripped the purse tighter, not daring to put it back in its former hiding place.

"In the face of a DuBoise sloop like *The Golden*

Gull anyone can be caught off guard." He looked at the ship as if it were an unattainable woman. "She's beautiful, isn't she?"

"Quite," Beth said, suddenly aware that she was standing close enough to the stranger to smell the leather of his clothes, to feel the warmth of his breath as he spoke. Aware too that he was very handsome. She moved back, surprised by a conspicuous quickening in her chest. She had never faced eyes like his before.

"And the *Gull*'s only one of many," the stranger said. "I've heard that DuBoise has a veritable merchant fleet—frigates, snow rigs." He turned to face her and once again she felt the heat of his eyes. "You have of course heard of Seth DuBoise?"

"No. I'm afraid I haven't."

"Then you must not live here in the city." He grinned. "Nor come from the manors across the river."

"No, I don't," Beth said defensively, adding, "and I wouldn't want to."

The stranger laughed. "Oh, no," he said mockingly, "you'd probably rather be drawn and quartered than forced to live in a mansion like Clearview."

Beth stiffened. Clearview! The very name brought forth the image of Regina DeWitt and memories she wanted no part of. She tossed her head arrogantly. "That I would, sir, most definitely." She started to walk away.

"Wait!" The stranger caught her arm. "You're not going to disappear before the sun's even set."

"I'm afraid I am," Beth said, pulling her shawl more tightly around her. A sudden breeze caught her bonnet. Before she could hold it, the wind swept it toward the river.

"My hat!"

The stranger chased it, catching it only inches from the water. By the time he returned, Beth's hair had come unpinned and blew recklessly about her face.

"Your hair's much too pretty to hide in this old woman's cap. I should have let it sink."

Beth went to take it, but he lifted it out of reach. "Really, sir," she said annoyed, "I appreciate the compliment, but I would prefer my cap." She lunged for it and stumbled, falling forward into the stranger's arms.

"Well, now," he said, drawing her to him, his face so close to her own that she felt as if her breath had been slammed from her lungs. "I thought you were a friendly sprite, but I daresay I like more privacy for things like this."

She jerked back, but not before she'd become aware of his desire for her. She reddened fiercely.

"You're crude, crude . . . awful," she said.

"Oh, come now. Let's not play lady. Ladies don't stroll alone on the Kingston waterfront with their wages pinned in their skirts." He moved toward her. "How much?"

Beth swung her hand hard across his face. "I may not live in a fancy house across the river," she said savagely, "but I'm more of a lady than the likes of you will ever meet!" She grabbed her hat from him, turned and ran.

She ran until she felt a stitch in her side, ignoring the odd glances of the people she pushed her way past. Of all the outrageous things to happen! And to think he mistook her for a . . . common whore. It was humiliating. And to desire her like that, right there . . . ooooh! It was awful! She craned her neck to see if she could spot Clay and Margaret. *Damn them.* For weeks she hadn't been able to get rid of either and now both were nowhere in sight. Wasn't it just her luck? The only thing she could do was walk back to where Clay had left the wagon and wait.

She took a shilling from her purse and bought a hot potato from a vendor. It was as good to eat as to hold, warming her spirits as well as her hands. She turned up Green Street and was taking her second bite when she stopped suddenly. The potato fell to the ground.

Near the corner, wrapped in a blanket and propped into a rolling chair, was Peter Avery. His sister, Elmira, stood behind the chair, which had gotten stuck in a rut, and was trying to push it free.

"Peter!" Beth shouted, and raced forward.

He turned. His drawn cheeks and lifeless eyes added years to his unsmiling young face. Beth stopped, hesitated. Then all at once he smiled and she rushed to him.

"Beth. It's you?" His voice sounded strange, timberless.

"Oh, Peter!" She sank to her knees and clasped his hand. She looked briefly up at Elmira and said hello. The stare that answered her was bitter and cold.

"I have nothing to say to you," Elmira said. She looked away. "Peter, we'll have to be going."

"Just a moment," Peter protested. "We're not going anywhere."

"Mother—"

"Mother's at the milliner's." He turned back to Beth. "Where have you been? I tried to get word to you after that night, but I couldn't find out where you'd gone."

"I'm staying with a family right outside Kingston. They have a farm. It's—it's very nice, but—" Her voice broke. "Oh, Peter, it's been so long since I had anyone to talk to. I asked the widow to get in touch with you, but she said you had moved."

"Yes, we're living—" He never finished the sentence.

A palm slammed Beth between the shoulder blades, sent her sprawling to the ground.

"Get away from my son, tramp! Haven't you caused enough pain?" Violet Avery glared down at Beth.

For a moment Beth was too stunned to react.

Violet Avery pushed at the back of Peter's chair. "Come, Elmira. We're leaving."

"Mother!" Peter protested. "What are you doing?"

"Mrs. Avery, please," Beth pleaded, scrambling to her feet. "I would never hurt Peter. He's my dearest friend."

"Such a dear friend that your brother nearly murdered him, eh?" Mrs. Avery said savagely. "That you left all our neighbors thinkin' *he* sired your Tory bastard."

"Mother!" Peter shouted. "That will be enough!"

"Enough? There you sit with a leg as useless as a rotted turnip and you tell me that will be enough?" She whirled on Beth. "You heard me once—stay out of our lives!" And with that, she heaved her weight against Peter's chair and wheeled it rapidly, despite his protests, down the street.

Beth leaned back exhausted against a building. It wasn't fair! Not for Peter, not for her. It was neither of their faults. Oh, God, if only she could wreak the vengeance she longed for.

She covered her face with her hands. She did not see Margaret and Clay come toward her. Even if she had, she wouldn't have known that they'd been hiding in the alley nearby, groping each other in a frenzy of revived lust, and had heard everything that Peter's mother had said.

Chapter 8

It took Margaret several minutes to absorb what she'd heard the woman pushing the cripple shout at Beth. It wasn't one of those times when she was in the mood to eavesdrop. After losing Beth, she had shared a beer with Clay and offered him what she knew Beth never would. Clearly he missed the liberties she had given him, and with the unspoken promise of more had guided him into the alley. There, blocked from view, she had let him fondle her breasts while she put her hand inside his breeches and touched his hot throbbing flesh.

It was at this inopportune time that she heard Beth shout to the young man Margaret had seen earlier being wheeled in a rolling chair. Both Clay and Margaret composed themselves at once and were about to walk out into the street when the young man's mother had appeared.

So, Margaret thought, the little priss not only knows more than she's let on, but has *done* more. And to have had a child—with a Tory at that! It was difficult to believe. But oh, yes, she was going to pay for her false innocence. She smiled inwardly. Oh, yes, she was going to pay dearly.

Margaret noticed that Clay wasn't smiling at all, that his face had the look of someone betrayed. Served him right, she thought, elevating that little twit to some sort of goddess. But he would have his revenge. They both would. And a lot of fun too. Clay Matthews wasn't very inventive, but neither was he one to say no to a good idea.

Margaret whispered her plan in his ear and his face changed instantly.

"Yeah," he drawled. "It would serve her right. Putting on airs and all."

Margaret dropped her hand and let it brush against Clay's breeches. He was interested in her plan, all right. She straightened her skirt and smoothed her hair. "Follow me," she said. They walked into the street toward Beth.

There was an unpleasant grin on Margaret's face as she approached. Beth wiped her eyes quickly and tried to look as if nothing had happened. Coughing, she fussed with her bonnet.

"Where have you been?" Margaret asked gently. "Clay and I have been looking all over for you. Haven't we, Clay?"

"Uh . . . yeah."

"I don't know what happened," Beth explained. "There were so many people. I just turned around for a moment and you were gone."

"We thought you'd run off." Margaret winked at Clay, giggled.

Beth glanced from one to the other. Something was amiss. Margaret was up to no good, and whatever it was, Clay Matthews was in on it. And whatever Clay Matthews was in on, Beth didn't like.

"Isn't it time we were getting back?" she asked.

"I suspect so," Margaret said sweetly. "Ready, Clay?"

Clay nodded, rubbed the back of his hand across

his lips. "Sure. Whenever you are." He avoided Beth's eyes.

Whatever had happened in the time those two were left alone was not good. Beth felt an uneasiness growing inside her. When they reached the wagon, the uneasiness had mushroomed uncomfortably—especially when Margaret *insisted* that Beth sit next to Clay.

The sun had just set when they reached the outskirts of Kingston. Margaret was happily thrumming her fingers on the side of the wagon. Clay was particularly quiet.

"Did you see that beautiful sloop, *The Golden Gull?*" Beth asked, uncomfortable with the silence.

Clay shook his head. Margaret looked up as if she hadn't heard. Something was definitely wrong.

Clay turned the wagon off Old Kingston Road and instead of heading for the Stillwell farm, went in the opposite direction.

"Hey! Where are we going?" Beth asked.

"It's a shortcut," Clay said.

"But the farm is over that way."

"Clay wants to show us his cabin," Margaret explained.

"Yeah. I—um—want you to see it."

"We've plenty of time before Mama expects us."

Beth sighed. "I guess so. I just don't look to catching it from your papa. Where is your cabin, Clay?"

"Oh, it's not far. Just about a ten-minute ride from here." He stared straight ahead, and ran the back of his hand several times across his lips.

What had gotten into him, and to Margaret? Beth wondered. The two were acting mighty peculiar.

"Saw you talkin' to that cripple fella," Margaret said lightly. "A friend of yours?"

"Yes," Beth said cautiously. How did Margaret see that? She wasn't anywhere around when Peter was there.

"Good friends, huh?"

"Seeing that you're so fascinated, yes. Good

friends." A chill began to crawl her spine. What was Margaret getting at?

"Well," Clay said, reining in the team, "this is it."

A small gray clapboard shack, smaller and less substantial than Vly and Black Annie's, stood off to the side of the road. It had only one window, and the small door was mostly obliterated by a mound of drifted snow.

"Very nice," Beth said politely.

"Let's go inside," Margaret said. "Don't you want to look around, Beth? Clay built it himself."

"Isn't it time to be getting back?"

"Oh, come on," Margaret chided. "We'll be home in plenty of time." She jumped from the wagon and reached up for Beth's hand. Reluctantly Beth gave it.

The interior of the cabin was dark and bare, except for a chair and an old straw mattress in the corner. It smelled of mildew. Clay lit a piece of candlewood and set it in the corner of the fireplace.

"Brrrr. It's freezing," Margaret said. "How about a fire?"

"I've got some wood out back."

"But we've got to get home soon," Beth protested.

"Oh, don't be such a sour tart," Margaret said as Clay went for the wood. "Besides, we have some questions we want to ask you."

"What sort of questions?"

Clay returned with an armful of wood, placed it in the corner, then set about starting the fire.

Margaret sat down on the mattress. "Oh, personal questions. Right, Clay?"

Clay waited until the fire began to blaze, then went to Margaret and stood behind her. He folded his arms and stared oddly at Beth. He nodded.

"What's going on?" Beth demanded. She felt cornered and didn't know why.

"Well, we want to know that it felt like," Margaret said, an ugly grin twisting her lips.

Unthinkingly Beth took a step backward. "What *what* felt like?"

"You know. Doing it."

"What are you talking about?" Beth looked to Clay. "Take me home this instant! If you two want to play your dirty games, you can do it without me."

She started for the door, but Clay caught her shoulders. "I don't think you should be the one to be talking about dirty games," he said.

Beth felt her breath catch in her throat. They knew! But how could they . . . unless . . . Mrs. Avery, that was it! They'd heard Mrs. Avery shouting at her! Beth threw her arms to the side and broke Clay's grip. "You keep your hands off me, you hear?"

"Whoa." Margaret stood and sauntered over to Beth, hands on her hips. "It's a bit too late to play the virgin, I'd think. Especially after giving birth to a child, eh?"

Beth kept her face expressionless, said nothing. It was almost sacrilegious to allow someone like Margaret to even refer to Suzannah.

"All we want is to hear a little about it, right, Clay?"

Clay didn't answer. He stood close and unmoving next to Beth, his breath coming in deeper pants.

"And then, the more you tell us the less we'll say about it to anyone. Promise. But if you don't tell us, well, I'm afraid I'm going to have to ask Papa about it. And I'll bet Papa can make you tell *him* everything." She touched her finger to the tip of Beth's nose.

Beth slapped her.

"Why, you—" Margaret's hand swung out and caught Beth on the side of the head. She staggered backward, and Clay grabbed her, locked her arms behind her. He was perspiring.

"Let go of me!" Beth brought her heel down hard on his foot. He yelped and she broke free.

"Get her!" Margaret yelled.

Beth raced to the door, but Clay blocked her. "Oh, no you don't." His face was flushed, his eyes wide with excitement.

"Let me go," Beth warned. "Or I'll . . . I'll . . ."

"You'll what?" Margaret said. "Scream? Who's going to hear you?" She stood next to Clay and ran her hands up and down his arms. "Don't be so prissy. We're just going to have a little fun."

Clay's eyes glistened, and he licked his lips repeatedly. "Yeah."

"You know, Clay," Margaret said, "Beth's never been kissed the French way. Why don't you show her how."

"Don't you dare, Clay Matthews," Beth warned.

Clay moved quickly, catching Beth off guard and pushing her back and down upon the mattress. He fell on top of her, pinned her. "Hold her hands!" he shouted.

Margaret climbed upon the mattress, gripped Beth's hands and pinned them above her head.

Beth thrashed from side to side to avoid Clay's mouth. Her head began to spin. *Oh, God, no. Please make them stop.* Then Clay's hands held her face and his lips came down hard upon hers, his tongue furiously invading her mouth. She felt queasy and weak.

"Oh, yes," Margaret breathed, her voice trembling. "That's it. Show her what it's like."

Clay's hands slid down over Beth's shoulders to the bodice of her dress, his mouth never leaving hers. The pressure of his body obliterated everything but her fierce desire to break free. Helplessly she felt his fingers begin to knead her breasts. She had to get away. She swung herself to the left just enough to free her knee from beneath Clay's thigh, and without hesitation brought her leg up hard.

Clay groaned and rolled over to the side, doubled up. Margaret screamed, let go of Beth's hands and reached for Clay. Beth raced for the door.

Outside she climbed aboard the wagon, turned it back toward the main road. She heard Margaret's shrill voice shouting after her as the horses broke into a fast trot. She did not look back.

Returning to the farm was out of the question. But if she didn't get out of the area by nightfall, Clay

Matthews would surely find her. And that was one confrontation she was not prepared to repeat.

The widow! That's where she'd go. Widow Brinks would hide her. Beth snapped the reins hard. With luck she could make Peekamoose Ridge in an hour. But as she looked at the ever-darkening sky, she realized it would take more than luck to make the climb with the wagon in that time. Clay Matthews could borrow a horse, easily overtake her. The only thing to do was to leave the wagon.

Beth pulled the rig to the side of the road and unharnessed the team. Using Clay's baggage rope, she fashioned a makeshift bridle and mounted one of the horses. She smacked the other, knowing it was close enough to the Matthews's place to trot home, and headed her own mount for the ridge.

It was already dark when she got there, but an orange glow filled the sky. *Fire!* Beth could smell it. But where—? Her heart seized with terror. It was coming from the widow's house. Beth dug her heels into the horse, hoping all the while that it was just a local bonfire, a celebration. Dear God, don't let it be the widow's place, she prayed.

Her horse began to shy before it even reached the house. Beth gaped in horror. Flames spewed from the widow's windows. The shutters were already burning and showers of sparks were falling to the ground.

Beth slid from the horse and ran toward the burning building. The widow's wagon was in the yard, which meant she had to be inside.

"Widow Brinks!" Beth screamed. "Widow Brinks!"

From inside Beth heard the widow's voice. "Stay back! It's going to fall. Stay back!"

Beth did not stop to think. She threw open the front door, covered her mouth with her shawl. Coughing violently, her eyes stinging, she tore through the kitchen to the widow's small bedroom.

"Widow Brinks!" Beth shouted. "Are you in there?"

"Run, child!" the widow's voice cried. "The house is going to fall. Forget about me."

Beth pushed at the door, but it wouldn't open. Coughing, she hurried back into the kitchen and picked up an andiron. "I'm coming in," she cried, and hurled the heavy metal at the door, smashing it open.

Beth made her way into the room. She could barely see through the smoke. "Widow, where are you?" she called.

"Here," came the weak reply.

Beth felt her way to the bed. The Widow Brinks lay wrapped in an old Indian blanket, her face almost skeletal.

"Oh, my God," Beth murmured.

"Child, you must get out," the widow said.

"Not without you. Here, put your arms around my neck. I'm going to carry you."

"Don't be foolish. You'll never—"

There was a crash and one of the huge crossbeams fell, bringing a good portion of the house flaming down.

"Put your arms around my neck," Beth ordered. "Now!"

The widow struggled to lift her arms. "I don't know if I can."

"You can. Now hurry." Beth put her arms beneath the widow and lifted her. She was startled by how much weight the widow had lost, how frighteningly light she was, but dared not stop to think about it. Without hesitating she carried the frail form outside to safety.

They hadn't even reached the wagon when the entire frame of the house collapsed. Beth sank to the earth, the widow still in her arms, and sobbed with relief.

The widow reached up, fingers trembling, and touched Beth's tears. "You must not cry. You need your strength."

Beth looked down at the emaciated woman in her arms. "Why didn't you let me know that you were ill?"

"There was no point."

"Come. Let me carry you to the barn. You'll be protected from the wind there at least." Against the widow's protests, she lifted her and carried her into the barn and placed her on a bed of hay.

"There's a lantern in here somewhere, isn't there?" Beth asked.

"On the side beam."

Beth stumbled in the darkness, sending a few chickens squawking, but eventually found the lantern. She lighted it. Bringing it close to the widow, she sat down.

"You need a doctor," Beth said.

"It is too late for that." The widow sighed.

"No! We'll go now. I'll take you there. You'll be fine."

The widow shook her head; a small smile played about her lips. "How like a child to pretend, to keep a fantasy to the last."

"Don't talk like that."

"No, child. I'm going to be with Everett soon. I've known it for many months. What eats me inside has only a bit more to go. It has already been written and will come to pass, just as all that I've told you will."

Suddenly Beth remembered the widow's words the night Suzannah was born. *You will risk your life to save mine and in so doing will alter your own forever*. And now it had happened. She couldn't return to the Stillwells and she certainly wasn't about to leave the widow. She wrapped the blanket more tightly around her.

"I don't want to hear any more," Beth said sternly, with more authority than she felt. "I'm taking you to Doctor Baker's and that will be that."

The widow shook her head. "No. You are going to take me to a cabin on the Bushkill. It's about five miles from here."

"But—"

"Do not argue. There's little enough time. Take the crate from the wall over there and put three hens in it."

"But why?"

The widow raised her hand, cutting off further discussion. Beth sighed and caught the hens easily, putting them into the crate.

"Now?" Beth asked.

"Now put them in the wagon, along with Everett's shovel and ax, and hitch up the horses. We must leave within the hour. The men that ride to stave these flames are not friends and one of them would wreak a special vengeance upon you."

Clay Matthews! Margaret would have told him about the widow and he certainly wouldn't waste any time in coming after her. The widow was right. They would have to move quickly. Beth hitched up the horses and made a bed for the widow in the rear of the wagon, using hay and her own shawl as a pillow. After making her as comfortable as possible, Beth climbed into the driver's seat.

"Head up Watson Hollow," the widow instructed. "When you come upon three oak trees bent into a bower, turn right onto that path. We can walk to the cabin from there."

"But how will I be able to see?"

"You just drive the wagon. I can see my way to that cabin without eyes anytime."

Beth snapped the reins and the horses responded. The wagon groaned and creaked as it bumped slowly along the frost-crusted road. She dared not go faster. She turned around to check the widow every few minutes, when finally the old woman laughed.

"I'm not about to go right yet, so keep your eyes on the road."

Beth relaxed after that and concentrated on keeping the horses at a proper pace.

The widow knew they had reached the turnoff even before Beth saw the oak branches. Following her instructions, she turned onto the small path and stopped the wagon.

"I don't see any cabin," she said, her eyes squinting in the darkness.

The widow raised herself up on an elbow. "If it could be seen that easily, it wouldn't still be here. Help me out, and you'll see it."

With strength Beth didn't believe the old woman had, she climbed from the wagon with Beth's assistance. She flung her arm over Beth's shoulder to steady herself.

"It's over there." She pointed into what looked like a clump of ash trees. "Come on."

Beth wondered if the old woman was having hallucinations. They were heading for nothing but the river. "Widow Brinks," she began, "I think . . ." Before she could finish, a small wooden cottage appeared before them.

"Pull the latch string."

Beth did and the old door swung open, creaking loudly. A smell of must and damp wood enveloped them, but it was not unpleasant.

Widow Brinks instructed Beth on where to find dry candlewood and within a half hour there was a fire blazing in the fireplace and water boiling for tea.

Beth put the widow on a small pallet next to the fireplace and propped her up with pillows. She seemed so little and helpless, her frizzy white hair now sparse as cat's whiskers, so unlike the robust woman who only months before had taught Beth how to split logs and gut hares.

"It's pretty, isn't it?" the widow asked, waving her hand weakly about the cabin. It was well built, with whitewashed mortar between the logs to keep out drafts, and a cobblestone fireplace that rose majestically to the peaked ceiling.

"Very," Beth said. "It's your honeymoon cabin, isn't it?"

The widow smiled. "We kept it up all the years Everett was alive, and I just continued after he was gone. I always said that I wanted to die here. Thanks to you I'll have my wish."

"That's no way to talk."

"The truth is always the way to talk. Now you hush,

I have things that have to be taken care of and there's little time." The widow beckoned and Beth sat down beside her.

"There will be a thaw in the next three days, and the ground will soften. I will not be here to see it, but you must wait for it. Beside the stream, out back, there is a cairn of stones. Next to it you will dig my grave."

"Widow Brinks!"

"There is no time for arguments. Everett lies there and so will I. Promise me that."

"But—"

"Promise me that."

Beth lowered her head. "I promise."

The widow sighed and fell back against the pillows. "Come closer."

She reached inside the bodice of her dress and took out a small purse. "Here," she said, "take this. There are twenty-seven pounds in it."

"Oh, but I couldn't."

"Of course you can, and you will. I won't be buying salt pork where I'm going. But don't get too excited about it, because it won't take you as far as you think. On the other hand, it's possible it might save your life."

"I don't understand."

"Don't try. Hide out here as long as you must, then make your way north on the other side of the river, for that is where your future lies."

"But my daughter—Suzannah." The thought of abandoning the mountains that, somewhere, hid her precious golden-haired child was almost too much to bear.

"You must forget her for now," the widow said sharply. "Follow your fate, find your fortune. It is all as carefully planned as it is randomly played on this earth. Patience. You will pay dearly for what you want, but time will reward you."

Reward her? But how? And why did her future lie in the north? Oh, if only she could get the widow to a doctor.

"I told you it's too late for a doctor," the widow said, as if reading Beth's mind. "Just let me say . . . good night. I'm tired now, very tired."

Beth leaned forward and the widow kissed her forehead. "God be with you," she murmured.

In the morning she was dead.

Beth didn't remember much about the next three days, only that the thaw came as the widow had predicted and the ground next to the cairn of stones turned over easier than Beth had anticipated.

After the burial, she cleaned the cabin, latched it as it was when they'd first arrived and hitched up the widow's wagon. She was headed toward the Hudson, the north, and her future.

Chapter 9

Seven miles out of Rhinebeck, an axle broke. To make matters worse, Beth's hike to find someone to fix it resulted in the horses' being stolen. The wagon slumped in the road like a gray rotting vegetable. She closed her eyes, asked the Lord for forgiveness, then began shouting every cuss word she'd ever heard.

She was still cussing, though more quietly, when a large rig came down the road. Two young men, in their late teens, sat in the driver's box.

"Well, lookie, lookie," the fairer-haired of the two shouted out. Pulling the wagon to a halt, he grinned broadly. "Seems you've come 'pon some difficulty. Well, rest easy 'cause help is at hand."

"My horses were stolen," Beth said dully.

"*Your* horses?" The youth raised his white-blond eyebrows. "Your father's perhaps, eh?" He laughed.

Beth's face turned cold. "*My* horses," she said defiantly, and immediately regretted it.

The youth pushed back his hat and turned to his friend. "Did you hear that, Frederick? *Her* horses.

Why, I don't know how we could have thought she was anything but a lady of property, do you?"

Beth didn't like their smiles, nor the way they were studying her. Her dress was frayed and patched, her shoes still soot-stained from the fire. And that awful ferry ride had left her hair matted and limp, making her look like heaven knew what. She felt the beginnings of fear.

She forced a laugh. "Well, I thought it would be a bit of a joke. Of course they're my father's horses. He's right back there." She pointed to the woods. "I'll call him. Pa! Pa!"

Frederick pushed his companion's shoulder. "Let's get movin', Stephen. I don't need a shotgun beadin' down on me. Besides, I don't think Raleigh would like it." He cocked his head toward the rear of the wagon. "Especially on his birthday."

So there was still another inside the wagon! Beth felt her throat tighten. She mustn't let them see that she was frightened. "Pa!" she called again. "Pa!"

The blond, Stephen, was about to start up the team, but changed his mind. He folded his arms. "Maybe we can give your pa a hand rehitching the wagon, should he come upon those missing horses. Or maybe we can just give you folks a lift, eh?"

"That's very kind, but I think we'll make out just fine. I—we wouldn't want to hold you up."

Stephen handed the reins to Frederick. "Here. Hold these for a while." He jumped down to where Beth was standing. "Maybe I should go into the woods and take a look for your pa, huh?" He took her arm. "Why don't you show me which way he went."

Beth tried to pull back, but Stephen held her with a good grip.

"No. He told me to stay with the wagon. He—"

"You're lying, little lady. It's written all over that pretty dirty face of yours." Stephen gripped her chin tightly and turned her face toward his. "Aren't you?"

His fingers dug into her flesh, but Beth didn't wince. "Take your hands off me, you pig."

"Well, now, I suspect that I have my answer."

"Aw, leave her be," Frederick said. He ran his fingers through his dark greasy hair nervously. "We got a long ride to Claverack Landing."

"Don't I know it. And once we get there it's going to be a long time between draughts if we sign on them whalers. I believe in feasting before a fast." He grinned at Beth. "And this one looks like she sure could fill the bill for all of us."

"I'd rather die first," Beth said scornfully.

Before she even knew what happened, the point of Stephen's knife was at her throat. "Your choice," he said evenly.

She dared not move. Even her slightest breath caused the point to sting her. She remained rigid. There was no doubt that this animal would slit her throat as easily as he'd gut a jackrabbit.

"Put it away," she said.

"That's better." Stephen returned the knife to its sheath. He circled Beth, his eyes appraising her with the cool detachment of a horse trader. "She needs a little cleaning up, but she'd make a fine birthday present for Raleigh, don't you think?"

A birthday present! Of all the humiliating . . . Why, she wouldn't stand for it. She . . . And then she remembered the feel of Stephen's knife against her skin. She remained motionless.

"Hey, she sure would," Frederick said. His small beady eyes glinted. He turned and looked into the wagon. "But he's going to be out cold for a good three hours more."

"That'll give me time to get her presentable," Stephen said. "After all, Raleigh deserves more than still whiskey on his twentieth birthday, 'specially considering that he saved you from jailing and me from a watchman's billy by taking us aboard this fine wagon."

Frederick leered at her. "Whatever you say, Stephen, but my thought would be it wouldn't hurt none to try her out before we give her to Raleigh."

Beth turned her head away. *Dear Lord, make them*

leave me be. The wagon creaked as Frederick stepped down.

"She's a good looker."

There was a slap. Beth turned, startled. Frederick was holding his cheek. "Now what did you do that for?"

Stephen pointed to the wagon. "Get back up there. What kind of present is it when you get it third hand, eh? Where are your brains? We'll keep her for the trip. Raleigh's good at sharin'. We'll just let him have the first of the wine." He turned to Beth. "We want you good as new for our friend Raleigh. And you're going to be nice to him, understand? 'Cause if you ain't, I'll mess you up so that you'll have to beg people for the rest of your life to be nice to you."

Beth shook her head. It was a nightmare. How was she to escape? Whoever this Raleigh was, she had to get away before he awoke. Suddenly she heard the sound of another wagon approaching. Her body became instantly alert.

Stephen took out his knife and pressed it to her side. "If you have any ideas of shouting to the cart that's coming down the road, get them out of your head now." He pushed the knife slightly and Beth yelped. "You hear me?"

"I hear you." She rubbed her side as Stephen held the knife behind his back. He smiled at the wagon as it passed and told Beth to wave. She did as she was told. When the wagon was out of sight, she felt tears well behind her lids.

"All right," he snapped, "we haven't got all day for this. There's a stream back there. Get to it."

"What do you mean?"

"I mean you're going to clean up." He pushed her forward. "Now get going."

Frederick reached in his rucksack and tossed a towel to Stephen. Stephen grabbed it, jabbed the small of Beth's back hard with his fingers. "Come on, come on."

At the bank of the stream, he pushed her down on

the damp leaves. "Now get that grime off your face and arms," he said.

Beth put her hands in the water and her fingers grew instantly numb. "It's freezing," she protested.

"Either you do it, or I do it for you," he said. "Now hurry it up."

Beth lifted the water to her face in cupped hands and washed. When she was through, she asked for the towel.

"Not until you take off that blouse and clean those arms."

"No." Beth clutched herself.

Stephen took the knife from its sheath and ran his finger over the blade. "Take off your blouse and clean those arms, or else I'm going to get angry and give you a real bath. Do you hear me?"

Beth nodded. With her back toward him, she unbuttoned her blouse, shivering in the late March chill. He walked around to the side to watch. She pretended not to notice his eyes staring at her nipples as they hardened beneath the thin fabric of her chemise. When she was through, he tossed her the towel and told her gruffly to get dressed and return to the wagon.

Frederick lifted her onto the driver's seat. Stephen followed, pulling her into the rear of the wagon.

"What are you going to do?"

Stephen pointed to a man sleeping in the corner. "You sit here, and fix your hair. I don't think he'll wake up until we camp for the night, but if he does, you say, 'Happy Birthday from Stephen and Frederick.' Understand?"

She didn't answer.

Stephen grabbed her hair tightly and pulled her head back. "I guess you don't," he said softly. "So let me make it clearer. If you don't do exactly as I've told you, you're going to wish for the rest of your life that you did. Now do you understand?"

Beth made a small animal noise of pain.

"Good." He threw her head forward, then climbed back on the driver's seat with Frederick.

"I sure hope Raleigh likes his birthday cake." Frederick's laugh was like a donkey's bray.

"I'll take it back if he doesn't," Stephen said.

"I thought we were both going to get a piece anyway," Frederick said, concern rising.

"I told you we were, so stop talking about it."

"Okay." Frederick was silent for a while, then he took a coin from his pocket. "I'll toss you for seconds," he said.

Beth sat huddled up, her arms crossed and hugging herself. Where was all *this* in the widow's prophecy? She had been tempted to offer payment in exchange for her freedom, but all that would have gotten her was an empty purse and the same predicament. At least she still had her money. When she broke away she'd be able to buy passage somewhere.

The body in the corner moaned. Who was this mysterious Raleigh celebrating his birthday in an unconscious stupor on the floor of what was more than likely a stolen wagon? He was evidently the leader of the three. Stephen seemed to have respect for him, which boded ill.

She lifted the canvas flap of the wagon. Maybe if she jumped now she could get away. Then again, if she didn't make it and they caught her . . . Maybe she should have let Stephen kill her and been done with it.

The wagon hit a rut, bounced. Beth hurtled forward. Before she could stop herself she was sprawled across Raleigh's back.

"What the—?" Raleigh snapped awake, rolled over, spilling Beth to the floor and a pile of blankets and supplies atop of her.

Her skirt and petticoat hiked up to her thighs. She struggled to free herself, only to become more tangled in a mass of cloth and stores.

"What the devil is going on?" Raleigh roared.

Stephen turned around and laughed. "Happy birthday. We thought you'd appreciate the present."

Raleigh pulled the blankets from Beth, tearing a

bag of flour as he did. The flour mushroomed into a
dusty white cloud that covered them both, leaving
Beth coughing and too shocked for fear.

Raleigh laughed and wiped his face. He handed
Beth a towel. "I don't suspect that was part of the
surprise."

Beth said nothing, kept her eyes lowered.

He put his arm around her shoulders. "You look
kind of young to be a professional 'birthday present,'
but I won't hold it against you. Let's see that face."
He took his hand and gently uptilted her chin.

Beth's surprise equaled the look on Raleigh's face.
He was the same young man she had met on the
Kingston wharf!

"Well, well, well," Raleigh said, his dark eyes spar-
kling with merriment. "So we meet again after all.
And to think you almost fooled me into believing you
were a proper young lady."

"I am," she said icily.

"Oh, come now, didn't the boys offer you enough?"

"Ooh!" Beth swung her palm hard against his face.

Raleigh looked confused. "Now what the devil was
that about? I thought the boys bought you for my
birthday?"

"I am not for sale. For you or for anyone else.
Your *friends* kidnapped me."

"Kidnapped?" Raleigh narrowed his eyes, then
threw back his head and laughed. "Oh, you are indeed a prize. Whatever they offered you, I'll match
it, so keep up your act. Only no scratching, please.
It is my birthday."

"Why, you—" Beth raised her hand, but Raleigh
caught it and pushed her back on the blankets. His
mouth found hers and before she could pull back he
was kissing her slowly, possessively. Mockingly.

She felt as if she couldn't breathe, as if she would
faint. Oh, God, would his mouth never leave hers?
Her head felt light. His other hand caught her about
the waist and pulled her tighter to him and she felt
his maleness quicken.

She tried to turn her head, but his lips and tongue were relentless in their slow assault on her mouth. The more she struggled, the more he seemed to desire her. She dared not move, could not think.

No one had ever kissed her like this before. Every flick of his tongue seemed to sear her mouth with sensations she had never experienced or imagined. And then slowly his hand released hers and slid down over her hair, to her shoulder, and on to her breast. He cupped it gently, his fingers pressing hard against her nipple, while his other hand moved down from her waist to her buttocks, lifting her to him. And all the while his mouth never leaving hers.

Dimly she was aware of her skirt being lifted, of his warm palm pressing the cold flesh of her leg. Everything seemed to be swirling around her, and through it all his lips relentlessly devouring hers.

Somewhere inside a molten flame began to rise, engulfing her in a terrifying wave of emotion. She panicked. *What's happening to me?* she thought wildly. She seemed to have lost control of her body, her senses. It was as if something, someone, had her under a spell. For one mad moment she felt herself returning Raleigh's kiss!

His hold loosened and he raised his head slightly. "You're the nicest birthday present anybody ever had," he murmured. "Whatever you cost, you're worth it."

That did it! Like a douse from an icy rain barrel! Beth felt herself spring back to her senses. Seething with rage, mindless of Raleigh's hand sliding up between her thighs, she flung her arm on his back and dug her nails deep into his flesh. She tore at him with catlike fury.

"You bitch!" Raleigh howled. He rolled off, slapped her face hard.

Beth felt her cheek. "Go on, beat me. I don't care. It's . . . it's better than having you . . . *use* me." Without warning she began to cry.

"Goddamn! What the hell is this all about?" Raleigh shook her shoulders. "Would you stop that and tell me? I thought you were my birthday present." He turned to the front of the wagon. "Stephen! Frederick! What's going on?"

Stephen stepped into the back of the wagon. "How do you like your present? Nice, huh, Raleigh?"

"Nice? Look at my back, goddamn it. Some birthday present. What do you owe her? I'll double it to unload her."

"Why, you little—" Stephen reached for Beth but Raleigh stopped him.

"I'm not inclined toward beating up women—or raping them. Just tell me the price you agreed on and we'll let her off at the next town."

"Price? What are you talking about? We just picked her up on the road."

Raleigh looked from Beth back to Stephen. "You mean you really kidnapped her?"

"Ah, hell, Raleigh. Anyone could see that she was a runaway, fair game. We just thought—"

Raleigh ran his hand through his hair, pushing back the bangs that fell to his brows. "You thought wrong. Get back up front with Frederick. I have an apology to make."

"Apology? To that little—"

Raleigh's voice grew angry. "Watch what you're saying. There'll be no kidnapping and raping when you're riding with me. There are enough willing ladies in this world without bothering the others."

"But—"

"You heard me."

Stephen grumbled as he went back to the driver's box.

Beth stared coldly, dry-eyed, at Raleigh. He returned her stare, but said nothing. His eyes just traveled the length of her body and back. Then he said, "I should have known you weren't a prostitute. You can't kiss worth a damn."

Beth felt as if she had been slapped again. Certainly she should be flattered *not* to be mistaken for a loose woman, but somehow the idea of being unable to kiss properly, or rather desirously, outraged her, and she wasn't sure why.

"Is that your idea of an apology?" she said cuttingly.

"I don't write billets-doux, and we didn't get far enough to warrant more."

"Why, you—"

"Calm down. Your honor's intact. If you want to put on airs you can get out now. But if you're out of money, luck, and want a ride to Claverack Landing, you can ride with us. Can you cook?"

"Yes."

"Good. At the rate we were going with Frederick at the fire, I thought we'd all have no stomachs left. What's your name?"

"Beth . . . Beth Talbot."

"Talbot . . . Talbot?" Raleigh shook his head. "Sounds familiar, but I can't place it. Doesn't matter. I don't like people poking into my past, so I don't poke into theirs." Raleigh leaned over to the front of the wagon. "Hey, boys, we got ourselves a *cook.*"

Stephen turned around, was about to say something.

"A cook," Raleigh repeated. "And nothing more. Is that clear?"

Stephen shrugged. "Whatever you say."

Raleigh turned back to Beth. "You look tired. Why don't you lie down and get some rest?" He waved his arm toward the blankets.

Beth flushed scarlet. The recent memory of his body pressing on hers, his hands taking liberties she'd vowed no one would ever take again, made her sit straighter still. "I—I'm fine, thank you."

"Your eyes are circled big as a coon's," Raleigh said. "I suspect that it's been a while since you had a rest, so if I were you I'd take it when I could."

Beth looked at the blankets and turned her head away.

"Oh, my God," Raleigh said disgustedly. "You don't think I'm going to molest you, do you?"

Beth felt her cheeks grow hot. That the thought had crossed her mind embarrassed her, and that Raleigh knew it had humiliated her. It humiliated her even more because somewhere, deep inside, the memory of his kisses was not all that repulsive. In fact, not repulsive at all. She looked away.

Raleigh grabbed her wrist. "You do think that, don't you?"

"No—no I don't," Beth stammered.

"You don't lie much better than you kiss," he said, still holding her wrist.

"Let go of me!"

"Not until we get something clear between us." His eyes were obsidian, fevered with unreadable emotion. "I'll admit I was drawn to you the day I returned your purse on the Kingston wharf; admit the same when I awoke earlier with a headful of whiskey and found you sprawled about me with your skirts aloft. But I've never pillaged nor begged for a woman's favors. And I never will."

"You're hurting my wrist."

"I just wanted to make sure you understood. Oh, I'll have you yet—and you know that as well as I— but that will be at *your* invitation."

Beth gaped at him wide-eyed. Smiling, he lifted her hand to his lips.

"And one hopes," he said softly, "that by that time you'll have learned how to kiss."

Chapter 10

Through the entire three-day journey to Claverack, though Raleigh behaved, was the perfect gentleman, and made sure that Stephen and Frederick did likewise, Beth could still feel his hand gripping her wrist, his mocking voice saying that he'd have her yet . . . that she knew it as well as he . . . and that it would be at *her* invitation! *And she could not sweep the words from her mind.*

He spoke little of himself, creating an aura of mystery that was heightened by occasional cryptic references to life in New York. Against her will, he fascinated her. Who was he? Why was he traveling with the likes of Stephen and Frederick to sign on to a whaler?

The night before they reached Claverack, camping not far outside the town, he spoke for the first time at some length about New York, calling it at one point a city of bad manners and worse smells.

"But the *haut monde* is there," Beth said.

Raleigh raised his eyebrows. *"Haut monde* indeed?

And where does a farm girl come to know of the *haut monde?*"

"I know how to read," Beth said saucily, "and how to write."

Raleigh gave her a look of mock sobriety. "And how to split logs, and skin a rabbit, and cook a stew. My, my. Just about everything—except how to kiss."

Beth felt her anger rise, grow stronger because there was no way to refute his accusation without compromising herself. She picked up a stick and stabbed at the ashes from the fire vengefully. She was grateful for the darkness.

"I fear I've offended you," Raleigh said. There was unmistakable laughter behind his words. "I'd best say good night."

"Good night," Beth said icily.

She watched him take his bedroll and disappear into the shadows. He was awful, just awful. He made her feel like a foolish child no matter what she did. The day before, she'd washed her hair and fixed it the way she remembered Regina DeWitt had fixed hers, wrapped and curled with tendrils falling softly about the face. And what had happened? He'd laughed! He'd actually thrown back his head and laughed, until she hurled a skunk cabbage at him and refused to speak to him for the rest of the day. She'd rather burn at the stake, drown in the ocean, fall off a cliff than encourage the likes of him to intimacy! She kicked a log at the fire and winced at the pain in her toe.

She opened her blanket and lay down, tried to sleep. Stephen and Frederick were snoring loudly beside the wagon, their slumber abetted by a large amount of whiskey.

Maybe that's what she needed. Whiskey. She made her way quietly to the wagon and got the bottle. She choked on the first swallow, and wondered how anyone could stand such burning. But the second went easier and the third easier still. When she walked back to her bedroll, she felt much better. But not in the least tired.

She lay down, tossed from side to side and tried to get comfortable. Whatever soporific qualities the whiskey had for others, it didn't have them for her. She looked over to the clump of pines where Raleigh was bedded. He was probably sleeping dreamlessly. Damn that man. It wasn't fair. He either treated her like a child or insulted her as if she were a common bar wench. Damn him! Damn him! She smashed her fist into the earth.

Who was he to think *he* was so desirable that she would come to him? Oh, he was handsome, that was for sure. Forced to be honest, she'd have to admit that more than once she'd brought her mind back to the way his mouth felt upon hers. And when she had, it made her stir, way up inside, in a way that both frightened and excited her. Thinking of it now, she writhed beneath the blanket and grew angry at herself because of it.

She got up and began to pace back and forth before the fire, her fury mounting. It enraged her that he slept so peacefully. After insulting her the way he had, he didn't deserve to. The more she thought about it, the angrier she became. What was wrong with her kisses anyway? Frederick and Stephen would find no fault with them, she was certain of that. Peter once said she had the lips of an angel. But they weren't good enough for Mr. Raleigh Eckert!

Beth stopped pacing and tapped her chin. So, they weren't good enough, eh? Well, maybe it was time for a retesting. She headed, a bit unsteadily, for the pines.

Raleigh lay on his back, barely visible in the fading firelight. Beth tiptoed closer, then kneeled down beside him. Can't kiss, eh? Well, we'll see about that. She leaned forward and was about to bring her mouth down on his, when he sprang suddenly awake and hurled her to the ground, throwing himself on top of her, his knife drawn.

"No!" Beth cried out. "I—it's me."

"What the—?"

"I was . . . I was . . ." She looked up into his eyes,

stared at them for a long moment and felt the now familiar stirring inside her, tried to ignore it.

"You were what? Do you realize I could have killed you?" He was genuinely upset.

Beth giggled. "I was going to make a big mistake, I guess."

Raleigh lifted her by the shoulders. "By Jesus, you're drunk!"

"I am not drunk," Beth said indignantly. "I have had a bit of whiskey, but I am not drunk."

Raleigh relaxed. "Can you sit up by yourself?" He let go of her shoulders and she teetered, about to flop back on the ground. He caught her and laughed. "What was the celebration?"

"I just thought it would help me get to sleep."

Raleigh raised one brow. "Over here?"

"Well . . ." She began to stammer. "I—I—" She suddenly was very, very sober.

"Tell me," he said softly.

"I was going to prove to you . . ."

"Yes?" His fingers held her ever so gently, but firmly.

"Well, if you must know, I was going to prove to you that I could so kiss."

"Really?" He regarded her with bemused amazement.

"Yes, really," Beth said, her temper rising.

"Lord knows, I'm not the one to stand in the way of someone out to prove a point. Give everyone a fair chance, my daddy used to say." He closed his eyes, dropped his hands to his side and lifted his face toward Beth. "Go on. I'm ready." He puckered his lips like a suckling possum.

"Oh! You're despicable!" Beth shouted. She started to get up, but Raleigh caught her around the waist and pulled her down.

"I'm not despicable, and you know it." His arm tightened around her. "If I were, you wouldn't be here right now."

"Raleigh, I—" She felt her body loosening, relaxing all over.

"I knew you'd come. I told you that." He ran his hand softly over her hair. "And you're at *my* bedroll, I'm not at yours."

"I just wanted to . . . to . . ." She shrugged, dropped her hands.

"Prove that you could kiss well?" He chuckled softly. "That's as good a place as any to start." He bent her slowly backward. "Here's your chance," he said softly, and covered her mouth with his own.

Everything that Beth had planned was forgotten in the moist warmth of Raleigh's kiss. Within moments the strangeness became familiarity. Her lips matched his, motion for motion, and when his tongue entered, her own, tentatively at first and then assertively, caressed his.

Her whole body became charged with feeling. It was as if every part of her was aflame and only the sweet soft wetness of Raleigh's mouth could extinguish the burning. She moaned, and he drew her closer to him.

"I want you," he whispered, his tongue flicking the corners of her ear. "And I want you to want me. Tell me that you do."

Before she answered, the vision of another night flashed before her. Instantly her whole body tightened. "Raleigh," she breathed, "I'm afraid."

"There's nothing to be afraid of." His fingers glided softly down her back over her hips. "We're going to make love. But I want you to want me. You must tell me that you want me."

"Oh, Raleigh." Beth pressed her mouth against his in answer, pushing away the fear.

His hand slipped beneath her sweater and shift and cupped her breast. She shuddered with pleasure. "Tell me," he whispered. "Say it."

"I—I want you to make love to me."

"Love," he said, as if it were her name, and drew her beneath the warmth of his bedroll.

His fingers were cold to her hot skin, but so gentle that she knew only pleasure as he removed her smock and skirt, her chemise and underthings. His hands and mouth caressed her ceaselessly as he sparked her body to unbearable throbbing hunger.

She moaned in need and ecstasy, her naked body moving against his, rhythmic, beseeching motions. Her bare breasts rubbed against his chest. He removed his breeches.

"Hold it. Know it," he said.

For a moment Beth felt panic returning and she was afraid. She drew back.

Raleigh stroked her face. "There is nothing to fear." He reached down and brought her hand to himself, held it there. "I want you to know me." He guided her hand gently back and forth.

"Like that, yes—oh, Beth, yes!" he whispered, his voice a muffled groan. His breath came faster, heavier.

Beth felt emboldened with power, and gripped him tighter. Her own body, unfettered from all restraint, gave itself freely to the pulsing of her desire. She writhed beneath the bedroll, every part of her craving release. "Raleigh, Raleigh," she murmured.

His hands stopped hers, pinned them momentarily to her sides. His mouth, so gentle before, came down hard and demanding against her own, so hard it was almost painful. But the pain merely excited her more. It was incomprehensible that this was happening, that her body was arching wantonly toward him, her hands gripping his hard-muscled shoulders and pulling him into her.

"Say it," he urged, his mouth against her ear.

She felt the throbbing heat of his passion pressing against her thighs, felt his hands part them. His fingers worked upward, caressing her.

"Make love to me," she moaned.

"Oh, yes . . . yes . . ."

He rolled her gently to her back, his hands holding her firmly. Bringing his knee between her thighs, he held them parted and entered her. Suddenly her body began to tremble, ache with an ecstasy that drove her shamelessly to match his thrusts. Her mind no longer functioned. She sought only to climb higher and higher, to reach release. Raleigh fondled her, gripped her, and then slowly, slowly, as if counterpointing the maddeningly beautiful acceleration of their bodies, lifted her up to him and held her there, muffling her cry and his own with his lips.

They lay entwined for several long moments, their bodies heaving heavily, spent, slick with the sweet wetness of their fervid passion.

Beth's head reeled. So that was what the poets meant when they spoke of making love; so that was passion. She looked up. Raleigh's dark eyes were staring down at her.

"Is there something wrong?" she asked. He looked confused, hurt. She ran her finger down his cheek.

"No. I guess not," he said. But his voice was cool, distant. He rolled off her and lay on his back, staring up at the star-filled sky, as silent and chilly as the night.

"Raleigh? What is it?"

"Nothing. You'd better get dressed. You'll catch cold."

Beth felt as if he had plunged a dagger into her. It didn't make any sense. Just moments before they had been one, truly one. And now? What was wrong?

"Raleigh . . . I don't understand. I thought—" She broke off, unable to express more.

"I thought things, too, and I was wrong also, so that makes us even."

Beth dressed quickly. All the warmth that had filled her to overflowing only a short while before was now destroyed by Raleigh's silence, replaced with a chill that cut to the marrow. She threw her shawl about her but did not move. Raleigh stood with his back toward her.

She approached him cautiously. "Raleigh?"

"Go to sleep. It's late and we have a long ride to-morrow."

She swallowed hard. "Sure. Okay. I'm sorry I *bothered* you. I just thought—"

He whirled. "You just thought what?" he said angrily. "You just thought you could play your innocent game and have a good laugh on me? Well, you did, all right. You fooled me and now you can have your laugh. I wish you would have told me, though, I feel rotten about depriving Stephen and Frederick."

"Why you—" Beth raised her hand to slap him. He caught it, twisted it fiercely.

"Quit it! I don't give a damn whether you're a professional or just an experienced amateur. But you were no virgin, that was for sure." He threw his head back and put his hand on his hip. " 'Oh, Raleigh,' " he said in a mocking falsetto, " 'I'm afraid.' "

Beth stepped back, not believing he was saying this.

"Y-you . . . you're awful. Horrible."

"I'm what? I'm honest, that's what I am, which is more than I can say for you. But you sure took me in."

For a moment, Beth thought she was going to faint. The woods began to swim and the ground tilted ominously. She put her hand on the tree to steady herself. The lovemaking, the hour, the wine, and now Raleigh's accusation all seemed to crash around her at once. Then, like the passing of a storm, she became fiercely calm. She raised her head proudly, squared herself directly before him.

"I didn't lie to you. I have never made love with a man before. You are the first. But—" she looked away, "but it is true that I am not a virgin."

"What sort of nonsense game is this now?" Raleigh said disgustedly.

Beth kept her gaze steady. "When I was thirteen," she began quietly, "I was tied to my bed and . . . and violated. It was an act no more related to what happened between us than a war cry is to a baby's gurgle."

"Beth." Raleigh looked stricken. "Who did such a thing?"

Her face turned ashen. "It doesn't matter. It will never matter. Don't ask me, don't ever ask me."

"Forgive me. How could I have known?" He reached out, but she turned from him and returned to her blanket by the fire. Her lip was bleeding where she had bitten it to keep back the tears.

Chapter 11

Beth was dry-eyed when their wagon rolled into Claverack Landing the next day. She had refused to discuss anything further with Raleigh during the ride, despite his increasingly irate persistence. When they had stopped for lunch she'd even gone so far as to stay inside the wagon feigning girl cramps so that he wouldn't dare intrude.

It was Raleigh, though, who told her they were entering Claverack, and pulled her forward to the driver's box so she wouldn't miss anything. Loath as she was to admit it, she was not unaffected by his touch, or, for that matter, his proximity on the driver's box. Every time the wagon threw them against each other, she was acutely aware of it.

Driving down the main street, she forgot her anger and found herself unthinkingly squeezing his arm, pointing animatedly to the odd wooden houses on the riverbank.

"I've never seen any like them! They look like tall saltboxes," she exclaimed.

"Nantucket style," Raleigh explained. "That's where the whaling families come from."

His shoulder bumped hers again and she looked away.

"Oh, for heaven's sake, stop it!" he bellowed.

"Huh?" Stephen jerked back on the reins.

"Not you! Just head for the river and mind your business."

Frederick chuckled, but stopped when Raleigh threw him a warning glance.

"Damn it! Stop the wagon!" Raleigh shouted.

"Stop it?"

"You heard me. Beth and I will meet you down at the pier. We're going to walk."

"I'm glad you consulted me," Beth said. "I hate to disappoint you, but I'd much rather ride."

"That's a shame," Raleigh said, "because you're walking." And with that he lifted her to the ground.

"You can't do that." Beth pounded his chest, but to no avail. Raleigh stayed firm, and the wagon left them standing in the street.

"Come on." He grabbed her and she stumbled forward. Taking her arm, he linked it through his and held it there. He walked quickly and she had difficulty keeping up.

"Where are we going?" She stumbled again. "Would you slow down?"

Raleigh said nothing and continued at the same pace.

"If you don't stop right now, I'm going to scream."

"Scream." He didn't miss a step.

Beth opened her mouth, took a deep breath. She pulled back and Raleigh stopped.

"Well?" he said. "What are you waiting for? I thought you were going to scream."

Beth looked down the street to the quay. Ship after ship lined the river docks, masts and rigging spearing the blue of the April sky. She wondered which one Raleigh would be on, how soon he would leave, and what would she do when he did?

"I changed my mind," she said quietly.

"Beth." He lifted her chin. "Look at me."

Reluctantly she brought her eyes to his. He tied the strings of her bonnet. "I don't want to have to chase it," he said. "Though if we weren't in town I'd pull it off and let your hair blow free."

"That's not why you took me from the wagon," she said, turning away again.

"No."

"If it's about last night, I don't want to discuss it."

Raleigh grabbed her shoulders. "Yes, by God, it is about last night, and you damn well will discuss it. Or . . ."

Beth stared at him coldly. "Or what?"

"Or I'll . . . I'll turn you cross my knee and spank you."

"Ha!" Beth tossed her head. "Right here in the middle of Claverack Landing. That'll be the—" Beth had no chance to say more. Raleigh swung her to the side and brought his palm down hard on her bottom.

She gasped, blushed fiercely. Two old women strolling across the street looked aghast and quickened their pace, pretending to avert their eyes.

"She's been naughty!" Raleigh shouted. The women hurried along, their heads raised with indignation.

"You . . . you . . ." Beth stammered, adjusting her bonnet, her cheeks still burning with embarrassment.

"Now can we talk about last night?" Raleigh asked calmly.

Beth folded her arms, huffed angrily. "Have I a choice?"

Raleigh unfolded her arms, locked one again in his and started walking. "No," he said pleasantly.

"Well, then, have your say, and let's get it over with."

"Beth, I'm sorry. I didn't . . . I had no idea about your past."

"Please. I can't talk about that." She stopped, stared at the ground.

"I understand. But someday you will, you should, and when you do it will stop haunting you."

"It will never stop haunting me," Beth said tonelessly. "Please. I don't want to discuss it. If that's what you have to say, I'd rather not hear it."

"No. That was only part of it." He hesitated. "The other part is that it wouldn't have mattered if you were just some ordinary girl. But you're not. You weren't since the first day I met you. You're special."

Beth felt her heart begin to quicken. His words, his voice, sent butterflies tumbling inside her, against all will and reason. She wanted to say something, but could think of nothing. She looked into his face and grew ashamed of the hunger she suddenly had for his arms. Almost as a reaction against her desire, she spoke sharply.

"Do you say that to all your ladies?" Instantly she regretted the words.

Raleigh's face clouded. He released her hand and glared. "If you're curious as to the women I've taken to bed then ask, and if you're not, then don't insinuate numbers and words I've spoken."

"I—"

"You what?" he said angrily. "You want me to grovel and apologize? Well, that I won't do. You can believe as you wish, but what I've said to you I've never said to another woman." He started walking toward the docks.

Beth ran after him. "Raleigh, wait."

He whirled, and, before she could stop him, caught her around the waist, pulling her close. "Listen to me, you foolish, damnable girl. I don't want any more nonsense out of you. You see those ships down there? By tomorrow night, I'm going to be signed aboard and shipping out, either for whales or God knows what. But if you think I'm just going to leave you here for the fates to sport with, you're mad."

Beth felt her head spinning. Raleigh's arm was tight around her as if nothing could break it loose, and yet there he was telling her now he was leaving her and not leaving her.

She put her arms around his neck. "Oh, Raleigh. I

feel like such a fool. I didn't mean to—" She noticed a couple walking toward them and immediately dropped her arms to her sides.

Raleigh laughed broadly. "Women are always saying good-bye to their men in this town. I'm sure they wouldn't be shocked by an embrace. A kiss, perhaps. Let's see." As the couple drew alongside, Raleigh brought his mouth down upon Beth's.

Beth heard the woman gasp, as did Raleigh, and the two broke apart in explosive laughter.

"Come on," he said, "before they summon the constabulary."

Beth held her bonnet, which was being buffeted by the wind. The closer they got to the river, the stronger the breeze became and the more concentrated her efforts to keep her hat on.

"Damn that thing," Raleigh shouted. "How can I talk to you when you're clutching your head like a beaten fighter?"

"I can't help it. It's my only bonnet and I'm not about to let it fly off."

"There's a tearoom at that inn up ahead. We'll go there. I can't battle you *and* the elements."

The tearoom was damp and more than slightly brine-smelling, but the smell of herbs and warm pastry amply compensated. It was the first time in many months that Beth had tasted real tea, and she sipped it slowly, savoring each swallow.

"Now that we don't have to worry about your damn bonnet, may I continue?"

Beth grinned impishly. "Clever way to trick you into putting up for a cup, eh?" She felt his hand search beneath the table for her leg, and giggled.

"Listen, you Circean devil, enough foolishness. There's lots to be done before I go, and little time."

Beth's smile vanished as she recognized that Raleigh spoke the truth. Though she had known all along that when they reached Claverack she'd be on her own, she hadn't given it much thought. Traveling with Frederick, Stephen, and Raleigh had made her feel secure, part of a family again. Family. Her spirits sank visibly. It seemed so long since they'd left. Did John miss her terribly? Would she ever see him again? And what of the wondrous child God had wanted her to have—Suzannah, golden-haired Suzannah? She had to be all right, for they would be reunited someday. And as long as that someday existed, Beth knew they both would survive.

She no longer even thought of Adrianne.

The thoughts cast a heavy pall over her, and Raleigh could not help but notice.

"Dear Lord," he muttered looking heavenward, "what now?"

"I'm sorry. I was thinking of the past."

"You have enough to handle with the present and the future. I'd advise you to keep retrospection for more leisurely occasions. Now, as for what's to be done with you while I'm gone . . ."

"To be *done* with me?" Beth was irate. Was she not enough of a woman to decide her own fate? "Am I to be disposed of as livestock?"

"Don't be an idiot. This is neither the time nor the place to ring in your independence. A whaling town is not known for its chivalry to unchaperoned females. I have some money to give you, which will hold you for a while at one of the boardinghouses. I'll tell them that you're my cousin and your mother died en route here from New York. Then we'll see if I can arrange a job for you at the candleworks. I believe there's a large one here."

Beth's jaw dropped. Give her some money? Get her a job? Did he think her totally incompetent? Why, she had money of her own and was certainly qualified to find work. He was still treating her as a child! Did he think she knew nothing?

"I appreciate your offer," she said frostily, "but I'm quite capable of paying my own way at a boarding-house. And of finding employment."

"Damn you, girl. You know nothing of the world. I tell you again, this is not a city where innocence is of value. A single female of your youth would be exploited instantly, without some sort of protection."

"And *you* can supply that protection?"

"I have a certain amount of influ— Never mind. Just follow my instructions." He slugged down the remainder of his tea. "Stephen and Frederick will be wondering what's happened to us. We'd best get down to the docks." He took a pound note from his pocket, paid the proprietor and waited for change. "Oh, and don't mention any of this to them. It would make them . . . curious."

Make *them* curious! Pound notes! Where did he get money like that?

"Just a moment." Beth put her hand to his arm. "You're not a drifter like Stephen and Frederick, are you? What you said before, about having influence. What did you mean?"

"Nothing. Let's leave it at that. I won't ask you questions about your past; you don't ask me questions about mine. Fair?" His tone was curt.

"Fair," Beth answered slowly. "But—"

"No buts. Now let's be on our way."

Raleigh left her with Frederick and Stephen. An hour later he returned. He had rented a room for her in a pretty boardinghouse on Pine Street and arranged for a job at the Niessen Candleworks.

The house was nicer than Beth would have imagined herself living in. Her room was on the second floor, in the rear, and had a long French window that swung out and offered a beautiful view of the river and ships. Centered in the room was a four-posted canopied bed of cherry wood, with a thick down comforter. Two chests with mirrors above each stood on either wall. Mrs. Peterson, a round-faced woman with a warm smile and slight limp, told Beth that her sister had just passed on and left her a houseful of furniture.

"Will I be able to afford to stay here?" Beth whispered to Raleigh. "I mean, with my job at the candleworks?"

"Just give Mrs. Peterson a hand in the kitchen now

and then, and don't worry. You're all paid up for a year."

"A year!"

"Shhhh." Raleigh closed the door to the room. "I told her it was your mother's money. I'm your cousin, remember?"

"A year! Raleigh, where on earth did you get that sort of money?"

"No questions. I've put on to the *Onteora,* a whaler. That's twelve months at sea. What was I going to spend money on aboard ship?"

"But—"

"It's done. Tomorrow you go to see Mr. Niessen at the candleworks. I've arranged it all, but if you're asked anything, tell him that you worked as a maid for William Eckert."

"Eckert? A relative?"

"I said no questions."

"All right. But everything is happening so fast. I won't know what to say, or think."

Raleigh put his arms around her. "You can start by saying good-bye." He kissed her gently. Then he guided her back toward the bed and began unbuttoning the bodice of her dress. "And you can think about this while I'm gone."

"Raleigh! You can't . . . Mrs. Peterson—"

"She doesn't appeal to me."

"But it's broad daylight!"

His hand cupped her breast, his fingers began to work her nipple. "Shhh," he said. "The other boarders will get jealous."

"But, Raleigh, this is madness."

His mouth muffled further protest. They made love silently, urgently. When it was over, Beth closed her eyes; and wrapped in Raleigh's arms, sun still streaming through the window, she fell into exhausted, dreamless sleep.

When she awoke, it was dark. And Raleigh was gone.

Chapter 12

Christopher Niessen was a portly man with graying hair arranged in a puff on top and tied in a queue behind. His cheeks were splotched with red patches and his eyelids drooped disconcertingly, giving Beth the feeling that he was tremendously bored with her presence, which was anything but the case.

In the month she'd been working at the candleworks, he had called her into his office at least a dozen times. At first it had been to instruct her on the length of wicks and the cleaning of the molds, but afterward it had been for no discernible reason, which made Beth more than a little uncomfortable in his presence. This was especially true when he'd walk around her, sizing her up as one did a dray horse, all the while pulling at the seat or crotch of his pants with the utter disconcern of a toddler.

Beth was careful to avert her eyes. Once, when she hadn't, she noticed a bulge in Niessen's britches. She'd blushed so fiercely she could barely answer his questions, which, curiously, seemed to please him. Almost always he would make some reference to her "former employer," William Eckert, whom she gathered, from his tone of respect, was a man of substance.

Today when she entered the small dark-paneled office, which reeked of jasmine—a futile attempt to mask the all-permeating scent of the whale fat used in the candles—she knew something was different. Wrong. There was an unpleasant smile on Niessen's face, and as he strutted around her he tapped a letter against his thigh.

"I thought you'd like to know that I received a missive from William Eckert today," he said, stopping in front of her.

His inflection put Beth immediately on guard. She tensed, tried to cover with feigned curiosity.

"'Oh, really? I do hope he's all right."

"He's fine. I wrote to him when you first began working here, thinking he'd be pleased to know that his valued housemaid was now safe in my employ. But not only wasn't he elated to be apprised of this news, he was distressed to learn that someone was *posing* as his former employee." Christopher Niessen narrowed his eyes and pushed his puffy face closer to Beth's. "So! You are a fraud. And the young man purporting to be Eckert's son, he was a fraud too, eh?"

"No. His name is Raleigh Eckert. I—I'm sure whatever he told you was the truth." But she wasn't sure at all! "He only wanted to help me get a job, that's why he said I had worked for his . . . his father."

Christopher Niessen slapped the letter against his hand. "And where is young *Mr. Eckert* now?"

"Why, he's at sea. On the *Onteora,* whaling." Beth felt her stomach knot as Niessen slammed the letter to his desk.

"Whaling?" He tossed his head and laughed unpleasantly. "William Eckert's son gone whaling? There's a good joke. If he told you that and you believed him, then he probably sold you other bills of goods too."

Beth's stricken look brought an evil grin to Niessen's lips. "Well, well," he said. "And by your pretty little face I have a good idea of those other goods, haven't I?"

"Your insinuations are inappropriate and vulgar," Beth said icily.

"Are they?"

"Most certainly," Beth said, with more hauteur than she felt. Had Raleigh lied to her as well as to Niessen? Was Eckert not really his name? And who was William Eckert that it was so incomprehensible his son would put on to a whaler? Damn! If Raleigh had only signed aboard the *Rachel Lee* he would be home in another six weeks, but the *Onteora* wasn't due back for a year!

"I wouldn't play at sanctimony at this point if I were you," Niessen said, flicking his tongue against his lower lip. "There aren't many jobs in Claverack for a girl of your years."

"Are you trying to tell me that I'm fired?" Beth asked stonily.

Niessen tugged abstractedly at his britches, his eyes fastened on Beth, glistening.

"Not necessarily," he said pleasantly.

He put his hand on her shoulder and a wave of revulsion swept her. She froze, stared at the window. Maybe if she didn't move he'd leave her and sit down behind his desk as he usually did. But he didn't. Suddenly Beth felt his hand sliding down toward her breast. She whirled and brought her palm smartly across his cheek.

"Don't you dare touch me!" she commanded.

Niessen was visibly stunned. He held his cheek, glared at her. "Why, you little slut. Who do you think you are to raise a hand to me? I could have you arrested for that."

"I wouldn't advise it. With nothing to lose, I'd make sure that Mrs. Niessen was vividly informed of a less than business relationship between us, as mythical as its grounds would ever be in reality."

"Get out!" Niessen growled. "Get out this moment and don't ever return!"

"With pleasure," Beth said bitingly. She left the office, slamming the door behind her.

"You'll be sorry," he called after her. "Very sorry. Nobody threatens Christopher Niessen and gets away with it!"

She didn't even look back.

Later that evening, when she told Mrs. Peterson that she'd lost her job, the sprightly old woman patted Beth's hand and said she believed she could find her some employment. But the following morning, when Beth came downstairs for breakfast, Mrs. Peterson was ghostly pale and wheezing.

"What is it?" Beth asked anxiously.

The old woman pointed to her chest. "Hurts. Hard to breathe. Get Doctor Wesselman. Two houses down on Bell Lane."

Beth helped Mrs. Peterson to the parlor couch, then raced down the street for the doctor. When she told him what had happened, he grabbed his bag and followed her.

Entering the parlor, Beth knew at once that they were too late. Mr. Broock, a middle-aged widowed hat maker who rented the front room, was standing beside Mrs. Peterson, crying. Dr. Wesselman pushed Broock aside, took out his stethoscope and pressed it to the old woman's chest. A few moments later, he returned it to the bag.

"She's gone." He sighed, then went to the desk and wrote something on a piece of paper. He handed it to Beth.

It was the name of a mortician and coffin maker on Dyne Street.

The week after Mrs. Peterson's funeral, a lawyer appeared at the door of the boardinghouse and informed Beth and Mr. Broock that the house had been sold to a Mrs. Niessen and they would have to find other lodgings. When Beth explained that her rent had been paid for an entire year, the lawyer told her she'd need necessary proof in order to get a rebate from the new owner. Without that, she was out of luck. And, according to the lawyer, who had gone through all of Mrs. Peterson's papers, no such proof existed.

Beth found another room, much closer to the docks and not nearly as nice, but realized that unless she found employment soon, she'd be homeless and very hungry in less than a month. Bustling and growing as Claverack Landing was—it was already being called the city of Hudson—there were few jobs of respectability for an unchaperoned young girl. And with Christopher Niessen against her, there might as well have been none.

After several unsuccessful weeks of seeking employment, doing occasional slop work for shillings, her clothes began to fray and few proper establishments welcomed her through their doors. As the days passed, she looked worse, sometimes eating no more than a biscuit and a bowl of soup in twenty-four hours. When her rent was more than a month overdue, the landlord threatened to have her jailed.

She paid what she owed with the last of the widow's money, then gathered her few belongings in a shawl and headed for the docks. She set up a bed in an abandoned wagon. Alone, frightened and weak with hunger, she began to imagine that Christopher Niessen was hunting her. Thinking she saw his leering face everywhere, she took to hiding out in daylight. In the evenings she fought dogs and rats for the scraps thrown from the taverns. It would be months before Raleigh returned, and God only knew how long before she'd see Suzannah again. What would happen between her and Raleigh, time would tell—but for the miracle child Suzannah *she had to survive*.

How long had it been since she'd eaten real food? Six days? Seven? She sat at the edge of the dock, her feet dangling above the water. The wind sent a fine spray across her face. She stared down into the blue-blackness of the river. Her head began to spin. It was odd the way the sun twirled round and round, spinning out sparks of color. All so pretty. Suddenly she felt herself falling, slipping into cool, clear nothingness. For a brief moment it reminded her of when she and Peter would splash barefoot in the icy spring waters at Red Rocks. And then there was only blackness.

"She's comin' 'round," a male voice said.

Beth smelled potato broth and beggar's tea. Was it a dream? She heard murmurs, unfamiliar voices, and caught the scent of ale. Where on earth . . . ? Her eyes fluttered open but she couldn't be sure if she was asleep or awake. If the former were true, it could be the beginning of a nightmare; if the latter were the case, she had surely died and gone to hell.

A gaunt, one-eyed man with a long, puckered scar on his cheek and lips that drooped to one side, as if imparting a secret, peered at her over a tankard.

"Yep. She's comin' 'round all right," he said.

"Am I in hell?" Beth asked, quite sure that she was.

The one-eyed man turned to the woman standing behind him. "Did you hear that, Ternice?" He laughed. "In hell she's thinkin' she is." He slugged another draught of ale, wiped his mouth with the back of his hand. Then he took the bowl the woman was holding and offered it to Beth. "And do they give you potato broth in hell?"

Beth blinked several times before she realized the room itself was dark and no amount of blinking would lighten it. "I— How did I get here? And where am I?" She sat up with some difficulty. She seemed to be in a cave of some sort.

"Plenty of time for answering questions," the man said. "First put a little of Ternice's broth in you. It's bad dealin' into an empty pot."

Beth took the bowl and spooned the broth up gratefully. It seemed the best she'd ever tasted, and she said so.

"Well, thank you." The woman stepped out of the

shadows and closer to the fire where Beth was. "It ain't nothin' fancy, but it stops the growlin'."

She was not an unpretty woman. Long dark hair, upswept and fastened with a comb, but with a face unsuccessfully painted to make her look younger than her years, which, Beth estimated, to be about thirty-six. Beth recalled having seen her on the docks with another woman. They spent their days and nights near the Driftwood Inn, pleasing men for money.

Beth spooned the soup up quickly, keeping her eyes to the bowl.

"Now, you've got to admit it's a lot better to be swallowing that than the bilge you set out for on the river," the man said, taking another swig from his tankard.

"Did I fall in?" Beth asked.

"Is that what you did? Fall?" Ternice asked. "Tom here was sure you were doin' yourself in."

"Well, I was watchin' you and you were certainly the most doleful soul I'd seen sittin' on the wharf in a long time. And then when you bent over, I was sure that you . . ."

"Oh, no. I wasn't trying to kill myself." She paused, then laughed ruefully. "Maybe I ought to have been."

"Now, what sort of way is that for a beautiful young girl to be speakin'?" He scowled and wagged a finger at her. "There'll be no more talk like that around Tom Longeye—" he cocked his thumb toward himself, "or I'll dunk you in the river myself!"

Ternice laughed. "And he means it, too." She refilled the bowl.

Beth looked from Tom Longeye to Ternice. "Are you sure there's enough?"

"I had a good night's tally," Ternice said. "We have potatoes, carrots, and soup meat to banquet on."

Beth blushed slightly. Ternice was the first prostitute she had ever met.

"So," Tom Longeye said, "you're wantin' to know where you are, and, I suspect, who you're with? Well, you're in the Lair, as we call it, and in the company of two of Hudson's most outstanding sharpers." He bowed. "I'm Tom Longeye, and I've seen more land from mizzenmasts than anywhere else. I sail when I can and cut purse when I can't." He cupped a hand beside his mouth. "They say I've the lightest fingers this side of the Hebrides."

"He's modesty himself, ain't he?" Ternice said.

"Truth is truth." He took another swig of ale. "And that's Ternice."

Ternice nodded, then looked inquiringly at Beth. "And what do we call you?"

"Beth. Beth Talbot." She smiled weakly. The soup had brought back her clarity, though peering into the darkness of the Lair, she wondered if she were ready for it. The cavelike room was dank, and every so often there would be a recognizable scurry in one corner or another. There were no windows.

"Where is this place?" she asked, slowly becoming aware of sounds from above. Creakings and scrapings . . . more voices.

"Below the Driftwood Inn," Tom said. "It's a private club, so to speak, for those of us who . . . well, just don't want to run into a constable for one reason or another."

"Others live here?"

"Not all the time, but on occasion, yes. Once one picks a pocket or involves himself in a bit of speculation, he's not up to company."

A thieves' den! So this was where she'd ended up. It was almost enough to make her laugh. Here she was, spooning up potato soup with a prostitute and a one-eyed cutpurse, while downriver in Rhinebeck her own daughter was more than likely swathed in fine linen and having her pheasant puréed by a mammy. But then Adrianne DeWitt was never really her daughter. Suzannah was that, and for Suzannah she'd sup with Bluebeard himself.

Tom Longeye interrupted her thoughts. "Hey now, not a smile for your hosts? What sort of thanks is that?"

"You're quite kind. I do appreciate it. Really." She smiled.

"We're not likely to be fishin' you out again, so how'd you get there in the first place? Tom said he's seen you hidin' about. From anyone in particular?"

"Christopher Niessen." Beth explained how he had fired her from the candleworks, and, after evicting her from Mrs. Peterson's boardinghouse, had successfully prevented her from finding work.

"Niessen's at the root of your discomfort, eh?" Tom Longeye shook his head. "Ain't surprising. That son of a water varmint is a pox on the human race."

"He wasn't worth the Lord's time in creatin', I'll tell you that," Ternice said. "When he gets to sousing, he comes down to the Driftwood and has a go with one of us. One of us that'll have him, that is. He pays fancy prices, but what he wants is more than most of us are willing to give. Once he overheard Vivienne telling me that he has a wick the size of his pinky and he beat her terribly. She had welts for weeks. He's a mean one, that Niessen. I give him wide berth, and"— she lowered her voice—"whenever anyone of us can do something to stick him, we do it!"

"I'm glad of that," Beth said, "but meanwhile I'm starving and haven't a place to live and—"

"Hold it there," Tom said. "You've food in your belly, girl, and you're with us now, that is if you'd like to stay."

"Here?" A dugout cellar beneath a waterfront bar wasn't much better than sleeping in an abandoned wagon, but the company was welcome and the potato broth terrific. "Are you sure it will be all right?" she asked.

"If you don't mind a little crowdin' now and then," Tom said. "Our rooms aren't fancy."

"Rooms?"

"We share 'em in the shack behind the Driftwood. We only come down here to meet . . . or when one of us finds it necessary to disappear for a while."

"But I have no money. I don't know how I would be able to pay, or repay you."

"There'll be nothin' to repay," Tom said. "Give me a little time and I'll teach you all you need to know to pull your own weight here." He took her hand and looked at her fingers. "Do you weave?" he asked.

"Why, yes."

"Good. Then they're nimble enough for working."

"You mean"—Beth's eyes widened—"picking pockets?"

"It requires skill, virtuosity, and courage. As such, my girl, it is an art. And artists, as I'm sure you are aware, are certainly deserving of recompense."

Beth grinned. There seemed no arguing with Tom Longeye's logic. "I'm afraid I couldn't ever—"

"Ah, ah!" Tom stopped her. " 'Couldn't ever' is a phrase to be avoided if you plan to survive." He drained his tankard, drew the back of his hand across his lips. "But more of that later. Right now I'm going to get me another ale."

He disappeared into the shadows. Beth heard the creaking of hinges. A slice of light cut through the darkness as a trapdoor opened from the Driftwood Inn above. The light vanished when Tom dropped the door behind him.

Ternice took the empty bowl from Beth. "Well, I got to be gettin' back to business." She sighed, laughed. "As my friend Vivienne says, a woman's work is never done."

Beth blushed and was grateful for the darkness. Not only had she never met a prostitute before, she'd never known any female as outspoken as Ternice. Nor any, she had to admit, quite as nice.

"You listen to Tom," Ternice advised. "He knows more about gettin' by with your wits than anyone around. And besides, I think he's taken a special liking to you."

Beth stiffened. Ternice saw it, looked confused, then tossed back her head and gave out a gusty laugh.

"My Lord, girl, not *that* way. I meant because

you're about the same age his daughter was before she died." Ternice looked toward the trapdoor to see if Tom was coming. "He doesn't like to talk about it," she said, lowering her voice, "but he never got over Meagan's passin'. It was the fever. She was gone in a week. I'd nursed her best I could, so did Vi and Lizzie, but it was no use. It hurt us all 'cause we'd raised her since she was six. Sad, sad thing. Tom stayed at sea three years after she died. But I'll tell you, I haven't seen him smile the way he did tonight in a long, long time."

The trapdoor creaked open.

"Don't tell him I told you," Ternice whispered.

"I won't."

"Won't what?" Tom called across the room, his voice evidencing high spirits.

"Won't get out of bed until she's feeling stronger," Ternice supplied. She winked at Beth. "I'll see you later."

Ternice stopped Tom, took a drink from his tankard and kissed him on the cheek. "She needs sleep, Tom," she warned, "so don't go keepin' her up with tales. She'll be here in the morning."

"Not even a quick tellin' of my ten days in a longboat?" Tom asked.

"Just behave yourself, Longeye," Ternice scolded. "The girl's tired."

"I'm not, anymore," Beth said. In fact, she felt wide awake. Like a child about to taste something forbidden, she was almost eager for Ternice to leave.

"I think you're both going to be hopeless!" Ternice shook her head and left.

"Well," Tom said, tossing a log on the fire and then coming to sit at the foot of Beth's mattress, "how would you like to hear about how I brought down an elephant with Captain Cook . . . ?"

Chapter 13

Under the guidance and protection of Tom Longeye in the months that followed, Beth became an accepted denizen of the Lair and member of the Pack. Aside from Ternice and Tom, the Pack included Vivienne and Lizzie, two seasoned prostitutes; Jeb van Riever, a confidence man who hoodwinked sailors out of their pay and seamen's wives out of their fidelity with equal aplomb; Brinker, a surly, ill-tempered burglar; and Ernst, a quiet, blond giant with several missing fingers and a gift for picking pockets equal to Tom Longeye's.

The Pack readily accepted Beth, treating her as a sort of mascot. Even Brinker, who rarely had a nice word for anyone, behaved fondly toward her, occasionally bringing her a scarf or pair of shoes that some burgher's daughter would never miss. She helped Ternice and Vivienne with the cooking (Lizzie, who could just barely make tea, by common consent was forbidden access to any pot) and spent long hours attempting to teach Ernst to read simple signs.

But most of Beth's time was spent with Tom, learning about the sea and how to behave like a young man.

"There's only one sort of woman walks the docks," Tom told her, "and since you're not that sort, you'll just have to become a boy." So, with her hair tucked under a workman's cap, wearing britches and a vest that successfully masked her bosom, she accompanied Tom almost every afternoon on walks along the docks. Before long she knew a sloop from a brigantine, and a frigate from a bomb ketch. To her own surprise she even mastered the principles of an astronomer's quadrant—a wedge-shaped device with a plumb line falling across a scale of degrees for charting courses.

"By God!" Tom had exclaimed at one point, "if only you *were* a lad, I'd lay out for Tahiti with you tomorrow."

Beth felt it was the nicest compliment anyone had ever given her. Disguised as a boy, she discovered a new sort of freedom. Not only did she have access to knowledge usually denied women but she was at liberty to walk where she pleased, climb and bend when she wished. What a relief not to be concerned about her skirts! The masquerade delighted her.

"It's a man's world, Beth," Tom said. "And had Meagan lived, I would have taught her the same. I can see no reason to keep you ignorant just for being the beautiful creature you are. You're ahead of many by your ability to read and write, but there's no reason why you shouldn't know how to shoot a gun or cut a purse or wield a knife too. The more you can do in a man's world, the more you'll expect of a man —ay, and the better the man you'll get."

On clear afternoons, Tom would borrow Jeb van Riever's horse and buggy and take Beth out into the woods. In a glade away from the road, he made a target with a piece of muslin marked with a bull's-eye and wrapped around a bale of hay. She soon became proficient with a flintlock pistol, and dangerous with a knife.

Using "Billy Boy," the double-edged, five-inch

blade he kept concealed in his boot and called his best friend, Tom set up threatening situations and showed Beth how to respond to them automatically. They both enjoyed the sessions, but one day when she dropped Billy Boy and giggled during the practice, Tom exploded.

"It's not a game!" he shouted. "My wife was murdered by a pair of thugs, and she didn't have to be."

It was the first time Tom Longeye had ever mentioned his wife, and to learn that she had been slain was stunning. Beth sobered instantly.

"I'll not go into details, except to say that she was avenged. But all that is beside the point and a past long dead. But you, you've a long life before you in an ugly world. What I'm teaching you now are skills that will serve you better than carding and weaving. But remember, this is no game. Never bluff. If you draw the knife, be prepared to use it."

Beth knew from his tone not to take his instruction lightly. She learned fast and well, so well that by her sixteenth birthday she could wield a knife with mean accuracy and fire a bull's-eye from forty paces.

Dressed as a boy in baggy britches, she became familiar to the regulars on the Hudson docks, though none was aware that it was she who was so blithely and successfully picking the pockets of the tourists disembarking there.

"You've become a real sharper," Tom said proudly when Beth deposited her day's haul in his lap. "But now it's time to stay low for a while."

"Why?" Beth pulled off her cap and let her long russet hair fall free. "I won't get caught. And if they ever get on to me, all I have to do is get to the Lair and back into my skirts." She shook her head and began brushing her hair.

She saw from the corner of her eye that Tom looked concerned. She had come to enjoy the danger, and that could be a sharper's downfall. It made one cocky and careless. But she wasn't about to become careless. So what if she liked the thrill of it? It was better than battling rats for a piece of stale bread. And besides, she was good.

Tom stood, gripped her hand, and stopped her brushing. "Listen to me, girl. I didn't teach you all I know to have you wasting away in Hudson jail."

His one eye glinted angrily. Tom Longeye rarely displayed his temper. Something more serious than her arrogance was troubling him, that was for sure. He drained the tankard he was holding.

"Something's wrong, isn't it?" she said.

"Could be better."

"What's happened?"

"Your old friend Niessen has become councilman and chief of the constabulary. The word's out that he's under pressure from DuBoise and the other ship owners to clean up the waterfront. Seems the passengers getting off here aren't pleased with being filched before they even reach their lodgings. Hudson's become a lively port, and a lot of political bigwigs are going to be passing through in the future. It wouldn't be good for Niessen, especially with his ambitions, to have the gateway to his grand city awash with cutpurses."

"I can think of nothing I'd enjoy more than making him look like the incompetent ass that he is." A light smile played around Beth's mouth. If picked pockets could destroy Niessen's political future, then she would lift purses with gusto.

"I know what you're thinking, but forget it. Niessen's out for the mayoralty, and blood. He'll be nastier than ever with anyone who stands in his way." Tom paused and looked away. "And without Ernst or me around, there'd be no one to pull you out if you fell into anything over your head."

"What are you talking about? I'm not going to get into anything over my head, but even if I did, why . . . where would you and Ernst be?"

No sooner had she asked the question than she grew uneasy about the answer. Something *was* wrong.

Tom was keeping something from her. He licked his lips, studied his boots.

"What is it? What's happened?" Beth demanded. "What aren't you telling me?"

"Ernst is in the bloody cage," Tom said angrily, "and from what Lizzie's heard, he won't be getting out."

"No!" Beth's hand flew to her mouth. It wasn't fair. The childlike giant who only last week had read his first page of print was more honest than a dozen Niessens!

"What will happen to him?" Beth asked, her voice anxious.

"It's not his first time in the cage." Tom kept his head down.

"You mean they'll—they'll hang him?" Beth said incredulously.

"There'll be a trial. But with most of the jury worrying about their own pockets, I can't say they'll care about a cutpurse's neck."

"There must be something we can do?"

"Ain't a one of us that Niessen wouldn't haul in next to Ernst if he had the chance."

Beth covered her face with her hands. Ernst only picked pockets, and that because he was hungry. Christopher Niessen crushed people. Oh, if only there were a way to crush him!

Tom took her hand and clasped it in between his. "There are other matters too, and little time."

A coldness spread over her. There was something in Tom's tone that boded ill.

"What other matters?"

"I've signed on the *Meadowlark,* and we'll be sailin' in two days' time. It's England, then down to the islands. I'd say eight months, but more likely it'll be a year."

Beth felt her lip begin to tremble. First Raleigh and now Tom Longeye. Raleigh's ship wasn't due for another month, and who was to know if he'd really keep his promise to return? He'd deceived Niessen, why not her? Moreover, time could have altered his feelings. And if Ternice was to be believed, those feelings might never have even existed.

"Why, all sailing men make grand gestures before they set to sea," Ternice had said when Beth told her of Raleigh. "If I could remember how many men swore they'd marry and make me an honest woman upon their safe return, why, it would start your head spinning. It's what sailing men do. Their nature, I guess."

When Beth protested, Ternice had conceded that perhaps Raleigh was different. But the silent, knowing laugh in her concession still echoed in Beth's ears.

She looked beseechingly into Tom's craggy, weathered face. "W-why didn't you tell me before?"

"No sense. You'd only get upset, like you are now, but sooner."

"Oh, Tom." Beth threw her arms around him. He hugged her tightly. Then, taking her shoulders firmly, he moved her back.

"You won't forget all that I taught you?"

Beth bit down hard to still her quivering lip. "Uh-uh."

"And there'll be no more picking pockets, hear? I spoke to Patrick, and he said he'll be able to use you in the inn kitchen, which will keep you away from the drunkards and earn you enough for your keep. But outside, you dress as a lad unless you're accompanied. Understand?"

Beth nodded.

"Since the day I pulled your sodden carcass from the river, you became my kin in all but blood—though Lord knows why I'd go and saddle myself with a sassy, troublesome female like you," he said gruffly. "Anyway, seeing that, makeshift or not, you're the only kin I have, I want you to take this." He reached down into his boot, withdrew his knife.

"Billy Boy. Oh, Tom, I can't." She pressed the knife back into his hands.

"Don't anger me, girl," Tom said harshly. "I'll not

leave any kin of mine unprotected. You take Billy Boy and keep him with you all the time."

Beth took the knife, stood on tiptoe and kissed Tom's cheek. "I'll take good care of him."

"You do that," Tom said, "and he'll take good care of you."

Two days later, with Billy Boy comfortably concealed in her boot, Beth stood on the dock and waved as the *Meadowlark* set sail downriver for the sea.

With Tom Longeye gone and a job that kept her indoors, constantly at the inn's ovens, Beth sank into a hard depression. Ternice's implication that Raleigh, like any other seaman, had made empty promises, dug at her heart. Though she didn't want to believe it, the thought that he had used her nettled. When he had thought she was a prostitute, he'd been willing to pay for his amusement. Maybe the rent at Mrs. Peterson's and his sweet words were just another form of payment? It had been so long since she'd seen him, so very long. Sometimes she'd remember that afternoon before he left, lying next to him in the bed. She could almost feel his hands caressing her, his mouth and tongue sporting with her flesh. And then other times, times that frightened her, she couldn't even be sure she remembered his face.

Then too, there was the matter of Ernst's impending fate. His trial was certain to be a travesty of justice.

"Isn't there any way at all we can help him?" she asked Ternice, who'd stopped into the kitchen for her usual respite between customers.

Ternice picked a scone from the tray Beth had just removed from the oven, took a bite. "Ouch! That's hot!" She licked her fingers and blew at the pastry, ignoring the question. Beth pushed the tray back so she couldn't take another.

"Aye! What's that?" Ternice looked indignant.

"Why don't you answer me about Ernst? There must be something we can do?"

Ternice's shoulders sagged. "Sure, there's something we can do. We can pay the guards a tidy sum and Ernst will quietly escape. But none of us has enough money, so forget it."

"I can't forget it," Beth said angrily. "How much money would it take?"

"About a hundred pounds."

"Between all of us, we could raise a hundred pounds!"

Ternice shook her head sadly. "Girl, be realistic. Vi, Lizzie, and me, we only bring in five, maybe ten pounds a night. And you, you're making shillings."

"What about Brinker and Jeb?"

"Brinker's got to stay low for a while, else it's his own neck in the noose. And Jeb's off somewhere in Albany."

"Well, when is he coming back?"

"Whenever it is, it won't be before next week, and by then it'll be too late. Face it, girl, it would take a very rich miracle to bring in a hundred pounds in the next three days." She patted Beth sympathetically and left.

Beth put another pastry tray in the oven and sat down, tried to think. Laughter and raucous shouts from the men in the taproom cut into her consciousness. Suddenly she was on her feet. That was it! She could get more money out of that crowd than Lizzie, Ternice, and Vivienne combined if she were picking pockets! So what if she'd promised Tom that she wouldn't. That was before it had become a matter of life and death. Besides, she knew how to be careful —and the men who left the Driftwood were usually drunk enough to be easy marks. She wouldn't bother with small fish, or the workers. Just the gents, the ones from the hill who came to the Driftwood for whatever their wives weren't giving them.

She feigned dizziness and hurried back to the shack. Quickly, without candlelight, she put on her leather britches, shirt, and vest, pinned up her hair beneath a cap and tucked Billy Boy inside her boot.

Sneaking into the alley alongside the Driftwood,

she crouched down and waited. A well-dressed though slightly disheveled gentleman headed unsteadily for his carriage. Beth rushed out, bumped into him and nearly knocked him to the ground. Pretending to be running from a gang of bullies, she picked his pocket. The man was grateful to be warned of approaching thugs—as were the others on whom she successfully repeated the ruse throughout the night.

By dawn she had nearly forty pounds.

She slept only a few hours. The following morning, tired but elated, she was out on the street again. Donald Rogers, a carver and friend of Tom Longeye's, whose shop was in a vacant sail loft near the wharf, saw her and waved a greeting.

"I suppose you're waiting to see what's come back on the *Hawkline,* eh?" he shouted. "She's been to the Caribbean and DuBoise is expecting a rich haul." He pointed at the figurehead on the sleek three-master. "Looks like my hawk took a beating. Must 'ave been a rough voyage."

"Seems so." Beth lowered her voice to sound more like a male. Even though the carver was Tom's friend, no one outside the Pack knew her secret.

A number of people had gathered at the pier for the docking of the *Hawkline,* and, to Beth's delight, they all looked like ladies and gentlemen of means. Once they began to crowd near the gangplank, it would be easy for her to mingle among them and bump just enough to perform her "sleight of hand," which was how she preferred to think of it. Picking pockets seemed so . . . criminal, so beneath what was definitely an art.

She strolled through the crowd to select her marks. Two gentlemen in particular stood out, one about twenty, the other handsomely gray haired and in his late fifties, apparently a man of more than just peripheral importance. Beth noticed that people greeted him formally, kept respectful distance. She did not catch his name.

One strike like that and she might not have to do

another. But then again, a casual bump against such
a man would be unlikely to go unnoticed. I can't, she
told herself, and scanned for more feasible possibilities. But each time she surveyed the crowd, she came
back to him.

Don't be a fool, she told herself angrily. It wasn't
worth it. If she were caught, it would be like pulling
the rope on Ernst. Still, time and again, her eyes returned to the same man.

He had a strong, surprisingly weathered face for a
man of his means, with a slightly aquiline nose and
thin sharp lips that looked as if they skinned back in
feral grimace more than they smiled. His lids drooped
low over piercingly unreal green eyes. Dressed in the
very latest of fashion, with a high collar and short-
waisted coat of plum-colored silk, he stood out like a
pheasant among grouse. Or, more appropriately, a
lion among lambs.

A temptation began to rise inside her. The chal-
lenge of taking a man like that was very appealing.
No. She mustn't think like that. The only reason she
was breaking her promise to Tom Longeye was to save
Ernst. She had to remember that. But then, almost as
if she were watching it from afar, the crowd began
to gather around the gangplank and she was beside
the man with the silver hair.

Without a moment's hesitation, her hand darted
out, seemingly invisible, seeking its target.

What happened next was a blur of pain. Her fingers went excruciatingly numb, as if they had been
crushed by an anvil.

"In England they'd chop your hands off," the gray-
haired man said without looking down. Still gripping
her hand, he smiled politely as a short man approached.

"How good to see you, Mr. DuBoise," the man
said, bowing. "The *Hawkline*'s cargo must be special
to bring you out."

For a moment, Beth forgot the pain. Seth DuBoise!
the most powerful ship owner in Hudson, if not the

colonies themselves. Of all the dumb, bad luck she could have caught!

"It is," DuBoise said coolly, dismissing the man with a pleasant nod and tightening his grip on Beth's hand.

She was barely able to keep from crying out. Surely her fingers were broken.

"Sir . . ." she managed to rasp. "Please . . ."

DuBoise looked at her as if he were surprised to find her there. There was an odd glint in his chillingly clear eyes, and were circumstances different, Beth would have sworn it was a smile. "My good lad, what can I do for you?" he asked pleasantly, his hand still not releasing hers, keeping it low and out of view.

"I—I'm sorry, sir. Please let me go," she whispered. Tears of pain blurred her vision.

"It's a job you're wanting, you say?" This time he *did* smile!

"M-my hand," Beth gasped. "It's breaking. Please, sir . . ."

"Well, how does houseboy suit you?" DuBoise said loudly.

The pressure lessened. What was the man doing? Was he mad? Whatever insane farce he was playing out, she had no choice but to go along.

"Just fine," she said, nodding.

"Good. You'll start immediately. My last houseboy died of the fever two weeks ago." Slowly he released her hand. She was just about to run when she heard, in an almost inaudible whisper: "Try to escape and I'll have you at the gallows before the sun's up."

Chapter 14

There was little doubt in Beth's mind that Seth Du-
Boise meant what he'd said. Though she'd never seen
him in person, his reputation was legend. Tom Longeye had told her that DuBoise was once an ordinary
seaman. How he'd gotten money to purchase his first
three-master was unknown, though gambling was suspected. But once he had her, the *Valkyrie,* he took
her on a trading voyage to the West Indies and came
back with one hundred percent profit—and another
vessel. That was the beginning. He'd privateered during the Revolution and now owned enough ships to
make him one of the wealthiest men in the colonies.
And, from what she'd heard, one of the most influential. Ternice had told her that two years ago General
Washington himself had paid DuBoise a visit.

It was also common knowledge that Seth DuBoise
was an infamous libertine.

Beth shivered beneath her vest. Her eyes darted in
every direction for a way to escape, but DuBoise
stayed close to her, a bemused smile playing at the
corner of his mouth.

Beth saw the captain of the *Hawkline* approaching.

"Sir," the captain said when he reached DuBoise, "we hadn't expected so impressive a welcome."

"I hope I'm not presuming that you deserve it," DuBoise said.

The captain smiled. "We've brought back enough sugar, molasses, cocoa, and cotton to make the two hellish storms that wrecked our masthead worthwhile."

"Good, good. I'm anxious to survey the holds." He turned and called to the young man whom Beth had considered as her alternate mark. "Philip!" he shouted. "Over here."

The youth was no more than twenty-one, tall and slender with a pouty face and darting rodentlike eyes. DuBoise introduced him to the captain as his nephew.

"Philip," DuBoise said, nudging Beth forward with his cane. "This is . . . I'm sorry, I forgot your name, lad."

"B-Bob," Beth said quickly. "Bob Talbot."

DuBoise nodded approvingly. "Philip, Bob is going to be our new houseboy."

Philip looked at Beth, his eyes appraising her outfit and definitely finding it wanting. "But, uncle—"

His protest was cut short with a sharp phrase from DuBoise. "You will take Bob at once to Alain's old room, and explain his duties. I'm going to inspect the cargo with Captain Rumney. Oh, before you go, tell Hugo I want to see him."

"Yes, sir," Philip said, his displeasure evident.

Beth watched as Philip crossed the dock and spoke to a tall Negro who stood at attention next to a large gold-trimmed coach. A few moments later the black man, dressed in a magnificent green jacket and britches, was before them. DuBoise excused himself from Captain Rumney. Tapping Beth's ankles with his cane, indicating that she should follow, he took Hugo aside.

"Hugo, this is Master Bob. He's going to replace Alain. He's not quite sure he wants the position, but I am. Make certain he doesn't leave before I return."

Hugo nodded. "I understand." He cast Beth an odd look, his eyes momentarily slitting closed like some jungle cat's, then opening slowly with suspicion. "This way," he said. They pressed through the dockside crowd to the coach where a bored, distinctly displeased Philip was waiting.

Philip said little during the ride from the docks to Wildwillow, the DuBoise mansion, for which Beth was grateful. Her head was whelmed in a maelstrom of fear, confusion, and a totally alien excitement, an excitement so redolent with apprehension that it made her giddy. At one point, when Philip deigned to acknowledge her presence with a rather rude, unsolicited appraisal of her clothes, she felt as if she would laugh.

But humor was far from what she was feeling. She was bewildered and scared. Why would a man of DuBoise's stature hire a pickpocket for his houseboy? And what would happen to her when he discovered she was not a boy at all? How long would she be able to keep up her pretense?

Whenever Philip glanced at her, she tucked her chin into her jacket and looked away. If she were any judge of character, though, this Philip wasn't interested in anyone but himself. The driver, Hugo, on the other hand, was a different story. She hadn't liked the way he looked at her. It was almost as if he saw through her disguise. But if he had, wouldn't he have said something to DuBoise? And if not, why not?

Her introspection was interrupted by the slowing of the horses and the sound of metal gates being swung open.

"Thank the Lord," Philip said, half to himself and half to Beth. "I'm famished."

Beth looked out the window and her eyes widened. The DuBoise mansion made the DeWitt manor seem quaint. Never had Beth seen such elegance. The white columns of a lofty portico gleamed against the lush woodland surrounding the house. Set high on a hill that overlooked the river, Wildwillow was as impressive an edifice as Seth DuBoise was a man. Its mass, its power, its eminence were evident from its overall structure to the finest hand-carved detail in the capitals of the columns.

The interior of the house was no less awesome. Following Philip to her quarters, her eyes flew from one oil painting to another, from a crystal chandelier to an embroidered satin couch. Never in her life had she even envisioned such an abundance of luxury. The rooms were huge, with high ceilings, brilliantly polished floors, and grand marble fireplaces. And the mirrors . . . the mirrors seemed everywhere. In the halls, in the parlors, around every turn, flooding the house with light. And each time she caught a reflection it would startle her, for she would not see herself, but an unfamiliar, sadly dressed working boy.

Philip made no attempt to introduce her to any of the servants they passed, nor did any of them question her presence. They merely stood back and nodded. In silence.

When they reached the west wing, they climbed a narrow circular staircase to the second floor. There Philip booted open a door.

"Here's your room," he said tiredly. "My uncle's is down the corridor on the right. He likes his breakfast coffee brought to him at seven, his baths hot, his toilet laid out precisely, his boots glossed daily, his snuffbox filled twice morning and evening. You're to call him Mr. DuBoise, *sir,* in private and never address him at all in front of others."

"I—"

"You're not supposed to understand," Philip said. "You're a servant and it won't sit well with my uncle to think above your station. My uncle runs Wildwillow like a ship, and mutiny here is met as it is at sea. Need I explain further?"

What manner of lunatic asylum had she fallen into? A house run like a ship, a servant committed to silence? Jesus, Mary, and Joseph, how long would she be able to keep up the pretense? Surely not long if

she was to be engaged in drawing baths for Seth Du-
Boise and other such intimacies! And when DuBoise
learned of the deception, what then?

"Well?" Philip said. "Have you any questions?"

Beth cleared her throat, deepened her voice. "Uh-
no. No."

"You take your meals with the rest of the staff. If
you have any problems, speak to Beardsley or Jane."

"Who are they?"

"You'll meet them,' Philip said, annoyed. "I can't
be expected to explain *everything*." With that, he left.

Beth sat down slowly on the bed. She felt as dazed
as someone who'd been socked a good one. There she
was this morning with forty pounds toward Ernst's
freedom, and here she was this afternoon a prisoner
herself. She walked to the window. The sun was just
above the hills across the river, and the water looked
like a long golden ribbon in the glow. But the beauty
was lost in thoughts of her predicament. How in heav-
en's name was she to escape from this place? She
looked down at the gates. Hugo stood there with his
arms folded resolutely across his massive chest. Then
slowly, like a panther, he began to pace back and
forth.

Dear God, she was trapped!

It was nearly dark when she heard the wheels of a
coach on the drive. She sprang up from the bed to go
to the window and a wave of dizziness took her. It
had been hours since she'd eaten, but she had dared
not expose herself to further scrutiny by going down
to the kitchen. Later, when everyone was in bed, she
would sneak to the pantry. Meanwhile she would
wait. Maybe DuBoise would forget about her. Maybe
something would happen to Hugo and she'd be able
to get away. Maybe . . .

She beat her fists against the mattress angrily.
Damn! Why hadn't she listened to Tom?

The creaking of her door startled her. There had

been no knock. When she looked up, Seth DuBoise was in the room.

"There are candles," he said. "But you can get them later. Follow me now."

He looked larger and more leonine in the confines of the house than he had on the dock, and more frightening. Beth shivered as she approached him. It did not escape his notice.

"I am not an ogre, though I fear my physical resemblance to one might be increasing these days."

Beth said nothing and kept her head lowered.

"The least you could do is tell me how wrong I am," he said with mock severity.

Beth swallowed with difficulty. "You're nothing like an ogre, Mr. DuBoise, *sir.*"

"Your sincerity overwhelms me." He left the room, indicating with a flourish of his cane that Beth was to follow.

At the door to his chamber, he stepped to the left, nodded to Beth, and waited. She fumbled with the knob, and in her nervousness nearly tripped over her own feet when she entered the room.

It was a grand bed chamber. A fire crackled in the bronze fluted fireplace, and its glow reflected in the lavishly mirrored walls, creating an almost sinful aura.

DuBoise put aside his cane, stood perfectly straight. "My jacket," he said.

Beth stared at him, unsure of what he wanted. "Sir?"

"You may remove my jacket."

"Oh." Beth moved quickly behind him and did as he asked. DuBoise seated himself on the lounge near the fire.

"Boots." He stretched his legs forward.

Beth felt his eyes on her as she approached, examining her, marking her. She could not raise her head. As she kneeled before him and took his boot in her hand, his voice sounded deeper and more intimidating than before.

"I see it's going to be manners and protocol that'll

be first on the list for you," DuBoise said. "Don't you know it's impolite to keep your cap on in front of a gentleman?"

As he reached for her hat, she jumped back, her eyes round with fear.

DuBoise smiled. "Did you think I was going to beat you about the ears? I was merely going to remove your cap."

"Y-yes, Mr. DuBoise, sir." She remained motionless.

"Well?"

"Well what, Mr. DuBoise, sir?" She felt nearly as foolish as she did frightened. What was she stalling for? Minutes?

"Take off your cap," DuBoise said, annoyed.

"Yes, Mr. DuBoise, sir." Gritting her teeth firmly, her heart feeling somewhere in her throat, she straightened her back, brought her eyes directly to DuBoise's, and, without expression, removed the hat.

Two pins fell to the floor, and her thick russet curls tumbled to her shoulders.

DuBoise's jaw dropped. He blinked, stared at her. "What the—?" And then he threw back his head and began to laugh, laugh uproariously.

Beth didn't dare move. She felt as if she were standing before a wild animal who at any moment could spring upon her, and she was not that wrong. Mercurial moods were among Seth DuBoise's more amiable characteristics.

"A wench, by God! A wench. And a pocket-picking wench at that! Now if that doesn't whip everything." He waved her forward. "Well, don't just stand there like a mooring mast, get over here so I can have a look at you."

Beth walked toward him slowly, but with her head high. If she were going to be sent to jail, that was that; but she wouldn't grovel. As Tom would say, When your number's up, go like a winner.

"Well, now." DuBoise eyed her appraisingly. "You made a pretty lad, but even in that outlandish costume you're wearing it would be an idiot not to see nature intended you to be a woman. Step closer."

Beth hesitated.

"Come on, come on. I'm not about to ravish you; I'm too old for that sort of horseplay. Besides, I prefer my pleasures cultivated to my taste. There are few things I find more boring than engaging in sexual activity with an inept, untutored female."

Beth colored profusely. Seth DuBoise's candor was totally unexpected and she didn't know how to react. Her hauteur vanished in a mushrooming swell of embarrassed self-consciousness. She lowered her head.

DuBoise stood, took her chin in his hand and tilted her head upward. His grip was firm, almost harsh, and his sea-green eyes relentlessly mined her face, as if trying to unearth some invisible secret. Then, his gaze unswerving, he said: "Ladies never lower their heads except in the presence of royalty or the pretense of prayer. But that's irrelevant if you want to be a boy."

"I only dressed that way because on the docks it was too dangerous to be a woman," Beth said quietly. "I mean, Tom Longeye thought it safer for me to dress as a boy."

"Longeye, eh? Leave it to that sly fox to know how to bury a treasure." DuBoise ran his fingertips across her cheek. "I haven't touched flesh like yours for years. So smooth. So exquisitely delicate. Like porcelain."

Beth trembled slightly. DuBoise's touch and voice made her uneasy. There was a sensuality about them that both repulsed and fascinated her. She stepped back, but DuBoise's arm snaked her waist with unexpected agility. Instinctively she stiffened.

"Relax," he said softly. "I told you before, I'm too old for the brawling lusts of youth. I have more discriminating passions." He looked at her a moment, then released her and crossed to the fireplace. "How old are you?"

"Sixteen."

"Sixteen." He said the word as if he were tasting a rare wine. "Incredible. And you are alone, without money, without friends?"

"I do have friends," Beth said defensively.

"Your friend Tom Longeye isn't around. That I know because I was there when he signed on the *Meadowlark*. Who are the others?"

"I don't see where that's your affair."

"There's no need for hackles. I'm trying to make you a fine offer. Obviously you're in need of money, else why would you have been out picking pockets. True?"

Beth didn't answer, turned her head away.

"That's quite rude, but I'll forgive it. *For the moment*." His voice changed, became cooler, harder. Beth's earlier trepidation returned.

"And to select me as your target means one of two things. Either you were very desperate or very dumb. My instincts tell me that the latter is unlikely. So the former seems to be the case. What was the cause of such desperation? Surely you had a source for your next meal."

"It wasn't for me that I needed the money. It was for—" she hesitated, "for a friend."

"May I be so bold as to ask the nature of your friend's needs? You realize that since Claverack Landing has expanded and become the fine city of Hudson, our laws governing such crimes have become more severe. You took a foolish chance. Were I to turn you over to the authorities, you might never see the light of day again." He waited a moment, then added. "And if I cared to, I could have you hung for it. So tell me of your *friend*."

Chilling realization coursed through her. DuBoise was not exaggerating, and he was aware that she knew it. What choice did she have? She told him about Ernst.

"How much money do you need to buy his freedom?"

"One hundred pounds," she said disconsolately. "Which might as well be one million."

"His freedom means a lot to you?"

Beth turned slowly to face him. "Why do you ask?"

"Because I have a proposition."

"What sort of proposition?" Beth asked suspiciously.

"A thoroughly honorable one, I assure you." He smiled a very private smile. "I will have your friend out of jail in the morning. But you must agree to stay on here at Wildwillow."

"Stay on? Here?" She was confused. "For what purpose?"

"My dear young lady, not everything in life needs a *purpose*. Frivolity and pleasure, like virtue, are their own reward."

"I still don't understand. Am I to be a servant?"

DuBoise's cold eyes warmed with an inner merriment. "Should I be so foolish as to take on a pickpocket as a servant?"

"I am not a thief!" Beth said angrily, her eyes blazing.

"And well I know that. But neither are you a servant." He circled and appraised her like a buyer inspecting an expensive statue; like a wolf assessing his prey. "No, my delightful lass in lad's clothing, you are the raw material for something much more pleasant."

"And that is . . . ?"

"Appellations are misleading. Let us just say that the artist in me is attracted to your Galatea-like qualities."

"Who or what is Galatea?"

"Have you never heard of the Greek sculptor Pygmalion?"

Beth shook her head.

DuBoise smiled. "Well, you will. You'll learn all about the Greeks, as well as the Romans. And more. Wildwillow has been lacking in one of the primal luxuries for a long time now, but for the first time I can see my way clear to rectifying the situation."

Beth was aware only that his eyes were studying without seeing her. It was as if *she* weren't there—but someone else was!

"You speak in riddles beyond my comprehension."

"Only for the moment. It will take time and effort, but I will make certain there will be little beyond your comprehension."

"Please, sir, can you not explain more now?"

"I will tell you only that you must trust me, and that if you do I will see to it that you become the showpiece of Wildwillow."

"Am I to understand that you want to groom me to be a lady?"

"Grooming is for horses and ladies are boring," Du-Boise said disdainfully. "I am going to make you much more than a lady. In the truest Greek sense of the word I am going to make you a courtesan—and the most desirable woman in the colonies."

Beth was aware only that his eyes were studying
without seeing her. It was as if she weren't there.

Chapter 15

"Do you like it?" Seth DuBoise asked.

Beth looked up from her French lesson. Seth Du-
Boise stood in the doorway holding a magnificent pale
green gown with a luxuriant long-sleeved bodice. "Oh,
sir!" she cried. "It's beautiful."

"It's the rage in England, I'm told. This kerchief is
very bouffant when tucked in." He laid the dress over
a chair, added the scarf for effect. "Something like
that."

Beth fingered it with reverence. It was still difficult
to believe that she wore fabrics like these, even after a
year at Wildwillow. Sometimes it disturbed her to accept such presents, made her feel as if, somehow, she
had sold her honor. But had she really? Seth had never
touched her, never even tried. He seemed to enjoy
looking at her, but was always the gentleman. Was it
better for her to suffer in virtuous poverty, clinging to
memories of a man who had obviously sported with
her for amusement? She pushed the painful thought of
Raleigh from her mind. Love was a myth, like Sinta

Klaus. Someday she would find Suzannah and know it again. Until then, she would think neither of that nor honor. Whatever DuBoise wanted, he would have; whatever she needed, she would get. *That* she vowed.

"There's a green silk hat, faced with blue, to go with it," DuBoise said. "It will do wonderful things for your eyes."

Beth took the dress and held it against herself. "It's magnificent."

DuBoise sat down on the window seat. "Let me see how it looks on."

Beth hesitated, as she always did when Seth asked her to try things on in front of him, her face flushing slightly. Each time she'd have to remind herself it was all simply part of her training, then she would tilt her head to the side, nose elevated, and casually, unconcernedly, let whatever she unfastened fall by its own weight to the floor. Today, though, she was anxious to see what the new gown looked like. She pulled her bodice lacing quickly, stepped from her dress awkwardly and tossed it hurriedly on the settee.

"You're not pulling off a pair of work boots," Seth said sternly, but without anger. It was difficult for him to reprimand her, especially when her excitement over the gown was so in evidence. She looked lovely even in her childish haste. In fact, he found her very unconcern about his presence as titillating as he usually found her maidenly embarrassment. Few things in life had given him as much pleasure as watching Beth in her white cotton chemise, her fine unbounded young breasts, their nipples raised demurely, swaying melodically beneath the thin fabric as she moved about the room.

She'd balked when he had first asked her to disrobe. But once assured that he was interested solely in her education and that the only difference between a body clothed in underthings and one fully dressed was the layers of material, she learned to do so easily.

But he did so enjoy the tint of embarrassment, the first hesitation that still remained. And though he concealed it well, albeit often with difficulty, it unfailingly aroused him—a condition not easily come by in recent years. More often than he cared to admit these days, it required practiced hands and inventive tongues to bring about what Beth could with a simple switching of fabrics.

One day, perhaps, when she was ready, he might take her to his bed. But for the meanwhile, the exquisiteness of his deprivation provided him with a unique pleasure. And no one knew better than Seth DuBoise how few of those there were left.

Beth pirouetted in front of him. "There. How do you like it?"

"I fear I've set about my own destruction. You'll outdo the *Experiment* with that outfit."

"The *Experiment?*"

"She's a sloop that's sailed all the way to Canton, China. New York's agog over her cargo: porcelains finer than England's, taffetas and silks, but they'll pale in your shadow."

"Do you mean we're going to New York?" Beth exclaimed excitedly. Most all of the ships that came to Hudson had stopped first in New York. It had libraries, a college, even a museum. And Raleigh Eckert had lived there. "Oh, sir, when?"

"We'll go downriver a week from tonight."

"Oh, a week," Beth said disappointedly. "Can't we go sooner?"

"You're always in a rush. You must learn that life's most glorious delights are those that cost time. There is a richness in something one has waited for that can't be equaled by immediate gratification." He gave her hair the lightest touch. "You shall see. Meanwhile, I'm expecting guests on Wednesday, so you can please yourself by wearing the new frock then."

"Guests? And I'm to be there?" Beth was totally unprepared for the invitation. Not since she'd come to Wildwillow had Seth DuBoise allowed her to socialize with any of the visitors. When there was company, she was confined to her room, taking all her meals there

too. As compensation, he always saw to it that she
had the latest fiction. Just last week she had devoured
Christoph Martin Wieland's *Oberon* in Mr. Adams's
translation. It was wonderfully romantic and she didn't
feel she'd missed anything, judging from what the
cook had told her of the company.

"I believe you're ready to be presented," DuBoise
said. "It's time that Wildwillow's reputation began to
spread. And you, my dear, are going to be the tinder
that ignites it."

"And what am I to make of that?" she asked.

"What you will. Suffice to say I expect you to keep
a sharp ear for my instructions. I have information to
gather at this 'social' get-together, and I'm going to use
you for the harvesting. Without taking offense, you
should know that there is much said by drinking men
in the company of women that they'd not dare let slip
in front of others; thinking as they do of women having scant more interest than pretty ponies in politics or
business."

Beth acknowledged DuBoise's compliment to her
intelligence with a gracious nod.

"I'll attempt to keep Philip in the background, since
my nephew has the unconscionable habit of allowing
his enthusiasm to betray our interest when feigned
boredom would serve us better. Though I realize it will
be difficult with you around. I've noticed his attentions."

Beth kept her face immobile. Noticed his attentions
indeed! It would be difficult for a blind man not to
see those! The arrogant, cabbage-faced dolt, who'd totally snubbed her at first, had in the past three months
become a constant nuisance. His *attentions* were as
obvious as his *intentions,* and both were as irritating
to Beth as a sack full of itching powder. Whenever
he could corner her, he would bother her for walks or
games of cards or a horseback ride. Under ordinary
circumstances, she would have enjoyed company on a
country walk or a pleasant horse ride, but with Philip
there weren't ordinary circumstances. He was forward

to the point of discomfort. Beth would have loved to tell DuBoise of his nephew's attempts at liberties with her, but Philip was sly enough to deny them, and she knew how much DuBoise disliked squabbles. As long as she could handle him herself, she'd do so. Though she fretted about how long that would be. When she last refused to accompany Philip on a ride, he pinned her arms and pressed himself grossly against her. She warned him if he ever tried it again, she'd tell DuBoise he'd assaulted her. He merely laughed. They were both lying, but neither knew for how long.

"I've never thought of myself as a spy," Beth said, pushing the unpleasant thoughts of Philip from her mind.

"And I don't want you to start now," DuBoise said. "You must only think of yourself as a woman. That is indeed sufficient."

The guests were expected at six. DuBoise came to Beth's room earlier with a small box of powder.

"I don't approve of powdered hair," he said, "but this new lightly dusted fashion of, what do they call it . . . ?"

"Mouse color?" Beth offered.

"Offensive, but yes, that's it. Anyway, here." He handed her the box. "It always impresses men to be around women *au courant* with London and Paris fashion."

Beth sat down in front of the mirror, opened the box and took out the small brush.

DuBoise leaned back against the wall and watched her apply the powder. She wore only her undergarments, the tops of her smooth white breasts rising like two gentle swells above the stays, her ankle and bare foot peeking from beneath the petticoat. His eyes savored her unawareness of him, and once again he found himself desiring her. He experienced the full pleasure of the feeling before he forced it away with the same iron will that had forged his shipping empire.

He cleared his throat. "The gentlemen will be arriving shortly, so I'll keep this brief. I want you to pay particular attention to any comments made by Mr. Hamilton. He's on his way to Philadelphia for the Constitutional Convention, and I'd like to know anything I can about what the future holds, especially since rumor has it that he'll be in charge of finance. Oh, and also, I want you to see what you can garner from conversation with James DeWitt. He's—"

Beth swung around. "DeWitt? The same DeWitt who lives at Clearview manor?"

"You know him?"

Beth flustered. "I—I don't. Not really. I saw his wife once or twice, that's all. I used to live on the manor lands." She turned back to the mirror. DeWitt. James DeWitt. Adrianne DeWitt's "father." She laughed silently. *Well, at least I'm on the same social footing as my daughter now.*

"I see," DuBoise said. "Well, what I want you to do besides enchant him into bragging about his plans, is to use the *talent* you claim to have perfected since we met and see if he's signed an agreement with LeFevre to take over the *Versailles*. I heard he met with him this morning."

Beth raised her eyebrow. "Am I to understand that you want me to do something unlawful?"

DuBoise grinned. "Only if you can do it without getting caught."

She turned back to her mirror and fought to keep the smug smile from her lips. So, the times she'd showed DuBoise her skill at picking pockets he *had* been impressed! Well, well, that pleased her, pleased her more than she would have thought.

James DeWitt was seated on a sofa in the oval parlor talking to Philip; Seth, Mr. Hamilton, and another man, with powdered white hair, stood near the fireplace drinking wine. When Beth entered, their conversation stopped. Philip and DeWitt hastened to their feet.

"Gentlemen," DuBoise said, walking to Beth and putting an arm about her waist, "I'd like you to meet Miss Beth Talbot. The new—" he hesitated, searching for a word, "*hostess* of Wildwillow."

DeWitt moved forward first, took Beth's hand and kissed it. He was younger-looking than Beth had expected him to be, remembering him only vaguely as a tall slender man with black hair and thin lips that looked as if they were created for spewing invective.

"A most extraordinary pleasure," he said. Then turning to DuBoise he said, "My compliments, sir— and my envy."

Beth pretended not to hear, greeting Hamilton and the white-haired man, whose name was Fritchett. She nodded to Philip as coolly as she could without being too obviously rude.

"Beth, I think we could use drinks," Seth said softly. "Would you mind?"

She suppressed a smile. They had rehearsed scenes like this so many times, it was difficult to believe it was real. She noticed the surprise on the men's faces when she went to the sideboard to pour the wine. Seth had told her it would disconcert guests to have a beautiful woman perform tasks usually reserved for servants. Especially an intelligent woman.

When she handed James DeWitt his wine, she let her fingers touch his, as Seth had taught her. It was the most innocent body contact, but as he had explained, quite provocative.

"I've met few besides Franklin who know how to enjoy a woman," he'd told her. "And even Ben doesn't appreciate the finer delights of sensuality."

Beth had never realized that female wiles could be used so effectively. Why, all she had to do was raise and lower her lids at DeWitt and he tripped over his words. Mr. Hamilton was more concerned with business, though she did turn his head when she adjusted the strap on her shoe, "accidentally" exposing her ankle. As for Fritchett and Philip, it took skill just to keep them at arm's distance.

She sat next to Mr. Hamilton at dinner and was flattered when he told Seth that he'd rarely had so lovely and intelligent a dinner partner. He spoke of how the Spanish real was becoming the accepted coin of value and how soon there would be American dollars to replace the fluctuating values of pounds and guilders. Beth surprised him with her comprehension of financial problems—which Seth had explained to her at great length and with hefty sighs—and had James DeWitt practically leaning in his potatoes to catch her eye.

After dinner, at Seth's signal, she followed the gentlemen back into the parlor and served brandy. DeWitt had already drunk more than he could handle, but showed no inclination of stopping. Beth encouraged him to take more, knowing well that his inebriation would only facilitate her task. When she felt he had enough, she ambled seductively into the hall and waited for him to follow.

"Miss Talbot," DeWitt called, standing unsteadily in the parlor doorway. "You're not leaving to retire so early, are you?"

"Not at all," Beth said sweetly. She slipped her foot out as he came toward her, and he stumbled, falling to the floor.

She moved quickly, her hand slipping in and out of his jacket pocket, removing everything and putting it into her own waistband as she helped him to his feet. "Are you all right, sir?" she asked.

DeWitt brushed himself off. "Of course. It was nothing, nothing."

Seth DuBoise entered the hall. "My dear DeWitt, have I plied you with too much of my spirits?"

"On the contrary," DeWitt said. "I think a little more brandy is what I need."

Seth took his arm and led him back into the parlor, casting Beth a fine wink.

She hurried into the library and closed the door behind her. Removing the contents of DeWitt's pocket from her waistband, she laid them on the desk: a billfold, a watch, and two letters. She quickly pushed the billfold and watch to the side and opened the first of the two letters. It was merely a statement of introduction from General Washington to someone named Preston in Philadelphia. She refolded it and opened the other.

This was it, a letter from Monsieur LeFevre accepting terms for the purchase of his ship, the *Versailles*. Just what Seth had wanted to know. Beth wrote down the amount of money involved, quickly scanning the rest of the letter and the ship's roster attached. Suddenly the pen fell from her hand. Listed as second mate was *Raleigh Eckert!*

But that was impossible. Raleigh had signed on to the *Onteora,* a whaler. Besides, mates on brigs like the *Versailles* had to be naval officers or gentry. How could . . . ?

She heard Seth's cough, her signal to return. She scooped up DeWitt's belongings and barely managed to reach the spot where he'd stumbled, pretending to have just picked up what fell, when he appeared.

"These must be yours," she said, holding out the letters, billfold, and watch.

DeWitt snatched them quickly and the watch fell to the floor.

Beth picked it up. "I don't think it's broken," she said. "It's still . . ." Her voice trailed off as she looked at the timepiece lying open in her palm. Inside was a finely painted miniature of a little girl with dark black curls.

Beth stifled an involuntary gasp: Adrianne!

DeWitt noticed her attention. "That's my daughter," he said. "She'll be three in October."

"She's—she's lovely," Beth said, mesmerized by the frightening resemblance the child had to the man who'd spawned her.

"A little hellion, that one." DeWitt shook his head as he looked at the picture. "Lord knows what she'll be like as a young lady. Has nice eyes, though." He flipped the watch closed. "Same color as yours."

Beth smiled weakly. "Thank you. I—I guess we'd best join the others now that you've reclaimed your possessions." She turned to go, but DeWitt caught her arm.

"Sir?"

He pulled her to him. His breath was heavy with the scent of brandy. "I don't mean to be impolite, but I find you exceedingly attractive."

"She is exceedingly attractive." Seth DuBoise stepped through the doorway, his eyes cool. "And you are, I'm afraid, being impolite."

DeWitt released Beth's arm. "My apologies, DuBoise. It must be the brandy that's riddled my manners. I realize that I should have approached you." He straightened his coat. "Your *hostess* appeals to me more than any of the bejeweled and buxom damsels they foisted upon us in Paris." He winked at DuBoise. "Let's just say that I would, um, be most appreciative if she could join me for the remainder of the evening?"

Without answering, Seth pulled the servant's bell cord. Within moments, Hugo appeared.

"Hugo, Mr. DeWitt is not staying the evening after all."

"I say, DuBoise, what are you talking about?"

Seth continued as if no one had spoken. "You may have his man bring his coach."

"Very good, sir."

"Say, what in blazes is this?" DeWitt demanded. He laughed uneasily. "Some sort of joke, eh?"

"Good night, Mr. DeWitt," Seth said with finality. "Beth, you may go to your room."

"Now wait a minute," DeWitt said, his speech slightly slurred. "You're not telling me that you're up in arms because of this . . . this"—he waved his arm loosely toward Beth—"pretty little trollop—or should I say *hostess?*"

Seth DuBoise's eyes turned thunderously dark. "There is a difference, sir, and I am offended by your disregard for it. You will pay for your rudeness."

DeWitt laughed. "With my life?"

"You insult me again by thinking I'd ask for something of such insignificant value. No, sir, not your life. But you will *pay* . . ."

Tame the Rising Tide   165

sailed on the Outward, hadn't he? Her thoughts reeled

Chapter 16

Beth's head was a whirl of confusion. The picture of
Adrianne, Raleigh's name on the *Versailles* roster as
second mate, and then Seth's unprecedented display
of . . . of possessiveness. What was that all about?
He had virtually thrown James DeWitt from the house
because of her. It made no sense. He had schooled
her in the arts of a courtesan, not the guarded sensi-
bilities of a lady. Surely he had expected his guests
to desire her.

But his reaction had been so definite, so angry. It
was almost as if he were—jealous. But that was ridiculous. He was more than forty years her senior, and,
by his own admission when she'd first arrived, he valued her no more or less than any of his other possessions. Still . . . Well, there was no point in pondering
his motives. Trying to outthink Seth DuBoise was like
trying to comprehend the heavens, and with that even
the heavens had an edge.

Yet Raleigh was something else. How could he
have become second mate on the *Versailles*? He had

sailed on the *Onteora*, hadn't he? Her thoughts trailed off as Ternice's words about sailing men came back to her. So there it was. He'd lied to her all along. What had been doubt before was now irrefutable.

She flung the scarf from her dress to the bed and began to pace the room. Engrossed in thought, she didn't hear Seth enter.

"It's not becoming to walk back and forth like a caged animal," he said. "We've discussed that before."

Beth started. "Oh, sir. I didn't—" She sighed and lowered her head. "I'm sorry. I was upset about the incident with Mr. DeWitt."

"Forget it. He's an unpleasant man and not worth fretting over. Besides, he probably won't remember it in the morning. All I want to know is, does he or does he not have the *Versailles?*"

"He does. I wrote down the purchase price in your study."

"That interests me less than his destinations. To know what ports he's heading for is to know what goods he's after, and how I can best leave him begging in the market."

"It said nothing of destinations."

"Crew?"

Beth hadn't expected the question and it flustered her. "Crew?" she repeated.

"Yes. Was there a roster?"

"I—I don't recall the captain's name. But one of the mates was a man named Eckert. Raleigh Eckert."

DuBoise's brows rose. "William Eckert's son, eh? That's a bit of luck."

"You know him?"

"I know his father. One of the most influential bankers in New York. With luck the ship will still be in port when we get down there." He glanced at Beth. "Is something wrong? You've got the look of someone who's just swallowed a raw egg."

"No. Nothing's wrong," she said quickly, keeping her voice steady. But everything was wrong. There was no denying it now. Raleigh *had* lied. Pretending to be a runaway going to sign on a whaler, when he was as much about to do that as she was to become the Queen of England! The son of a wealthy banker. No wonder he could afford to pay so royally for his dalliance. And to think she'd actually been waiting for him to return to her. She gave a silent rueful laugh. She'd be waiting until the frosts of hell for that!

Seth took her hand. "DeWitt didn't bother you in any other fashion, did he?"

Beth blinked. "Oh, no. Really, sir, he didn't do anything. He just had too much to drink, I suspect."

"You forgive disrespect too easily."

"But, sir, you told me that I must be prepared to handle such overtures as a courtesan."

"That'll be enough of that," Seth said sharply.

Beth was shocked by his tone. "I—I'm afraid I don't understand. You said—"

"I've changed my mind." His voice still rang with anger. "It no longer pleases me to have you as a courtesan. You will do much better as a lady."

Beth blinked, bewildered by this new attitude.

"You will act accordingly and be treated the same way."

"I don't understand why you're so angry. What have I done?"

"Nothing." He swung round and left the room. There was no way he could tell her that for the first time in his life he wanted something he knew he could not have.

He wanted her love.

"Hugo!" he roared.

The giant Negro appeared at the foot of the stairs. "Sir?"

"Send the coach for Miss Liliana. And tell her to wear black!"

For a long while after Seth left, Beth remained standing, motionless. Not only had she been betrayed by Raleigh, but somehow by Seth too. She had heard him call for Miss Liliana, and knew well who and what Miss Liliana was. They'd met at breakfast on several occasions, for this was not the first late evening he had called her to Wildwillow.

Miss Liliana, Seth once told her, was a poor man's substitute for a courtesan. "A knowledgeable bed partner in a nice package, but little more," was what he'd said.

Beth picked up her pillow and hurled it angrily against the wall, and didn't really know why. She'd accepted the fact that Raleigh had used her, that her months and months of waiting and hoping had been foolish, but still, somewhere deep inside, it stung. The laugh he must have had at her expense. To think she had given herself to him, believed his kisses, his selfish passion. Oh, how it galled her! She threw herself across the bed and hammered her fists against the mattress.

Well, she would show him. She stood, went to the mirror and studied herself in the glass. She was no longer the helpless, hapless wench he'd so cavalierly left behind. She took the pins from her hair and brushed it back over her shoulders. She was a woman, as fine-looking as any and more capable than most, and she knew it. What she wanted now was enough money and power to push that fact in Mr. Eckert's smug, lying face.

And there was only one way to do it—through Seth DuBoise.

It was an insane plan, but what did that matter? It was a way to get back at Raleigh, a way to get a lot of things.

She sat down and began brushing her hair, listening carefully for the arrival of Miss Liliana.

When she heard footsteps on the landing, she opened her door quietly and beckoned to Miss Liliana. Bemused, Miss Liliana sauntered into Beth's room, accompanied by a heavy scent of violets. She was a tall, firmly built woman in her twenties with a bounty of carrot-red hair.

"Well, well. What manner of intrigue is afoot?" she asked.

Beth carefully closed the door. "It's a . . . a surprise for Mr. DuBoise. A little joke."

Miss Liliana raised an eyebrow. "Mr. DuBoise has never struck me as someone enthused about 'little jokes.' But then again, I am, so do tell me what you have in mind. It's obviously something to which I'm to be a party."

"Well, that's just it," Beth said. "You're not going to be a party to it. I mean, that's the little joke. I'd like to change clothes with you and take your place." She said it quickly and cast her eyes to the side as she did.

Miss Liliana let her mouth drop open, and then burst into a rich delighted laugh. "Oh, my dear girl, that is indeed a *little* joke—and one I fear I'd rather not be party to. When Mr. DuBoise requests my company, he's not likely to be pleased with substitutes." She patted Beth under the chin. "Lovely as you are, I'm afraid you'll have to wait for your own turn." She headed for the door.

"No, wait," Beth said, thinking quickly. "I—I wasn't supposed to tell you, but it was he who thought this up. He knew I'd have trouble convincing you and wagered two hundred dollars that I couldn't do it. I wasn't thinking of splitting my winnings," Beth said with a sigh, "but a hundred is better than none."

Miss Liliana perked up. "You mean I would get a hundred dollars? Hmmm. That's a pleasant bit more than the thirty I get for . . . performing."

"And you have a holiday to boot," Beth said. "But hurry, we must do this quickly."

Miss Liliana flung off her cape. "Why not?" she said delightedly, untying her laced bodice. "I've had queerer requests, believe me."

Beth undressed and Liliana helped her into the black stays that Seth DuBoise had specifically requested.

"You could use a bit more on your bones," Liliana said, "though what's there is rather pretty."

Beth flushed and murmured, "Thank you."

"As long as you're doing this," Liliana said, "would you like to rouge your nipples? Mr. DuBoise does admire nicely rouged pointers."

Beth colored more deeply, bit on her lower lip. "Yes, please," she said with much more firmness than she felt.

Miss Liliana opened her reticule and took out a pearl-covered box of fine red powder. She licked her finger, then tamped the rouge. "Come here."

Beth stood in front of her and kept her eyes on the ceiling as Liliana applied it.

"Delightful," Liliana said, "if I do say so myself." She held up her black and red gown and helped Beth into it, tying the laces of the bodice tightly so that Beth's breasts swelled beyond the fabric's edge. "There now." Liliana pointed to the mirror. "Go have a look."

Beth stared at her own reflection and for a moment felt light-headed with a sense of her own power. There would be time enough for her to learn to be a lady, but right now there was no doubt that she was a woman.

"How do I look?"

Liliana put her hands on her hips, leaned back. "You can come down to my place and work anytime," she laughed.

Beth gave Liliana's hand a small squeeze. "I guess you ought to wish me luck," she said.

"With DuBoise, you'll need it," Liliana said. "He requires more tending than most, but at his age it's to be expected, if you know what I mean."

Beth didn't, but was too embarrassed to press for details. All she wanted to do was wash Raleigh from her mind and get Seth to realize she was more than his Galatea!

Liliana lay down on Beth's bed. "I'll wait here for

the return of my clothes. Take your time. It's not often that I have the opportunity of being in bed alone."

Beth walked down the hall to Seth's room conscious of every heartbeat. Her hands were cold, yet small beads of perspiration had begun to form on her upper lip. She was mad to try this. For all she knew, DuBoise would be enraged by the ruse. And what of Miss Liliana when it came time to pay off money she didn't have?

There was no point in thinking of any of that now. She took a deep breath and rapped gently on the polished mahogany doors.

"Come in," Seth called.

The room was dark, except for the glow of the fire. Seth DuBoise stood in his dressing gown next to the mantel, his back to the door, his large frame almost in silhouette. Beth remained motionless in the doorway.

"You can enter, Liliana. I know you're theatrical, but I—" He turned around and froze. "What the . . ."

Beth pushed the door shut behind her and sauntered forward. "Liliana was feeling poorly," she said boldly, "so I've come to take her place."

She crossed the room and stood before him, her forehead coming only up to his chin.

"You look ridiculous in that outfit," he growled, though there was no anger in his voice.

"No, I don't," Beth said brazenly. "And I don't believe you think I do either."

"You're a foolish child," he said sharply. "Go back to your room and get out of those clothes."

"If it's the clothes that offend you . . ." Beth brought her gaze straight up to his and began to unlace the bodice.

DuBoise said nothing. His eyes fastened on her fingers as they drew back the fabric, pulled the sleeves from her shoulders and let the top of the dress fall to her waist.

"No," he said. It was hardly more than a rasp.

"Yes," she murmured, and stepped out of the gown.

The firelight played on her body, giving her skin a shimmering luminescence. Seth DuBoise was acutely aware of the small beauty mark on the crest of her right breast, the endless silken smoothness of her white skin as it met the black satin of the stays. His eyes traveled down further to the shadowed dark triangle enclefted between her faintly downed thighs, and his breathing became audible. But he didn't move.

"You wanted Liliana to wear black. Does it look as well on me?" Beth closed her eyes and pushed her bosom forward. One breast came free, its nipple hard and prominent as the stem on an apple. She freed the other and stepped closer.

Seth gave a low moan. The blood surged to his loins in a rush of unprecedented desire.

"Have you nothing to say?" Beth asked huskily.

"Turn around."

Beth pirouetted slowly until her back was facing Seth. The heat of the fire felt hot on her naked buttocks.

"Bend forward," he said, "as if you're picking flowers. Slowly, very slowly."

Beth leaned forward uncertainly.

"That's it," Seth said. "Like that."

Suddenly Beth began to be afraid. This wasn't going at all as she expected. She stood up and turned around.

He had his robe open, and even in the shadows she could see his tumescence.

"I was not going to hurt you," he said. "I was simply enjoying the awkward innocence of the posture. There is much to be learned in the art of lovemaking. If that is what you truly want to know, I will teach you."

"I did not come here seeking knowledge for myself," Beth said, "but to give you pleasure."

"Life could offer me no greater pleasure than teaching you the myriad ways of love." He reached out and took her hand, led her to his bed. Effortlessly, he unfastened her stays and tossed them to the side.

He spoke with difficulty as he gazed at her in naked-ness. "Are you sure this is what you want to do?" he asked. His fingers touched her shoulder and began to trail down across her breasts.

Beth shivered with apprehension and an unex-pected excitement. Despite Seth's fifty-seven years, his hands were deft and thrilling. "Yes," she whispered. "Oh, yes."

Seth eased her gently back upon the satin com-forter and removed his robe, lay down beside her. "You don't have to do anything now, for a good part of learning how to give in love—as in life—is being able to receive. I want you to just lie here and take my pleasure."

His hands cupped her head, stroked her hair, spreading it out across the pillows as if it were flax of gold, murmuring softly: "Pretty one. Pretty little one. My own sweet pretty one."

Then Beth felt his lips on her shoulder, moving slowly down. She opened her eyes and saw the back of his head, his silver hair glinting in the fire's glow, as his mouth reached her breast. She gasped in a mix-ture of shame and ecstasy. How could she be allowing herself to submit to this?

As if in answer, her body squirmed with unbidden pleasure, and Seth's tongue began its slow sensual descent.

When she realized what he was about to do, she stiffened and pulled back, frightened by her own de-sire.

He ran his hands gently across her belly. "You must take fully or you will never be able to give fully."

No, she told herself. This was wrong. He was a man older than her own father, a man she didn't love, a man . . . His tongue flicked about her thighs, his lips softly pressing her. No! It was wrong, bad. But sud-denly she did not want him to stop. His hands slipped beneath her and drew her more tightly to him.

Her body rose and fell as if she were being tossed on crests at sea.

"Oh, God," she moaned. "Dear Lord . . . don't . . .
yes . . . I mean, don't . . . you mustn't . . . oh, please
. . . please, don't."

She arched and suddenly, dizzily, spasmed in release. Her heart hammered wildly as she tossed her
head to the side and fought to bring herself back to
control.

Seth took her hand and kissed her palm. "What
great delight it gives me to pleasure you. You are so
young, so refreshingly new to everything."

Beth said nothing. She felt guilty and ashamed;
guilty for so calculatingly wanting to use DuBoise and
ashamed for having experienced so sinful a pleasure.
Was she now a fallen woman?

"So quiet," Seth said. "Don't tell me there's re-
morse?"

There was an anxiousness in his tone that caused
Beth to roll to her side and look at him. Even in the
semidarkness she could see his face clearly. Tanned,
lined by the years, but still powerful, there was a
vulnerability in it at that moment that Beth had never
noticed before. It was almost as if he were afraid of
something. But that was absurd. Seth DuBoise would
never be afraid of anything. Why, he'd thumb his
nose at death itself.

"No, of course not," she said quickly, looking away
again.

"You would prefer that I was thirty years younger
and devilishly handsome, wouldn't you?" He laughed
half to himself. "And so would I, believe me."

"That's not so." Hesitantly, she raised herself up on
her elbow. Never before had she heard such loneliness,
such sadness in a voice. She reached out and pressed
her fingers against his lips. "That's not so at all."

"Such innocent hands," he murmured.

"I—I'm not so innocent," Beth said. "I'm really
not."

"For the likes of me, you're purity itself." He
stretched his fingers toward her breast, then suddenly

stopped himself. He grabbed his robe. "Go on. Get back to your room."

"What?"

"You heard me. I told you I was going to make you a lady, and I am. It would be all too easy for me to turn you into a tart." He picked up her clothes and tossed them at her. "Get dressed. You'll need your rest, we're sailing for New York tomorrow." He went to the fireplace and tossed on another log.

Beth pushed the clothes to the side and slipped from the bed, tiptoed across the room and came up behind him. However it happened, she wasn't sure, but it was no longer a matter of connivance or calculation. She *wanted* to give herself to Seth DuBoise. No, it wasn't passion, but neither was it pity or cold-hearted greed. In one way, it was a kind of gratitude —in another, though unlike anything she'd ever felt for Peter or Raleigh, it was a sort of love.

Brazenly she pressed herself against him. "I'm not going back to my room . . . yet."

Seth whirled, almost knocking her off balance. He grabbed her shoulders. "You'll do what I say. You'll . . ." His eyes took in her nakedness and an almost agonized moan broke from him. His mouth came down hungrily upon hers. Beth put her arms around his neck and suddenly felt herself being carried across the room.

He lowered her awkwardly to the bed and with totally uncharacteristic urgency fell on top of her, his knee prying her thighs, his body thrusting with impatient desire.

"Wait, please," Beth begged, suddenly frightened by his roughness.

"No. Now." His breath came in short explosive gasps.

Instinctively, as if reliving the nightmare again, Beth tried to clamp her legs shut, began to push against Seth's chest. "You don't understand. If you could just—"

His mouth stopped her protests. She was no match

for his strength. Her legs spread and held apart, she felt him fumbling with himself.

No, this wasn't the way she wanted it. She wanted to scream, but his mouth was relentless. And then suddenly he entered her, and she did scream.

It was a garbled sound from her throat, but Seth reacted instantly. As unexpectedly as his roughness had begun, it disappeared. His lips pressed against her ear softly, whispering soothing endearments.

"Shh, my little one. I'm sorry. I'll be gentle. I should have known better. Relax now and let me love you."

He stopped all motion and just stroked her hair, waiting, every so often moving slightly. And slowly, slowly, Beth felt her own body untense, and then grow impatient. Like a wave rolling in to the shore, her desire gathered momentum. And suddenly she was moving beneath him, her body damp with the heat of wanting. And then magically they were a chord, their rhythms pulsing to the same surging beat. Beth no longer knew or cared where she was, who she was, what was happening—only that she knew she never wanted it to reach the ending that every fiber in her body strove for.

And all she could hear was Seth DuBoise repeating over and over: "Ohmygod, ohmygod."

At the point when she thought she could survive no further pleasure, there was a cry of ecstasy from her lips and a thunderous groan of release from Seth. And it was over.

It was a long time before either of them spoke, and then Seth said: "I don't know if you have the makings of a lady, but God knows, you leave nothing to be desired as a woman."

Before Beth returned to her room, Seth asked how she had gotten Liliana to let her take her place, knowing well how Miss Liliana was not one to lose an evening's wages. When Beth told him, he laughed and said it was a bet well made and that he'd pay happily.

"But if there is a next time," he said, "don't bother with disguises. It will be a lot cheaper that way."

He smiled and watched her dress, told her to go quickly to sleep so that she'd be wide awake for the sail in the morning, and kissed her chastely on the cheek when she left.

Only later, when the room was dark and the fire low, did he press his face into the pillow still scented with the fragrance of her hair, and cry with joy.

Read the Room Flier

"But if there is a next time," he said, "don't bother
with these to light a fire. Just use these."

Chapter 17

Beth had been aboard the *Golden Gull* before, but
had never sailed on it. The sloop was Seth DuBoise's
joy. Sharp-prowed and deep-keeled, the sleek twin
master was distinctively multicolored. Sailors from
Manhattan to Hudson could spot the vessel from
shore, and even ordinary valley folk would stop and
wave to it when it made its way up or down the river.

Beth removed her bonnet and let the wind ruffle
her hair as she stood at the rail. The day was magnificent, with only a wisp of a cloud to mar an otherwise flawless blue sky. The sails billowed with the
breeze that had sped them down to the Highlands in
what the captain said was near record time.

"You're enjoying it," Seth said, coming up behind
her quietly.

"Oh, ever so much." Beth turned to face him and
found herself embarrassed meeting his gaze. What
had happened between them was still so unreal. Had
she really . . . ? She pushed the memory from her
mind for more reasons than she cared to admit—
even to herself.

"You know there are supposed to be wood nymphs in those hills over there." He pointed to the high rock cliffs that flanked the river. "They repeat travelers' songs. Shout something. They'll answer you. Go on."

"What shall I shout?"

"Anything you're inclined to."

Beth bit her lip thoughtfully. "I know!" She cupped her hands on either side of her mouth. "Make way for the *Golden Gull!*"

The words bounced off the hills and rolled back to her in a chorus of echoes.

"I wish I could sing," she said. "What marvelous fun that would be!"

"You have no need for song," Seth said. "Your voice has a special music of its own."

Beth flushed at the compliment, and looked away.

"Modesty is becoming, but perpetual embarrassment is not. I'd hate to have to refrain from addressing you in any sort of flattering fashion for fear you'll redden to apoplexy."

Beth laughed. "I'm sorry. It's just that—"

"Almighty Christ, girl, do you really think I need an explanation?" He pushed hair from her eyes, smoothed it back from her forehead. "I just want you to be comfortable and happy," he said softly. Without another word he kissed her brow and went forward to talk with the captain.

Beth returned to the rail and stared hard at the shore. What had she done? What was she doing? She wished she had time to think, to plan, but there was none. And what was there to think about and plan for anyway? Seth wanted her and she needed him. What could be simpler?

She would not think more about it. Could not. *Not when she knew that her body had responded shamelessly to a man she did not love.*

Philip called her name, but she pretended not to hear. She'd seen the look on his face when Seth strolled the deck with her, his hand around her waist. As clam-brained as Philip was, he wasn't blind. And if she didn't miss her guess, what he saw was not to his liking. He was probably the most transparent heir apparent she'd ever meet.

He leaned on the rail beside her. "I was wondering when you were going to drop your neat little innocent act and get down to business."

"And that's supposed to mean?"

"Your visit to my uncle's bedroom?"

Beth whirled.

"Now, now, you're not going to deny it, are you? I saw you decked out in Liliana's stuff and was intrigued enough by your entrance to hang around for your departure, which surprised me by being a substantial three hours later. I didn't think the old boy had the stamina to—"

"Get away from me and stay away from me," Beth warned, "or I'll tell your uncle."

"I don't think you will—you know what happens to the bearer of bad tidings—but I'll leave you anyway. I'm patient, and your kind always tips their hand sooner or later. I just wanted to let you know that I'll be watching, so you can be on your guard. I thought . . ."

Beth didn't wait for him to finish. She left the rail and ran to the cabin.

She stayed inside for the remainder of the day, telling Seth her stomach had come unsettled with all the excitement. He was most solicitous and had the cook make her a special herb broth. He himself returned to the cabin frequently to see if she needed anything more.

She probably would have remained there, nibbling on her hatred for Philip and gorging herself on her own self-loathing for evading him, had it not been for the thundering splashes of the river sturgeon.

The sound was akin to boulders falling into the water, and her curiosity was keen enough to bring her back on deck. Seth's delight in seeing her emerge from the cabin did not, Beth noticed, slip by the beady brown eyes of his nephew.

"Feeling better?" Philip asked, his sarcasm only barely contained.

"Much," Beth retorted curtly. She smiled, walked to Seth and deliberately linked her arm through his, delighting in Philip's consternation.

"Can you see them?" Seth asked. He pointed across the darkening water.

"I don't— Oh, yes. There's one."

Like a great shadow leaping from the depths, a sturgeon hurtled up from the water and splashed down again.

"What are those lights over there?" Beth asked.

"Fishermen. They come out with torches and spears for these. The Indians used to do it all the time. Lovely. Like some primitive pageant, isn't it?"

Beth nodded. Philip joined them, positioning himself next to her.

"Delightful show, uncle," he said, pretending to be unaware that his thigh was pressing against Beth's.

Her first impulse was to retreat to the cabin. But suddenly she was conscious of the warmth of Seth's arm and from it drew a strength she hadn't realized, a strength all her own. It was almost as if something frozen inside her had finally thawed.

It was a true inner confidence she hadn't felt for a long time . . . a confidence that Peter Avery had encouraged, Widow Brinks had extolled, Tom Longeye had respected, and even Raleigh had known. And now it was back, ironically warmed to life by a man to whom she could give her body but not her heart.

She lifted her head high. "I believe, Philip," she said gaily, "there is enough railing for you to admire the great fish without wrinkling my frock."

Philip flustered, practically jumped back. She had caught him off guard and smiled triumphantly.

At that point Hugo came to tell them that dinner was served.

The *Golden Gull* had just passed Newburgh, and Beth was almost asleep when her cabin door creaked open and Seth entered. She could see him clearly in the moonlight, but made no move to show that she was awake. He stood at the side of her bed, his strong imposing frame casting a long shadow over her. She breathed more deeply, feigning sleep.

But her heart had already begun to pound.

She felt the thin coverlet being drawn back and beneath her cotton nightdress her nipples, like traitors, tautened against her will.

"Beth," Seth whispered, drawing his palm lightly across her breasts. "I want to make love to you in the moonlight."

Beth sat up, drew the cover to her chest. It was wrong, all wrong. She couldn't go through with it. "Seth, no. I— The other night was something else. I—"

He sat down on the bed and took her arm, kissed the crease of her elbow and felt her pulse quicken. "Go on," he said softly, stroking her skin.

"I—I don't love you," she said.

She felt him stop for just a moment, as if stung by a small insect, then he kissed the crook of her arm again. "I don't believe in big miracles," he said. "It's no surprise."

"But—"

"You have been truthful with me about your heart," he said, his hand pressing against her thigh, "now tell me about your body. Tell me that it doesn't want me."

Before she could answer, he lowered her back against the pillow and his hands fluttered over her like butterflies, igniting her.

She felt her breathing become difficult. "I—"

"Go on, tell me that you don't want me to make love to you and I'll go away and never bother you again."

Beth formed the words in her mind, but they would not come past her lips. Her body had taken control. Whether it was loneliness or longing, she did not know, but there was no denying her aching to be touched, to be fondled; no denying her fierce hunger for love.

"I can't," she said helplessly.

"Then forget about your heart, and let me show you how to be the remarkable woman you are."

But as she closed her eyes and gave herself to the passion, it was no longer Seth's arms that held her, nor his mouth upon hers. It was Raleigh's. And the pleasure that swept her upon release was as great as her guilt.

Beth awoke to a knock on the door. The sun was streaming in and the cabin was filled with fresh flowers.

"Do you want to see New York," Seth called, "or are your dreams more interesting?" He opened the door and smiled broadly.

"Where did these come from? I— Is it awfully late?" When he continued smiling, Beth jumped to the window. "We're here!" She scrambled from the bed. "Why didn't you tell me?"

"You needed rest, and New York abides. Besides, I have every intention of flaunting you, and I didn't think it proper for you to have large circles beneath your eyes. Now hurry and get dressed and meet me on deck. We're to stay at the Van Brundt's for the week, and they'll surely have their carriage here for us by noon—and I have things to do first."

Beth dressed hurriedly, but took care to wrap the kerchief over the bodice of her gown in a very bouffant fashion, as she had seen it on one of the last patterns to come over from France. Checking her image in the mirror, she pinned her hair beneath a wide bonnet so that it fell, almost in spirals, to her shoulders.

New York at last. It was difficult to believe she was about to walk upon the streets she'd only read about. And the theater. Oh, she did hope Seth would take her to the theater! The great Mrs. Hallam was too old to play Juliet or Portia these days, but she did still appear on the boards. What a thrill it would be to see her!

Beth swung round for a final check and her eyes caught the rumpled sheets of her bed. Her cheeks colored with the memory of last night's intimacy. *Some lady,* she thought ruefully. She returned her gaze to the mirror, and smiled brazenly. So I'm not a lady. Fainting was a bore anyway. She swung her hips shamelessly at her image and went to meet Seth.

The Van Brundt's home was an impressive new Georgian structure with a charming balcony above its front door and an ornate Palladian window facing out on Pearl Street. Lovely as it was, Beth wished the coach hadn't whisked them away from the docks so quickly. Neither in Hudson nor Kingston had she seen so many extraordinary ships. There were sloops of all sizes, tri-masted snow rigs and gun-heavy brigantines. What she hadn't learned about ships from Tom Longeye she had from Seth. It pleased him to have her so knowledgeable, almost as much as it displeased Philip. When she expressed her desire to see the DuBoise ships, the *Manitou* and *Victor* especially, he beamed and promised to take her touring the docks.

Seth introduced her to the Van Brundts as his ward. It made her feel more comfortable and she knew that he had done it for her sake. Propriety was not something Seth DuBoise concerned himself with.

Emily Van Brundt, a stylish, slender woman in her mid forties, seemed determined to show how delighted she was with Beth's presence. She took Beth's hand and clasped it awkwardly.

"As the mother of three boys, I'm always outnumbered. It's a pleasure to have female company for a change."

"Thank you," Beth said.

"Not that Seth DuBoise would be any less welcome alone," she added, casting him an affectionate look that made Beth wonder if perhaps Mrs. Van Brundt wouldn't have preferred a solo visit. A quick glance at Seth offered no clue.

Jan Van Brundt, a man of Seth's age who looked a

good ten years older, welcomed Beth with a warm smile. He was, Seth had told her, one of New York's most successful silversmiths, and, as such, a man of wealth and influence.

Beth wondered why, for a man of his success, his eyes had the look of a beaten dog?

"Well, come along, now," Emily chirped. "I'll have Dora Mae show you to your room and help you unpack. She'll be your servant while you're our guest." She turned to Seth. "I suppose you've brought Hugo for you and Philip."

"I left him on board the ship. I hear the docks are getting rough at nightfall."

"I don't know what this city is coming to. They're building houses all over, and nearly every ship that ports has a holdful of Lord knows what sort of riffraff. I've told Jan I don't know how many times that he and the others on the council ought to be doing something about it, but it's like talking to a wall. Anyway, let's not get me started on *that*. We've a dinner party planned in your honor and I don't want to tire you out before then." She rang for the servants.

"Now if there's anything you want," she said, looking pointedly at Seth, "you just ring." She patted Beth's hand abstractedly. "Oh, it is so nice to see another pretty face around here."

Seth suggested Beth take a nap, freshen herself for evening, but she was much too excited to sleep. From the window in her room she could see the river and the ships, and when she looked down, a whole parade of elegantly dressed men and women, children with hoops, and nannies with fancy baby buggies. Sleep? Her first visit to New York? Never. Besides, her only dinner party had been the one at Wildwillow, and the thought of meeting New York society was thrilling.

She spent the next few hours deciding what to wear and how to fix her hair, changing her mind when she'd see another style pass by below in the street. More than vanity was motivating her, though she wasn't sure what. She finally decided on a mauve crepe gown with a rather low bodice, simply because she knew Seth liked it.

The look in his eyes when she came downstairs that evening told her she'd made the right choice. Even Jan Van Brundt's tired visage sparked with appreciation. Surprisingly, though, it was Philip who stepped forward with a compliment.

"You look perfectly marvelous," he said, taking her hand. "May I?" He swept his arm toward the parlor, where other guests had gathered.

She looked quickly at Seth, who nodded his approval. Reluctantly she took Philip's arm.

"Come now," Philip said under his breath, "I'm not taking you to the slaughter. I'm trying to be friendly."

"Were I to believe that," Beth replied, "I'd seriously understand the world to be flat."

"Do you only take the word of men who've *known* you?"

Beth jerked her arm free just as Emily reached them.

"Stunning, child, just stunning," Emily cooed. "I must introduce you to our guests." She led Beth forward.

"Carolyn, Arthur," she said to a stout middle-aged couple. "I'd like you to meet Mr. DuBoise's ward, Miss Talbot. Beth, this is Mr. and Mrs. Elmdorf."

"Very pleased to meet—" Beth stopped midsentence. Across the room by the fireplace, a tall young man with dark eyes was staring at her, squinting slightly as if trying to place her.

Beth had no such difficulty from where she stood. The young man was Raleigh Eckert.

158   *Time the Rising Tide*

Klaus. Someday to rebuild that Suraswati and know it... Until then... he could steal neither of that ...

Chapter 18

"Something wrong?" Emily asked.

"Uh, no. No. I'm sorry." Beth smiled at the Elmdorfs. "Very pleased to meet you."

Emily eyed her oddly, but once assured that Beth wasn't about to be sick or faint or otherwise embarrass her, she relaxed. Only then did she notice the direction of Beth's gaze.

"Oh-ho," Emily said. "I see you've managed to pick out your dinner partner already. I thought you two would get on. Come, let me introduce you."

Beth stood frozen as Emily started across the room.

"Goodness, come along." Emily lowered her voice. "He's probably the most sought-after bachelor in New York. His father is William Eckert, one of the richest men in the city. Though it's true that Raleigh has always been the family's black sheep, he hasn't been irrevocably disinherited yet. Besides, just between us, he's more fun than the others."

Raleigh smiled politely as the two women approached. Then suddenly his eyes widened with disbelief and recognition.

Before he could speak, Emily began her introduction. "Raleigh, I'd like you to meet Miss Talbot. She's visiting us from upriver. She's Seth DeBoise's ward."

"I see," Raleigh said slowly, one brow rising. "Mr. DuBoise is a most fortunate guardian."

Beth kept her gaze locked on Raleigh. Two years had toughened his skin, added a small scar to his cheek, but other than that his bear-black hair still fell to his shoulders and his eyes still had the mocking piercing quality that inexplicably enraged and aroused her.

Beth acknowledged the compliment with an awkward nod of her head while Emily completed the introduction.

"Now you must excuse me while I make sure that the kitchen has everything prepared. Servants are not what they used to be." She tapped her fingers lightly against both their arms, pleased with the correctness of her pairing, and left.

Neither Raleigh nor Beth said anything for what seemed an interminable moment.

Beth broke the silence. "You're looking quite well for a *whaling man*. Especially after so long a voyage." She wanted to sound disinterested, but could not keep the bitterness from her voice.

"For an orphaned waif and candlemaker, you've not fared badly yourself."

"I survived," she said coolly.

"*That's* quite obvious."

"Your innuendo is uncalled for."

"Is it? Seth DuBoise's *ward*." He laughed. "Really, Beth. You can't expect me to believe that."

His words stung, but she could not deny them. How could she explain what it was like living on crusts of moldy bread, never knowing if there would be a next meal? How could she tell him about picking pockets to save the life of a criminal, when he'd never had to deal with such matters? Their lives were worlds apart. He was the highborn son of a banker, and she was a tenant-farmer's daughter. His expedition to Hudson had been a lark; hers had been a necessity.

"You may believe what you like," she said. "It seems we have both been victims of mistaken impressions."

It appeared pointless to attempt further explanation. Neither was the person the other believed him to be, and that was that. . . . Or was it? After all, she was no longer the tenant-farmer's daughter. She was the ward of one of the most powerful shipowners in the colonies, and as such entitled to equal footing with Mr. Raleigh Eckert. The recognition of this gave her a certain vindictive pleasure.

She tossed her head gaily. "Well, now that the past can be put behind us, do tell me all about yourself. You look like someone who's had a fascinating life."

"Artifice does not become you," he said. "I prefer an honest tart to a false lady anytime."

"For your edification, Mr. Eckert, I am neither," she snapped angrily.

"I see your temper hasn't lost its short fuse." His eyes glinted with mockery. "But it has attracted the attention of your *guardian's* nephew. He seems to be regarding us with great interest."

"I'm not surprised. His avocation seems to be the earnest study of my every move."

"How flattering to have that much attention from still another DuBoise."

"For someone of your fine breeding, Mr. Eckert, I find you crude and offensive. I should introduce you to the young Mr. DuBoise. You might find you have much in common."

"*Touché.*" Raleigh laughed.

"I'm glad I afford you such merriment," Beth said frostily. "Unfortunately you don't provide the same. Now if you'll excuse me, I'll take some fresh air."

Beth turned quickly and made her way to the balcony. The cool night breeze soothed her burning cheeks. How could she allow a low-lying, deceitful cad like that to infuriate her so? That she had wasted nearly two years of her life pining for him was bad enough. But now to see his true colors and still find herself affected was unconscionable.

And to think that just the other night in Seth's arms she had imagined . . . Oh, how she reviled herself for it! Never again would she be so foolish as to believe the likes of Raleigh Eckert. Why, he could die tomorrow for all she cared. In fact, few things would delight her more.

She put her hands on the railing, took a deep breath, and let it out like a boiling kettle.

"My, my. Another whistle like that and they'll think fife and drum are marching."

Beth whirled. "For a gentleman, Mr. Eckert, you have the sensitivity of an ox. A lady usually desires to be alone when she excuses herself from company."

Raleigh shrugged. "What does an ox know? Besides, if I didn't come out here and catch you alone, how would I be able to tell you how lovely you look."

Whatever Beth was about to say flew from her mind. Raleigh put his hand on her waist. With just the pressure of his fingers, he drew her toward him and into the shadows.

"How would I be able to greet you in the manner to which I suspect you've become accustomed?" He pulled her closer.

"Why you—" But her words were lost in the hungry urgency of his kiss. She tried to struggle free, but his arm gripped firm and his mouth was inescapable.

When he released her, her heart was pounding violently and rage had engulfed her.

"How dare you—you animal!"

"I dare because I have questions that need answering and little time to wait for you to play out proprieties. When I returned to Hudson, I went to the boardinghouse and found you'd left. Then I checked the candleworks and Niessen said you'd quit and run off."

"That lying rodent!"

"I didn't know what to believe—and still don't. I

came back to New York and wanted to put to sea immediately. There was an opening on the *Versailles*. Arrangements were made, and I was on the water again before the month was out."

Beth was speechless. So he had returned to Hudson. He had come back for her after all!

"When can I see you—alone?"

"I don't know." She felt flustered, shaky.

"Damn you, woman. I'm sailing in a week for China. I'll call on you here tomorrow. Emily will probably be delighted. We'll go riding."

"Tomorrow. No. I—I can't. Seth—uh, Mr. DuBoise is taking me to see his ships."

"Oh." Raleigh turned and looked out over the street. "How foolish of me to forget about your *guardian*."

"Raleigh, it's not what you think. N-not really. We have to talk."

"When?"

"Where can I find you?"

"I'll be aboard the *Versailles* most every day."

"I'll let you know just as soon as—"

"There you are," Seth said. He stood in the doorway to the balcony, limned by the candlelight from the Van Brundt's tiered chandelier. It was difficult for Beth to see his face.

"It's almost time—" He noticed Raleigh in the shadows. "Oh, you must be young Eckert. I didn't see you there." He looked strangely at Beth, then back to Raleigh. "I'm Seth DuBoise. I know your father quite well."

The two men shook hands. Beth did not fail to notice the coolness in Seth's gaze. When Raleigh escorted her to the Van Brundts' table, she was aware of Seth's almost palpable scrutiny.

With Philip in earshot, Beth's conversation with Raleigh was limited to innocuous pleasantries. But it was difficult for her to keep her face from betraying her when Raleigh's knee would, every so often, press firmly against her own beneath the cloth.

Beth waited until Seth and Philip had both adjourned to the library before whispering to Raleigh that she would meet him in two days.

"It will be impossible for you to board the *Versailles* without your guardian knowing it," Raleigh cautioned. "It's not a common practice for ladies to—"

"Let me be the judge of what ladies do. Now you'd best join the gentlemen, or we'll become conspicuous."

"Standing by your side, even the invisible would be conspicuous."

"Go," Beth said urgently. "Before Emily gets a bee in her bonnet for gossip."

Raleigh laughed ruefully. "Such intrigue seems to belie your innocent relationship with Mr. DuBoise, my dear." Without waiting for a response, he bowed his head politely and went into the library.

"You seemed to get on quite well with Mr. Eckert," Philip said casually the following morning as they walked to the Van Brundts' carriage to join Seth.

"He's quite personable," Beth said.

"Why don't you tell that to my uncle? Personable second mates are not easy to find. He might offer him a job on one of the DuBoise ships."

Philip was goading her, pushing her into betraying something. He was suspicious by nature and his jealousy made him even more so.

"I'm not qualified to judge Mr. Eckert's sailing abilities." Beth paused and smiled sweetly. "*Yet.*"

Philip scowled and dropped the subject. He was sensitive about Seth's continued tutoring of Beth in business matters; especially his occasional comments on how well Beth was learning.

"You two walk as if you're becalmed," Seth called from the carriage. "We'll never get to see anything at that rate. Hurry on."

Beth sat beside Seth as they rode to the docks and avoided Philip's eyes whenever Seth patted her affectionately on the knee.

The DuBoise ships were exhilarating. Seth was delighted by her enthusiasm and more than once left Philip behind in the tour.

"You have salt somewhere inside those delicate veins," Seth said, running his thumb gently across the back of her wrist as they strolled on the quay. "And I continue to find it marvelous."

"It was Tom Longeye who prompted the infatuation I suppose," she said. "His tales were mesmerizing."

"But it's more than that. You've got fine business sense." It was the sort of keen eye that had, so many years before, led Seth himself to trading the right goods for the right prices and more ships. How strange, he thought, that in the body of an angel dwelt the acumen that spawned titans.

"Oh, is that the *Versailles?*" Beth pointed and stumbled on a cobblestone.

Seth caught her arm, and felt the same cold gnawing at his gut that he had the previous evening when he'd walked out onto the Van Brundts' balcony and found her talking to William Eckert's son. Had he become that possessive already? That insecure? Surely it was his imagination that more than a casual conversation had transpired between them. But still, the feeling persisted. There was something about the way Beth had tossed her head, the way Eckert smiled, that seemed to indicate—as impossible as it was— that they had known each other before. That they had known each other well. And the more he attempted to dismiss the thought, the more annoyingly it returned.

"Yes, it is," Seth said. "Did young Mr. Eckert happen to say where she's headed?"

"China. They're leaving . . . at the end of the week."

"China, too. Well, then, it looks as if the *Victory* will have to take on stores more rapidly if she's to leave before DeWitt's vessel. Philip!" Seth turned to his nephew, who had been keeping a discreet distance behind.

"Yes, sir?"

"Go to Captain Roberts and tell him to speed up

the loading. I want the *Victory* to sail in three days."

"Three days? But they weren't planning to leave until next week."

"There's a change in plans. We have to beat De-Witt's *Versailles* to Canton if we want to uphold our reputation. If the *Experiment* made it, the *Victory* certainly can. She's a better ship any day."

Beth said nothing, feeling somewhat like a traitor, though it surely didn't matter to Raleigh when the *Versailles* arrived in China. Besides, knowing when and where to sail was the nature of the shipping business. Being a seaman was something else. And as far as she was concerned, anything that was disadvantageous to James DeWitt was worth pursuing.

Seth seemed preoccupied through the remainder of the afternoon, and only later, when she thought about it, did Beth recognize a direct connection between the altering of his mood and her mention of the *Versailles*. But was it only the ship that disturbed him? she wondered.

She retired soon after dinner, feigning a headache. Alone in her room, she tried to sort her thoughts, but found herself more confused and upset. She could not reconcile her relationship with Seth and her desire for Raleigh. Try as she did to convince herself that neither demanded rationalization, she could not, and tossed about the bed with a soul-deep unrest.

She heard the door creak open. Lying perfectly still, she pretended to be asleep. Through her nearly closed eyes she saw Seth approach the bed. She kept her breathing regular and waited. He didn't move for a while, just stared down at her, and then, as he had on the ship, he trailed his fingers almost imperceptibly down through her hair. But this time she did not respond. She heard him sigh. He left the room, closing the door softly behind him.

When the room was dark again, she blocked Seth from her mind and guiltily recalled Raleigh's lips upon hers, and the feel of his hard-muscled arm clasping her to him.

At that moment, Raleigh was in Seth DuBoise's thoughts too. Sitting in his room, Seth thrummed his fingers against the arm of his chair and wondered what it was about young Eckert that puzzled him. Over the years Seth had learned if not to completely understand then at least to trust his feelings. His lack of control over anything made him uneasy, and the fact that he had no strings leading to Raleigh Eckert distressed him. Controlled, like fire in an iron stove, Eckert could be a great asset; let to burn his own path, he could prove dangerous. Especially where Beth was concerned. She knew his name too easily, remembered details about him too well. *Were I twenty years younger,* he thought, *I'd never have noticed.* The years, as he'd come to know well, had sharpened his wits as well as his defenses and had given him the power he possessed today. But were there a devil to barter with at this moment, he knew he'd make the fool's deal without hesitation.

But there was no devil to bargain with. His age would remain the same. Raleigh Eckert was a threat, and somehow he would have to be watched.

The following day, Emily Van Brundt took Beth to the gardens on Golden Hill. They sipped tea, while watching a troupe of jugglers and a man with a dancing bear, chatting about the latest fashions and the guests at Emily's dinner party. Emily brought up Raleigh's name frequently, watching hopefully for a reaction. Beth did her best to appear disinterested, to Emily's undisguised disappointment. The woman was either a matchmaker or a troublemaker. Beth suspected the latter. Her questions about Wildwillow also led Beth to believe that her earlier suspicions about Emily's interest in Seth were well founded. That distressed her, but not nearly as much as the fact that she still hadn't come up with a plan for getting out of the Van Brundts' to meet Raleigh aboard the *Versailles*.

The plan did not come to her until dinnertime, and

when it did, she became so excited her face flushed and everyone thought she was ill.

She protested her health, wolfed down her food to prove it, and then waited until the men went into the library to make her excuses to Emily, who'd had quite a bit of wine with dinner and didn't mind being relieved of her hostess's smile for the remainder of the evening.

Beth told one of the servants to inform Mr. DuBoise that she was retiring early to rest for their return journey the following day. Then she hurried to her room and bade Dora Mae to follow.

The young black girl was disturbed by Beth's urgency and looked frightened when Beth bolted the bedroom door.

"I need your help," Beth whispered.

"Yes, ma'am." Dora Mae nodded, shifted her weight.

"I need some old boy's work clothes and a cap . . . and boots, too."

"Ma'am?"

"Mrs. Van Brundt's coach boy, Waldo, is about my size. A pair of his britches and boots would work fine. And a cap too, mustn't forget that."

Dora Mae shook her head. "I don't understand."

"Just get me the clothes and don't tell a soul about it. Here—" Beth reached into her valise and took out a small purse, pulled out some silver coins, "take these, and be quick about it."

Dora Mae smiled. "Yes, ma'am!"

"And not a word, remember?"

"Silent like my daddy's grave," Dora Mae promised, and hurried out. When she returned, she had the clothes Beth had asked for.

Beth undressed, tossed her gown and stays on the bed and, to Dora Mae's amazement, put on the clothes, taking Billy Boy from her valise and dutifully slipping it into her boot.

"Hand me those hairpins."

Dora Mae's eyes bulged as Beth pinned up her hair and covered it with the soiled cap.

"Lord, Miss Beth," Dora Mae exclaimed, "you look just like the boy who rides over with the dairy stores."

"That's what I want. Now I need another bit of help." She took more silver coins from her purse. "Can you get me down through the kitchen and have Waldo bring the carriage out back?"

"Oh, Miss Beth, I don't know about that. If Miss Emily finds out about taking the carriage, she'll—"

Beth dropped a few more coins into Dora Mae's hand. "She's not going to find out. And these are for Waldo." She shook her purse.

Dora Mae's eyes twinkled. "Follow me."

Waldo was reluctant to drive to the docks, but a few more coins eased that and they were off.

When they reached the *Versailles,* Beth stepped down from the carriage and told Waldo to return for her at the first ray of dawn. Without waiting to hear his protest, she ran to the ship.

When she reached the gangplank, she pulled her collar up and shouted to the sailor on guard: "Message for Mr. Eckert."

"Yeah. All right. What's the message?"

"Personal. From Mr. Seth DuBoise," Beth said, keeping her voice as deep as possible. "I've been told to deliver it m'self."

"All right, all right. Aboard with you, lad." Beth climbed the plank and the guard called to another man, who was sitting on the railing.

"Hey, Taylor! Show this lad to Eckert. And no funny business. He's a messenger, hear?"

Taylor was a tall gap-toothed man with a particularly ugly grin, which widened when he saw Beth.

"Why can't we find a cabin boy like this for the China trip, eh?" he chortled.

"You heard me, Taylor," the guard shouted. "No funny business. Leave the boy alone. Just take him to Eckert."

"Sure, sure." Taylor winked at Beth. "How'd you

like some real tobacco, laddie?" he whispered. "I got some below deck, along with some nice sugarcane."

Beth drew her head back. "I've come to see Mr. Eckert, that's all."

"He'll be in his cabin all night. What's your rush?"

"I have a message for Mr. Eckert," Beth said loudly.

The guard at the top of the gangplank turned around. "Taylor, I'm warning you . . ."

"All right," Taylor grumbled. He narrowed his eyes and sneered at Beth. "Try that again, laddie," he said softly, "and you might find those pretty apple cheeks of yours slashed apart. Gibbs Taylor doesn't like being made the fool."

Beth's skin grew cold. Even in the darkness, she could see the man meant what he said. "Yes, sir," she said hesitantly.

Taylor looked as if he were about to grab her arm, then dropped his hand to his side, turned. "Come on," he said tiredly. "I'll take you to Eckert. There's plenty more that's willing."

Taylor rapped his knuckles dutifully against the cabin door and left.

"Who is it?" Raleigh called.

Beth waited until Taylor was out of earshot. "Me!" she whispered hoarsely.

"Who is it?" Raleigh's voice was annoyed.

Damn. "Message for Mr. Eckert," she shouted back.

Raleigh unlocked the door. He wore a white shirt, open to the waist, and tight black britches with a wide silver-buckled belt that only barely concealed a pistol.

"Who the devil is—" Raleigh stopped, stared at Beth, then tossed his head back and laughed.

"May I come in?" Without waiting for his answer, she stepped inside the cabin and closed the door behind her.

"You are a cagey wench, aren't you?" he said. He took a step back. "Let me have a look at you." He shook his head in appreciation. "Madam, you have my compliments. You've done what I thought it impossible to do, while I sat here wondering if you would come. You've stilled my ardor."

Damn him. Could he ever greet her without raising her hackles? "Should I consider that a triumph?"

"A minor victory." He removed her cap, letting her hair spill down over her shoulders. "And a short-lived one at that." He caught her about the waist and drew her to him.

"Raleigh, we must talk. There's so much I want to say, to expl—"

His mouth pressed hungrily against hers, his tongue darting from side to side . . . caressing . . . assaulting . . . demanding. She could barely breathe, move. She put her hands against his chest and tried to push him back.

"Don't be foolish," he said softly. He began unbuttoning her jacket, his lips against her neck. "It's been too long to waste time with words. I don't want excuses or explanations now. I want you."

His hand slipped easily inside her jacket, beneath her camisole. Beth felt his fingers gently stroke her breast.

Dear Lord, she thought, *why don't I stop him?* Was she no better than what he obviously thought she was? She lifted her hand again to push him away, but let it fall to her side as his lips moved to her neck.

"Oh, Raleigh . . . Raleigh," she murmured. Something shameless stirred inside her and she arched her back, pressing herself against him. His hands slid down to her buttocks and pulled her closer.

"I want you now more than I wanted you that night on the way to Claverack," he said hoarsely. "And you'll never know how much that was."

"You said I didn't know how to kiss." Beth pulled her head back. "Am I any better?" She put her arms around his neck and pulled his mouth to hers, parting her lips and inviting his tongue into wondrous exploration with her own.

She felt his maleness stiffen, his arms tightened

around her. His desire ignited her own and she dug her nails into his shoulders and writhed against him.

"Take off your clothes," he breathed. "I want to love you with my eyes before my body devours you."

Beth's heart beat wildly and an urgent pulsing began inside her. Shame and desire mingled. All she wanted was to give herself to Raleigh, completely, without restraint. Give herself to him as she had never given herself to Seth. And in giving herself to him, she wanted him to take her, have his way with her, so that not even the smallest spark of passion would remain unspent.

She undressed before him slowly, deliberately, moving against his hands as they pressed each part of naked flesh as it became exposed. Her own body was infused with a hunger so keen it possessed her. Her nipples tautened against his palms; her thighs became moist with her own longing.

"Lie down," he commanded. Laying his pistol aside, he unbuckled his belt and came toward her.

Brazen with a passionate thirst beyond slaking, she stared at his nakedness and knew even greater excitement. What was she doing? It was as if she had no control over her actions, but she knew it was that she wanted none.

Almost trancelike, she watched him approach. Then, as he leaned over her, she reached down and encircled his sex with her hand.

Raleigh moaned with pleasure, and she guided him to her.

"Take me," she murmured.

He thrust hard inside her. "Do you want me to be gentle?" he asked.

"I want you to be you."

"I can be an animal as well as a gentleman."

She opened her legs and arched upward. "Be both . . ."

Chapter 19

Beth made it back to her room only moments before
the Van Brundt servants began morning chores. Her
body ached with the delicious, swollen afterglow of
pleasure as her mind attempted to sort out all that
had happened.

How would she tell Seth that she could no longer
live with him? How could she tell him that she was
in love with Raleigh Eckert and he with her? Raleigh
had suggested she wait until he return from China,
but only because she'd lied about the true nature of
her relationship with Seth. It had seemed pointless to
discuss . . . well, incidents. That's what they were,
weren't they? She and Seth didn't . . . weren't really
lovers. What had transpired between them was more
or less a mutual satisfaction of needs. Nothing more.
Someday she would tell Raleigh about it, but later,
when he could understand. Right now it was best that
he believe Seth to be just a possessive rich eccentric.
Still, how was she to continue living with Seth? In one
way it might be easier to just tell him and leave, but

then in another it seemed unnecessary to hurt him. There would be time before Raleigh returned. Somewhere in those months there would be a simple way to say good-bye.

Beth called Dora Mae and asked her to draw a bath. But before it was ready Beth had fallen asleep. Dora Mae felt it was none of her business to wake a guest. Besides it was easier to keep an eye on someone who was sleeping, and that's what Mr. DuBoise was paying her for.

Seth DuBoise paced his room. His eyes were dark and his brow furrowed. He had been right about that young Eckert. He did not enjoy using spies for things like this, but his suspicions had been too strong. Only now that they were confirmed, he was more distressed than when he'd been uncertain.

There were many courses of action open, but none of them pleased him. He could toss Beth out, let her see for herself how her dashing Mr. Eckert would provide for her. From what he'd heard, Mr. Eckert had a wide array of ladies who considered themselves foremost in his affections. But when he thought of doing this, he saw an emptiness in his life that he couldn't bear. No, he had to keep in mind what *he* wanted. And what he wanted was Beth. Eckert was the problem. It would be a year or more before he returned from Canton, but once he did there would be trouble again. Yet if Seth were prepared, had more control over Eckert, things could be different. Yes . . . things could be very different. For the first time that morning he smiled.

He was going to pay a visit to Mr. Eckert. And, if he didn't miss his guess, Mr. Eckert's own ambition would be all that was necessary to arrange things. He was going to make Raleigh Eckert a first mate on the *Manitou,* an offer it was unlikely he'd refuse, and send him to the Caribbean. Once there, it would be easy to direct him to France and back again for several lucrative runs. It would be a good two years before he set foot in America again. At the very least it would tamp down whatever girlish infatuation Beth had for the youth; at best it would make her forget him completely.

He rang for the carriage and headed for the *Versailles.*

Two hours later, on the ride back, Seth DuBoise looked as if a great weight had been lifted from him. And it had. Raleigh Eckert at that very moment was aboard the *Manitou,* a handsome purse in his pocket, and readying to lift anchor for Saint Dominique.

Seth took from his jacket the note Raleigh had asked be given to Beth. He fingered it for a moment, then without unfolding it to read, tore it in shreds and cast it to the cobblestones.

"Hurry up, driver!" he shouted. He was anxious to return to Beth, for both of them to return to Wildwillow.

Beth felt the change in Seth on the ride upriver. He had not attempted any intimacy, but seemed to be waiting for her to do so. Naturally she had not, but his curious shift in attitude made her wonder how much he knew? She would have to tell him about Raleigh soon. There would be no way to avoid it.

The first night back at Wildwillow was strained from the start. Before dinner, Seth had sent one of the servants to Beth's room to request that she wear her green gown. He only made requests for special clothes when he was feeling amorous. Beth dressed with extreme trepidation. She had hoped she'd have a few more days, but maybe it would be better this way. She'd tell him and it would be over. She could not go on living a lie, and deceiving Seth for any amount of time was impossible.

Dinner seemed interminable, and Philip's comments on her silence only aggravated her already heightened anxiety.

"Philip's right, my dear," Seth said when the dishes

had been removed. "I've never seen you so subdued. Are you feeling ill?"

"A headache . . . I've had it all day."

"Well then, why not go to your room and lie down for a while? A headache that has already spoiled a day should not ruin an entire evening." He smiled genuinely, but she could not meet his eyes.

Beth paced the floor of her room. A penned lamb waiting for the knife, she thought. How long would it be? He'd give her a reasonable amount of time to nurse her headache and then he'd be there. There was no mistaking his glances during dinner. No, there was no other way. She would tell him tonight. She lay down on the bed to wait.

She hadn't heard his footsteps in the hall and the soft knock at the door startled her.

"Beth?" she heard him call. "Beth."

She took a deep breath, sat up, adjusted her skirt. "Just a moment." Tossing her head back, she crossed the room to the door.

Seth was wearing his robe. He had a glass of brandy in his hand, and his eyes glistened in a way that indicated it was not his first. He stepped inside, closing the door behind him.

"How is your headache?" He put his glass on the dresser.

"Much better."

"I'm glad."

He stepped toward her and she backed away. "N-not completely gone," she added quickly, "but better."

"I have a cure for headaches." He reached out and pressed his fingers against her temples, rubbed slowly. "There, doesn't that feel good?"

"Seth . . . I have something I must tell you." She drew away from him. "We can't . . . I mean, I can't be the way I was with you anymore." Her cheeks flamed and she turned her head to the side.

"I'm afraid I don't understand." He turned her toward him. "What do you mean?"

"I—I'm in love with someone . . . someone else."

She felt his body stiffen. *"Someone,"* he repeated. "Who is this mysterious *someone,* may I ask?"

"Raleigh Eckert."

"Ah, Mr. Eckert. The second mate whose name you just *happened* to remember."

"We—we knew each other before I came to Hudson and—"

Seth's voice was cold, edged with a kind of cruel malice she'd never heard before. "And you managed, over Emily Van Brundt's mediocre beef roast, to rekindle an old passion?" He gave a hollow laugh. "I'd be impressed—if I were a fool."

Beth suddenly felt frightened, trapped. "We knew each other before. You see—"

"I saw," he said bitterly. "Do you take me for addled? Don't you think I know you sneaked out of the Van Brundts' so you could get to his bed!"

Beth gasped, drew away from him. His face was twisted with rage.

"Were you so deprived that you couldn't hold your body from him? So bored with an old man's efforts that you couldn't wait to offer yourself up on a young man's pallet?"

"Seth, no. Please."

"Were his thrusts harder? His maleness greater?"

"Seth, stop, please. I didn't mean to hurt you."

"Hurt me?" He grabbed her wrist and squeezed. "Why should *I* be hurt? He's at sea and you're here with me."

"But that's no more. What has happened between us is over. I love Raleigh. I never *loved* you. I'll leave tomorrow."

He thrust her back savagely, and she fell across the bed.

"You'll go nowhere without my telling you to," he growled. "Is that clear?"

"Seth, you can't keep me here against my will."

She tried to struggle to her feet, but he pushed her back down, pinning her arms. "I can do anything I want." And with that he gripped the bodice of her gown and tore it from her. "They're mine," he said, squeezing each breast painfully. "You're mine."

Beth felt afraid, truly afraid. His mouth came down brutally upon hers before she could turn away, and she tasted the cognac that fired his lust. His hand came up hard between her legs and she cried out. His fingers tore at her undergarments. She clamped her legs together and tried to roll away, but he was too strong.

"Open your legs," he ordered, tossing his robe to the floor. "Now!"

Beth squirmed beneath him trying to escape, trying to keep her thighs together as his knee rammed between her legs to wedge them apart.

"Spread them for me like you did for your sailor, how about it?" he panted.

Beth pressed both her hands against his chest, but to no avail.

"Come on, come on," he urged. His fingers pinched her flesh as his knee pressed open her thighs.

"No. Seth, no!"

"By God, yes!" he roared. He gripped her hair and pulled her head back until she screamed. "Now take me," he said softly, "take me in your hand and guide me where I want to go. And if you don't . . ." He tightened his grip on her hair.

Beth could hardly breathe; but the longer she refused to comply, the more painful his grip became. Finally, tears streaming down her cheeks, she took him.

She lay motionless as he pummeled her with his body, dazed and empty of comprehension. After a few moments he shuddered and collapsed on her, breathing heavily.

She remained perfectly still, too terrified to move or speak. Then she heard odd choking sounds. It took a moment for her to realize that Seth was crying.

"Dear God, forgive me," he moaned. He looked

down at Beth, then quickly turned away. "God, God, what have I done?"

Stunned, Beth listened to his sobs in utter disbelief. It was all a bad dream.

Seth sat up, put on his robe and covered his face with his hands. Beth drew the sheet around herself, and only then did she realize that she was trembling.

"My God," he murmured. "My God, my God."

"Seth?" she said softly, tentatively.

He turned, looked at her and then, wincing as if in pain, fell to his knees. "Forgive me. I don't know what madness possessed me. The agony of waiting a lifetime for something I never dreamed possible, attaining it, and then having it snatched from me was too great." He buried his head against the sheets.

Beth opened her mouth, but found herself unable to speak. Hesitantly she reached out and stroked Seth's hair.

Seth looked up. "Sweet beautiful child, tender marvelous woman. Perhaps I ask too much in my plea for forgiveness. If you scorn it, I'll not blame you. My only defense is that . . . is that I've never before wanted something that I knew I could not have. And I will say to you what I have never said to another woman—I love you, Beth."

"Oh, Seth." Beth looked away, fighting back tears.

He clasped her hand. "It is not to be a burden upon you. The hungers of my flesh can be sated by any number of talented females, but only you can fill the void in my spirit. I want you to stay here at Wildwillow until Mr. Eckert comes for you."

"But how can I?"

"There will be no repetition of tonight, you have my word. Your room will be your sanctuary. You will become in reality what you've only been in pretense: my ward."

"I don't know what to say."

He smiled. "Yes is simple enough. My life is too short to let sunlight slip away any sooner than necessary. Will you stay?"

Beth nodded. "Yes."

Seth kissed her hand. "If there is a God in heaven," he said quietly, "He is good."

Over the months that followed, Seth became a model guardian. Aside from the clothes and tutors he plied Beth with, he continued her apprenticeship in the shipping business. And, true to form, Philip continued to resent it—just as he continued to desire Beth.

Philip knew she and his uncle weren't sleeping together. Vera, the upstairs maid, assured him of that when she came to his room. And nothing escaped Vera. But they shared an intimacy that excluded others and it enraged Philip; especially since he could not establish a similar intimacy with Beth. Perhaps what galled him most was his own inability to push her from his thoughts.

With Vera's cooperation, he had several times been able to spy upon Beth in the bath. The vision of her soaping her breasts had often awakened him from sleep with throbbing desire, and, occasionally, would reappear during the day, causing inconvenience and embarrassment. Someday, he assured himself, he would have her. In the meanwhile, Vera was an accomplished palliative.

Beth had grown accustomed to evading Philip's advances. In fact, after a while, dodging them became a game. He reminded her of a poisonous snake. Handled correctly, he was harmless. But one always had to be on guard.

Ten months after their visit to New York, with Washington firmly installed as President of the new United States and news of the storming of the Bastille in France causing some consternation among American shipowners, Beth accompanied Seth to the Hudson waterfront for a meeting with two of his captains aboard the *Golden Gull*. He had become accustomed to her presence at such meetings, and often asked her to take notes, which had proved invaluable in planning stores and allotting money for future voyages.

Hugo had just stopped the carriage in front of the pier, when Beth rose excitedly from her seat.

"It's Tom," she cried, pointing to the man standing outside the Driftwood Inn. "Tom Longeye!" She put her hand aside her mouth to call him, then hesitated, looking questioningly at Seth.

He clasped his hands on top of his walking stick. "It's extremely unladylike, you know. And Longeye is hardly proper company for Seth DuBoise's ward." He looked dramatically somber, and then a small smile curled the corners of his mouth. "Well, go on, you silly woman, call him. I have nothing but good feelings for anyone who looked out for you as well as Longeye."

"Oh, thank you!" Impulsively Beth kissed him. Then she shouted to Tom.

Tom looked at the carriage warily, confused.

"Tom! You will-slugging, bilge-water devil, get over here or Billy Boy will claim your hide!"

Seth cleared his throat. "I think his name would have sufficed," he said quietly.

Beth waved her arms. "Over here."

"Why, I'll be!" Tom shouted. He headed at a run for the carriage, then slowed when he saw Seth DuBoise.

Beth jumped down and ran to him. She threw her arms about his neck, hugging him tightly. "Oh, Tom. I never thought I'd see you again. It's been so long."

Tom looked uneasy and pulled awkwardly away, aware of Seth DuBoise's scrutiny. "And time has been good to you, girl." He nodded toward the carriage. "You've got yourself a fine friend. A sure cure for a rumblin' gut and the little scallywags that crawl and bite in the night, I'd say."

"Mr. DuBoise is my guardian," Beth said, speaking quickly. "He's been very kind to me. Come. He's heard so much about you." She took Tom's hand and pulled him to the carriage.

"Mr. DuBoise, I'd like you to meet Tom Longeye," Beth said proudly.

"Your reputation precedes you, Longeye," Seth said.

"And yours the same, gov'nor."

"Are you with a ship now?" Seth asked.

"Laid off, that's what I am," Tom said. "With all that burning and blood in France, DeWitt and Carey are holding back. I could always go to the coast and whale, but I've lost my stomach for that hunt. I like the merchants. I'll find me something good for these bilge bones down in New York."

"Tom's one of the best seamen anywhere," Beth said. "He knows as much about ships as Guerney, if not more."

Guerney was Seth DuBoise's dock foreman and jack-of-all-trades for most ship repairs.

"Go on, girl," Tom said, embarrassed. "Guerney's the top, and ain't no bloke 'round here goin' to argue that."

"I think so," Seth said, "that's why he works for me. But if you're as good as Beth says, which I've no reason to disbelieve, I don't see why you can't work for me too."

"How's that again?"

"Guerney can't be all places at once. He's been shuttling back and forth between here and New York. If you like, the job here is yours, you know most of the men anyway, and Guerney will stay in New York permanently."

"Do say yes, Tom," Beth said excitedly. "It would be wonderful having you around again."

"I don't know."

"It would be a lot safer than picking pockets," Seth said quietly.

Tom looked from Beth to DuBoise. His expression didn't change, but Beth could tell that he was reweighing Seth's offer.

"Please, Tom?" Beth begged.

He shook his head and laughed. "All right, all right. Old Guerney could use a little nippin' at the heels."

He faced Seth. "When do I start and what'll you pay me?"

"Now, and you'll collect fifteen dollars at the end of the week."

"Not exactly a fortune."

"Not a gallows rope either," Seth said.

"Right you are." He extended his hand and Du-Boise shook it. "Just tell me what to do."

"You might as well join us aboard the *Golden Gull* now. I'm working on a plan to put two ships on a regular China run. And I want each of their sailing times cut as much as possible."

"Well, with the *Versailles* down, China should be wide open."

Beth grabbed Tom's arm. "What did you say about the *Versailles?*"

"Haven't you heard? She went down off the cape about a month ago."

"No . . . no." Beth shook her head dazedly, staggered back. "It couldn't. Raleigh . . ." The pier began to rock beneath her feet, then suddenly the whole world turned upside down and everything went black.

When she opened her eyes, her head was in Seth's lap and the carriage was hurrying back to Wildwillow.

She sat up unsteadily. Seth put his arm around her shoulders.

"It's all right," he murmured. "Everything will be all right. We're going home."

"Raleigh's dead," she said tonelessly. "Dead." But that wasn't possible. He was coming back for her. He had promised. All the plans they'd made that last night aboard the ship. No, it wasn't true. It couldn't be true.

"There were no survivors," Seth said.

Beth began to sob.

"Cry," Seth said, "it's the only comfort I can offer you."

Beth buried her face in his chest and wept. He patted her head rhythmically, rocked her gently in his arms. Her tears pained him, but he did not say what he knew would stop them. He did not tell her that Raleigh Eckert was *not* aboard the *Versailles,* that he was safe in Saint Dominique and on his way to the south of France. He would probably lose her forever when she discovered his deceit. But until then she would belong to him alone. And that was worth any consequence.

It would take time. She would want to grieve and mourn the future she'd never have. But she was young, and that would not last. Her mourning would end eventually. And when it did, she would be lonely and aching. And he would be there.

It was a voyage as carefully calculated as any fortune had ever delivered into his hands to plan.

On Christmas Day, 1789, in the great hall at Wildwillow, Seth DuBoise's voyage came to its successful conclusion. Twenty-year-old Beth Talbot became Mrs. Seth DuBoise.

Book Two

Chapter 1

"Why, Mr. DuBoise, it's beautiful!" Beth said, holding up the pear-shaped diamond pendant Seth had just given her.

"It's to mark the beauty of this past year. The happiest year of my life." He poured her more wine. "Come, let us toast our anniversary." He raised his own glass. "To continual smooth seas of love."

"To contin—" As she lifted her glass, her sleeve caught the arm of the chair, spilling the wine and sending the glass crashing to the floor. "Oh, damnation. Look what I've done."

"The wine isn't gone," Seth said. He went to the cabinet for another glass. There was always more wine. It was the moments that were irreplaceable. He could almost feel them slipping away. The year with Beth had been all he could have hoped for and more. She was the perfect mistress for Wildwillow; the perfect helpmeet. If the world ended tomorrow, he would not feel cheated.

For Beth, a good part of the year had been consumed in mending and healing. Though it had been more than two years since the *Versailles* went down, her heart mourned long after she had married Seth. Even now there were occasional twinges and, when she was alone, tears. All she had left to dream of was Suzannah.

But Seth had been good to her, and for her. He never once pressed her for affection or passion, and because of this she found herself freer and more willing to give both. Under his tutelage she had become almost as adroit at spotting lucrative shipping ventures as he. And though in his absence many of the merchants still preferred to deal with Philip, enough of the others recognized her power in the DuBoise operation and treated her with a respect that filled her days with satisfaction and pleasure.

It was a pleasure dimmed only by Philip's jealousy, which had grown uglier with each passing month. Her marriage to Seth had squelched his advances toward her, at least for a while. But when she became more active in managing the line, more able than he to handle the workers and seamen—thanks to Tom Longeye—Philip's resentment had become almost palpable. He missed no opportunity to hurt or humiliate her in private. She was reluctant to complain to Seth, knowing how he wanted to avoid seeing any faults in his sister's son; but Philip's recent sexual advances were going to force her to do so.

"There," Seth said, handing her a new glass. "Now we can toast our good fortune."

There was a knock at the door.

"It seems," said Beth softly, "that we'd best just drink the wine and save the epigrams for later."

Seth laughed. "Come in," he called.

One of the servants from the gates stood in the doorway looking uncomfortable. He held his cap in his hand, worked it nervously with his fingers.

"Yes? What is it, Tyro?"

" 'Scuse me, Massa DuBoise, but there's a gentleman here asking for Miss Talbot."

Beth frowned. "For Miss *Talbot?* Who on earth could that be?" She took another sip of wine. "Sinta Klaus, perhaps?"

Seth looked distressed, his face lost its color. "Where is he?"

"In the front hall. I tol' him there was no Miss Talbot no more, jest Missus DuBoise, but he didn't seem to understand. Or . . . well, he jest didn't seem to take that answer as enough. And he . . . well, he raised his voice a bit and told me to get you."

Seth rose unsteadily to his feet, put his glass on the table.

"Seth!" Beth went to him, put her arm around his waist. She glared at Tyro. "You're upsetting Mr. Du-Boise. Didn't this man give his name?"

"Oh, yes, ma'am. He said he was a mate on one of Mr. DuBoise's ships; said his name was Mr. Eckert."

"Eckert?" A frightening thumping began in Beth's chest. What sort of bizarre trick was being played? There was no Mr. Eckert on any DuBoise ship. She looked to Seth for an explanation, but he stared straight ahead.

She shook his arm. "Seth, what is this? What does this mean? Who is it out there?"

He threw his shoulders back, took a deep breath. "I believe," he said evenly, "that Tyro said it is Mr. Eckert."

"Raleigh?" Beth breathed, the name barely audible. Seth said nothing.

"But Raleigh's dead. The *Versailles* sank. No survivors, you said."

Seth did not even look at her. His eyes stared ahead blindly.

She grasped his arms, her voice trembled. "Answer me! Who is that out there?"

"Does this answer you?" a voice boomed from the doorway.

Beth whirled, clutched her bosom. A tall swarthy figure, bear-black hair falling across his forehead, strode into the room.

She opened her mouth to speak, but neither words nor thoughts would come. Raleigh . . . alive . . . here . . . how?

"So," he said, his voice redolent with disgust, "two years of waiting for a first mate didn't appeal to you. Or was your dramatic little shipboard tryst with me just an amusement? Or were you bored with your *guardian's* tutoring?" He said the word as if it left a bitter taste in his mouth. "I assume you had a good laugh over my proposal."

"Proposal . . . laugh . . . I— Your ship sank . . . I don't understand." Beth dug her fingers into her hair, shook her head. It was a nightmare, it couldn't be real.

"My wife is upset, Mr. Eckert," Seth said quietly. "I think it best that you leave."

"You're damn right. I can't stand bad acting." He stomped toward the door. "Oh, by the way." He turned to Seth, ignoring Beth entirely. "You'll need another first mate. I'd rot in hell before I'd sail another ship of yours."

"Raleigh, wait!" Beth cried, trying to collect her wits.

He whirled, eyes blazing. "Wait? Wait for what? What do you know about waiting anyway? I spent more than two years waiting to return to you, thinking that you were waiting for me. Ha! Good laugh there, isn't it? What were you doing while I ate enough hardtack and salt meat to last a lifetime, eh?" He looked at both of them and spat. "Spare me your explanations." He stormed from the room.

"Raleigh!" Beth shouted. She started after him, but Seth held her arm.

"Let him go," he said.

Beth jerked free. She stared into Seth's face, her own slowly contorting in rage. "You tricked me," she said through clenched teeth.

"I didn't trick you. I simply—"

"You simply didn't tell me that you knew Raleigh wasn't aboard the *Versailles*." Her voice was controlled, but its intensity was fevered. "Simply didn't tell me that you had made him a first mate on one of the DuBoise ships, because you knew I wouldn't be interested in that, right?"

"Beth, please."

"You lied to me. You watched me grieve and professed concern, while all along you *knew* he wasn't dead. You . . . you tricked me into marrying you."

Seth came toward her and she stepped back. "Stay away from me, you . . . you vicious old man!" She burst into tears and bolted from the room.

In the hall she grabbed Tyro. "Where did Mr. Eckert go?"

"Why, ma'am, he took off in his carriage as if the devil was ridin' his heels."

"Well, the devil will be riding your heels if I don't catch up to him. Get the carriage."

"Beggin' your pardon, missus, but Mr. DuBoise told Hugo he could have the night off to spend with his family."

"Forget about Hugo. I can drive the carriage myself. Now hurry."

"But it's startin' to snow."

"I don't care!" Beth shouted. "I want the carriage *now!*"

"Yes, ma'am," Tyro said, stunned by Beth's uncharacteristic shouts. He nodded several times and then ran down the hall.

Beth grabbed her cape, threw it over her shoulders.

"Beth, no!" Seth came into the hall, breathing heavily.

She flashed him a look of raw hate. "Don't you ever try to tell me what to do again."

Without waiting for his response, she ran for the door.

The wind whipped the hood from her head and snow stung her face, soaked her hair, as she made her way down the hill into town, driving the horses faster than it was safe for them to go with angry snaps of the reins.

He'd probably be at the Driftwood. If not, Tom would surely be able to find him for her. She had to explain, and he had to listen. *He had to.*

The Driftwood Inn was rowdy and packed with drunken sailors when Beth entered. The smoke was thick and it was difficult for her to make out faces.

"Well, well, blokes," a tall staggering young seaman exclaimed. "Look what Sinta Klaus brought us." He reached out to put his arm around Beth, but she backed away.

"How 'bout a Christmas drink, sweet one?" A fat sweaty man pushed his tankard in front of her.

She ducked to get away, but suddenly found herself in the arms of an equally robust and unsavory character.

"Hey now, this is tender, eh?"

She jammed her elbow in his stomach. "Let go of me."

"Ow. Damn little tart, what's that about?" He tried to grab her, but she moved quickly. Only not quickly enough to avoid having her breast rudely squeezed by Felix Dimanche, one of the waterfront's infamous regulars. Dimanche was known for his remarkable lack of enemies; anyone who was his enemy didn't exist for long.

"A firebird on Christmas," Dimanche said. "What a present, indeed. Come here, little one." He beckoned.

"Hey, Felix," someone yelled, "that's DuBoise's wife."

Felix Dimanche cocked his head to the side and studied Beth. "Is this true?"

Beth nodded. "Yes," she said haughtily. She was shaken by the crowd, by the dawning recognition of danger and the heavy scent of sweating, drinking men, but dared not show it.

"Oh?" Dimanche raised his eyebrow. "So what does Mr. DuBoise's wife crave on Christmas Eve that she comes here, eh?" He turned to the onlookers and laughed.

They laughed with him.

"Eh?" He smiled broadly at Beth.

"I'm looking for Raleigh Eckert," she said coldly. "It's . . . it's important that I find him immediately."

"Dimanche knows no Raleigh Eckert, but will I not serve for the same purpose?" Suddenly he grabbed her wrist and pulled her onto his lap, laughing. "Shall we see?"

Before she could stop him, his mouth covered hers, the rank scent of ale sickeningly pungent. She struggled fiercely, but his grip was iron and she succeeded only in raising her skirts to the cheers of the onlookers. She had to get away from this animal. As his hand reached around for her breast, she clamped her teeth hard into his lip.

Dimanche pushed her to the floor. "Bitch!" he screamed. He took a handkerchief and pressed it to his bleeding lip.

"Pig!" Beth spat.

"Why you—" He pulled her roughly to her feet and pinned her hands behind her back.

"Be careful, Felix. There will be trouble. She is a lady of influence."

"Good. All the better to humble." He jerked Beth's arms and pulled her until she bent backward. "So, you're a lady of influence. Well, we'll see how much influence you have." He slammed his hand against the table. "Silence!" he shouted. "We're going to have a Christmas party, everybody."

The tall young seaman who'd first accosted Beth tapped Dimanche's arm. "Felix, I think you had better not."

"Don't give me orders," Dimanche growled.

The young man disappeared back into the crowd. Beth looked around desperately for a friend, but most were Dimanche's men. Then she saw Patrick Gerrity come from the kitchen, and felt a wave of relief. He knew her from the days in the Lair. He'd stop this.

"Hey, Dimanche!" Patrick shouted. "There'll be none of that here. Let the girl—" Before he finished, a bottle crashed on his head. He collapsed to the floor.

Beth watched horrified as he was dragged to a corner and pushed under a table.

There was a cheer from a few in the crowd. The others began to shout for Dimanche to begin the party.

Dimanche climbed up on a table and dragged Beth with him, wrenching her arms painfully as he did.

"Attention, mes amis!" Dimanche shouted. "I am going to show you the difference between a lady and a slut. Hey, Bunko!" He shouted to a huge fat man drinking in the corner alone. "Bring me one of the sluts from upstairs."

Bunko nodded, raising his massive hulk from the chair with difficulty.

"What I will demonstrate, my friends, will make you all feel much better about sleeping with tarts. Believe me—oh, here she comes now."

Beth stared as Bunko pushed a disheveled Ternice toward the table.

"Quit yer pushing, you big oaf," Ternice said. "Lord knows I can—" She stopped and looked up at the table. "Beth! Child, what are they about?" She glowered at Dimanche. "Let her go, Felix, you fool. She's married to DuBoise. Do you want Niessen down here hunting all of us?"

"I'll worry about it from the coast of Africa. Now get up here."

One of the men jammed a hand between her legs and lifted her to the table. Ternice screeched, and kicked him in the jaw.

"You pay for my prizes if you want 'em," she roared.

The man staggered, cursing, to his feet and tried to get at her, but the others held him back.

"All right!" Dimanche shouted. "Enough!" He took five Spanish reals from his pocket and dropped them into Ternice's hand. "There. Now pull down your dress."

"What?"

Dimanche, still holding Beth with one hand, gripped Ternice's bodice with the other and ripped it to her waist, tearing her black chemise and leaving her breasts flopping dolefully over the rent fabric.

A cheer went up from the crowd.

"Damn you, Dimanche!" Ternice cried. "You've ruined my best dress."

Dimanche ignored her. "And now, let us see how different the lady is." He took out five more reals and extended them toward Beth. She tried to kick him.

"Your choice, madam." He grabbed the collar of her dress and yanked hard.

There was a sharp tearing sound as the seams of the gown gave way. Beth gasped as she felt the moist hot air of the inn against her exposed flesh. Her nipples tautened in fear and humiliation.

There was shouting and whooping. Two burly men pushed their way forward to the table and tried grabbing her leg, but Dimanche drew his pistol and they backed away.

"Are you ready for more?" he shouted into the crowd.

The men roared their answer.

Beth saw that Ternice was scared, and that frightened her more than Dimanche did. Dimanche was inciting the men to a point where even he could no longer control them. Beth could see it in their greasy, panting faces. They were all drunk. They'd been at sea for months . . . been without women. Tom had warned her about sailors aroused, how he'd seen murders committed for little more than a lady's handkerchief. She had to act quickly.

She flung herself against Dimanche, knocking him to his knees.

"Run, Ternice, hurry," she cried. Ternice jumped from the table, distracting some of the mob. Beth slipped her hand into her boot. Her fingers clamped round Billy Boy's handle.

"You little silk slut!" Dimanche grabbed for her.

She drove the blade through his arm.

Dimanche screamed.

"Hey," someone called, "she's cut Dimanche. Don't let her get away."

Hands grabbed at her. She kicked savagely and slashed out with her knife.

"Get her!" Dimanche roared.

She saw Bunko approaching and screamed.

Suddenly a voice boomed out. "Stay right where you are, my hefty friend, or you'll be feast for the worms!"

Raleigh stood in the doorway, hatless, his hair white with snow, his pistol drawn and cocked, his face as dark and unreadable as the night itself.

As he walked toward Beth, the men moved back making a path for him.

"Cover yourself," he said coldly.

Beth's cheeks flamed with shame as she pulled her cloak around.

"The woman stays, stranger." Dimanche's bloody arm hung at his side. His other was raised. In his hand was a pistol.

"I don't think so," Raleigh said. He pushed Beth toward the door and started after her.

"No one disobeys Dimanche!" he cried, and pulled the trigger.

There was a deafening explosion, then screams as men dashed for the door. The room filled with smoke.

"Raleigh!" Beth cried. She saw a man slump to the floor. Another shot rang out. She looked up just in time to see Dimanche fall from the table . . . and Raleigh's smoking gun.

"We'd better leave quickly," he said.

"Not out there. Dimanche's men will kill us. Come. I know another way." She grabbed his hand and pulled him toward the kitchen.

Raleigh balked. "You're crazy. They'll trap us like rats back there."

"Follow me. There's a way out. I lived here when

I left the candleworks. No one knows of it except friends. You have to trust me."

"Trust you? That's a laugh."

There were angry shouts from the men.

"Come on," Beth urged. She headed for the pantry. "There's a trapdoor under the table. Hurry."

Raleigh followed Beth down through the trapdoor, closing it behind them.

"Where are we?" he whispered.

"Shhh. We're in the Lair. Follow me."

A small fire burned in the fireplace, relieving the darkness enough for Beth to point out the exit hole that led outside. "You can squeeze through. It leads to an alley on the other side of the inn."

"They'll be looking for fresh tracks in the snow now. We'd better wait for a while."

Beth rested her hand against the wall, and suddenly the enormity of what had happened upstairs hit her. Her knees felt weak and she feared she was going to faint.

She let herself sink slowly to the floor, too tired to talk, to think.

Raleigh was silent for a long while. Then he said: "Is the tavern where you come when no other assignations are available?"

"I came here looking for you," she said. She had no strength to shout the anguish inside her, to force him to listen, to believe her.

He laughed bitterly. "Why? To convince yourself of your innocence at my expense again?"

"Raleigh, please. That's not true. Why won't you listen to me?"

"Listen to you? I should not even be near you. For years I've walked in and out of taverns, among the surliest riffraff, and never had to draw my pistol. Now, I have killed a man because of you, and whatever catlike needs drive you."

"Oh, God, Raleigh." Beth buried her head in her hands. "You cannot think that of me."

He grabbed both her hands. "What else can I

think? Do you expect me to believe that you never knew DuBoise signed me on as first mate of the *Manitou?* That he never gave you my proposal? That you never got my letters? That in all your knowledge-able access to the DuBoise shipping records, you never saw the lading bills I sent monthly from the *Manitou?"*

"But that's true!" Beth reached for his face and her cape fell open, revealing her bare breasts. She pulled at the torn bodice in an attempt to cover herself.

Angrily, Raleigh pushed her hands away. "No, by God, let's have no false modesty. Two years at sea should entitle me to something. Here, face the fire so that I can see those treacherous peaches." He gripped her by the shoulders and turned her harshly.

"Raleigh, you're wrong. You have to believe me. I knew none of what you said. I married Seth DuBoise only because I thought you were dead, and he had been so kind to me."

"His money made it easier to share his bed, I sus-pect," Raleigh said viciously.

"Raleigh, please. I love you."

"Do you really think I am fool enough to fall for your lies a second time? *Guardian!* I should have known the truth that night at the Van Brundts'. Tell me, did you enjoy his spotted hands upon you?"

Beth swung her palm hard against his face. Rage, fierce tearing rage coursed through her. Where love and anxiousness for forgiveness had dwelt, now raw loathing overflowed. Damn him to hell! If he could not accept the truth from her heart, the devil could have him because she certainly wouldn't.

"You're vile," she said. "Whatever love I insanely nurtured for you was a madness from which you have just freed me."

"Surely such feeling doesn't come and go so easily," he said mockingly. "Maybe I did misjudge you." He unbuckled his pants. "Come. You can show me how much you love me."

Beth drew back. "You animal."

He grabbed her behind her neck, pulled her head

toward him. "Let's have more from those lips than lies. Use your mouth on me!"

She struggled to pull away, but his grip on the back of her neck was too painful.

"And you'll do it right—or else," he warned.

"Never!" she spat.

He pushed her back on the dirt floor, and, despite her kicking, hoisted her skirts and pinned her legs with his own.

"On second thinking," he said huskily, "there are certain things I will not risk even for love. This will be much safer."

Beth tried to reach the knife in her boot, but Raleigh pinned her hands behind her head.

"You're supposed to be a lady now. Why not be gracious and entertain me properly?"

In the next instant he was inside her. And against her will her body was responding.

"That's much better," he said softly.

"I hate you. I hate you. I hope you die," she murmured, trying desperately to remain still. But the more she attempted to keep herself motionless, the more acute the sensations became. Her body arched toward him.

His movements increased in intensity and she matched each thrust with her own. The pleasure made her light-headed. All thoughts of time and place fled her mind. She wanted to scream, to laugh, to cry. His breath was warm against her ear; his fingers hot upon her flesh. Was she so weak that she could not fight this man? Or was she so foolish as to actually love the damnable rogue?

"Oh, God!" she cried out, her body convulsing in an unbidden ecstasy; Raleigh's moan signified his nearly simultaneous release.

They lay quiet and spent for a long while. Raleigh was the first to speak.

"Why did you come to the tavern tonight?" he asked quietly.

"To find you. To convince you that what I said at Wildwillow was true."

He looked down at her. "I want to believe you. Fool that fate might prove me to be, I love you."

"Oh, Raleigh." She flung her arms around his neck and kissed him. "Don't leave me again."

"I must. I'm sailing downriver tomorrow."

"I'm going with you," she declared.

"Your husband wouldn't approve. You are still Mrs. DuBoise," he reminded her.

"I never belonged to him. I'll always belong to you. I'll arrange for a divorce once I'm in New York."

"You're not lying to me, are you? Playing me for the fool while you remain secure as mistress of Wildwillow?"

"My love, what must I do to convince you?"

"Very little," he conceded. "If you mean what you say about leaving DuBoise, be at the sloop *Dixon* tomorrow morning at eight."

"I'll get my things and come aboard tonight."

"Your appearance tomorrow is sufficient proof. Besides, it will be safer. There's little enough of this night left, and we'll have to make the best use of the darkness to get away. It seems advisable, just in case any of Dimanche's men are still sober—or drunk enough—to want revenge."

He stood, brushed himself off. Beth got to her feet and clasped his hand between hers.

"You go first," he said. "I'll see that you get to your wagon."

"You will be careful, won't you?" she asked anxiously.

"Either that, or dead."

He cocked his pistol and followed her out.

Chapter 2

Beth clutched her cape tightly around her as she entered the main hall. The snow of early evening had turned into a fine misty rain, and the ride back to Wildwillow had chilled her, though it was as much the anticipation of facing Seth as the elements that caused her to shiver uncontrollably. Odd, she thought, that all the candles were still lit at that hour. Had Seth demanded the servants keep a vigil for her? Odder still, there were no servants to be seen.

She started up the stairs, then stopped. Hugo, drawn and haggard, stood on the landing.

"Hugo. What on earth are you doing here?" Her voice trailed off. There was something very wrong. "What is going on?"

Hugo said nothing. His eyes took in her torn clothes, her disarray. He continued down the steps. When he reached her he stopped.

"Your husband is dying," he said, the disdain in his voice unmistakable.

"Dying? What are you talking about?"

"While you were *out,* ma'am, Mr. DuBoise had a heart attack. The doctor says he doesn't have long."

"No . . . no." Beth shook her head, as if by denial it would be any less true.

"He has been asking for you." Hugo's voice was cold.

"I—I'll go to him at once." Beth started, but Hugo held her arm.

"Begging your pardon, but I'd suggest you put on other clothes first."

Beth flushed, pulled her arm free. They stared at each other for a moment. Hugo's devotion to Seth could have been measured by the hatred for Beth in his eyes. Whatever she had done, she'd hurt his master, and now that hurt was going to kill him. Hugo would not let his master see her in so sordid a condition, would not let the man who'd taken care of him for so many years leave the world in further pain.

Beth dropped her gaze. "I'll change," she said quietly.

Philip was in a chair outside Seth's bedroom when Beth came down the hall.

"Where have you been?" he asked, more piqued than concerned.

"Never mind that now. Is he . . . ?" Beth dared not complete the question.

"Still alive? Yes. But you'd best see him now."

Beth opened the door slowly. Seth lay in the huge four-poster bed, his face ashen, his eyes closed. Four of the slaves, Hugo's wife among them, stood silently at the foot of the bed. When they saw Beth, they nodded and filed silently out.

Beth drew closer. It was strange how old he looked. She had never seen Seth as old. He was always so vital, so alive, so . . . so indestructible. Dying was incongruous to someone like Seth.

His lids fluttered, then opened. "Beth . . . Beth."

She pressed her hand on his. "Shhh. I—I'm here."

Tears welled in her eyes. She tried unsuccessfully to blink them back.

"I must . . . I must apologize."

"No, you mustn't talk. You have to relax so you can . . . can get better."

"Don't be foolish, child. I always know when a voyage is—" he wheezed, "is ending. Now let me speak, for there isn't much time."

"But you must rest."

"I don't want to go to my grave with your hatred. I did what I did with Eckert because I loved you. I knew from the moment I saw you with him at the Van Brundts' that he alone could take you from me. I . . . I knew I couldn't keep you forever, but I wanted you for as long as—" His voice broke and he began fighting for breath.

Beth lifted his head. "Hugo! Come quickly," she called.

Hugo rushed in and raised Seth up, holding him until he regained his breath. When he did, he lowered him to the pillow.

Hugo started for the door, when Seth called his name.

"Hugo. I want you to look out for Miss Beth after I'm gone."

"Whatever you wish, suh." Hugo lowered his head.

The resentment in his voice did not go unnoticed by Seth. "Hugo," Seth said, with surprising sharpness, "Miss Beth has done nothing but give me happiness, do you understand? Her flight this evening was . . . was my fault. Bear her no grudges, my dear friend, I beg of you . . ." His voice trailed off in another bout of wheezing.

"Please, you must not talk," Beth pleaded. She held his hand, pressed it to her cheek. All the anger and hatred that had filled her earlier were gone. Neither meanness nor lust had driven Seth to deceive her—it had been only love. She knew that now. And, in truth, that love had not been unrequited.

"I . . . I don't have long, my dear. But whatever

time is left, I want it to be with you. You will stay with me, won't you?"

Tears welled in her eyes. She swallowed hard and tried to smile. "Why, Mr. DuBoise, what ridiculous questions you ask. Of course I'll stay." She turned her head quickly, and bit her lip.

She wasn't aware of the time, until suddenly it was almost dawn. Raleigh would be expecting her in a few hours at the *Dixon!* She had to *get a message to him.*

She made sure Seth was asleep, then stepped out into the hall. Bill, the gardener, a heavyset black man with silver-white, fleecelike hair, stood near the door.

"Where's Mr. Philip?" she asked cautiously. She didn't want him around now.

"He went to lie down for a while, ma'am. Is . . . is Master DuBoise . . . ?"

"No, not yet. In fact, he's . . . he's asked that you deliver a message for him."

"Whatever Master DuBoise wants, I'll surely be glad to do."

"Go to the quay and, aboard the *Dixon,* find Mr. Eckert. Tell him that Mr. DuBoise is dying, and that . . . that contact will have to be made next week in New York."

"Contact?" Bill repeated.

"Mr. Eckert will understand. Tell him that he can leave word of his whereabouts with the Van Brundts. Now do you have all that?"

"Yes, ma'am."

"Well, go now. And be quick."

Beth watched him hurry down the stairs, then quietly slipped back into Seth's room to continue her vigil.

Philip was in the kitchen when Bill came in looking for a coat.

"Where are you going at this hour?" Philip asked. Bill told him.

"Eckert, eh?" Philip stroked his chin thoughtfully. He had learned from the servants what had transpired

earlier, and figured out himself why his uncle had kept
Eckert a secret. The old man never was one to share
his favorite possessions. But now she was on her way
to meet Eckert, or so it appeared. A message sent
with urgency, eh? What, he wondered, would happen
if such a message were never delivered? He smiled.
If his uncle could pretend someone was dead, he,
Philip, could certainly pretend a message was delivered.

He told Bill that Miss Beth's message had already
been relayed to Mr. Eckert. But if she were to ask,
Bill was simply to say he'd done it. It would only upset her, Philip explained, if she thought there had
been another courier.

Upstairs Seth opened his eyes. Beth leaned toward
him.

"It's getting close," he said. "You mustn't interrupt
me. I haven't enough breath for arguments."

She nodded, pressed her lips to his hand. Oh, dear
God, she didn't want him to die. She loved Raleigh,
loved him with all her soul, but suddenly she knew
that if giving him up would keep Seth alive, she would
do it.

"Come now, where's that spunk of yours?" he said.
"Save that face for when I'm no longer speaking. I
want to take the image of your dancing eyes and
silken hair with me through eternity."

"Oh, Seth." She felt as if she would explode with
grief.

"Uh-uh." He raised a finger and wagged it at her.
"You're a grand lady now. And you must realize there
are only certain times when you are allowed to show
real feelings."

"I don't care," she wailed, all her control gone. "I
don't want to be a grand lady if that's the price."

"There, there." He patted her hand weakly. "I'll
wait if you *must* have your cry." He smiled.

Beth looked up and grinned through her tears.
"Forgive me," she said. "I never meant to hurt you."

"Nor I you—" He winced in pain and Beth felt as if a knife had entered between her own ribs.

When the pain subsided, he said: "Lawyer Slade has my will. Wildwillow, the DuBoise fleet, and all my assets are yours."

Beth's mouth opened but Seth held up his hand and continued.

"I've left my nephew a fancy stipend, which will enrage him, because he thinks I don't know he devoted his whole greedy, inept young life to being my heir. But you do understand that I wouldn't have left you in charge of what it's taken me a lifetime to build if I didn't think you were more qualified to run it."

"But, Seth, I can't."

"Of course you can—ow." He clutched his chest, waited until the pain passed. "Of course you can. And you will. Longeye's a good foreman. Keep him. And Philip, well, if you think you can get on with him, he's not a bad manager here in Hudson. And remember, pay off the customs men you have to, and always make sure you have a proper cargo list. Also, keep our ships away from the savages who got Cook. It's bad for the morale to have captains butchered." He flinched and began fighting for breath.

"Let me get the doctor," Beth said.

"Doctor be damned," he gasped. "It's too late." The wheezing turned his face bluish.

"No," Beth said aloud, and didn't know that she said it.

Seth struggled to continue speaking. "Make sure," he said, "that I am buried as soon as possible. No waking. I don't want to be stared at lifeless. Promise me that?"

Beth nodded. "I promise."

He seemed to relax. "Good. Now give me your hand."

Beth clasped his gently.

"Tighter," he said. "Tighter. I want to feel your life before I go." He began to gasp as if he were strangling.

"Seth," she called. No, no. Don't let it happen. Let him live, she pleaded silently. "Seth . . . Seth, I— *I love you.*"

He turned his head toward her, pursed his lips as if to speak, and then was dead.

Chapter 3

"What it is, Tom?" Beth pulled her shawl more tightly about herself as she looked up from the ship's railing.

"We'll be in New York Harbor in another half hour," he said. He bit off a wad of tobacco and began to chew.

Beth nodded. And in another hour or so she would be with Raleigh. God, if only she weren't so numb! Seth's death had sapped her of feeling. Not since Suzannah had been torn from her had she felt so empty. More than a husband, Seth had been her strength, her father.

Not that she missed her own father. Whatever had happened to Abraham Talbot only the Lord knew, and more than likely even *He* didn't care. The same held true for her brother Ansel. But she did miss little John. He'd be just about fourteen. And Suzannah, always Suzannah. She could still see the tiny crescent on the back of her neck. God's jewelry, Widow Brinks had said. Someday they'd be together again. Someday. She sighed.

"I sent word to the Van Brundts that we'd be arriving yesterday. I hope they haven't been inconvenienced."

Tom spit tobacco juice over the side. "Comin' downriver at this time of year is always chancy. In a week or so this whole river will be packed with ice."

Beth shrugged. They could hire a coach to take them back, or a sled if need be. Meanwhile, she would see what Raleigh had planned. She'd enclosed a letter to him in her missive to the Van Brundts. She wondered what Emily had thought of that, and smiled.

Emily Van Brundt, it was obvious, was determined to be the grande dame of New York's *haut monde.* She made it her business to let absolutely nothing in the way of news or gossip slip by her. As fond as she was of Seth, it probably distressed her not to learn of his death sooner. And receiving Beth's note to Raleigh without so much as an explanation must have left her apoplectic. Poor Emily. Well, it certainly wouldn't be long, explanation or not, before she put something together herself. After all, it wasn't often that she could act as go-between for one of the wealthiest young widows in the United States.

Beth didn't bring up Raleigh or the letter when she arrived, thinking it best to appear unconcerned about the matter. If Emily knew that Raleigh was a DuBoise first mate, she conceivably thought it a business communication. But when dinner was over and she still hadn't mentioned it, Beth thought it odd.

She waited until she was ready for bed, and then said: "Oh, by the way, did Mr. Eckert send an answer to my note?"

Emily looked surprised. "Oh, my dear, I thought you knew." She went to the desk and handed Beth back her note to Raleigh unopened. "Raleigh's gone to sea. I was sure you knew, but then with the funeral and all, I suppose it could have slipped your mind."

"Gone to sea?" Beth stared at Emily. "But that's

impossible. The *Manitou* isn't scheduled for a voyage for another three weeks."

"Then you didn't know?" Emily said, unsuccessfully trying to sound sympathetic. "It was a surprise to us, too. I had planned a marvelous dinner party, and Raleigh *is* such a fine addition. I was terribly disappointed." She lowered her voice. "I often think that Jan is jealous. Isn't that ridiculous?"

Beth's stomach felt weighted with stones. "Where has he gone?"

"Well, William Eckert bought a ship, a three-master, I think, the *Firebrand*. He's got it on a sugar run from France to Saint Dominique—and Raleigh has gone on as captain."

"Oh, no!" Beth looked stricken.

Emily didn't notice. "I know," she prattled on, "dreadful, isn't it? He'll be missed by all of us."

Beth stayed in bed till noon the next day, feigning a headache. Her eyes were puffed and swollen from crying. It was incomprehensible that Raleigh should leave like that. Even if he hadn't known when she was arriving, he should have waited. He must have realized it would take time for the funeral arrangements. And knowing that, how could he leave . . . unless he never really cared in the first place? Could that be possible? Could his outrage at Wildwillow have been merely wounded pride?

Before they'd made love, he had been cruel, almost savage. Had that been the truth and what followed the sham? Ugly thoughts shot at her like arrows. Was she really the fool?

No. Surely she was jumping to conclusions. It was just a mischief of fate that had separated them. She refused to consider any other possibility. Raleigh would return in a few months and everything would be fine. Deciding this, she felt enormously better. So much so, that she made up her mind to remain in New York until he did.

Within two weeks, she had purchased a handsome Georgian row house on Nassau Street, and within a month she had her furnishings and servants in residence. Three stories high, with an attic and gabled roof, the house delighted Beth with its romantic Ionic columns and graceful oval windows that afforded a marvelous view of the river.

It was a view she knew Raleigh would love.

She devoted her months of waiting to decorating the house, reorganizing the New York shipping office, and trying to find Suzannah. She hired nearly a score of detectives, each of whom claimed to have scoured the Catskills, all of whom found nothing. It depressed her, but kept her from wondering why Raleigh hadn't written.

The main DuBoise shipping office was on South Street. It was a large wainscoted room, with six desks and filing shelves for ledgers in which shipping dates and duties were diligently entered by three earnest young clerks, supervised by a curmudgeonly old man named Mead, who'd sailed with Seth DuBoise more years ago than any of the three clerks had been on this earth.

At first Mead resented Beth's presence in the office, but once she assured him that his duties would remain the same and his salary would increase, he was quite amenable to her suggestions for improving their operation. Especially when her revamping of cargo inventory sheets proved to save them all at least a day and a half's work.

On the other hand, Mr. William Haggerts, one of the three clerks, was quite delighted with Madame DuBoise's presence right from the start. Tall and blond, with eyes the color of spring grass, he could barely keep his mind on his ledgers when Beth was present. And whenever she spoke to him, his cheeks would humiliate him with color.

His attentions did not go unnoticed by Beth. And secretly she was flattered by them. He was the same age as she was, and, according to Mead, came from a fine Philadelphia family. It struck her as odd that he would be working as a clerk when his demeanor would indicate that he had no need for such employment. When she asked him one day, he blushed furiously, and admitted that he was preparing to enter the shipping business himself and was determined to learn all he could.

"So," Beth said, "we will be competitors one day? Is that it?" She smiled and tossed her fashionably curled hair to the side.

"Well—I—I wouldn't do that, no," he stammered. "I mean, well, yes. But not exactly, if you know what I mean."

Beth laughed. "Really, Mr. Haggerts, there's nothing wrong with competition. I don't take offense. It's the American way, at least that's what they say in the papers."

"According to my brother-in-law, the country will soon be in competition with itself. Half going with the President and the other half going against him. Like Jefferson and Hamilton are these days."

"Well, I don't know if that's about to happen just yet."

"My brother-in-law says yes. In fact, he's heard that Hamilton is planning to impose a tax on distilled spirits. That will hurt farmers and exporters alike. My brother-in-law says—"

"Lord, Mr. Haggerts, your brother-in-law sounds like the oracle. Who is this learned gentleman?"

William Haggerts looked embarrassed. "Well, he's a reporter for the *Evening Post,* but he's one of the most knowledgeable men I've ever met. Really. He doesn't even write all that he'd like to because Mr. Gaylord—he owns the paper—is wary of speculative editorializing. But I tell you, what he's told me about this General Bonaparte in France is frightening."

"Hmmm. Is that so? I'd be interested in what he has to say. I'm planning on sending two of our ships to LeHavre at the end of the summer. I would hate to run into unnecessary difficulty. What did you say your brother-in-law's name was? I'd like to meet him."

"It's Avery, madam. Peter Avery. He's—"

Beth put her hand on Haggerts' arm, startling him into rigidity. "Peter Avery?" Could it possibly be the same Peter Avery? Her Peter? "Tell me," she said anxiously, "is he tall with fine blond hair?"

"Well, yes, he is." Haggerts looked surprised by her question. That a lady of Madame DuBoise's stature would be acquainted with his brother-in-law seemed highly unlikely. And now the possibility of embarrassing her by having her make a wrong identification was setting his stomach aquiver. "I—I'm sure you must know another Peter Avery," he said apologetically. "My brother-in-law rarely goes on the social circuit. He's partly a cripple, you see."

"Peter!" Beth breathed. It was him! And he was here, in New York! She had to see him. How many years had passed? How many millions of miles had they grown apart? Dear, dear Peter. "Where is he?"

Haggerts was nonplussed and utterly disoriented by the excitement in Beth's voice. Just having her hand on his arm was enough to confuse him, but this inexplicable, urgent interest in his brother-in-law set him to stammering.

"I—I—why, he's home, madam. Or, of course, he could be at the paper, or . . . well, I'm not exactly sure where he is right now, but—" He looked on the verge of panic.

Beth patted his arm, which did nothing at all to help and merely raised his color to that of a fire beacon.

"I didn't mean to upset you, Mr. Haggerts, but I do believe that your brother-in-law is an old friend of mine whom I haven't seen in many, many years," she said easily.

Haggerts nodded weakly.

"I only wanted to know where he lives."

"On Liberty Street, with my sister and their children."

"Oh, I see." Why had that come as a shock to

her? Haggerts had said his brother-in-law. Peter married and a father. Strange how possessive one became of people without any reason. Peter had always been her friend, never her lover, though there were many times when he would have had it otherwise. How curious life was, how awfully curious.

"Well," she said, heaving a sigh as if after completing some heavy task, "you must tell him that he is invited to dinner Friday next at the house of an old friend." She saw that Haggerts was looking uncomfortable again. "Oh, and you and your sister as well."

Haggerts beamed. "Why, thank you, madam. I'm sure they'll be as honored as I am to accept." He hesitated. "Will my brother-in-law know you? I mean, he's never mentioned the acquaintance."

"Just tell him that Beth Talbot's making corn biscuits and turkey. He'll know."

Chapter 4

"Are you sure the turkey is just as I wanted it,
Manda?" Beth asked.

The tall black girl put the lid back on the pot. "My
word, Miz DuBoise, but you are nervous about tonight. I never seen you in such a state."

"Ridiculous," Beth scoffed, checking her reflection
in the glass of the kitchen window. "Does my hair look
right to you?"

Manda grinned. "You look beautiful as I ever
seen you. There sure must be something special about
tonight."

Beth looked away and didn't answer. How could
she face Manda when she was having difficulty facing
herself? There was no denying that she'd spent an in-
ordinate amount of time preparing for the dinner tonight, not the least of which had been having her
dress made especially for the occasion. It was a magnificent blue velvet gown that gave her the tiniest waist
possible and maximum bosom. When she tried to rationalize the cost and style of the dress, she couldn't.

No, the truth was that she wanted to look her best for Peter—or, more truthful yet, she wanted to look better than his wife.

If Raleigh were here, she thought, I wouldn't care what I'd be wearing tonight! But Raleigh wasn't there, and there had been no word from him at all, no word *about* him except that absurd rumor from Emily Van Brundt. What had she said? Something about having heard he'd taken up with a French count's daughter. French count's daughter indeed! Emily was always fabricating tales about Raleigh, just to make him more of an asset to her parties. When he returned, Beth would have to tell him the legend he'd become. They'd laugh about it in between making love.

God, he'd been gone a long time.

The knock at the front door shook her from her reverie. As Tyro went to answer it, she hurried down the stairs. When she reached the landing, the door opened and she froze.

Peter entered the hall first, limping slightly, keeping his hand tight on his cane. His hair had darkened somewhat, but it still fell across his forehead, almost into his eyes, as it had as a boy. He was followed by a thin young woman, with wispy unswept brown hair and china-fine features. Only in her reticence did she resemble her brother, who looked as uncomfortable in these surroundings as he did in all others.

Beth took a step down and her eyes met Peter's. For a dizzying moment time spun back and all she saw was a boy sitting by a stream, a boy hungry for the future and anxious to become a man. So anxious that at ten he had confided fears that he'd never physically become a real man, fears that vanished after his twelfth birthday when he'd told her of an initiation ceremony with his cousins and their maid. It didn't seem possible that time had swirled by so fast, that those buzzing summer days were gone, that the man before her whom she knew so well was a stranger.

"Peter," she said coming toward him. She held out her hand.

"I've waited a long time for corn biscuits and turkey." He kissed her hand.

The next thing Beth knew, tears were streaming down her face and she was laughing and crying all at once. Peter's wife looked as ill at ease as her brother.

"Beth, this is Laura," Peter said, putting his arm around his wife's waist in a proprietary manner that appeared to comfort her.

"Please forgive me," Beth said wiping her eyes. "It's been so many years, and Peter and I were such good friends."

"He's told me," Laura said, her voice and manner as reserved as her emotions. She was not one to commit easily to friendship.

"Well, come into the parlor. We must celebrate. I've invited the Van Brundts—who were quite impressed by the way that I managed to lure Peter Avery, of the rapier words, out into the open—and the Warrens, who were equally impressed. Thomas Warren, in case you didn't know it, is your landlord. He owns the *Evening Post* building."

"That will be more people than I usually socialize with in a year," Peter said smiling.

"You don't mind, do you? The Van Brundts were so anxious to meet you." There was a knock at the door. "And that's probably them now." Beth looked at Peter and tried to read his expression. Was he upset that she had invited others? She had thought about it and decided it would make things easier all around. At least Laura Avery wouldn't feel abandoned if Beth wanted time alone to talk with him. And from the way Laura Avery was already studying her, Beth decided she had made the right decision.

At dinner, Jan Van Brundt was happy to monopolize Laura, and Emily and Mrs. Warren were enchanted with the presence of young William Haggerts. Thomas Warren was involved with his food and looked up from it only occasionally to say, "How's that again?", returning to his plate without really listening to the answer, but nodding sagely.

Beth and Peter barely touched their food. Within the confines of their social graces they spoke animatedly, and, after dinner in the garden, without restraint about their years apart. Peter told of his months of convalescence, and how he confounded the doctors who said he'd never walk again, and the people who never believed he'd attend the university. He spoke of meeting Laura, who was doing charity work in the hospital where he'd gone for treatment.

"She reminded me of you," he said. "She had that air of beguiling innocence."

Beth looked away. "My innocence has been gone a long time."

"It's never left you." He covered her hand gently with his own.

Beth turned back to him. "Do you never see darkness?"

"Not in sunshine."

"Oh, Peter, how I've longed to talk to you."

"And I to you."

"Tell me, before you left Shokan, did you . . . did you ever hear anything about my daughter Suzannah?" Beth said the words quietly, but they seemed to resound. She'd never spoken to anyone of the twins except Peter, and he alone knew their heritage.

"I could never be sure," he said. "But I did hear that a family of tanners had an infant daughter, which surprised everyone, since the wife was almost surely past bearing years. But they moved on, and I never learned their name."

"Oh." Beth looked at her hands in her lap. "I've tried to locate her, but with no success. It's just that I've never stopped thinking of her, stopped feeling that I deserted her. I will find her someday, though. I know it. She's nearly eight now. I wonder if her hair is still blond? It was pure gold. Morning sunlight."

"I suppose you know that the DeWitts' daughter is in London," he said quietly. "I heard that Regina sent her there for proper schooling because she was getting too wild."

"I didn't know, but it doesn't surprise me. The child resembled her father too closely. I stopped thinking of Adrianne the moment she left my womb. She had never belonged to me—Pa and Ansel had seen to that." There was bitterness in her voice, and to Peter's careful ear, there was also sadness.

He put his arm about her shoulders in brotherly fashion. Beth, back in his life after so long. It was so easy, so familiar. And with the familiarity came an unbidden surge of desire. He forced himself to ignore it, tried to will it away. She had grown more beautiful with the years, more beautiful than he had ever fantasied her those lonely bedridden months when her memory had been his only outlet of release.

She let her head fall against him, and the rosewater scent of her hair incited his body to continue its defiance. He accepted his frailty, and refused to judge himself.

"So much has happened to me," she said, "so much that I want you to understand, but that I fear you may not."

"I'll always be your friend, Beth. Had things been different, I—" He stopped himself. There was never any point in pursuing ifs. "I'll understand, simply because you will tell me what it is you want me to know."

"Oh, Peter!" She hugged him. Her story tumbled forth, in bits and pieces at first and then in a rush like a spring flood all of it came out—her stay with the Stillwells, Margaret, Widow Brinks, and Raleigh; her months with Tom and the Pack, her marriage to Seth. Words and emotions mingling with tears of relief. When she finished she felt purged, and exhausted.

Peter sat quietly a moment, then he said, "So it's William Eckert's son who's caught your fancy."

Beth looked up suspiciously. "You say that in an odd way. Why is that? Do you know him?"

"By reputation only."

"He's not the rogue he's made out to be, believe me. I'm sure he's had his day with the ladies, but he's changed." She was grateful for the darkness because of the blush that warmed her cheeks. "What I mean to say is that he loves me. We'll probably wed soon after he returns."

"Has he asked you already?"

"Well, not exactly. But it is understood between us." She said this gently, as if Peter was a child who would not fully comprehend it.

"Perhaps it is a misunderstanding then."

Beth pulled back. "Whatever are you saying?"

"I don't like to come back into your life with bad tidings. Maybe it would be best to go back and join the others and let this matter drop." He stood.

"Peter, for heaven's sake," Beth demanded, "what are you not saying? Bad tidings be damned. Tell me."

"In tomorrow's paper there will be a notice. Mr. William Eckert had it sent over just today."

"Notice? What sort of notice?"

"A notice announcing the betrothal of Mademoiselle Marie Ouvrard to Mr. William Eckert's son, Raleigh, last month, on his plantation in Saint Dominique."

Chapter 5

"We're going, Tom. I've made up my mind. And
you're coming with me." Beth paced back and forth
across the oak floor of the office, making angry clicks
with the heels of her boots. She'd stared at that an-
nouncement in the paper long enough.

"Girl, you're mad. It will cost a bloody fortune to
outfit for a voyage to Saint Dominique when we hadn't
been planning on it."

"I don't care what it costs," she snapped angrily.
"I want a ship ready to leave as soon as possible. And
I want no murderers or rapists in the crew either."

Tom flung his hands in the air. "Now how am I going to know who's done what to whom before I take
'em on, eh?"

"You know damn well who's done everything, so
don't try to tell me otherwise. I know it won't be easy
finding a completely respectable crew, but whatever
we have to pay—pay it. I don't want to have to worry
about sea sickness and getting my throat cut or my
maid raped too." She slammed a ledger down on the
desk.

"What in the devil's drawer has gotten into you? You're not thinking clearly, girl, and that's what gets most people into their worst states. It has something to do with Eckert, doesn't it?"

"That's my affair, isn't it? Yours is just to get this voyage under way."

Tom shook his head sadly. "Beth, girl, come here." He held his arms wide.

"And what makes you think that . . ." She could not continue. She rushed into his arms and buried her face in his shirt.

"There, now. It's jealousy that's filling our sails for this one, isn't it?"

"And what difference does that make?" she sniffed.

"There's no reward in it. Never is."

"I don't care," she said. "I'm going down there. I—I want to buy a plantation. It will be a good investment, so I'm told."

"Beth, if he's fool enough to want another woman, then he's not man enough for you. Leave it at that."

"I don't believe he wants another woman. He can't. He . . ." She bit her lip. "There are certain things one has to see for herself."

The voyage took four days longer than Beth expected, but was much more pleasant than she'd feared. The *Windsweeper* was a fast compact topsail schooner with ample space below decks. (Tom called her a dainty vessel with the spunk of a brig.) Because of Beth, Tom had seen to it that there were better than usual stores aboard, which, along with the balmy weather, kept the crew in fine spirits all the way down.

Beth had taken her maid, Cora, along, as well as Hugo. Over the past months his animosity had softened to understanding, and, as Seth had wished, he became her protector in truth. Except for a squall that kept Cora bunkbound for two days, they both enjoyed the trip.

Emily Van Brundt had arranged for Beth to stay with the Mavannes at Havenhall. They were cousins of hers and owned one of the largest plantations on the island.

They were also, according to Emily, well acquainted with the Eckert family.

Beth tried to keep her mind off that and any meeting with Raleigh by busying herself about the ship, to Tom's unending consternation.

Three days out of New York she shocked Cora, Hugo, and the crew by appearing on the quarterdeck in boy's pants and shirt. Since her costume was for convenience and not subterfuge, she didn't bother with a cap, and her hair blew free and wild in the salt-sprayed winds, turning it in three days from its chestnut hue to a burnished gold.

Cora warned that it wasn't ladylike to take so much sun and Tom told her she'd have to stay out of the rigging, but Beth ignored them both, learning everything she could, from knot tying to navigation, with the dauntless enthusiasm of a sea-struck boy.

Only when they were two days from Saint Dominique did she realize how much sun she'd unwittingly taken. She couldn't meet the Mavannes looking like that. She begged Cora for ointments to lighten her skin. Cora didn't promise success, but she made a paste of lemon juice and ash for Beth's face and had her remain in her cabin during the day, allowing her to emerge only after sunset. When she did, she was in a state of frustration and pique, especially upon learning that the calluses on her hands wouldn't disappear for several weeks.

But neither her calloused palms nor tanned skin was on her mind when the *Windsweeper* sailed into Cap Français Harbor. Never having traveled farther than New York, she was startled by the sight of so many half-naked black workers, all carrying baskets of coffee or sugar to the anchored merchant vessels, while overseers lounged and joked and occasionally snapped a switch; the spectacle was enough to send her mind in a spin. The heat made everything more intense, and the smells of the dock were almost nauseatingly pungent. Unlike the odors of preserved fruit, spices, and sandalwood that she associated with ships, these new scents touched her in a way that sparked both excitement—and fear.

As she stood on the deck, trying to take in all that she saw, a low rumble of tom-toms could be heard from the steep hills beyond the city, and despite the hot sun a small shiver ran through her.

Her hands were still cold when she arrived at Havenhall an hour later.

The large sprawling mansion, strongly French in design, with a wide shaded veranda, was surrounded by lush bougainvillea vines and slim heavy-leafed trees.

Gabriel Mavanne was a good-looking man in his early thirties. He had a small reddish beard and a warm smile that was friendly and vaguely mischievous. He put her at ease immediately.

"We expected you several days ago," he said as they walked to the house.

"You should admonish the wind. It was capricious and sometimes barely filled the sails."

"I'll have it flogged at once."

"I'd say not," Beth laughed. "I prefer empty sails to those of a vengeful tempest."

"As you wish. Wind," he said looking skyward, "you're forgiven this time."

"It really was a fine journey, though. Clear skies almost all the way."

"I'm glad of that, but we had thought we could give you a rest before thrusting you into our island social whirl. I'm afraid, as it turns out, you've just time to freshen up. My wife, Denise, has planned a party tonight in your honor."

"And if I hadn't arrived until tomorrow?"

Gabriel grinned. "We probably would have celebrated anyway and had to tell you all about it. There's Denise now." Gabriel waved to the tall, willowy woman walking across the veranda. "Denise!"

Denise turned, waved back and came toward them.

Holding her hand was a pale blond miniature of herself about eight years old.

Gabriel made introductions.

"We're so glad you've come," Denise said. "You must tell us everything that's happening in New York. The news from Paris is so depressing these days, with all that violence and bloodshed. Emily does try to give us the latest gossip, but she is not the most diligent correspondent. Oh"—she stepped back and prodded her daughter forward—"I haven't even introduced you to our daughter, Enid. Enid, this is Madame DuBoise."

"Pleased to meet you." Enid gave an obligatory curtsy, then looked to her mother. "Now may I play?"

Denise sighed. "Go on."

Enid curtsied again, then ran into the garden.

"That child. She won't sit and embroider like other little girls. She prefers the little nigras' games, climbing trees, jumping through barrel hoops. I don't know how she'll ever become a lady."

"I'm sure she will," Beth said. "And probably a lot more."

"Now our son, Jacques, on the other hand, is just the perfect gentleman," Denise went on, not really hearing what Beth said. "By the way, Gabriel, where is Jacques?"

"Riding, I believe."

"He does love that. He's twelve and very much ready to be twenty. He's good with the slaves and could probably run the whole plantation by himself. But enough of that. It's sticky and I'm sure you'd like to change before the party. Gabriel did tell you?"

Beth nodded. She could see that Denise Mavanne was not one for abbreviated conversations, was indeed Emily's cousin.

"We're having lovely people. Well"—she cupped her hand archly by her lips—"some of them are not so lovely, but down here we all stick together, more or less. Even Madame Bescroft, who thinks she's better than just about everyone."

"I see." Beth felt the perspiration trickle down her back and hoped Denise wouldn't go into a detailed description of them all.

"Oh, and you might know one of the guests, he's a friend of Emily's."

Beth felt a funny tripping of her heart.

"Captain Eckert," Denise said. "Tall, handsome, dark-haired, with—"

Beth smiled. "Yes, I know him."

"Have you met his wife yet? Lovely girl. Marie."

Beth blanched. Wife? Raleigh married? It couldn't be. He was only engaged a few months ago. They wouldn't marry so soon. He couldn't. He . . .

"Are you all right?" Denise asked.

"Oh . . . oh, yes. It's the heat, that's all."

"You'll get used to it," Gabriel assured her.

"I'll have one of the servants prepare a tub. A bath and a nap and you'll be fine for dinner."

"I'm sure," Beth said, knowing well that she wasn't sure at all.

Chapter 6

The sun was setting when Beth stepped out onto the
balcony adjoining her room. She watched its orange
brilliance disappear behind the shadowy hills without
emotion, thought, or feeling. So, it was done. Raleigh
was married. She'd come too late. Perhaps it was
better that way. Any sooner and he once again might
have lied his way into her heart. Was ever there so
treacherous and deceitful a man?

She had thought she would cry, but strangely no
tears came. *Perhaps*, she thought, *I am at last grown
up. Maybe now I'll be able to recognize the difference
between a man and a bastard.* If there was one.

She felt the bitterness, tasted it. It would pass, and
she knew it. It always did. Only sometimes, like now,
it seemed as if it would linger forever.

She watched the blacks leaving the cane fields.
There was something about the way they walked, a
listlessness, a resentful submissiveness that had nothing to do with fatigue, that made her uneasy. And
the muted sound of the drums from the hills magni-

fied the feeling. Nothing of spirit stayed content in chains, not even the heart.

The clock struck six and Beth went to join her hosts with anger buried in her chest like a dagger. She smiled and graciously acknowledged Denise's introductions, deferred demurely to the eminent Madame Bescroft, exchanged pleasantries with Gabriel's friend Donald Tremain, and felt quite composed until Raleigh entered. Then the dagger twisted.

He came across the veranda with a pretty dark-haired girl on his arm. He smiled at Denise then turned slightly and the smile faded.

Beth had steeled herself for the encounter and nodded politely. It was a small and bitter triumph to see him struggle for composure.

"Oh, doesn't he look dashing in that white satin shirt?" Denise whispered under her breath. "Raleigh, how delightful of you to join us." She swept up her skirts with one hand and took Beth in tow with the other before she could protest.

"Beth, I believe you know Captain Eckert, and this is his wife, Marie. Marie, this is Beth DuBoise."

Marie smiled shyly and greeted Beth in French, perceptibly clutching her husband's arm tighter.

Raleigh's face was unsmiling. "You are the last person I'd expect to see on Saint Dominique."

Beth's eyes flicked for an instant to Marie. "I gather that. Congratulations on your marriage.'

"Thank you." He looked around. "And where is your husband?"

Beth was thoroughly taken aback. Did he actually think she'd married again? "Is that supposed to be amusing?"

Raleigh shrugged. "Not particularly."

What sort of game was he playing? Could he not know about Seth? That was impossible. Bill had told her he'd delivered the message. "My husband is dead," she said quietly, "as I was sure you had been informed."

"I regret that I've been out of touch for a long time. I'm sorry. My condolences." He bowed his head.

Beth seethed inwardly. How could he lie so badly . . . so blatantly? Dear God, why hadn't she listened to Tom and stayed in New York? Or better yet, why hadn't she returned to Hudson? Raleigh Eckert wasn't a rogue, he was a rotter!

"Well then, what brings you to the island?" he said amiably.

Beth controlled her anger. She would rather die than reveal the real reason for her visit. Never, never would Raleigh know what her feelings for him were. "I came to—to look at a plantation. There are large profits, I hear, to be made from sugar."

"So there are," Raleigh said, "if you don't mind the necessary dealing in flesh. I've found I am a poor plantation master. Perhaps you and I can talk business. I am thinking of selling Rondelle. It's a most lucrative plantation, I guarantee. Does the prospect interest you?"

"All lucrative prospects interest me," Beth said coolly.

"Ah, yes, so they do." Raleigh smiled.

Beth thought she would not be able to stop herself from slapping him. The arrogance . . . *the nerve!*

Denise coughed politely, a good hostess sensing tension and ready to remedy the situation. "There's Monsieur Cartine. Beth, I do want you to meet him. He's a widower who owns several merchant vessels and the largest cane plantation on the island. Raleigh, Marie, you will excuse us?" Without waiting for a reply, Denise put her arm through Beth's and whisked her across the veranda to a portly though vigorously good-looking gentleman in a white linen coat and trousers.

Denise told Beth that she and Monsieur Cartine should have a lot in common seeing they both owned ships and had suffered loss of loved ones. Before Beth could either laugh or protest, introductions had been made. Denise slipped away and Beth was trapped in a painfully dull discourse on the high cost of barnacle damage.

Beth was less concerned with barnacle removal than with breaking free of Monsieur Cartine, who had taken a fancy to her and was not easily rebuffed. She noticed that Raleigh was observing her and was convinced he was enjoying her present plight. He was standing alone against a pillar, sipping a tall drink, and she could swear that he was holding back a smile. Damn him! As much as she hated to do it, he was going to be her only way out of Monsieur Cartine's attentions.

As Monsieur Cartine rambled on, Beth interrupted.

"You must forgive me, sir, but there is a matter of great importance that I must discuss with—" she looked around desperately, "with Captain Eckert, and I see that he is alone at the moment."

Before Cartine could protest, she was off. Standing beside Raleigh she said under her breath: "If he's watching, pretend you are hearing me impart something of great importance."

"I would expect nothing less to fall from your lips," he said. He did not change his stance, continued to lean lazily against the pillar. "Though I must warn you," he said quietly, "that Monsieur Cartine is about to join us anyway."

"You must help me get—" She stopped and smiled sweetly as Cartine came alongside her. "Monsieur Cartine, you know Captain Eckert?"

"Of course. And how is your lovely wife?"

"Wonderfully well, thank you. She's inside. In fact, she was asking about you not two minutes ago."

"Really?" Cartine seemed to puff up a bit.

"Yes. She was wondering if you would like to come to dinner when her cousin Amy arrives." He turned to Beth. "Beautiful girl, Amy. The toast of Paris."

Cartine cleared his throat. "The toast of Paris?"

"Well, that's what we've heard. But who knows?"

"Where did you say your wife was?" Cartine asked, his eyes bright.

"Inside."

Monsieur Cartine excused himself, and hurried off to look for Marie. Beth forgot her animosity for a moment and smiled.

"Thank you for the rescue." She gazed across the garden.

"Don't mention it. Marie would like Monsieur Cartine to meet her cousin Amy."

"The toast of Paris?"

"Well, perhaps I exaggerated there. Nothing is the toast of Paris these days except the fires of revolution. *Liberté, Fraternité, Égalité.* He took a long swallow of his drink. "The words are shouted very loud and the feelings are strong. I wonder how far they will carry."

"How far what will carry?" Gabriel Mavanne joined them, smiling. "The beat of those infernal drums?"

"That too," Raleigh said, gazing thoughtfully into the hills.

"What do they mean?" Beth asked.

"Mean?" Gabriel laughed. "Nothing. That's just the slaves worshipping their tribal gods. They're really quite primitive, you know. Superstitious. Like children, actually."

Despite Gabriel's easy answer, Beth still felt unnerved. Perhaps it was only Raleigh's presence. Perhaps.

Gabriel left, and Raleigh suggested they walk to the garden. Out of sight of the house, behind a copse of palms, he stopped.

"Why did you come?" he asked.

"I—I told you."

"I don't believe you." He gripped her arms. "Haven't you toyed with me enough?" His eyes burned with searing fury.

"Haven't *I* toyed with *you?* What manner of perverse humor delights you? Could you not wait two weeks for me in New York? I know what you thought of Seth DuBoise, but for all his faults he had been good to me. I could not let him die alone that night. I thought . . . I was sure you would understand."

"What night? What are you talking about?"

"Why are you playing this game?" Beth asked, her voice distraught. "Haven't you put me through enough? I sent a servant to your ship that night, that Christmas Eve. He told me that he gave you my message."

"Beth." Raleigh gripped her shoulders. "Beth, I received no message. No one came abroad the *Dixon* that night. I waited until dawn without sleep, watching for you, waiting, not wanting to believe what was obvious. That you were not going to give him up."

"No. You're lying. I won't listen anymore." She turned her head away. "There are limits to how far you can pressure even a captive heart."

"Dear God, Beth, there is no purpose for lies. Romeo and Juliet were far less star-crossed than you and I. The fates have played us foul again. For some reason I do not know your servant spoke falsely. Perhaps he was lazy and was afraid to say he had not delivered the message; perhaps he was misinformed at the boat. I can only speculate. But by God, the truth is that I had no word from you. And I know only that I wanted, from that dawn on, to put your presence and your memory as far behind me as possible."

Beth searched his face and knew he did not lie. "Oh, Raleigh."

His arms came around her and it was as if they had always been there. She felt unafraid, secure for the first time since she'd landed on the island. She could not even hear the tom-toms for the roaring of blood in her ears. Slowly she looked up and saw that his face was twisted in a nameless agony. He took her firmly by the shoulders and pushed her from him.

"Raleigh, my love, what is it?"

"It can no longer be. I married two months ago." His face was dark, his eyes haunted.

"But—"

"Were it just Marie and I, I would attempt annulment. But there is another consideration. Last night

Marie told me that . . . that she is with child. She is an innocent in all this. I cannot cast her off, anymore than I can ask you to be less than my wife." His arms hung limply, futilely at his sides.

Beth began to reach toward him, then let her hands drop. So there it was. The end at last and one that neither of them wanted.

"Well then," she said with an audible sigh, "I guess we ought to rejoin the guests. All that has to be said has been said." She looked away.

"Beth," Raleigh called softly.

She turned.

"I love you."

She opened her mouth to speak, then changed her mind and bolted for the house, her heart anguished and hammering like the tom-toms in the hills.

Chapter 7

The drums continued to talk in the hills all night and the next day. Gabriel and his son, Jacques, teased Beth about her apprehensions. The summers in Saint Dominique were for pleasure, for cool drinks served by smiling happy slaves. Twice that afternoon, Gabriel called over slaves and asked them to tell Beth whether or not they were happy.

"Happy, mizzy, happy," they'd said, smiling, and bowing low.

"See?" Gabriel said. He'd tossed them pennies, laughed as they scrambled for them. "Like children. That's what they are."

Still, the rumbling distressed Beth. Maybe it was thinking about Raleigh too. She didn't want to do too much of that. It was pointless. She'd look around at a few plantations, see Raleigh and Marie's Rondelle when she felt emotionally stronger, and then leave for New York. She was restless. If one life was over and another had to begin, she wanted it to begin as soon as possible. Meanwhile, she would try to make the best of her visit.

She could not endure an entire day with Denise, who seemed to be able to gossip nonstop, and so feigned a great desire to go riding. Jacques gave her his horse, a beautiful roan who knew the trails and the way home just in case she got lost, and somewhere around three in the afternoon, she headed up the mountainside into the cool forest.

The horse was spirited, and riding him Beth lost all track of time. Confident that he would be able to find the way back, Beth gave no thought to direction. The sounds of the insects, the drums, all blended with the wind rushing past her and she had gone much further than she intended when the sun began to slip down toward the sea and she turned for home.

It had been a good ride. It had taken her mind off Raleigh. It had taken her mind off everything—except the drums.

The deeper she had gone into the forest, the louder the tom-toms had grown. Partly convinced by now that there really was nothing significant in the drums and that most of her apprehension stemmed from her own inner turmoil, she became curious about them. And when she heard them beating louder and louder, she tethered her horse and walked forward to explore.

Moving stealthily, she stepped out onto a large overhanging rock and knelt down. What she saw below her in the glade almost caused her to gasp, more out of surprise than fear. Black men, what looked like a hundred of them, were sitting silently in a large half-circle, facing a fire, behind which stood a tall voodoo priest who leaned ominously on an improvised altar made of stones.

What on earth . . . ? Beth inched closer to the edge of the rock so that she could hear what was being said without being seen.

The priest was incanting something that she could not make out. Suddenly a flash of lightning sizzled across the darkening sky and the blacks jumped to their feet and began screaming in some sort of religious frenzy.

Their intensity sent chills through Beth, but she was too fascinated to move. Something was about to happen. She could feel it. The priest raised his hand and gave a signal to two men, who proceeded to drag in a black pig. The pig squealed in protest, as it was tied down on the makeshift altar. Then to Beth's horror, there was a flash of a knife and the earsplitting screech of a dying animal.

Her stomach felt queasy, but there was something about the ceremony below that mesmerized her. She watched as the men slowly walked forward and dipped their hands in the blood of the pig, then raised them aloft, chanting. At first she wasn't sure what they were saying. But before the last man had drenched his hands for the ritual, the words were clear. *Liberté ou mort.* Liberty or death!

Suddenly Beth became afraid, afraid of what the ritual stood for as well as being discovered. Quietly moving backward to the path, she saw a statuesque young slave woman, naked except for red laurels twined about her brow, begin a frighteningly sexual and symbolic dance.

What it all meant was unclear, but that it boded ill was certain.

She ran for her horse and prayed as the animal raced down the mountain for home.

When she told the Mavannes what she had witnessed, only Denise looked concerned.

"That's their religion," Gabriel assured her. "They're always sacrificing something to their sanguine gods."

"But that *Liberté ou mort,*" Beth protested. "Doesn't that sound as if—"

"They've heard us discussing *Liberté, Fraternité, Égalité.* They're just imitating us. I told you. They're not men. They're children." Gabriel laughed. "You must learn to relax, Beth. Enjoy Saint Dominique. It's a paradise, really."

Beth slept fitfully that night and the next. She did not like the drums and wished she could speak to Raleigh about them, but knew it would be brazen to appear at Rondelle without invitation . . . unless of course she was seriously interested in purchasing the plantation.

And why not? She could leave a competent overseer in charge of the place. According to everyone she had met, plantations were sound investments. She made up her mind to ride to Rondelle the following day.

She dressed with extreme care and wore her favorite green taffeta dress, a soft pitched hat with a large plume cocked jauntily upon her head. She had Cora dress her hair in long curls, and when she checked her reflection in the glass before leaving, she felt she had never looked lovelier.

And for what purpose? She scolded herself for her vanity, then unthinkingly dabbed some perfume behind her ears. *Damn. Would she ever be free of him?*

Her anticipation of seeing Raleigh was great, and when she arrived at Rondelle and learned that he wouldn't be back until the evening, she was crushed.

Marie invited her to stay, but Beth declined and left word for Raleigh to call on her at the Mavannes' if he was still interested in selling Rondelle.

When she returned to Havenhall she was cross and hot and didn't give a damn if the whole island fell into the sea that morrow.

She was still in poor spirits when the Mavannes' dinner company began arriving, and felt it best to walk outside and cool off.

A carriage out front caught her eye. The driver was a tall gray-haired black man who sat barefooted on the box, smiling as he gazed at the hills. It was a strange, knowing smile. If the drums were talking, he was listening. And comprehending.

Beth approached him and he bowed from his box. She noticed that the carriage was from the Breda plantation. Denise had mentioned that there was a slave there who was reputed to be one of the most impressive on the island. A Roman Catholic, she'd said, who was literate in French and Latin and could mix the best herb potions anyone could want. Just by the way he held his head, Beth knew this was the slave.

"You listen to the drums?" Beth said.

The black man looked at her with more than casual interest. "They speak," he said quietly, "so I listen."

He smiled and Beth felt herself flush. He was not like other slaves. No part of his spirit had ever been shackled; no part ever would.

"Do you know what they say?"

"They say there will be blood, much blood, rivers of blood," he said coolly, still smiling.

Beth was too stunned for a moment to move, then she stepped back. "It's rude to . . . to say things like that. To shock people. What is your name?"

"Toussaint, madam." He bowed his head. "Toussaint L'Ouverture."

The slave Denise had spoken of. "I've heard about you, Toussaint. You know too much to indulge in lies. Why did you say that . . . about the blood?"

Toussaint shrugged. "I fell at birth. The August heat. I do strange things often." He returned his gaze to the hills, and continued to smile.

Back in the house Beth told Gabriel Mavanne what Toussaint had said.

"He's just pulling your leg," Gabriel laughed. "You must learn to relax. Here, have some sherry and come and join us."

Beth took the glass and was about to follow Gabriel, when one of the servants told her that Tom Longeye was in the kitchen.

"Tom? Here? I do hope nothing has happened to the ship?" She told Gabriel to make her excuses and hurried to the kitchen.

Tom was sweating and distraught.

"Tom, what is it?"

He looked around the kitchen, cocked his head toward the two servant girls preparing food. "Let's step outside."

"Whatever is happening?" Beth asked once they were outdoors.

"There's trouble, lass. It's bubblin' and about to boil over. Hugo's caught the drift of it. Those voodoo drums mean death. The slaves on this island are going to break loose. I don't know when it's going to happen, but when it does, it's not going to be pretty. I'd say let's haul anchor."

"I've tried to tell the Mavannes that, but they don't seem to believe me." She put her hands on her hips and began to pace.

"These are their slaves, it's their problem. I suppose they'll know how to handle it. But, lass, they treat these poor savages worse than I've seen most anywhere. And all this talk about the revolution in France has given the slaves ideas."

"Then we will leave. I'd planned on staying another week, but there seems no point to that. Set in stores and we'll sail in two days." She could have an attorney work out any deal with Raleigh if necessary.

"We're ready to ship out now."

"Well, I can't just *go!*" Beth snapped. She was annoyed that her plans hadn't worked out, that she hadn't seen Raleigh, sale or not. No. She wasn't leaving without seeing him. "We'll sail in two days," she repeated.

"That might be too late."

"Really, Tom, if there were that much danger, surely the planters would be aware of it. It's not as if every slave on the island is just waiting to kill. Look at the Mavannes' servants. They're devoted to the family."

"Lass, believe me—"

"Tom, that is the way it will be." She made a cutting gesture with her hand. "We'll sail in two days. Now go inside and get yourself a bottle. I'll have them prepare a room for you and you can spend the night here."

Tom sighed, shook his head, but followed Beth inside.

After dinner, Beth was attempting to look engaged by Denise's recounting of Enid's latest exploits when Raleigh entered.

"What a surprise," Denise said, getting up to greet him. "What brings you here at this hour?"

Raleigh looked beyond Denise to Beth. She felt his gaze and her heart lurched. *Damn him to hell,* she thought, *will I ever cut loose of this passion?*

"I've come to speak to Madame DuBoise about the sale of Rondelle," he said. "Marie and I have decided to leave the island."

"No." Denise made a moue. "You certainly can't be considering going back to France?"

"We would most likely go to Florence. Marie's uncle has a villa there. She is his only heir." He looked at Beth. "We would like to leave as soon as possible, so the faster we can resolve this transaction, the better."

"Of course." Beth stood slowly. She forced a smile. "Let us go into the garden and talk."

She didn't meet Raleigh's eyes, and with a heavy heart walked out into the early evening darkness.

Raleigh took her hand. "Come," he said softly. "Let us walk a bit further. Denise's laughter cuts the air like a machete."

They walked in silence until the noise and lights from the house could no longer reach them. Then Raleigh stopped.

He looked down at Beth. Her hair seemed to shimmer in the full moon's light, and her clean soaped familiar scent unexpectedly quickened him. He wrestled inwardly with an anguished desire, looked away when he spoke.

"So you want to buy Rondelle?"

"I—I had considered it."

"A favorable offer and it's yours."

"Whatever its value. I'll have my attorney contact you. I sail for New York the day after tomorrow."

"And I for Florence in a month's time."

"Well then," she sighed, "that is that. Shall we use a handshake to confirm the transaction, or is my word good enough?"

Raleigh stared at her for a moment, then slipped his arm about her waist and drew her to him. "I want more than your word, more than your hand for good-bye."

"Raleigh—"

"I want you. And if I burn in hell for my desire, it will be no greater than the torment I endure now." He brought his lips down slowly upon hers, savoring the sweet, moist warmth of her unsuspecting mouth, her surprise, her resistance, her slow and wondrous surrender.

His hand moved slowly up from her waist and cupped her breast. Even beneath the thickness of the brocade he could feel the heat of her body, the firmness of her nipple pressing into his palm. His groin throbbed with hunger.

He knelt down and pulled her with him, his body aching for hers. "Beth, Beth," he moaned.

And silently, as if in answer to unspoken prayers, he felt her hand caress his thigh, reach up for his tumescence, press it lovingly.

A chill of ecstasy ran through Beth as she held him. Fully clothed, in a garden where they could be discovered at any moment, her desire was great.

"Yes," she whispered. "Yes. Now. If it be sin, then I shall join you in hell."

He began opening the buttons of her bodice. "And we will make love on hot embers for eternity." He kissed the cleft between her breasts. "And we shall—"

A piercing scream and muted shouts came from the house.

"Dear God, what's happened?" Beth said. A horrible fear began to scale her flesh.

Raleigh jumped to his feet. "I don't know. Come on. Hurry."

He started running toward the house. Beth followed. As they approached, she saw a group of people on the veranda. At first she thought they were in costumes, festooned with makeup. But as she got closer she saw that the costumes were their ravaged clothes.

Their makeup was blood.

Chapter 8

"What's happened?" Raleigh demanded.

"The slaves," Monsieur Cartine gasped. His eyes
were wide with fear, his face covered with blood from
a gaping slash on his forehead. "They've gone ber-
serk. They're killing babies, women, everyone!" He
was almost screaming as he spoke. "We must arm ourselves. Kill all the blacks before they get us."

"There's one of the murderers now!" someone
shouted. "Get him."

Vadi, the Mavannes' houseboy, stood stock-still.

"Wait," Gabriel said. "That's my—"

Before he could finish, Gabriel's friend Donald
Tremain had shot the boy.

"Good God," Gabriel cried. "This is madness. A
few renegade slaves doesn't mean—" He turned as a
lathered horse galloped into the yard.

Beth recognized the man as the overseer she had
seen that morning at Rondelle.

"Mr. Eckert! Mr. Eckert!" he shouted. "You've got
to come quickly. They're killing . . . burning the fields.
It's awful . . . awful."

"Dear God, Marie!" Raleigh turned to Beth. "Stay here. Get a gun and keep it with you. I'll be back as soon as I can with Marie."

Before Beth could say anything, he was gone.

"This is awful," Denise said. "I thought it was odd when I didn't see any of the servants around after dinner. They must be frightened by all this too. Oh, poor Vadi."

"You don't understand," Monsieur Cartine said. "It's all of them. They've got knives, guns. They want us all dead." His voice verged on hysteria.

"Come inside," Gabriel said. "We can use the house as a fortress. Denise, bring the children down here. Jacques is good with a gun. We'll need all the help we can get."

Everyone followed Gabriel into the living room. Denise got bandages for Monsieur Cartine and the Tremains, then went upstairs for the children.

Tom Longeye came into the room with his pistol drawn.

"Oh, Tom." Beth ran toward him. "You were right. It's happened."

"And damned if I have nothin' but this one pistol." He slammed his fist angrily into his palm. "All right. How many men and guns have we?"

Gabriel took count. "Six," he said, "including my boy, Jacques."

Tom gave a chilling laugh. "By rough estimation there are about one hundred thousand of your island blacks out for all the blood they can spill. Our best chance is to try and reach Cap Français. The ships are all armed and we can keep any number at bay while we move out."

Donald Tremain stepped forward. "Are you mad, man? Do you expect us to just leave our homes to these heathens?"

"Your homes ain't goin' to be left to anyone. And hangin' around here, ain't none of you going to even be alive to sweep up the ashes."

"Really, Mr. Longeye," Gabriel admonished. "I

tend to agree with Mr. Tremain. I fear you are being unnecessarily alarming. Surely you don't believe that we can't bring this under control?"

"I believe that unless we get out of here fast, we're all dead."

Screams came from outside. Someone was pounding on the door. Tremain raised his pistol.

Beth rushed to the window. "Wait," she cried. "It's a white woman out there."

Gabriel unlocked the door and a heavyset woman, half nude, her face caked with dirt and blood, shrieked unintelligibly and fell into his arms.

"My God," Gabriel murmured. "It's Madame Bescroft."

Beth went for some water. When she returned, Madame Bescroft had regained consciousness and was screaming again. Beyond calming, she ranted like a mad woman about a nightmare of rape and the most heinous carnage imaginable. Her eyes bulged and rolled as she spoke until she once more, mercifully, lost consciousness.

"Where is your gunpowder?" Tom asked.

"It's—" Gabriel's face whitened as he heard his wife's scream from upstairs. "My God!" He ran for the staircase with his rifle.

Denise stood on the top landing holding Enid by the hand. "Jacques is dead," she said, almost like a bewildered child. "They've . . . they've taken his . . . head." She covered her mouth with her hand, turned and retched.

"They must be in the house," Tom said.

Gabriel ran for Denise, brought her and Enid downstairs, then started up again, his rifle ready. No sooner had he reached the top step, than smoke began filling the room.

"Fire!" Monsieur Cartine shouted. He raced for the door.

"Wait!" Tom called, but too late. Monsieur Cartine flung open the door to the veranda and ran out.

There was silence for a moment, then a bloodcurdling scream. They all listened, horrified. Helpless.

"We can't stay in here and burn alive."

"If we run out now, we've no better chance than he had," Tom said, pointing to the veranda. "When the smoke gets a bit thicker, we've all got to make a run for it. We don't know how many are out there. Maybe two, maybe fifty. Our only chance is to try and get to the harbor."

"What about Madame Bescroft?" someone asked. "She's still unconscious."

Tom didn't answer. "We'll leave through the parlor. Follow me."

Someone screamed. "They're coming in!"

"Run for it!" Tom shouted.

Gabriel turned, raised his rifle. Beth grabbed Denise's arm and pulled her and Enid toward the parlor.

"But my husband," Denise said. "I have to wait."

Beth pulled her. "We can't wait. He'll be along soon. Come on."

"Mommy, mommy." Enid began to sob.

"Shhh. Honey. It will be all right," Beth said. "But we have to run. We have to run fast."

The parlor was dense with smoke. "Hold on to me," Beth commanded. She led the way to the door. She pushed it open and someone grabbed her hair. She screamed.

Suddenly she was being dragged across the ground. The pain and shock melded and numbed her. From nearby she heard Denise pleading: "Please, no . . . no, she's only a baby. No . . . don't do that to her." And Enid shrieked in terror.

Beth struggled futilely against the slave who held her. He slapped her. She screamed as he ripped the clothes from her. There was no stopping the assault. His dark sweat-moist body covered hers, pinning her helplessly. He rammed savagely inside her.

He'll kill me after this, she thought. *I have only minutes, maybe seconds to stay alive.* And in that instant she made up her mind to live. She had to reach her boot, to reach Billy Boy. Fighting back waves of nausea, she raised her legs until they encircled his back. *Seconds,* she thought. *Only seconds.* His movements accelerated and he released his hold on her hands. Slowly she brought her hand up so that she could reach the knife.

Her fingers closed around the handle and she carefully eased the weapon from its sheath. Bringing her hand down to her side, she held her breath. *Just a few moments more . . .*

At the instant of his release, she brought the knife up hard beneath his ribs. He grunted, brought his head up for a moment, then his body spasmed. He collapsed on top of her.

Heaving him off, Beth got unsteadily to her feet. Denise and Enid, where were they? There were gunshots all around . . . screams, shrill awful screams, and the house was totally engulfed in flames. She staggered forward and nearly tripped over the body of Mr. Cartine. His hand was still clutching his unfired pistol. She took it from him.

She walked toward the bushes stealthily. She could hear Enid sobbing, calling her mother. Two burly slaves stood over Denise's naked, motionless body. Without thinking, Beth raised her pistol and fired.

The taller black reeled forward and fell; the other turned and leapt for Beth. She screamed, started to run. Another shot rang out and when she looked back, her pursuer had fallen to the ground. Tom Longeye stood with legs apart, his pistol still smoking.

"Tom!" She ran toward him, tears of relief streaming down her cheeks.

"It's all right, lass. They seem to be—*arghhh . . .*" he staggered sideways, clutching his side.

"Tom!" Beth cried. She caught him before he fell, and only then did she see the gaping hole in his side.

"Take my gun and load it, girl," he gasped. "Go on."

She eased him to the ground and did as he said.

"It's yours now."

"But—"

"I'm not . . . not going to be needing it, girl."

"Tom, no." Beth saw the widening pool of blood and shut her eyes. Dear God, this wasn't happening.

"You can make it to the *Windsweeper*. It's—" He started to cough and blood trickled from the corner of his mouth.

"Don't try to speak." Beth cradled his head in her arms.

"Blast, lass, it's my last chance to." He coughed again. "Don't grieve. I've done my travelin'. And I do have a lot of loved ones waitin' for me. You—" his body heaved and he struggled for breath, "you remember all I've taught you. Keep that powder dry, Billy Boy sharp, and get on the ship and hoist anchor."

"I will, Tom. I will," Beth promised.

"And, lass . . ."

"Yes?"

"Keep away from slavin'. Dirty business. Men don't like bein' in chains and sooner or later they'll let you know it."

"I promise."

"Now get movin', girl. I love you and don't want to have to worry about you."

"But—"

"Damn, girl. I have enough on my mind with dying, don't I? Now get—" His body stiffened.

"Tom!"

He looked up at Beth and smiled. Then his head dropped lifelessly to the side, and he was gone.

There was a movement in the darkness. Beth grabbed the pistol and waited. Her heart pounded heavily, while behind her she could hear Enid's plaintive wailing. *Come on, come on. Where are you, you murdering devil's son?*

She saw a figure coming toward her and she raised the gun. *Just a little closer . . . a little closer.* Her trembling finger circled the trigger.

And then the figure called her name.

"Beth!"

Beth lowered the gun and stood up. "Raleigh? Raleigh, is that you?"

He stepped into the clearing. His shirt was torn, splattered with blood, and even in the darkness she could see the shock in his deep-hollowed eyes.

"Thank God you're alive!" She rushed forward and collapsed against him.

"I thank God for little this night," he said, his voice hollow and bitter as winter fruit.

"Marie?" Beth asked.

"She's dead. I should have been there. Maybe I could have—oh, God." He groaned and covered his face in his hands. "What they did to her. I . . . I didn't even know it was a human being when I found her."

"You mustn't think of that now. We have to get to the harbor. It's our only chance."

"For what? Life?" He started to laugh. "Life in all this?" He laughed again and Beth slapped him.

"Raleigh. Raleigh. I need you. Help me. We have to get to the ship."

"Mommy, mommy!" Enid wailed.

Beth turned and saw the child shaking her mother. She went to her and pulled her close. "Hush, child. We don't want them to come back."

"Mommy. Why doesn't mommy say anything?"

Beth bent down. Denise's eyes were closed, but her body was warm. Beth pressed her ear against Denise's chest.

"She's alive! Raleigh, quickly. We'll have to carry her."

Raleigh stood for a moment without moving. Then, as if a silent decision had been reached, he hurried forward and picked Denise up in his arms. "There are two horses in front. Can you ride with Enid?"

"Of course."

"We're going to be riding fast. Enid, you hang on to Miss Beth, do you understand? And don't say a word or cry out."

The girl nodded. "Will my mommy be all right?"

"I—I pray so. Now let's go."

"Wait," Beth said. "We should find the others, tell them to get horses and follow."

Raleigh stared at her. "Others? *There are no others.*"

The voyage back to New York aboard the *Windsweeper* was somber and unremittingly painful. Denise was barely coherent for the first week and went into an almost catatonic stupor for the second. Enid wept daily and screamed whenever Hugo appeared. The two other survivors they had managed to bring aboard, a German named Schultz and an English schoolboy named Hardy, who had been visiting the Tremains, merely paced the quarterdeck and stared at the sea.

Raleigh was unreachable.

Beth attempted to console him, but his private agony was beyond consolation. There was no doubt in Beth's mind that he blamed himself for Marie's death; that he felt if he had not been there, in the Mavannes' garden with Beth, he would have been able to save her. And nothing Beth could do or say seemed to help. Her very presence seemed to increase his guilt, and after the first week she tried to avoid him as much as possible. When he was ready, he would come to her.

The night before they reached New York, he did.

It was late, but the breeze was weak, and even on the water the air was close. Beth couldn't sleep and had left her cabin for a walk on the quarterdeck. She stood by the railing, staring at the ripply silver moonstripe in the water. Raleigh drew alongside. He said nothing, but for the first time since they'd left Saint Dominique Beth felt he was with her.

"It's difficult," he said. "She was an innocent and should not have died. I feel responsible."

"Raleigh, there was nothing you could do; nothing anyone could do."

"I did not have to come to the Mavannes' that night. But I wanted to see you."

"You couldn't have known what would happen."

"I realize that. But it was my need for you that took me away. She wanted to join me for the ride, but I discouraged her because I knew I wanted to be alone with you." He covered his eyes with his hand. "God, it was I who deserved to die."

"No one deserved to die," Beth said quietly. Tentatively she stroked his arm.

"You're wrong. I had deceived Marie from the start, because I knew that I had never stopped wanting you. I married her to forget you and made love to her to remember you. I loathed myself for the deception and thought that time would render it to truth." He gave an empty laugh. "Like thinking time could turn clay into gold."

"Raleigh, you must stop this. Grieve yes, but not die yourself. You must learn to live again."

He looked down at her upturned face, took her in his arms and kissed her hard, urgently.

Beth had been wanting his kiss for days, but not this way. "Raleigh, wait. You—"

"No. Now."

Before she could protest further, he picked her up and carried her to her cabin.

Once inside, he locked the door and kissed her again, roughly, unpleasantly, desperately.

"Raleigh, this isn't what you—" Before she could finish he had brought her to the bed and was unbuckling his belt.

In moments he was on top of her, his hands touching but not caressing her, his mouth wanting but not finding her. There was need but no love, and soon it was obvious that there was not even desire.

Raleigh stood, walked to the window and stared out. Beth came up behind him.

"It's all right," she whispered. "Everything takes time to heal. We'll work it out."

"I won't be staying in New York," she said without looking at her.

"I don't understand." She felt the knot tighten inside her, felt her world slipping.

"I'll be sailing out as soon as I can."

"For where? For how long?"

"Anywhere. I don't care how long." He looked at her, his eyes narrowed and pained. "She's dead and I killed her."

Beth knew the words he didn't speak, read the accusation in his eyes: *And you're alive!*

When they reached New York, Raleigh was off the ship before she awoke.

He had left no message.

Book Three

"Yes. We were ... cousins."

Chapter 1

"Really, Peter, I insist that you, Laura, and the children come to Wildwillow with me next week," Beth said. "The fever has already started. Dr. Martin said he treated eighteen cases last week. It's foolish to jeopardize yourselves unnecessarily."

Peter stood on the balcony looking out at the river. "I have my job here, not up in Hudson." He turned and smiled. God, she was lovely.

Ever since Beth had returned from Saint Dominique three years ago, Peter had felt his attraction for her grow. What made it worse—or perhaps what saved things—was that she thought of him only as a good friend, a friend whom she could confide in, never realizing that as she detailed intimacies and her silent longings for another man, she scored him deeply.

How long, he wondered, would she keep that candle aflame for Eckert? How long, too, could his own fires smolder before they ignited?

"Couldn't you just leave the paper for a while?"

"You know I can't. But it would put my mind at ease getting Laura and the boys away from here. It's very kind of you."

"Kindness is not what motivates me. Selfishness is more like it. I'll miss your company up there. I always do."

"I can join you all for a few weeks in August."

"It's not the same. No one in Hudson talks to me the way you do. At least you believe I have a brain under my bonnet, not just curls." She picked up a book from the table. "I want you to read this Mary Wollstonecraft book. It's just been published in Philadelphia."

Peter took it from her. *"A Vindication of the Rights of Women?"*

"It's time, don't you think, that half the population got the recognition it deserved? I'm quite excited about it."

"Next thing I know you'll be wearing those boat britches of yours in public."

"You're the only person outside of my crew who knows about those. Besides, you don't expect me to climb a rigging in skirts, now do you?"

"Ladies, dear heart, don't climb riggings at all," Peter pointed out.

"True." She put her hands on his shoulders, wrinkled her nose at him. "But I've never been much of a lady."

Peter remained perfectly straight, his arms rigid at his sides. Being alone with her had become increasingly difficult. She looked more beautiful than ever these days, her chestnut hair worn full, sideswept with thick curls that fell past her shoulders and delicate tendrils wisping provocatively about her face. Her waist, corseted, was barely wider than a hand's clasp.

He tried not to compare her with Laura, but that, too, was difficult. In the past two years, after Hiram's birth actually, Laura had taken to sweets and had rounded considerably. She was as loving and attentive a wife as any man could want, excellent with the children, and of a good inquisitive mind. All of which only upset him more about his feelings for Beth.

"I must be going," he said. "Laura will wonder what's happened to me. She worries these days."

"Then Wildwillow will do wonders for her. At least she won't have to be concerned about the boys coming down with the fever."

"You realize, of course, that there is a totally odious part of me that will resent your leaving with Laura. I've come to consider you both my women, and the prospect of being left without either is distressing."

Beth tilted her head provocatively. "Oh, really? Both your women, eh?" She sauntered forward, smiling. "I daresay that's a thought one wouldn't suspect entering the mind of the right proper Peter Avery, journalist." She chucked his chin.

Peter looked away. "Don't do that," he said.

"Do what?"

"You know very well what. I'm not oak."

"I'm sorry." She lowered her head. What had gotten into her? She'd been flirting with Peter for the past several months, and they both were aware of it. How could she? Raleigh would return to her. She knew it. He'd promised, hadn't he?

Immediately after they'd returned from Saint Dominique, Raleigh had sailed for England. He'd written to her from there, declaring his love. He was signing on an American brig headed for Africa, he said, to heal his wounds, and would return by Christmas. (*Don't count the days, for I shall make them all up to you in kisses,* he'd written.) That was the last she or anyone had heard from him.

After two years, she'd been ready to accept that he was dead. But then the news came that the Barbary corsairs, aware that American ships carried no real naval protection, had captured dozens of vessels and taken hundreds of seamen prisoners. Raleigh's ship was among them. She told herself it was only a matter of time before he returned to her—but some days that time was almost too much to bear. Wildwillow would do her good. Would do everyone good.

"I'd better leave," Peter said.

"You'll let me know about Laura and the children?"

"I'm sure the answer will be yes. They can visit my mother in Kingston on the way." He picked up his hat.

"Peter?"

"Yes?"

"I'm . . . sorry about before." She touched his arm gently. "It won't happen again."

He leaned on his cane, studied her. Then slowly he said, "Yes, it will."

Sailing upriver in the fresh June sun was always exciting for Beth. Whenever the ship passed Newburgh, she felt as if she were entering a new world. The mountains grew higher and darker, rich with velvety black conifers, and the air was sweet with burgeoning flowers. And somewhere in that world, she would imagine, a golden-haired eleven-year-old girl running barefoot and happy through a stream. Suzannah.

Sometimes, if they docked in Poughkeepsie or Kingston, Beth would find herself staring into the crowds on the quay, searching each young face for traces of her own. Searching for Suzannah. *When I find you, I'll make up for all the years apart,* she would promise silently. And then, as always, she would pray.

The countless detectives she'd hired had come up with nothing, but her dream of locating her golden child, and Peter's comforting presence, were what had kept her going without Raleigh. Whether he was in an Algerian dungeon or chained to the thwarts of one of the dey's galleys, or even alive, was still unknown. But as long as there was hope, she'd continue to believe he would return.

Only these last few weeks had her conviction wavered. She'd written President Washington herself, demanding that the government do something about the situation, but received only the satisfaction of a personal note from the President's secretary saying that a law had been passed authorizing the building of six warships which, it was hoped, would vanquish the corsairs and liberate the seamen. The ships would be three years in building. Nothing more could be done.

Staying afloat for so long, clutching at straws, took its toll. Even though some days she would throw herself into work, checking books and cargos, overseeing repairs, there were others when she'd fall into a deep depression and close her doors to everyone but Peter.

She'd discouraged suitors for so long that she'd acquired the nickname "Ice Maiden." Sometimes, when she sat alone, hugging herself, aware of her body crying out for love, the appellation made her laugh tears.

Only Peter was really aware of her loneliness; and of all the men she knew besides Raleigh, Peter was the only one who could assuage it.

But he was married and Laura was a good friend. *That's all there is to it,* Beth told herself.

She knew there was more, and every so often it aroused and frightened her.

It would be good to stay at Wildwillow. Good for everyone. The only bad part about it, as usual, would be Philip.

Philip DuBoise was on the portico when the carriage pulled into the drive. The months since she'd last visited had been rude to him. His skin was pale, his eyes underlined with dark circles of wine-full nights, and he'd developed an indolent paunch. He had come to think of Wildwillow as his own, and it was obvious he resented Beth's presence—just as it was obvious that he still coveted her body.

Beth introduced him to Laura and her sons, and, while the Averys were getting settled, suffered his mildly vulgar recounting of several purportedly amusing anecdotes, related, no doubt, with a hope of titillation. She wondered if she would be able to tolerate his presence for three months.

Surprisingly, at dinner that evening, mellowed by wine, he was perversely pleasant. In fact, before retiring, Laura commented that she found him "charming," an adjective Beth would have wagered could never be applied to Philip.

When they were alone, though, whatever elements had charmed Laura vanished.

"Well, Ice Maiden, how have things been between your frigid thighs?" He poured himself another glass of wine.

"Don't you ever change, Philip? Aren't you bored by your own foulness yet?" Beth started for the door.

"Oh, come now. I was only joking. That is what they call you, though, did you know that?"

"So I've heard," Beth said tiredly.

"Still waiting for your Captain Eckert, right?" He drained his glass and poured another. "Seems to me like you're waiting for Neptune to spit him back, and that's a long wait."

"I don't care to discuss Captain Eckert with you, or much else for that matter."

"You must be getting hungry though, eh? They might call you Ice Maiden down in New York, but I used to hear you with my uncle. You were about as frosty as—"

Beth slapped him. "Listen, Philip, and listen well. I own this house and I own DuBoise shipping. It is only out of deference to your uncle that I keep you on and allow you to live here. Mind your manners and keep your place, or else I swear you'll be picking scraps for the rest of your days."

"No need to get testy, *auntie*."

"Keep out of my way while I'm here. Just keep out of my way."

Philip bowed. "I'll do my best, mum. Though there will be times when we'll have to put on a slightly more cohesive appearance. Next week, for instance."

"Next week? What's that supposed to mean?"

"You told me to purchase two more ships for the line, didn't you? Well, we'll be closing on the *Deliverance* next Wednesday when the DeWitts arrive."

"The DeWitts? Coming here?" Beth felt a lurch inside her, and then a scrambling of emotions.

"The whole family's sailing upriver for holiday. I couldn't very well *not* extend hospitality, could I?" Philip looked annoyed.

"The whole family?"

"I don't believe it's very large," he said sarcastically. "You needn't fear being put out of your bed. My, but you do look upset."

Beth shrugged. "It's nothing. James DeWitt is unpleasant after indulging in spirits."

Philip scratched his chin thoughtfully, smiled. "Vaguely I remember some sort of altercation when my uncle was alive. Nonetheless that's gone under the bridge, and I doubt if the silly sot even recalls the incident. I've been dealing with him on various things for several years now. Besides, I hear that when his wife is around he's the very pillar of temperance."

"I'm not surprised," Beth muttered.

"You know the woman?" Philip asked.

"In a manner of speaking."

"What's that supposed to mean?"

"Nothing. Nothing at all." Beth excused herself and retired to her room. So, after all these years, she would once again come face to face with Regina DeWitt and the child she had bought from Beth's womb.

It would be a long week until Wednesday.

Across the ocean, in a dark and fetid, dirt-floored cell, Raleigh Eckert tried to figure out what month it was. When he had arrived at the prison, he had marked off the days and weeks on the damp stone wall. But after a while, the lines no longer made sense. How long had it been? How long would it be? He reached inside his tattered shirt and fingered the paper he'd hidden there. The guard had gotten it for him in exchange for a ring worth several hundred dollars. The ring was worthless to Raleigh, but the paper, and the promise from the guard that he would send the letter to America, was worth everything.

He'd had the paper several days now and still had not written a word. There was so much he wanted to say, yet so much he couldn't. How was he to write to someone he loved of the vile horrors he had witnessed? Could he put to paper accounts of comrades meeting their death by sword or starvation? Describe the nerve-stretching boredom of endless days in a dank, windowless cell where spiders, a variety of multilegged insects, and an occasional rat were the only diversion? Was there any way he could relate the sordid fiasco of the whores' visits? The stale bread and rank meat that floated like jetsam in the broth that sustained him? No. He could say none of it. It would only give her pain, and he had already inflicted enough of that.

In the end, he wrote only two sentences:

I write you from the bowels of hell to declare my love for eternity. I live only to return to your heart.

He gave the guard the letter, and, for weeks afterward, drifted to sleep imagining Beth pressing the missive to her breast.

He would not have rested as comfortably had he known the letter never left Algiers.

The morning the DeWitts were expected, Beth awoke early, put on her boy's britches and cap, and sneaked out to the stable. She had Tyro saddle up the fastest horse. It was a beautiful black gelding, champing at the bit as he came from his stall. *He wants to run as much as I do,* Beth thought, *but neither of us is free to go where we'd like.* She rode at a gallop across the damp fields and through the woods, still smoked with morning mist, reveling in the sweet wind that stole her breath, relaxing in the thoughtless quiet of her mind. She wished the ride could go on forever, but both she and the horse tired by midmorning. There was never an easy way to run from yourself. She slipped back into the house through the servants' entrance and was bathed, dressed and properly resigned to greeting her guests as the mistress of Wildwillow when they arrived.

She wasn't really prepared for Adrianne.

When the carriage pulled up to the entrance, the girl was the first to step out. She was tall with jet black curls, and quite mature for her eleven years, looking astonishingly more a young lady than Beth would have imagined. Then again, Beth herself had reached bleeding age at nine, as had her mother before her. Still it was a shock to see the girl so womanly.

Adrianne surveyed the house with a glance as arrogant and superior as any her "mother" could muster. Regina had done a good job. There were as many redeeming features in the girl as there were in her "parents."

Regina and James DeWitt followed their daughter from the carriage and Beth joined Philip to greet them.

Philip made the introductions. Beth thought she saw a quizzical flicker in Regina's face when their eyes met, but it was probably her imagination. The years of motherhood had made little alteration in the woman. She was, in her thirties, as she'd been in her twenties—beautiful, treacherous, and cold-blooded as a copperhead. How odd it was, Beth thought, to meet again the woman who had totally altered so many lives.

"I've looked forward to meeting you," Regina said. "Your name and remarkable reputation seem to come up at every dinner party we have lately." She said the words sweetly, but it was clear to Beth that she was annoyed at anyone besides herself and daughter getting such attention.

"Even James has been curious about you," she

went on, "and for my husband to be interested in anything outside of spirits, ships, and gaming tables is truly remarkable. James?"

James DeWitt stepped forward and kissed Beth's proffered hand. If he remembered her, he chose not to show it. "A pleasure indeed, Madame DuBoise. I knew your late husband. Admirable man, admirable."

He thought you a toad, Beth said silently, while she thanked him for the compliment.

"And this," James said, "is our daughter, Adrianne. She's just returned from London."

Adrianne curtsied reluctantly. "Most pleased to meet you," she said politely.

Her voice startled Beth. Though it was cultured and held traces of recent British schooling, there was something in the timbre that was strongly reminiscent of Beth's own. What also startled her was the child's strong resemblance to her real father, and her faint but unnervingly discernible resemblance to Beth herself.

Adrianne narrowed her eyes and studied Beth quite intently, until Regina poked her gently in the back. Beth ushered them inside, made further introductions to the Averys, and then excused herself as the servants showed the DeWitts to their rooms.

Dinner that evening began awkwardly, with Adrianne making a scene about being served with the children. Regina had tried reasoning with her, telling her that she was in fact only eleven and still a child, to which Adrianne had retorted that she was more of an adult than most of the "ninnies" who dined at Clearview, which resulted in a slap from Regina and a tearful dinnerless exit from Adrianne.

"She's at a difficult age," Regina told Beth offhandedly, obviously clamping on a fury.

And one that will follow her to her grave, Beth thought. "I see." She kept her face properly somber.

The remainder of the evening was uneventful until Laura, more talkative than usual, turned to Regina and said, "Difficult as your daughter is, she's quite beautiful. In fact, she looks a little like Beth, don't you think?"

Beth felt her own face drain of color as she watched Regina bristle.

"Wouldn't that be lovely if she did?" Regina said tightly. "Though I'm afraid she's consigned to favoring me."

"Oh, I can see where she's like you," Laura said, blithely prattling on, sipping more wine, "but there's something about her mouth and eyes—"

"Really, Laura," Beth interrupted, laughing. "Madame DeWitt's daughter is practically her mirror image. I think you've imbibed a bit too freely."

Laura agreed that perhaps she had and soon after took her leave.

Philip and James went into the parlor, leaving Regina and Beth alone. The two women sat in silence quite a while before Regina spoke.

"There *is* a resemblance between you and my daughter," she said coldly.

Beth laughed uncomfortably. "I'm flattered that you think so, but I can't see it."

"Talbot," Regina said, spitting the name. "That's who you are, isn't it? Beth Talbot." Her eyes flashed angrily, as if she'd been betrayed.

Pretense was pointless. Beth raised her head, returned Regina's icy stare. "Yes, Talbot was my name."

"But you were supposed—"

"Supposed to leave the country. You had it all planned, didn't you? Neatly planned. You were going to toss us all to the mob because you wanted us out of the way. Meanwhile I lost my father, my brother, and . . . and more."

Regina said nothing, her back stiffened.

"Well, it's true, isn't it?"

Regina ignored the question. "James doesn't know," she said. "He must never find out the truth about Adrianne. It would destroy both of them."

"I've no intention of saying anything. Adrianne is your daughter. She always has been."

"James had considered spending another day here. I think it best that we leave tomorrow."

"As you wish."

Regina stared at Beth. "Well, you've come a long way for a tenant-farmer's daughter, I'll give you that."

"Spare me your benevolence." Beth stood and without a backward glance left the room.

She didn't see Regina pick up a wine glass and hurl it savagely to the floor.

The following day, after the DeWitts had departed, Beth wrote a long letter to Peter detailing what had happened. The whole matter upset her more than she cared to admit, and somehow, just telling Peter about it made it easier for her to reconcile. Before she'd finished, though, there was a great commotion in the hall, and she dashed out to see what had happened. As it turned out, it was nothing more than little Hiram Avery swallowing a butterfly, but by the time the story was drawn out of his brothers, dinner was nearly ready and she'd forgotten about her letter.

When she returned to her room that evening the letter was gone.

She searched under the bed, bureaus, chairs, anywhere it could have fallen or blown. She never considered that someone might have taken it.

Philip knocked on her door at midnight.

She pulled on her dressing gown and let him in. He was drunk, his jacket was askew. Her letter to Peter was clutched in his hand.

"Well, well, well." He slurred his words, his head lolling to the side as he shook the paper in front of her. "Guess what I have here?"

Beth reached for it, but he held it out of reach. "Uh-uh-uh. It's not polite to grab. Besides I need this tender little missive. It's going to get me all the sweet things I've always wanted." He staggered to a chair and slumped into it. "So, your bastard daughter is DeWitt's brat. If that isn't the joke of all."

"If you think I'm going to pay you money to protect the DeWitts, you'll have to think again. That's their problem. And make sure they pay you plenty, because you'll be through with DuBoise shipping forever."

"Not so fast, *auntie*." Philip held up his hand. "I may be drunk, but I'm no fool. I have no intention of dragging the DeWitts into this at all. It's your dear friends, the Averys, that I know you'll protect. How do you think that sweet Mrs. Avery will react when she learns that her dear husband sired a child with you?" He clicked his tongue. "Such a scandal. Those poor little boys."

"It wasn't Peter's child."

Philip raised his brows. "Oh, no? Dear me, it certainly sounds as if it were. Nonetheless, once his wife sees this letter I doubt if she'll believe that it wasn't." He smiled. "In any event, there will be a good deal of damage done."

"You're disgusting."

"Enterprising, dear auntie. I'm just protecting my future."

"What do you want?" she asked stonily.

"A lot, but I'll start with money. Oh, and I'm tired of staying here in Hudson all the time. You do have room for me in that lovely house of yours in New York, now don't you . . . ?"

attentions toward her had already upset Laura enough.
Besides, she had involved him once before in a con-

Chapter 2

"You'll not bring your foul friends here again," Beth shouted.

Philip lit a cigar and put his feet up on the Hepplewhite table. "Temper, temper, auntie. If you recall, you are in no position to issue ultimatums. Your dainty letter is safely ensconced in the bank, where I alone can reach it."

"What I witnessed when I returned last night was enough to sicken me. Alley cats have more morals, swine more restraint, than those filthy degenerates you brought in."

It had been three months since Philip had taken up residence in the house on Nassau Street and Beth's nerves and patience had been stretched to breaking. She'd seen little of Peter, due as much to his support of Jefferson's Republicans and Citizen Genet (which, as a shipowner, enraged her since British capital was indispensable for profitable trade) as to Philip's presence. She had made up her mind early on not to involve Peter in the matter, having realized that his attentions toward her had already upset Laura enough. Besides, she had involved him once long ago in a matter that wasn't his concern, and she'd never forgiven herself for the outcome.

"Really, auntie, I wish you wouldn't speak so rudely about my friends." He stood and crossed to her. "In fact, I'd like very much for you and I to be friends too." With that he grabbed her about the waist and pulled her body tight against his.

"Let go of me!" She brought her heel down hard on his instep.

"Ow!" Philip flung her backward and she fell onto the couch. "You dirty little—" He came forward menacingly. "You're going to pay for that." He reached out quickly, grabbed her breast and squeezed it brutally.

Beth bit his arm.

He screamed and backed away, cursing.

She ran to the desk and pulled out Tom Longeye's pistol. She aimed it at Philip.

"Get out," she said. "Get out and don't come back."

"I'll get out, all right. But tomorrow I'm collecting your billet-doux from the bank and paying a call on that sweet Mrs. Avery. She's such a nice woman. And the boys are—"

"Get out!" Beth shrieked, her hands trembling as they held the gun.

Philip shrugged, snuffed his cigar. Straightening his jacket he went to the door. "By the way," he said, his hand on the knob, "if you change your mind—it'll be too late."

When he was gone, Beth sat down and found herself shaking. She rang for one of the servants, told him to go to the *Evening Post* office and fetch Mr. Avery at once. And to tell him that it was a matter of utmost importance.

"But why, Beth? Why didn't you tell me right away? I could have made Laura understand." Peter's face was taut and troubled, but he held her hands gently.

"She resents me, Peter. I've sensed her jealousy from the first time we met. The letter would only confirm her worst fears and destroy your marriage. I ruined your life once already." She lowered her head. "And now I'm going to do it again."

"Shhh." Peter cradled her in his arms. "I'll speak to Laura tonight. I'll explain." He stroked her hair, the tips of his fingers just barely touching her face, sending unbidden sparks of desire through him.

Beth looked up into his eyes, and something stirred inside her, something that had lain dormant since Raleigh had gone. It was a need, a longing that seemed to intensify with each passing second. And there was no doubt in her mind that Peter felt it too.

"It's wrong," she said, "we can't."

"I know. But we will."

"Peter?" Her voice was quizzical, her eyes almost frightened.

He cupped her face in his hands. "It seems as if I've waited for this moment all my life." He kissed her softly. "Come." He took her hand and guided her to the bedroom.

They made love for a long time, gently, shamelessly. Peter adored her body with his eyes, his hands, his mouth, until she felt as if she'd melted. Everything she had pent up was released, sated. Everything he had dreamed was fulfilled.

Finally, exhausted, they lay wrapped in each other's arms in a darkened room that hid their sin, made their knowledge of it easier to bear.

"Peter?"

"I love you, Beth."

"Don't say that." She turned away.

"It's the truth. I've loved you as far back as I can remember."

"Peter, don't."

"Don't what? Don't tell you what I can't hide, what you can plainly see?"

"Peter, you're a married man, and I—I'm still in love with Raleigh."

There was silence. Then he said simply, "I see."

"Do you? Oh, Peter, you don't see at all. What just happened between us *had* to happen. I needed you and reached out for you and you were there. I don't want it to change anything between us, except perhaps bring us even closer together, as friends. Do you understand?"

"I understand. In one way it saddens me, but in another . . ." His voice trailed off and his hand found hers, clasped it.

"Friends, Peter?"

"Friends."

Later that night, after Peter had gone, Beth had difficulty falling asleep. Somewhere around two A.M. she got up to pour herself a glass of wine. As she started downstairs, she heard someone knocking at the front entrance. Philip? Would he have the gall to return?

Wrapping her robe more tightly about her, she went to see who it was. She was quite surprised to be confronted by two constables.

"Madame DuBoise?"

"Yes."

"I'm afraid we have some bad news for you about your nephew, Philip DuBoise. May we come in?"

Bad news about Philip? What in heaven's name could . . . "Yes, of course." She ushered the two men into the parlor.

"Well, you see," said the tall one, coughing uneasily into his hand, "he's, um, dead."

"Philip? Dead? But how—?" It took Beth a moment for the words to sink in.

"Well, ma'am," said the other, "he's been murdered."

"Dear God!" Beth gasped. "How did it happen?"

The tall constable looked at the other, and the other shuffled his feet. Finally the shorter one spoke.

"A lady of the evening cut 'im, ma'am."

"I beg your pardon?"

"He was stabbed to death by a prostitute in a club

on Kruger's Wharf. We've got the harlot in custody, if it's any consolation. And enough witnesses to make sure she'll hang."

Beth turned away. "Please excuse me. It's a shock." She walked across the room trying to push away the question in her mind: What unspeakable act had he tried to foster on the woman to goad her to killing?

She thanked the constables and told them she would make arrangements for the body in the morning. When they'd gone, she surprised herself by crying. She wasn't sure whether they were tears of sadness or relief.

The following day she went to the bank. As next of kin, reclaiming the letter was merely a matter of a few forms. It was ironic that it was so simple. She read the letter once, then burned it. It gave off an unpleasant odor as it turned to ash.

She had Philip's body sent up to Hudson for burial. After the funeral, she stayed on at Wildwillow. She planned to spend several months, thinking it best not to see Peter for a while, but his unexpected letter a few weeks later changed all that.

12 December 1794

My dearest Beth,

I had promised myself that I would not write to you, but as you see I have broken my own word. Though I miss you deeply, as do Laura and the boys, who ask for you often, something other than your absence has prompted this quill to paper. Your brothers Ansel and John are in New York! In covering a story on gambling for the Post *two days ago, I found myself at a gaming club on South Street. And who should be there dealing a deck? None other than your brother Ansel. I recognized him instantly, having long ago committed his surly countenance to that sector of memory that preserves hatreds, loathings, and small piques, but, and fortunately I suppose, he did not recognize me. This I suspect was due in large part to a healthy inebriation. When I questioned the owner about him, I was told that he had arrived just recently and was living above the club with his brother, an eighteen-year-old lad who worked odd nights in the kitchen. Were just Ansel alone in New York, I would certainly have held the news until your return. But knowing your feelings for John and not knowing how long either of them will be around (gaming being the chancy business it is), I thought it best to let you know at once.*

I realize this is a letter of mixed tidings and hope you bear me no ill for imparting them.

Your loving friend,

Peter

Two hours later she was aboard a coach and headed for New York.

Chapter 3

"You can't go there alone," Peter said sternly.

Beth continued tying her bonnet. "Hugo will drive me. If there's any problem, I'm sure I can call on him."

"But he won't be inside the club with you. There are all sorts of strange types there."

Beth sighed. "Peter. I've taken care of myself for many years now, and I have been in far worse places than Kahill's gaming club. Besides it's early in the evening."

"But, Beth, you're known in New York. Your carriage is recognizable. People will wonder—"

"I don't give a damn what people wonder," Beth said sharply. "And I'm surprised to hear that you do."

Peter slapped his forehead. "Blast you, Beth. You know that's not what I'm getting at. Or maybe you don't. I'm just thinking about Ansel. He's treacherous, and as soon as he finds out you have money and status, he'll find some way to weasel in on it. Mark my words. He'll use you until he gets what he wants, and then he'll try to destroy you."

Beth felt herself growing defensive, not of Ansel but of her own motives for wanting to see him. Motives that she knew it best not to impart to Peter.

"Thank you for your advice," she said coolly, "but no matter what's right, I'm going to handle this my way."

Peter shook his head, smiled. "Do you know any other?"

The Kahill Club was located in a rather ordinary-looking graystone building on the river side of South Street. The neighborhood had come into some repute a few years back when Madame Leila opened her fancy bordello, which, it was rumored, boasted girls from the four corners of the world. Beth wondered if the expensive carriages that lined the street were for Madame Leila's or the Kahill Club. Probably the former, but at least Beth's own wouldn't look out of place.

She told Hugo not to worry, and marched, head high, to the entrance of the Kahill Club.

She'd prepared herself, or thought she had, for any kind of reception. As it turned out, she was taken totally by surprise. Behind the dapper well-dressed proprietor, who opened the door and greeted her with mild suspicion, stood a tall, blond-haired giant of a man. He stared at her, let his jaw drop, then came around, put his hands on her waist and hoisted her in the air.

"Damn me and damn me again if it ain't Beth!"

"Ernst!" Beth cried. "Ernst. It's you."

"And it wouldn't be, or rather I wouldn't be, had it not been for you getting to DuBoise."

Beth hadn't seen Ernst since before that fateful day when she'd set out to steal money for his release from prison. The day she'd met Seth. The day that had, for all intents and purposes, changed her life.

The proprietor looked enormously distressed by their reunion. Ladies were certainly not patrons of Kahill's gaming club, and other sorts of women were discouraged, unless accompanied by a gentleman. Though the woman who'd just entered looked like a lady, her friendship with Ernst, the bouncer, seemed to belie it. He would have to ask her to leave.

"Madam, I'm afraid that—"

"Mr. Kahill, sir," Ernst said, "this lady is Madame DuBoise." He said it proudly, and with a hint of superiority at being able to make the introduction.

"The shipowner?" Kahill asked, coloring slightly. He was a man who held high stock in recognizing the right people and did not enjoy being caught ignorant.

Beth nodded.

Kahill bowed. He was not unfamiliar with the widow DuBoise's name or reputation. The tales of her beauty had not been exaggerated, but for the Ice Maiden to appear at a gaming club, ah, that was indeed peculiar. And to have a friendship with a brute like Ernst . . . Perhaps the Ice Maiden's tastes in lovers did not run to gentlemen? If that were the case, even Nevin Kahill could forsake propriety for an evening.

"Has madam come to try her luck at the tables?" Kahill asked.

"I'm looking for one of your employees. Ansel Talbot."

Ernst frowned. Kahill flashed him a warning look. Whatever made a woman like Madame DuBoise happy would be good for the club. "Why, yes," Kahill said, "he's here. I'll have someone relieve him and I'll send him right out. You can wait in my office if you'd like."

"Ernst, show Madame DuBoise into my office."

Ernst nodded. When Kahill moved away, he took Beth by the arm and guided her down a hall to a small but opulently decorated room.

"What are you wanting with Talbot?" he asked. "He's a bad one."

Beth removed her gloves. "He's my brother."

"Your brother!"

"It's too long a story, Ernst. We were separated many years ago. Were it only Ansel, believe me, I'd not be here. But I've learned that my other brother is with him. And it's John I've come for."

"You've done right. He's a nice lad, and I hate to see the way Ansel treats him." He glanced toward the door. "They're coming now. I'll leave. Remember, though, I'm here and at your calling. I know what you did for me, and Ernst doesn't forget. Ever." He took her hand and kissed it awkwardly. "God bless," he whispered, then left.

Beth stiffened as Nevin Kahill entered the room with Ansel behind him. He'd grown thicker. His shoulders were broad, arrogant, and there was a belligerence in the thrust of his chest. His eyes had dark circles beneath them, and his obsidian hair was greased to a snakelike sheen. He squinted for a moment at Beth, then suddenly his eyes widened in recognition.

"Well, kiss my bootstraps if it ain't my baby sister." A grin spread across his face. He licked his teeth and came toward her. "If this ain't the coincidence to end them all. You're looking right fancy." He stared at her appraisingly. "Right fancy." His smile broadened. "You must be getting by all right."

"Hello, Ansel."

Nevin Kahill coughed. "I'll leave you two to say your greetings. When you're through, Talbot, I'll expect you back at the table." He bowed to Beth. "A pleasure meeting you, ma'am."

Nevin Kahill left. Ansel nodded and walked around Beth. "Kahill was right. You sure are a fancy lady."

"How's Pa?" Beth asked coldly, ignoring his glances.

"Dead. Got hisself shot in bed with a lady. A fancy lady, like you."

Beth listened, felt nothing. Her father had died so long ago for her that whatever his real end was didn't matter. "And John?" she asked.

"Why, he's fine. He's here with me, doin' odd jobs for Kahill. Come on. I'll take you upstairs to see him."

"Wait. Before we go, I want to settle something with you. Private."

Ansel leaned back against the wall, crossed his legs. "Oh?"

"Two things. The first is I want to take John to live with me, if he'll come."

Ansel laughed. "He's all grown now. Eighteen. He don't need a mother, unless of course it's somethin' else you're thinking of being for him."

She flashed hatred at him. He hadn't changed. He was as vile as ever. And no doubt, as untrustworthy.

He reached out and flicked the fabric of her skirt with his finger. "Looks like you have someone paying well for your pretty little smile, eh?" He laughed again.

Beth moved back, didn't answer. "So it will be all right if I take John?"

"Hell, it will be a pleasure. He's always gettin' preachy about my ways anyway. Maybe if he lives with you he'll start gettin' interested in girls. He's shyer than any virgin I ever met."

"Good, then that's settled." She pulled her gloves on nervously. "The second thing is Suzannah."

"Suzannah?" Ansel looked bewildered.

"My baby," Beth said icily. "The one you stole. I want to know where she is. I want her back."

"You're crazy. Besides, I wouldn't know where to find her—"

Beth opened her purse, took out a wad of bills, slapped them into Ansel's hand. "That's one hundred dollars. I want Suzannah. Tell me where I can find her and there will be more money for you."

Ansel stroked his chin. "Well, well, well. This certainly changes things. I suppose I can trace her down."

"Name your price."

"My, but you must have a nice gentleman stashed away."

"I said name your price."

"How about a thousand?"

"Done. I'll have five hundred delivered to you tomorrow, and you'll get the other five hundred when I have Suzannah. But there's not a word to be said to anyone about who she is or why I'm searching for her. Do you understand?"

"Dear sister, for a thousand dollars I can seal my lip tighter than a tomb."

"Good. Now lead me to John."

When they got upstairs, Beth stopped outside the door. "I'd rather see him alone."

"Whatever you say."

She took a card from her purse on which she had written her name and address and gave it to Ansel. "Contact me when you find her, and not before."

"I don't like taking orders," Ansel said.

"You like money, though, so you'll do as I say."

In the darkness of the hall, Beth did not see the smile that played about Ansel's lips. Oh, he liked money all right. And as long as it was clear that his sister had it, he would find a way to get his share. Meanwhile, there was no point in upsetting her. Besides, the future suddenly looked very bright.

"So right you are, sister," he said. "So right you are." And he left her, laughing as he went down the stairs.

Beth knocked on the door. A sleepy "Come in!" was called from behind it.

The room was dark except for a single weak candle on the table in the corner. A tall, slender, and shirtless young man with longish blond hair was stretched on a bed next to the wall. Had Beth not known it was her brother, she would never have recognized him. The last time she'd seen him, *she* was four years younger than *he* was now.

"John?" she said hesitantly.

He bolted instantly to a sitting position. "Y-yes, ma'am?" He grabbed frantically for his shirt, stood hurriedly and pulled it on.

"John. I'm your sister, Beth. Do you remember me?"

"Beth? Is that really you?" He stepped toward her, staring at her face. "I—I remember. It is you. It really is you!"

"Oh, John." Beth threw her arms around him and hugged him. He stood awkwardly for a moment, and then he hugged her back. Tightly.

"How did you find us? How did you——?"

She put her fingers to his lips. "Hush. I'll explain it all. Just gather your clothes. You're coming with me."

"With you? I don't understand."

"It's all right. I've spoken to Ansel."

"But I have a job here. I make six dollars a week."

"How much do you know about ships?"

"Well, not much, but I've done some sailing."

"Good. You'll be doing a lot more, and learning too. And making more than six dollars a week. Would you like that?"

John ran his fingers through his hair. "Would I like it?" He shook his head. "I'm all confused. What's happening? I mean, am I awake? Is this real?"

"Oh, John, yes. Yes, it's real. Didn't I tell you that forever would be too long to wait to see an imp like you again——though you're hardly an imp anymore."

John shrugged, embarrassed. "Guess not. You're not the way I remember you either."

Beth smiled. "Am I a disappointment?"

"No, ma'am. I——I mean no."

"I'm glad."

"All the time we were in Halifax, I never forgot you. I always prayed that you were all right and living with good folks. I guess, by looking at you, that my prayers were answered."

Beth reached up and stroked his face. "I guess mine were too."

"How did god find us? How did you—"

Chapter 4

"And not only can John do sums faster than I can put them down, but he's excellent with the sextant. William says he's become a great addition to the business."

Peter shifted his weight and made himself more comfortable on the couch. Damp weather always stiffened his leg. It was the only time he was forced to acknowledge his handicap.

"My brother-in-law William would say anything to make you happy," Peter said with a sigh. "He's been enamored of you for years."

"William? Really, Peter." Beth brushed some imaginary dust from her skirt. She knew that Peter spoke the truth, but William always struck her as so young and innocent that she felt guilty just being the object of his desire.

" 'William? Really, Peter,' " he mimicked gently.

"Well, don't you think that John has done well?" Beth demanded.

"Of course I do. He's bright, personable, and shares his sister's delightfully reticent omnipotence."

"I don't know why I put up with you."

"Because I don't keep trying to marry you off to someone, that's why."

Beth laughed, but it wasn't all that untrue. Everyone she knew in New York, with the exception of Peter, seemed determined to align her nuptially. Even Peter's wife, Laura, though she knew about Raleigh, would occasionally try to arrange a more than casual dinner match with an available bachelor.

"You're a true friend," Beth said.

"My motives are not totally altruistic, unfortunately," Peter said. He caught Beth's eye for a moment, then looked away. What was past, was over. That it once had been, was enough.

"Then perhaps I should question the purpose of this visit?"

"I was just passing by."

"Liar."

Peter shifted his weight again. "Bad liar, I guess."

"Come on. What is on your mind?"

"What's on my mind is none of my business, that's the problem."

"That has never stopped either of us from involving ourselves. So what is it?"

"It's the money you've been giving Ansel," Peter said quietly.

Beth walked to her desk, picked up a paperweight and stroked it absently. "How do you know about that?"

"Never mind. It's enough that I know that for a year now you've been feeding him a lot of cash, and that he's been gambling it all away on ships headed upriver."

"It's only happened twice," Beth said defensively, knowing full well that Peter was right. She probably was a fool for giving *any* money to Ansel. But he'd told her five months ago that he had several leads on Suzannah, only without more money, more trips upriver, he wouldn't be able to follow them. But she knew what Peter would say if she told him. He'd tell her what she didn't want to hear: that Ansel didn't know any more than those detectives she'd hired, and that she never should have offered him money in the first place. And more than likely he'd be right. But Ansel was her only hope. And she wouldn't give up hope for Suzannah any more than she could give up hope for Raleigh.

"What are you hiding?" he demanded.

Beth remained silent. Peter took his cane and got painfully to his feet. "Never mind. I'm sure you have your reasons. And if they're good enough for you, they are more than satisfactory to me." He kissed her good-bye and left.

Three days later Ernst arrived at her door with a message from Ansel. It was scrawled on a whore's fan.

Have found Suzannah. More expensive than we planned.

Once Ansel had told her he'd located the family that had Suzannah, nothing mattered. Their name was Dedericks, and they ran a tannery about twenty miles north of Kingston in Olivebridge. He gave Beth a small map drawn on a page of the evening paper. She gave him half of two thousand dollars.

Beth smelled the tannery about a mile before they reached it. A wide, thick cloud of yellow smoke hung above it. Hugo pointed and Beth nodded. The wagon continued its bumpy climb through the woods where felled naked hemlocks, like battle casualties, lined each side of the narrow road. It was a new industry, good for the people, but there was going to be enough money in it to make men greedy, and Beth knew that would mean death for something. Though it hardly seemed possible, judging from their inestimable number, Beth sensed the victim would be the hemlock.

The Dedericks' tannery was little more than an enormous shed under which bark was ground and vats filled and tended for hide tanning. A small house stood adjacent to the tannery, and when Hugo pulled the wagon in front of it, Beth saw a young girl run back inside. Her heart skipped. The girl was about twelve, and her hair was as gold as the sun.

A grizzled man with an unfriendly pocked face approached the wagon.

"Ezra Dedericks is the name. You looking for someone?"

"How do you do," Beth said. "I'm looking for a child who was left in your care as an infant thirteen years ago. Suzannah Talbot?"

"Ezra Dedericks narrowed his eyes. "No such person here."

"Wait. I—I'm her cousin. Her mother wanted to find her desperately. That was . . . that was her last request. I swore to her on her deathbed that I would find the girl and raise her. I know that she was brought here."

Ezra Dedericks licked his lips nervously. "Not here."

At that moment the door to the house opened and the girl Beth had seen before stepped out.

Ezra turned and shouted. "Get back inside there, Divinity!"

"Just a moment," Beth called.

The girl froze.

"Who's that?" Beth asked.

"My daughter, Divinity."

Beth swallowed hard. "Divinity," she said, "please come here."

Ezra glowered, but said nothing. The girl walked forward shyly. She was dressed in a shabby dun-colored smock, but shapeless as the garment was, a young woman's figure, not a child's, was in evidence beneath it. Her blond hair was snarled and matted, but her face was beautiful. Beth trembled with anticipation as the girl approached. It was Suzannah, wasn't it? She had to be sure.

"Hello, Divinity," she said.

The girl curtsied, lowered her head. "Ma'am."

Beth reached out and casually brushed the girl's

hair to the side, revealing the small crescent-shaped birthmark on her neck. She nearly gasped. "What . . . what lovely hair you have."

The girl blushed. "Thank you, ma'am."

"Get back inside, Divinity," Ezra said gruffly.

The girl's eyes grew frightened and she hurried back to the house.

"Now you, get your nigger and get off my land," Ezra said.

Beth opened her purse. "That girl is my kin. I realize you've raised her as a daughter and losing her would mean losing a good houseworker and a loved one"—though Beth had her doubts about the loved one—"so I am prepared to compensate you for her leaving."

She signaled Hugo to bring her a small box that was beneath the seat of the wagon. When he did, she took it from him and opened it.

Ezra Dedericks's eyes bulged. It was not difficult to surmise that never in his life had he seen so much money.

"There's a thousand dollars in gold here. It's yours if the girl leaves with me now."

Ezra grabbed the box. "I'll tell her that her kin is here."

"Do you like sailing, Divinity?" It was difficult for Beth to call her by that name, but it would be easier for her to get used to, than for Divinity to begin calling herself Suzannah.

"I ain't never been in no boat on the big river before." She turned and looked at Beth. "Are you really my kin?"

"Uh-huh."

"I always knew I wasn't mam's real child. Well, not always. Lester told me so when she died. Lester, he's my . . . he was my not real brother. He told me how I got brought to mam in a blanket by a man on horseback, and how all the kids were to say that I was her real baby. Did you know my real mam?"

"Yes. We were . . . cousins."

"Was she as pretty as you?"

"People said we looked a lot alike."

"Why did she give me away?"

"She didn't. She never would. She—" Beth struggled to find words. "She got sick and they thought she would die, so they took you away without telling her, when she was asleep."

"Didn't she try to find me?"

"Oh, she did. Believe me, she did. But she was poor and had no way of knowing where to look. I thank the Lord that I was able to find you after all these years."

"And my pa, did you know him?"

Beth stared out over the water. "He was a fine man," she said with difficulty. "It was everyone's loss when he died." There was no point in saying otherwise. What was one more lie?

"Where are we going?" Divinity asked, changing the subject.

"To a house in Hudson. It's called Wildwillow. I hope you will like it."

"Will you be there?"

"Most of the time."

Divinity smiled broadly. "Then I'll like it fine."

Beth put her arm around her daughter. She had her God's child, and no one would take her away again. She would contact Ernst at once. He would be happy living upriver. And Divinity, Beth could be sure, would be safe.

For the first time in a long while, Beth knew joy.

April 12, 1796

Dearest Peter,

As I told you in my last letter, Divinity thrives on knowledge, and now, with Mr. Brinktmann as her tutor (I can't thank you enough for commending him to me) she is positively blooming! Her hair has finally regained its natural luster, and, with the help of three meals a day, she's relinquished her skeletal demeanor and become a real beauty. She has heard so much about you and John that she is incessant in her requests to visit New York. (You see that all I say about you when not in your presence is not awful.) But I feel it best to wait until she learns enough to feel comfortable in society and with the frenetic pace of the city. I, though, will be coming down next month for John's birthday. I'm planning a small gathering on the seventeenth and expect that you and Laura will join us.

You inquired about my spirits. They soar when I am with Divinity and sink like a rock in a swamp when I am alone. But I have heard that Washington might be readying a ransom for the Algerian prisoners, and I pray nightly that there is substance to the rumor. I know you are warning me not to raise my hopes too high, but what good are hopes otherwise?

My love to Laura and your fine young men.

And to you.

Beth

Peter raised his glass. "To John, and two decades of good living. Happy birthday."

John smiled sheepishly, looking eminently younger than his years.

Beth put her arms around her brother, raised her glass and added: "To a fine future on land and at sea with the greatest merchant company in the nation."

"Belay there!" John said. "What if I decide to become a trapper?"

"Best not," Beth said, "else I'll put sails on your pony and have him swim to Canton."

Everyone laughed. John drank his wine then, walked out into the garden with two of his friends, while

Beth, Peter, and Laura sat down to chat. One of the servants approached, looking disturbed.

"Yes, Cassie, what is it?" Beth asked.

"It's Mr. Ansel, ma'am. He's at the door with . . . with a lady."

"Ansel here? With a lady?"

Cassie bent forward. "A painted lady," she whispered.

"Damn him," Beth muttered. "He'd spoil heaven if he could." She stood and started for the door. Ansel marched into the room, a frowsy-looking carrot-haired woman clinging to his arm.

"Well, well, if it ain't a party," Ansel said, listing slightly. The carrot-haired woman giggled, steadied him.

"What do you want, Ansel? You're not welcome here and you know it."

Ansel squinted, looked past Beth to Peter. "Now wait a minute. Do my eyes see who I think they see? Is that old Peter Avery over there?" He laughed and slapped his thigh. "By God, it is, isn't it?"

Peter took his cane, stood. Laura reached for his hand, but he shook her away. "It's me," he said coolly, coming forward.

"What's with the cane, Peter boy? You're too young to be doddering. Strikes me that I remember you used to pack a pretty good punch."

Peter's knuckles whitened on the handle of the cane. Beth put her hand on his arm.

"Leave, Ansel," she said. "And take your lady friend with you."

Ansel nodded. "I will, I will. But I came by to ask you for a little something so that me and my lady friend can celebrate."

John walked back into the room, took one look at Beth and the others and turned angrily to Ansel. "Get out. You're drunk and not welcome, can't you see that?"

Ansel's eyes narrowed. "Watch your mouth, boy." He pointed his finger warningly. "My business here is with your sister, not you." He faced Beth. "I need money."

Beth bit her lip, said nothing and went to the desk.

"Sis!" John shouted. "You're not going to give it to him? He's only going to drink it away."

Beth said nothing. Ansel knew she was keeping Divinity's real identity a secret. Except for Peter, only he knew the truth. Even John thought that Divinity was a long-lost cousin. It was better that way, especially for Divinity. And if Beth had to continue paying to keep Ansel quiet, that's what she would do.

She took out an envelope with cash inside and handed it to him. She avoided Peter's eyes. "Now get out," she said.

"Sure enough." He picked up a glass of wine and downed it. "You have a right nice celebration too, just like they're having at Washington's place." He pulled a newspaper from his pocket and slapped it. "He's paying a million dollars for our American boys, which is a real laugh. Some of 'em sure as hell ain't worth two cents."

Beth grabbed the paper. It was true! Washington had agreed to pay the ransom for the Americans imprisoned in Algiers. Raleigh would be coming home!

"Peter, look." She handed him the paper.

Ansel looked from one to the other, shrugged. "Keep the paper." He gave the woman at his side a quick squeeze. "We won't have much time to read tonight."

They both snickered and left.

"Bastard," John called after him.

"Forget him," Beth said excitedly. "Do you know what Washington's ransom means? It means Raleigh will be coming home."

"But from what you told me, you're not even sure he's alive."

Beth hugged herself. "I'm sure." She spun around and ran to Laura and hugged her. "I'm so happy. Oh, Peter, isn't it wonderful?"

Peter said nothing. His hand with the newspaper hung at his side, his face was somber.

"Peter?" Beth said quizzically. "What's the matter?" Her eyes dropped to the newspaper. She crossed the room and quickly took it from him, opened it.

Below the story that had buoyed her heart was a small article. It was wedged between an advertisement for guns and an appeal for hospital volunteers. The headline was:

DEWITT DAUGHTER KILLED
IN BOATING ACCIDENT

The paper fell from her hand. An anguished, unbidden cry broke from her. Though she could deny Adrianne in life, she could not in death. Her heart ached for all the years it hadn't; ached as if it had been torn by the Almighty Himself.

Chapter 5

"But I don't understand," John said. "Why should I go to Hudson if I'm doing so well here?"

"Because the Hudson office could use an infusion of new ideas. Besides, it will give you a chance to get acquainted with your cousin Divinity, who is dying to meet you. It will also keep you out of the hot city and away from the fever, and, quite bluntly, I'd rather be alone to meet Raleigh when he returns."

"You're not sure he's even going to be on the *Ravenswing*."

"His letter said he'd be on the first rescue ship back, and he will."

"But with all those men returning, it will be something of a miracle if—"

"I believe in miracles," Beth said staunchly. Raleigh's letter had been nothing less. Scrawled on the back of some indecipherable public notice, he'd managed to get it to England and a DuBoise ship. Captain Roberts had brought it to her personally, regretting only that the *Ravenswing* and *Flintlock* would be a good four weeks later in reaching New York.

John put his arms around his sister. "It's just that I don't want to see you hurt again. Even Peter says you're walking the roofbeams for a fall. Raleigh has been gone a long time. People change."

Beth put her hands over her ears. "I don't want to hear any more from you or Peter. Your good intentions are distressing me more than you can imagine."

"All right." John held up his palms. "No more advice. I'll go to Hudson, baby-sit Cousin Divinity, and see who has his hand in the company apple barrel." He smiled. "How does that sound?"

Beth grabbed a pillow from the couch and tossed it at him. He sidestepped and it landed in the potted ivy. They both laughed.

"Go on with you," Beth said. "And pack enough to last the summer!"

It was only the first week in June, but the heat was already warm enough to bubble the tar on the ships at anchor in the harbor. Beth had risen early that morning, bathed in lilac water and spent more than an hour at her toilette. M. Sabret, whose wigs were the finest in Paris and New York, had arrived at nine to dress her hair. He charged exorbitant prices for his service, but Beth did not care. He spent at least five minutes on each curl, but what was cost? Raleigh was coming home.

Cassie had brought breakfast, but Beth had been too excited to touch it. Now, waiting in her carriage in the hot quayside sun, surrounded by throngs of boisterous seamen, relatives, and friends of returning prisoners, she thought that surely she would be sick.

Hugo had been against her coming to the docks. The crowd waiting for the *Ravenswing* had swelled alarmingly, and he was concerned. He renewed his request that they leave. When she refused, he suggested that at least she wait aboard one of the Du-Boise vessels, reducing the chances of being mauled when the rescue ship dropped anchor. She remained firm in her decision to stay, until the carriage horse spooked and began to paw the air.

Hugo drove her to the DuBoise shipping office. She asked Mr. Higgins, the supervisor, to see her aboard whatever ship of theirs would be closest to the arriving *Ravenswing*. Ironically, it was the *Manitou*.

She waited demurely on deck until the large trimasted frigate *Ravenswing* entered the harbor. Then, without warning, her own excitement and the fever of the crowd caught her. She ran down the gangplank into the seething throng.

Prodded and buffeted by damp, sweaty bodies, she pushed her way forward. Her bonnet, which she'd so carefully chosen to fit perfectly over M. Sabret's hairdo, was pulled off and trampled. But the closer she came to the ship, the less she cared.

A roar went up from the crowd when the roster of returning seamen was posted. People pushed and shouted, vying for position to read it. Beth fought her way forward, her heart was thumping like a war drum. Quickly she scanned the names . . . Evanston, Ely *Eckert!*

She wasn't sure if she screamed or if the shout came from someone else. She struggled through the mob toward the gangplank, toward the long, wavering line of gaunt, bearded, emaciated seamen who seemed to pour slowly down the ramp, melting into the crowd.

Sweat dripped from her forehead, slid down her sides. She hardly noticed. Her eyes clamped on each man as he came into view, her breath catching hopefully. Where was he? His name was on the roster. He had to be aboard. He had to be . . .

Then she saw him.

He was frighteningly thin and his eyes searched the crowd like those of one demented. But neither his gaze, nor the beard that covered his face, nor the scar that zigzagged like miniature lightning across his cheek made her hesitate a moment. With strength she never knew she possessed, she forced her way through the mob, shouting his name.

She saw him turn, squint.

"Raleigh! Raleigh!" She waved frantically.

His eyes found her. "Beth!" he cried, and plunged into the crowd toward her.

Within moments they were in each other's arms, clutching each other with a desperateness born of loneliness and hopes and fear. Embracing each other as loved ones, and as strangers.

"Beth," he began, his voice strained and raw.

"Hush. There will be time to talk. We're going home."

They held hands and said nothing in the carriage, but with every turn of the wheels the years apart slowly disappeared. When they reached the house it was as if they had never been separated.

There was so much to say, where did one begin? She wanted to tell him about Divinity, the empty years, her prayers, Peter, John . . . everything. But when she finally spoke, it was to ask him if he liked the house.

"It's large enough for the first regiment."

"Is that all you think of it?"

"Just an observation. You realize I've been in cramped quarters."

Suddenly and explosively Beth laughed, tears of relief and happiness streamed down her cheeks. "What I realize is that your infuriating contentiousness has gone through hell and remained unscathed. We've not been together an hour and you've managed somehow to raise my hackles." She wiped her eyes. "I bought this house because I thought you would like it, believe it or not."

He pulled her close. "I believe it. And it's lovely."

"There's a balcony upstairs. Come." She took his hand. "I've not once stood on it when I didn't—" Her voice broke off as they entered the living room. Ansel sat on the couch smoking a cigar.

"Good day, sister," he said. "I see by your visage that I've picked an inappropriate time?"

Cold fury raged through her. "Raleigh," she said, her voice tight, "this is my brother Ansel."

Raleigh looked from one to another, frowned. "How do you do?"

"As well as I can as long as my luck holds," Ansel replied. "You must be the returned prisoner, eh?"

"What do you want?" Beth asked curtly.

"No time for amenities, is that it?" Ansel stretched and stood. "Well then, I'll just take what you owe me and be off." He winked at Raleigh. "Leave you two to get reacquainted."

"Owe you—?" Beth stopped, forced a smile. "Of course." She excused herself and hurried into the parlor, where she now hid her cash box, since Ansel had taken to dropping by unannounced when she wasn't home. She grabbed some bills and stuffed them in an envelope. A hundred? Two hundred? What would satisfy him so that he'd leave her alone?

She knew the answer and didn't want to think about it: Ansel would never be satisfied. She slammed the drawer.

Ansel poured himself a drink.

"How about a toast to celebrate Raleigh's return?" He extended the glass to Beth as she entered the room.

Beth ignored it, handed him the envelope. "Another time, Ansel."

He shrugged, pocketed the money. "Well, I can see that you two have your own toasting to do." He laughed, then downed the drink. "Raleigh"—he nodded—"sister, dear." He placed the glass on the table and left.

Raleigh stared after him.

"I'm sorry he was here," Beth said, clasping her hands together. "He's—he's quite abrasive, I know."

"I must confess, I am not taken with him. And I am confused. Why do *you* owe *him* money? He dresses like a gambling man, and unless you have taken to wagering, I cannot see how—"

Beth waved her hand. "It's a . . . a family matter, really. Come. Look at the view."

Beth drew him to the balcony, but Raleigh did not look toward the river.

He took her face in his hands. "This is the view I've dreamed of. All those lightless days in that putrid prison, it was you I saw, you who allowed me those precious moments in my mind when I could escape."

"Raleigh." She flung her arms around him, pressed her head against him. "My love, come. Let me wash the memories of that hell from you."

She took his hand and led him to the bath chamber. The large porcelain tub had been filled and scented with mint. She rang a small bell and, as she'd instructed earlier, one of the servants appeared with two large buckets of hot water, added them to the tub, then left. Beth trailed her fingers in the water, then put them against Raleigh's forehead. "It's the same temperature as your body, but it will cool you."

Raleigh pulled her to him. "For what purpose? I will only be feverish again the moment my eyes are upon you."

She pulled back, pretended to be indignant. "I've waited for a lover, not a rutting bull."

He looked down, calling attention to the swelling beneath his britches. "Bath or no, it seems this rutting bull is here to stay."

Beth blushed, as much from excitement as embarrassment. "Go on with you." She turned her head away.

"Whoa, now." He walked round in front of her, uptilted her chin. "You're the one who suggested this bath. Wash the memories of that hell away is what you said you'd do." He unbuttoned his shirt. "There's a lot of memories that need washing."

"Well, I meant . . ."

He threw his shirt to the floor, unbuckled his belt. "You know what you meant as well as I."

Beth felt herself flushing furiously. He was undressing, in broad daylight, right before her! Not touching her, not coercing her, just allowing her to stand there, fully dressed, and watch him.

She felt a strong sensual stirring. Brazenly she took his nakedness, let herself feel the heat of her own excitement. He had lost much weight, but his body was taut and firmly muscled, and his hunger for her was thrillingly blatant. Never had she allowed herself to look at a man so; never had she felt as helpless a victim of desire.

He stepped into the bath, slid down slowly beneath the water. "Well?"

Beth found it difficult to speak. "Well what?"

"Madam, I've spent two years in hell." He raised a washcloth. "If you would be so kind as to make good your promise."

Beth approached the tub slowly, bent down on one knee and took the cloth.

"You can start with my back," he said. "I enjoy anticipation."

Beth dipped the cloth in the water and ran it down over him. The touch of his flesh against her palm made her quiver.

"I think," he said gently, "that it would be a terrible shame to get water all over that lovely frock. Don't you?"

"I— No. I couldn't."

Raleigh reached out and stroked her neck. "Of course you could. Just take it off."

Beth stood and hesitantly began to unbutton the bodice of her dress. She started to turn away, but Raleigh insisted she face him. Her fingers trembled, and she half closed her eyes. Her breathing grew heavier.

"That's it," Raleigh said. "Take it off. Everything. Oh, you are exquisite."

She stepped out of her underthings and laid them carefully beside her dress. Then suddenly, emboldened by her own yearnings, she walked directly to the tub.

"Your back is done," she said quietly, bending over for the washing cloth. "I have other parts to attend to." As she lowered her hand beneath the water, Raleigh reached up and pulled her, squealing, down on top of him. Water splashed all around.

"Raleigh, dear Lord," she cried, "not here. It's insane."

"And what's wrong with a little madness?"

Till long after the moon came out, they gorged themselves on love, filling the dark, empty years of separation with a rich, effulgent passion. By dawn they were filled with each other and exhausted, but by breakfast they were relaxed enough to sit opposite one another and discuss politics. By lunch the next day they'd already had their first fight.

Chapter 6

The weeks following Raleigh's homecoming were the most tumultuous and the happiest of Beth's life. Their stormy courtship was the talk of New York society. Their shocking displays of affection in public, notably an extended embrace of an intimate nature in front of the Merchant's Exchange, were brought up at nearly every social occasion. Their fights were events. When banker Eckert's son spanked the Widow Du-Boise in a carriage parked in front of the Bowery Theater, even Peter Avery's conservative *Evening Post* carried the story.

Though Raleigh's residence was still the Eckert mansion on Cedar Street, it was common knowledge —and grand fodder for the gossips—that his breakfast tray was in residence on Nassau.

"I don't think it's proper to continue your relationship with Mr. Eckert in such a fashion," Laura Avery had whispered to Beth at the Midsummer Ball. To which Beth had replied in all sincerity: "You're right."

Beth knew that Peter disapproved of her flagrant romance too, but for reasons other than those that disturbed his wife. Still, he managed to remain a good friend, and Raleigh was fond of him.

Neither Beth nor Raleigh cared what was being said about them. But if one heard something about the other, she or he became enraged. In fact, the quickest way to mend an argument between them was for someone to take sides. But when either was asked about nuptials, neither replied.

At least not to anyone except Peter.

"I don't understand," he said one afternoon when he and Beth were alone. "You say you love him and he loves you. Why then don't you marry?"

Beth twirled the ribbon from her bonnet. "Oh, we will, I am sure."

"But when?"

Beth laughed. "When we stop arguing long enough for him to propose and me to accept."

Peter put his hands on her shoulders, turned her toward him. "You are too flippant. I've known you too long to believe that *you* believe what you said."

Beth sighed. "Perhaps not, but it sounds acceptable."

"What is it? Maybe I can help?"

She patted his hand. "You're a good friend, but time is my only ally in this matter. The guilt he bears for his wife's death has not been put to rest . . . and I have my own to wrestle with. He has yet to meet Divinity, and I will not marry him with a lie in my heart."

"But surely he'll understand about Divinity, and it will make no difference."

"I fear the difference it will make if I tell him the whole truth. And I cannot marry without telling it to him. So"—she clasped her hand—"we will continue to raise the eyebrows of New York."

"But—"

"There are no buts, Peter. You know I cannot tell

Raleigh what you alone know. Not yet. Not now. It would be . . . dangerous, much too dangerous."

"Dangerous? But how? After all this time, what would he do?"

"Do?" Beth repeated simply. "There's no doubt in my mind that he would kill."

"I want you alive," Raleigh said, tossing clothes into Beth's valise. "It's no fun making love to a dead woman."

"Raleigh!" Beth pulled her traveling bag away.

"The fever is spreading all over the city. We are going to Hudson. Besides, you've been spouting the praises of your brother John and cousin Divinity and Ernst, the guardian giant, like a trumpeting whale for weeks now, and it's time I got to meet them, don't you think?"

"Of course, but I thought perhaps around Thanksgiving time. I mean, it's . . . so soon. I—I didn't think you'd want to travel upriver."

Raleigh scowled. "Why on earth would you think that? You know I love those mountains. Is there some reason that you don't want me to come to Wildwillow?"

"No, no, of course not," Beth said quickly.

"Well then"—Raleigh smacked her on the behind, "let's heave to, lassie. The winds have never been better."

Raleigh sensed Beth's unease on the trip upriver and was bewildered by it. There was something about his coming to Wildwillow that distressed her. At first he thought it was because Wildwillow had been Seth Du-Boise's home, thought that perhaps she felt uncomfortable with the memories, but that was not the case. No, it was something else. Something that had to do with either her brother or this cousin, Divinity. And for some reason, Raleigh suspected it was the latter. And why was this Ernst there as a bodyguard? What wasn't Beth saying? Whenever he questioned her about the girl, she was evasive. It wasn't like her, not at all. She was anxious, drawn tighter than an Iroquois bow. Only after they made love and he held her in his arms did he feel her relax. And even then, he knew she did not sleep.

"There's John!" Beth waved, pointed to the tall blond youth on the dock. "Isn't he handsome?"

Raleigh smiled. It was the first time he'd seen Beth look even remotely happy since they'd left New York. "Indeed. Were he not your brother I would be jealous."

Beth ignored the remark. "Look, Divinity is there too."

"Where?"

"She's getting out of the carriage. There, next to John."

Raleigh squinted. "By God, she's lovely." He turned and looked at Beth. "Strong family resemblance, too."

Beth started. Did he suspect? No, of course he didn't. It was a natural comment. She was becoming too sensitive. She'd have to tell him soon . . . but not yet. She wasn't ready, and, she feared, neither was he.

When they reached the dock, Divinity ran forward to greet her, John following.

"Cousin Beth!" Divinity cried. "You look so beautiful." She hugged her, then stepped back and curtsied to Raleigh.

Raleigh bowed his head.

"Divinity, this is Mr. Eckert, a very good friend of mine."

"I'm most pleased to make your acquaintance, Mr. Eckert," Divinity said, enunciating each word as Beth was certain Mr. Brinktmann, the tutor, had taught her.

John hugged his sister, extended his hand to Raleigh.

"Raleigh, this is my brother John."

"I've heard lots about you," John said. "My sister thinks highly of you."

"The feeling is mutual," Raleigh assured him.

"Missy's fixin' pheasant," Divinity burst out excitedly, "and cream trifle for dessert."

Beth laughed. Though Divinity looked remarkably like a grown young woman, she was still a thirteen-year-old child, excited about fancy dinners and cream trifle.

Then again, Beth was only a year older when she had given birth to her. The thought was distressing.

"Where's Ernst?"

"I told him I'd watch out for Divinity," John said. "I wanted to bring the wagon out myself to meet you."

"Besides," Divinity said, "we planned a picnic up near High Point to watch for the *Gull*." She flashed John a conspiratorial smile.

It did not go unnoticed, nor did the small wink John returned to her. A cold unease gripped Beth.

"Come on," John said, "you and Raleigh can sit in back, and Divinity and I will ride up front."

"Young ladies don't ride with the driver," Beth said stiffly.

"Oh, Cousin Beth," Divinity pleaded, "we won't go through town or anything."

"It's not—" She broke off in a yelp as Raleigh hoisted her to the seat of the wagon.

"Hop up, Divinity," Raleigh said. "Miss Beth and I will be happy to relax back here." He climbed in.

Beth glowered. "Raleigh, you . . . you . . ."

He put a finger against her lips. "Hush, madam, there are children present."

Beth folded her arms, looked furious, then burst out laughing. What was she thinking? There was nothing between John and Divinity, they were just friends, the way any cousins would be. She was just sensitive, that's all. She leaned back and rested her head on Raleigh's shoulder.

Later that evening, after Ernst had entertained everyone with his sleight-of-hand tricks and John and Divinity had gone to bed, Raleigh suggested a walk in the garden.

"I'd forgotten how beautiful it could be up here," Beth said.

"I've never forgotten."

"Nor I, really. Actually I remember how it looked and smelled when we first came to Hudson."

"Love has a marvelous way of imprinting things like that on the mind."

"You are presuming that I was in love with you then?" Beth asked with mock hauteur.

"I am presumptuous, bold, and always right."

"Oh, Raleigh." She leaned against him, and he kissed her.

"Why do lips taste better in moonlight?" she murmured.

"Don't know, but they do, and," he whispered, "looks as if we're not the only ones who think so."

Beth lifted her head, followed Raleigh's gaze through a copse of pine trees. Her breath caught in her throat.

"John and Divinity!"

Raleigh chuckled. "What was that he was saying about 'early to bed'?"

"No!" Beth said.

She started to pull away, but Raleigh held her.

"Hey. They're just kissing. I'm sure that John wouldn't—"

"No!" She jerked free and ran toward them. John and Divinity jumped apart and stood sheepishly in the moonlight.

"Divinity, go to your room!"

"But, Cousin Beth—" Divinity protested.

"You heard me," Beth shouted. "Go to your room this instant!"

Ernst came running. "What's the shouting? I was digging some night crawlers over there when I heard you. Is there trouble?"

"No. Everything is all right, Ernst. Just see that Divinity gets back to the house."

The big blond man put his arm around Divinity's shoulder. Her lip began to quiver. She cast John a quick look, then broke from Ernst and bolted for the house. Ernst scratched his head and followed.

Raleigh put his hand on Beth's shoulder. "Now, Beth, the youngsters were only—"

She shrugged his hand off. "I'll handle this." Her voice was cold. "John, I want you to prepare to go back to New York at once."

"But, Beth, you don't understand. I love Divinity. I—"

"I don't want to hear about it. She's a child."

"Now wait a minute," John said, his voice growing angry. "I know she's young, but she's not a child. And . . . and I'm not planning on taking advantage of her, if that's what's worrying you. I'm planning on marrying her."

"She's too young to even consider marriage," Beth snapped.

"I didn't mean right now. And besides, you're no one to talk. You were only thirteen when—"

"That's enough!" Beth shouted.

"Only thirteen when what?" Raleigh said.

John's eyes sparked angrily. "Only thirteen when she got herself pregnant, and then had bastard twins!"

Beth slapped him.

"Well, it's true, isn't it? Slap me again and it'll still be true."

This wasn't the way she wanted Raleigh to find out, but there was nothing to be done. She hadn't planned on ever telling John, but now there was no choice.

And there was no lie.

She looked at Raleigh. His face was unreadable. "It's true," she said. "I—I was raped when I was thirteen and gave birth to twins."

"You never told me you'd had children."

"I thought it would be better that way." She turned to John. "You were too young to remember. But the babies were girls. Pa didn't know there'd be two of them, but he sold one while it was still in my womb to Regina DeWitt."

"My God," Raleigh gasped. "Then—"

"The child's name was Adrianne," Beth continued.

"She drowned last year. To this day James DeWitt believes she was his real daughter. The other girl, Suzannah, was ripped from my arms by my brother Ansel and given to a family of tanners."

"No," John said, shaking his head, "no. You're not going to— *No, that's not true!*"

"Divinity is not your cousin, John. She can never be your wife."

"But . . . but . . ." He ran his hand through his hair, fighting for words, grasping at straws. "But then she's my niece. There's no scripture law against marrying your niece, is there?"

Beth swallowed, raised her head and kept her eyes steady as she spoke. "She's more than your niece."

"I don't understand. What do you mean, 'more than my niece'?"

"Your brother Ansel is her father."

Chapter 7

"Raleigh, it's over, forget it. It happened fourteen years ago!" Beth pleaded.

Raleigh picked up his valise. His mouth was set in a hard angry line. "Don't tell me it is over. That scum has been blackmailing you for how long now? How much have you paid him? Oh, he must be a happy one, humming his dirty little secret to himself and raking in your money." He kicked the base of the bed. "And you've been lying to me."

"Raleigh, please," she begged, "believe me, it was the only way. I didn't want Divinity to find out."

"And you didn't want me to find out the truth about Divinity, is that it?"

"No. I was going to tell you, of course. But I wanted you to know the whole story. I didn't want you to find out the wrong way."

"Wrong way, right way." Raleigh slapped his forehead. "God, woman, the truth has only *one* way."

"That's not so. You don't know Ansel. He could

hurt Divinity. He'd use the truth—though his own version of it—like a lash."

"Then you should have told her yourself."

"But—"

"She's going to hurt more with a lie when she finds out that John is leaving and she can't understand why."

"I can't tell her that—"

"That you're her mother? Why not? She loves you, that's evident. She's going to find out sooner or later, somehow, and when she does she'll hate you for having lied to her. Listen to me, Beth"—he took her hands, "she's both young enough and old enough to understand now."

Beth turned her head away. "I can't."

"Then it's *you* you're trying to protect, not Divinity."

"That's not so."

"If not, then tell her. Don't you understand? You've become a prisoner of this lie. No, the truth is not pleasant, not easy, but it will set you free. You must tell her. Promise me that you will."

Beth nodded. "I promise."

"And between us, Beth, there can be no more lies and secrets. I could not bear to learn that you've been deceiving me in other ways."

"Never, oh, darling, never." Beth pressed his hand fervently to her lips. Somewhere in the very furthest reaches of her mind a spark of warning flickered. She knew what it was, it was the fact that Raleigh did not know that she and Peter had been more than childhood acquaintances, that they had—if only briefly—been lovers. But that was over, done with, there was no deception involved. She tamped the spark with her will. "Never," she said again.

He kissed her. "You stay here in Hudson. I will return just as soon as my business is taken care of."

Beth grabbed his arm. "Raleigh, please, don't do anything foolish."

"Foolish? Hardly," he assured her.

"You know what I mean. Ansel is dangerous, violent. I'm frightened."

"Don't be. I just want to have a short chat with your brother, an informative discussion if you will. I am going to make it clear to him that his money tree no longer bears fruit."

"You don't know Ansel. He—"

Raleigh pressed his fingers against her lips. "Have no fear. I have had long experience with vermin."

The following morning, before the sun was up, John knocked at Beth's bedroom door. He was dressed for travel, a satchel in his hand.

"I'm leaving," he announced. "I wanted to be gone before . . . before . . ." His voice broke and he turned away.

Beth put her arm around him, brought him into the room. "You can't leave her like this."

"What other way is there? Should I wait around to lie? Sorry, Divinity, it seems I've fallen out of love with you. Oh, you don't understand? Well, that's a shame, because I'm leaving and never coming back and—"

Beth shook him. "Stop it!"

She saw him look up at the ceiling, fight tears.

"You'll not sneak off like a coward; you'll say good-bye like a man."

"Like hell—"

Beth interrupted. "I'm going to tell Divinity the truth."

"What?" John looked incredulous. "But you can't. You can't do that to her."

"I won't be doing anything to her except perhaps allowing her to recognize that you are hurting as much as she, and, I hope, offer you both a chance to look forward to the day when time will heal your hurt and allow you to be friends again and kin."

"You expect too much."

"Perhaps. But if I get only part of it, I'll be happy. In many ways I have deceived myself as much as

I've deceived Divinity. I always thought of her as
God's gift, a golden child meant to be *my* salvation.
But she was not brought into this world to save me,
though for a long time she was all that did. She is a
human being in her own right. I think I understand
that now. It's time she understood it too."

Divinity sat in her bed. Her eyes were red from crying through the night. Seeing Beth, she turned her
face toward the wall.

Beth approached slowly, sat down and took her
daughter's hand. "Divinity," she said calmly, "I have
a painful story to tell you . . ."

Divinity walked back with Beth to the room where
John was waiting. Her face was drawn, but her hand
was clasped firmly in Beth's and there was something
about her that seemed to be shining.

John left two days later for New York. He had
planned to remain there a week before heading west.
But he had only been in the city a few hours when
he was aboard another coach and headed for Hudson
with a fury.

Ansel was dead, and Raleigh Eckert was being held
for murder.

"Why can't I see him?" Beth demanded angrily.

"Because there's enough of a scandal about this
whole thing already," Peter said, "and your appearance at the jail won't help him." He handed her a
glass of water. "Here, drink this, you look pale."

Beth took the water gratefully, sat down. She'd
been sick to her stomach the entire ride down.

"Have you spoken to him? What did he say? Oh,
God!" She stood up, tossed her head back and paced
nervously, hugging herself. "I don't believe this has
happened." Beads of sweat appeared on her brow.
She felt light-headed again and sat down.

"Are you all right?" Peter asked

"Fine," she said, brushing aside the question. "Now tell me what really happened."

"Whose version? Raleigh's or Kahill's?"

"Well, Raleigh's, of course—" She hesitated. "Why? Is Kahill's so different?"

"Substantially. According to Raleigh, he didn't do it. According to Kahill, Raleigh shot your brother in cold blood."

Beth covered her face with her hands. "Dear God."

"Why did Raleigh go to see Ansel in the first place? I thought you two were spending the rest of the summer upriver?"

Beth explained about Divinity and John, about Raleigh's anger upon discovering that Ansel had been blackmailing her. "I tried to stop him, but I couldn't. He was determined to tell Ansel that there would be no more money. But I know he wouldn't kill him, not deliberately."

"Jesus, Mary, Joseph," Peter whistled. "Tell that tale in court and Raleigh's as good as dead."

"Don't talk like that," Beth snapped. "If Raleigh says he's innocent, he is."

"Not by Kahill's account. He says Raleigh entered the club—and I quote—like a man out to kill. When he asked Kahill for Ansel, Kahill told him that Ansel was in back, in the office. According to Kahill, Raleigh pushed past him and went to the office. Kahill said he heard shouting, went back to see what was happening, and arrived just as Raleigh pulled out his pistol and fired."

"What does Raleigh say about that?"

"What one would expect. He says it's an outright lie. His account is that he went to the club, and, with a bit of force, extracted—along with Ansel's three front teeth—his solemn word that he would not bother you again, and that within two weeks he would leave New York."

"I don't understand," Beth said, pacing again. "It makes no sense. If what Raleigh says is true, then why would Kahill lie?"

"The obvious reason is that Kahill himself killed your brother."

"But for what end?"

"None apparent enough to satisfy the court, that's for certain. Aside from some minor altercations, Kahill basically got on with Ansel, so the others at the club have said."

"Then why would he lie?"

"If he is lying."

"Of course he's lying," Beth snapped.

"Calm yourself. I'm trying to figure this out too. Now if we accept the fact that Kahill had no argument with Ansel, then his only reason for killing him would be to get at someone he *did* have an argument with."

"But Raleigh didn't even know Kahill, I'm almost positive of that."

"But William Eckert does. He knows Kahill very well."

"Raleigh's father?"

Peter nodded. "William Eckert has been the force behind the committee to clean up South Street. The gaming club and the brothel, both of which are owned by Nevin Kahill, have distressed Eckert since they opened, mainly because of their proximity to his banking offices."

"But why—?"

"One imagines, in a situation such as this, that someone of Mr. Eckert's means will do his best to extricate his son from the matter. It's quite possible that Kahill needed a coin, other than money, with which to barter for the preservation of his establishments. An eyewitness account of a murder can be conveniently blurred for the right promise."

"You mean Kahill killed Ansel . . . just for that?"

"Men have been murdered for less."

"But unless we can prove that Kahill did it, Raleigh is still in jeopardy."

"True, unless—"

"Unless what?"

"Unless we can prove with a witness that Ansel was alive after Raleigh left the club."

Beth's stomach began to churn; she felt as if she were being rocked aboard a ship. For a moment she felt as if she would pass out. She grabbed Peter's arm.

"Beth! You are ill."

"It's nothing," she said sharply. "Just the heat." But she knew it wasn't. She had not bled in two months. There was no doubt in her mind that Raleigh's child had already begun inside her.

"Let me get the doctor," Peter said. "It could be the fever."

"It's just the heat. Please, let's not quibble about my health. Tell me where we can find this witness who saw Ansel alive after Raleigh left."

"That's the problem. There is none." Peter opened his hands, held them forward helplessly.

"Yes, there is!" Beth said suddenly. "You!"

"Me? What on God's earth are you talking about?"

"If Kahill can get away with murdering my brother and give a false eyewitness report about his killing, we can at least present a reputable witness in Raleigh's defense. All you have to do is say that you were with Raleigh when he left Ansel, and that Ansel was alive then."

"You mean perjure myself?"

"Peter, this is no time for scruples. Raleigh's life is at stake."

Peter walked toward the window in silence. Beth knew how much Peter valued integrity, knew that what she was asking him to do was more than she had any right to.

When Peter spoke, his voice was no louder than a whisper. "And what if Raleigh did kill Ansel?"

"Peter!" Beth said, shocked. "You can't believe that."

"Can't I? Ansel was not a difficult person to hate, and certainly one that many nights I myself, if the truth be known, longed to annihilate." He stared down at the street. "I've never denied you anything you've ever asked. But this time you ask too much."

Beth turned, covered her face with her hands and cried.

"Don't you understand, Beth? I can't do it. There's Laura and the boys to think of, too. They know I wasn't with Raleigh at Kahill's."

"Never mind. Forget I ever asked you." She did not look at him.

"Beth, please." Peter touched her shoulder, but she shrugged him away. "He'll have the best lawyer, his father will see to that."

"And he'll probably get him a lovely casket, too."

"Beth—"

"It will be a wonderful story to raise his child on," she said bitterly.

Peter froze. "Child? What child?"

"Never mind." She hadn't meant to let it slip. She wasn't even going to tell Raleigh until she thought the time was right. She wanted a proposal of marriage from the heart, not one extorted by necessity. Damn her loose tongue.

"Are you telling me that you are with child?" Peter asked.

"I'm telling you nothing."

"Look at me." Peter turned her to him. "You are pregnant, aren't you?"

Beth nodded.

Peter let his hands fall to his sides. "Does Raleigh know?"

"No."

"I see," he said quietly.

"I don't believe in muzzle-in-the-ribs wedlock," she said proudly.

"Well and good," Peter said, "but perhaps if Raleigh had known he was to become a father, he would have thought twice about his meeting with Ansel."

"Then you don't know Raleigh," Beth said.

"Perhaps not," Peter said, "which will make it all the more difficult to lie for him."

"Peter!" Beth's eyes sparkled with new hope. "Then you will . . . ?" Her question hung unspoken.

He walked again to the window. His back was to Beth when he spoke. "I will do what I can to see that your child is welcomed into this world with a father."

Beth ran to him, hugged him.

Peter put his arms around her, held her close, drinking deeply the clean sweet scent of her hair. It was a parting, a final severing of his childhood dream. The time had come to give her up in reality as well as in the privacy of his mind. But simply because he would love her no more did not mean that at that moment he loved her any less.

He would think of a way to explain to Laura about the lie he would tell to save Raleigh. In his mind, he would rationalize the matter, turn it into a moral act. But the love of a woman he could never have was his only motivation—and in his heart he would hide that truth forever.

Chapter 8

Divinity sat in the crowded courtroom clutching her mother's hand. The jury had reached a verdict.

Beth watched the men enter the box with a curious calmness. There was no longer anything she could do, and so for some strange reason she was more relaxed than at any other moment during the trial. She patted Divinity's hand. She'd done the right thing in acknowledging the child's request to come from Wildwillow to be with her.

During the weeks before the trial, Divinity's presence eased the emotional tension that had previously incapacitated Beth with headaches. More important, it had given Beth an optimism she thought herself incapable of.

It was an optimism not easily come by. Raleigh was bitter, and not even her visits to the jail changed that. She tried getting him to talk of the future, marriage, but he'd withdrawn into himself and remained unreachable.

And soon she would be unable to hide her condition.

It seemed so sensible to handle the situation her way in the beginning, despite Peter's advice. But now her gentle secret seemed more like a deception. Perhaps she should have told Raleigh right away. But she hadn't, and it was too late to rectify that now.

"Will the prisoner rise and face the bench," the judge said.

Raleigh, looking pale and gaunt, stood slowly and walked toward the judge.

"The jury will now tell the court how it finds the defendant."

Beth stopped breathing.

"Not guilty, Your Honor."

The courtroom erupted in noise and the judge hammered his gavel repeatedly. Beth paid no attention. She ran to Raleigh.

"It's all over. You're free." She pressed his hand against her face. "Free."

Peter came forward, extended his hand. "I'm glad it's over."

Raleigh regarded him strangely. "So am I. I . . . I want to thank you for what you did for me."

"Forget it." Peter seemed not to want to talk about it.

"It's not something one forgets that easily."

"You're acquitted, that's all that counts."

"Is it?"

The two men gave each other hard, searching looks. "Why did you do it?" Raleigh asked.

"Another time, Raleigh," Peter said. "Laura's waiting for me." He turned to go.

Raleigh stopped him. "No, now. I want to know."

"Raleigh, let's go home," Beth said. She felt the mounting tension and did not like it. "Divinity's with me. Look, here she comes now."

Raleigh did not look. He held Peter's arm. "Why?" he repeated.

"Because you were innocent and there was no other way to prove it."

"You believed that?"

"What I believed was less important than what the jury believed."

"Not to me," Raleigh said angrily. "I didn't kill Ansel Talbot."

"I'm glad to hear that."

"You think I did kill him, don't you? But you lied for me. Why?"

"Raleigh, that's not true," Beth interrupted. "Peter—"

"Ansel Talbot is dead," Peter said tonelessly. "Even the person who killed him is innocent. Justice has been done. Now if you will excuse me?" He bowed to Beth and Divinity and hurried off to where Laura was waiting.

Raleigh was silent riding home in the carriage. Beth did nothing to engage him in conversation. Divinity spoke animatedly of her visit to Delancy Square with Ernst, and of Mr. Brinktmann, who, from what Beth could gather, was rapidly filling the gap left by John in her daughter's life.

Raleigh listened politely, nodded occasionally, and darkened like a storm cloud with each passing moment.

In the house, after Divinity had left them, Beth could bear his silence no longer.

"This should be a time for celebration. What alum grips your spirit?"

"Nothing." He walked to the far end of the room, then turned. "Do you believe I murdered your brother?"

"Dear God, no!" She went to him. "How can you think that?"

"Peter Avery believes I did."

"That's not so."

He ignored her. "Still, he lied for me. Why?"

"Raleigh, stop this. Without his testimony you would have hung. Is that not reason enough for his stepping forth?"

"A man like Avery would not commit perjury without some sort of threat . . . or inducement."

"You don't know Peter then," Beth said defensively.

Raleigh's eyes narrowed. "But you do. Very well, I suspect."

She bristled. "I detect innuendo of such a low nature that I shall not embarrass either of us by recognizing it." She felt dizzy and held on to a chair.

"Are you ill?"

"Of course I'm not ill. I'm just angered by . . . by . . ." The room spun, and she passed out.

She awoke moments later on the couch. Raleigh had put a cold cloth on her head. He looked concerned.

"What happened?"

"You fainted. I've sent Cassie for the doctor."

"No!" Beth sat up quickly and almost blacked out again. "I don't want a doctor."

"Ridiculous," Raleigh said gently, smiling for the first time since the trial ended. "I refuse to make love to an unconscious woman."

"Oh, Raleigh." Beth put her arms around his neck. "I've missed you, missed you awfully."

"And I you, for some absurd reason that totally escapes me."

"I don't want us to be separated again."

"Perhaps we can work something out."

Beth felt her heart leap. It wasn't a proposal of marriage, but if the doctor came, Raleigh would find out about the baby anyway. She smiled up at him. "I hope so. I wouldn't want your son questioning me about your being around all the time."

"My son?"

Beth shook her head. "Maybe your daughter, but I have a feeling that it's a boy." She patted her belly. "Haven't you noticed I've put on some pounds?"

Raleigh stood, a stunned, disbelieving look on his face.

"Well, what's the matter?" Beth asked. "Are you that unprepared for fatherhood?"

"I—I'm just surprised." He walked to the bookcase, deep furrows wrinkling his brow.

"Is something wrong?"

"I don't know. You seem to have all the answers." His voice was cool, distant.

"Well," Beth began unsteadily, "I wasn't thinking of a formal wedding, if that's what you're worried about. We can get married right aboard the *Gull*."

"Really? I see you have planned this out rather neatly then. I'm sincerely impressed."

"Whatever are you talking about?" Beth felt uncomfortable. There was something in his tone that was hostile, hate-rimmed.

"Madame Innocent, forgive me." He walked to the wine decanter and poured himself a large glass. He held it aloft. "To the queen of machinations."

"Machinations!" Beth jumped to her feet. "What are you implying?"

"My dear girl, I am not implying anything. I am putting the simple arithmetical equation of one plus one together. I believe I know now why Peter Avery so willingly perjured himself in my behalf."

"Oh, really?" Beth said angrily. "And that is?"

"Repayment for your delightful services, though I doubt either of you planned on . . . the dividend."

"Why you . . . you . . ." Beth lifted a vase from the table and threw it at him. Raleigh ducked, but not in time to prevent it from hitting his shoulder. "You bastard!" she screamed.

"You are not one to be hurling epithets," he retorted.

She came across the room, her hands like claws raking for his face. He caught her wrists, twisted them roughly.

"I told you there was one thing I would not forgive you for," he said savagely, "and that was deception. Do you think I am a fool? Did you think I would believe that Peter would lie for me out of the sheer goodness of his heart? Tell me, how long have you two been lovers?"

Beth's foot shot out, the tip of her shoe catching his shin.

He let go of her.

She fled to the other side of the room. "Get out of here and never let me see your face again!"

"With pleasure, madam, though I doubt it is my face that you're so angrily banishing from your life."

Rage erupted within her. All the years of waiting for him, the endless lonely nights of imagining the happiness they were to share, the anticipation of his joy upon discovering she was carrying his child. All of this to add to nothing? She cursed. Enraged beyond feeling, she spewed forth words like mud from a spring flood. It was the anger and frustration of a lifetime of denial, of waiting, of dashed hopes and irreparable dreams.

Throughout the tirade Raleigh was silent, his face impassive. Whatever his thoughts, they were his own and not to be shared. When she was through and stood, shaking from emotion before him, he said simply: "May I go now?"

Her voice was cold, expressionless. Empty. "You may go to hell."

Chapter 9

"But why can't I go with you?" Divinity begged.

"Because Miss Winslow's school here in New York is better than any upriver." Beth chucked her under the chin. "And how are you going to impress Mr. Brinktmann if you have no education?"

Divinity blushed. "Why can't Mr. Brinktmann continue to tutor me?"

Beth crossed her arms. "Because, my dear, it has become more than obvious to me as well as to both of you that your student-teacher relationship has altered considerably. And if Mr. Brinktmann is to come courting, it would be better for all concerned if he doesn't have to spend that time quizzing you in French."

Divinity twirled a blond curl. "I suppose you are right. But I don't understand why you have to go away."

"I explained all that." Beth looked away. She didn't want to have to again. She'd told her about the baby and, perhaps unwisely, about Raleigh.

"But why is no one to know where you are?" Divinity pressed. "Why must I say you're in England?"

"Because that's the way I want it. I need time by myself, to sort out my life. You and Ernst know where I'll be, that's enough."

Divinity looked confused. Beth sighed and pulled her daughter close. "I can't expect you to understand, but you must believe me. I've spent a lifetime going one way, and now I must change course. It's not going to be easy, but I don't want any help—or hindrance."

"Can't I even tell Peter that you're at Wildwillow?"

Beth sighed. Peter, dear Peter. He would be distressed to learn of Raleigh's suspicions, and more than likely blame himself in some manner. "No," she said, "not even Peter. I must do this alone."

Divinity hugged Beth. "I still don't want you to go. It will be a long time until Easter."

"Not so long. Ernst will be company and Emily Van Brundt will be a good guardian. Her cook is marvelous, and you and Ernst will both enjoy the stay at her house. I guarantee by the time I see you in April you'll know everything about everyone in New York."

Divinity looked at the floor. "I don't care about *everyone*."

"Nor I," Beth said gently. "But because of the ones I do care about, I must leave." To stay in New York and be humiliated by Raleigh was more than she could bear. Wildwillow would be a haven where she could close herself off from the world, at least until she could face it again. Maybe, if she were lucky, she might even learn how to be happy again.

When the *Gull* sailed past Kingston, Beth looked to the black mountains beyond and thought of Widow Brinks and the prophecy she had made so many years before. *Through all your days, and all your men, only one shall hold your passion . . . and in so doing shall control your destiny.* Was Raleigh that man? And if so, was this to be her destiny?

"Damn him to hell!" she shouted at the heavens. Then she fled to her cabin crying, hating herself for her tears.

The first snow came early, and at about the same time the child moved inside her. Despite both, Beth spent most of her days at the DuBoise office, working on cargo ledgers and foreign accounts. She had her dressmaker design fuller clothes, and no one outside her doctor and the house servants even knew of her pregnancy.

She enjoyed the secret.

At night she sat in front of the fire, her hands upon her belly, and spun daydreams about the life that kicked for recognition inside her. This baby no one would take from her.

Divinity's letters were frequent and newsy. Almost always they contained long sections on the esteemed qualities of Mr. Brinktmann. From what Beth gathered, he was becoming a fixture at the Van Brundts, and apparently anxious to put a more permanent claim on Divinity.

The winter was cold and long. When the snow got deep and her belly too large for concealment, she took to stitching samplers and reading Shakespeare's plays in lovely leather editions from London. She tried not to think of Raleigh, and in so doing kept him in her thoughts daily. She chastised herself for it, begged God to erase him from her mind, but neither self-reproach nor divine imploring had any effect. He crept into her dreams and made love to her nightly, leaving her to wake alone and despondent more mornings than she cared to think about.

By the end of February, after a particularly bleak spell, she broke her resolve and wrote to Peter. She poured everything that had been walled up inside her for months into the letter, starting with her fight with Raleigh, though omitting his allegation that Peter had fathered her child. As she wrote, she found herself growing hungry for news of friends, of happenings, and of Raleigh.

Peter's reply came quickly. Beth laid the letter out on the table before her and savored the envelope for a full half hour before opening it.

She was unprepared for its contents.

5 March 1797

My dearest Beth,

Your letter, which under ordinary circumstances would have flooded sunlight into my day, only rent further a heart that has suddenly been torn asunder. My sweet-souled Laura is gone. A treacherous chill laid siege to her body and pneumonia took her just a short ten days ago. Before she died, she spoke of you and of the fine times she and the boys had at Wildwillow. I grieve only that you did not write sooner, that perhaps before she died she might have . . . But no, this is not to make you feel guilt. You suffer enough. I wish only that I could alleviate that pain.

I knew nothing of your break with Raleigh, though after you had gone and he shunned me without the slightest reserve, I suspected something of the sort. I cannot believe he has denied his child. Then again, he has not been himself since the trial. I am told he has taken to drinking to excess and rarely appears in public.

There is much I want to say to you, but it must come from my lips without interference of quill or paper. The boys are with Laura's mother. All I need is your invitation and I shall be aboard the next coach north. I await your reply.

With fond heart,

Peter

Her reply was simple and direct. It contained none of the sadness she felt at Laura's passing, at Raleigh's drinking, at Peter's bereavement. But it was, she knew, knew, what Peter wanted. It said only: Come at once.

The day Peter was to arrive, Beth felt strange. The baby was not due for another three weeks or more, but that morning, for some reason, she felt it was curiously imminent. *Most likely imagination and nerves,* she thought, and attempted to ignore the sporadic contractions that continued to tauten her abdomen.

When Peter arrived, the contractions had increased their intensity and regularity. To Beth's distress, she was forced to greet him from her bed.

"I—I had no idea your time was now," Peter said. He looked haggard, his bones fairly jutting through his drawn cheeks. But his eyes held love and warmth, and Beth cried in spite of herself when she saw him.

"Now, none of that. Lord knows I haven't traveled up here to see you cry. You could have done that in a letter."

She smiled, then grimaced as a ring of pain circled her body. When it passed she said, "I'm glad you're here."

"I had to come. I had too much to say to you, and you know that journalists are notoriously poor correspondents."

"I know no such thi—" She winced.

Peter put his hand on her swollen belly, held it there for a few moments. "Has the doctor been called?"

"I told Cassie to get him. The baby's not due until next month, though."

"I fear he doesn't know how to read a calendar. I was with Laura for our three, and I'd say you're only an hour away. Maybe less."

"Don't joke, Peter. The doctor won't get here for at least three hours." Beth made a face as another pain gripped her.

"I don't think the baby is going to wait that long."

"Ridiculous," she said. And her waters broke.

Through an unexpected blur of pain, Beth was aware of frantic preparations. Peter organized hot water and towels while Hugo raced off to find a midwife.

"Peter!" she cried. "There won't be time for a midwife."

He took a cool cloth, wiped her forehead. She was sweating more than he had ever seen Laura sweat, and she was pale, very pale. It wasn't right.

"Don't worry," he said soothingly. "I delivered ten calves and three sheep in my time."

"Peter, it's . . . it's going to come soon."

"I'm ready for it." He washed his hands and came back to the bed.

Beth tried to smile. "What will the servants think?"

"Whatever they damn please." He rolled up his sleeves and lifted the sheet. "Madam, your baby is about to be born. Push!"

Beth pushed and within minutes the baby was out. Peter lifted it by its heels and smacked its buttocks. There was a faint cry, then a louder one.

"Congratulations," Peter said. "You have a son."

"A son," Beth breathed.

"I'll let the doctor do the cord cutting." He wrapped the baby in a blanket and placed him in her arms. "A son."

The baby's face was bright red and wrinkly, but its eyes were an incredibly beautiful dark blue and his hair was long and black, like his father's.

"Beth," Peter said, "I was going to wait to ask you this, but I don't see why I shouldn't do it now."

Beth stroked the baby's cheek with her finger. "He looks just like Raleigh, doesn't he?" she said proudly.

Peter said nothing. He sighed and his shoulders slumped a bit.

"I'm sorry," she said. "What were you going to say?"

"Nothing." He patted her hand. "Nothing at all."

She smiled weakly, licked her parched lips. Peter put his hand on her forehead. It was burning.

"Do you feel all right?" he asked.

"A little light-headed. I'm probably just tired."

There was a knock on the door and Cassie entered.

"I got the doctor, ma'am. He was . . ." Her eyes bulged when she saw the bundle in Beth's arms.

The doctor, a portly man in his fifties, entered the room huffing.

"The baby's here," Peter said. "Looks fine to me, but Mrs. DuBoise seems to be running a fever."

The doctor went to Beth and touched her forehead; a deep frown crossed his own. "Leave us please," he said.

Beth saw the doctor come toward her and then he began to blur. She blinked her eyes, but her lids seemed to be on fire. And then the room began to swirl, swirl, swirl. . . .

It seemed a long time before the daylight came, a long time. Beth knew that she was dreaming, because everyone was floating. Peter, Ernst, Divinity, the baby, even Raleigh. She heard words, but they made no sense, felt cold and hot, then nothing.

For a long time there was nothing.

And then, like a wheel slowly spinning to a halt, the room began to come back into focus. But when she looked around, nothing made sense. There was a table in her room that hadn't been there before, two or three basins of water and a pile of sheets. And a minister was there, standing beside the bed.

When she opened her eyes, he crossed himself and sank to his knees. And the next face that appeared before her was Raleigh's.

She tried to lift her hand to rub her eyes, but her arm felt like lead.

"Raleigh?" she said, her voice barely audible even to her own ears.

"Yes. I'm here." He sounded anxious, as if he expected her to leave at any moment.

She found it difficult to speak. Her tongue was thick, her throat parched. Was she dreaming? "Raleigh?" she said again.

He touched her face with the tips of his fingers. "Yes? What is it?"

"The baby? Where is the baby?" She patted the bed beside her. "Where is he?"

"Shhh. He is fine."

"Where have they taken him? He was right here. I don't understand." She tried to sit up, but could barely lift her head. And then the room began to swim again.

She saw Divinity, heard her speak, but could not make out the words. Peter also. And then it was night and she slept. When she next opened her eyes, sun was streaming through the window, the minister was still at her bedside, and Raleigh was holding her hand.

"What's going on?" she demanded.

Raleigh smiled broadly. He looked as if he hadn't slept in days. "You could say hello first."

Beth looked around. Divinity rushed forward and kissed her.

"Oh, mother," Divinity said, half crying, "I prayed so hard that you wouldn't die."

Beth blinked. "Well, obviously it was a good thing you did."

Peter stood behind Divinity. "We all did," he said.

Beth looked incredulously from one to another. "I don't understand."

"You had childbed fever. The doctor said you wouldn't live, so I took the liberty of having Hugo summon Ernst and Divinity, and your daughter knew enough to get Raleigh. You were unconscious for most of two weeks."

"But the baby?"

"He's fine," Raleigh said soothingly. "And handsome."

"Do you really think so?"

"Would I lie to you about *my* son?" He pressed her hand to his lips. "Oh, Beth, can you ever forgive me?

I love you so much. I was a fool, an idiot to drive you away. I never want to lose you again."

Her eyes misted. "Raleigh," she murmured.

The minister coughed. "I'm glad to see that our prayers have been answered and that my services aren't needed after all."

"Just a moment." Raleigh looked at Beth, a long, loving look that made all the promises she would never have asked him to make; fulfilled all the dreams she had given up daring to dream. He slipped a ring from his finger. "This can work for now," he said. "It seems a shame to have called Reverend Thompson all the way out here for nothing."

"For *nothing!*" Beth said, indignant. "Why, of all the—"

Raleigh silenced her with a kiss. When they broke, she looked up at the minister.

"I think you'd better marry us quickly," she said smiling, "while we're still talking to each other."

Escape to the World of ROMANCE and PASSION

Romantic novels take you far away—deep into a past that is glittering and magical, to distant shores and exotic capitals. Rapturous love lives forever in the pages of these bestselling historical romances from Pocket Books.

_____	81961	BELOVED ENEMY Amanda York	$1.95
_____	82320	DAUGHTER OF THE FLAME Julia Grice	$2.50
_____	81817	DIOSA Charles Rigdon	$1.95
_____	82251	DULCIE BLIGH Gail Clark	$1.95
_____	82014	FAR-OFF RHAPSODY Anne Marie Sheridan	$1.95
_____	80944	FORBIDDEN RITES Joan Bagnel	$2.25
_____	81845	JEWEL OF THE SEAS Ellen Argo	$2.25
_____	82273	LORD OF KESTLE MOUNT Joan Hunter	$1.95
_____	81919	MARIE Margot Arnold	$2.50
_____	81043	TAME THE RISING TIDE Virginia Morgan	$2.25
_____	81135	TARTAR Franklin Proud	$2.50
_____	81486	VALLAMONT Pamela Gayle	$2.25

Romantic Fiction

by Mary Kay Simmons

the author of the
million-copy bestseller
A Fire in the Blood

_____	81026	CAMERON HILL	$1.75
_____	82423	MEGAN	$1.95
_____	81018	WITH RAPTURE BOUND	$1.95
_____	81022	YEAR OF THE ROOSTER	$1.95